W9-CCZ-260

PRAISE FOR *THE RUNAWAY*

"Petrie has a preternatural talent for ratcheting up suspense." —*New York Times Book Review*

"Explosive and engaging! Fasten your seatbelt, this is going to be a wild ride." —Lisa Gardner

"Each book is richer. Each new Peter Ash novel is deeper and more complex than the last. Nick Petrie raises the bar with each new book and every time exceeds himself." —Robert Crais

"Another violent, fast-paced thriller in this action-packed series." —Associated Press

"Downright frightening fun . . . This is one hellacious ride for crime fiction fans." —*Kirkus Reviews* (starred review)

"*The Runaway* laces a tense thriller with wry humor." —*Milwaukee Journal Sentinel*

"Nail-biting . . . Shifting points of view serve to heighten the suspense. This adrenaline-fueled ride will keep readers turning the pages." —*Publishers Weekly*

PRAISE FOR *THE BREAKER*

"Nonstop action at a machine-gun pace." —C. J. Box

"Another outstanding offering in the celebrated Peter Ash series, with Nick Petrie's trademark complex and fascinating characters inhabiting a tightly woven story that will keep thriller lovers riveted. The hype about Nick Petrie is real—he's just that damn good!"

—Mark Greaney

PRAISE FOR *THE WILD ONE*

"Nick Petrie's exceptional writing has earned him comparisons to many of the thriller-genre greats, but *The Wild One* announces that period has come to an end: Petrie is setting the bar, not reaching for it."

—Michael Koryta, author of
Those Who Wish Me Dead

"This kinetic, breathless masterpiece illustrates why Petrie is here to stay." —*Publishers Weekly*

PRAISE FOR *TEAR IT DOWN*

"Petrie is hell on wheels at mounting lethal action face-offs. A close cousin to Lee Child's more analytical Jack Reacher, Peter Ash is one of today's more exciting action heroes." —*Publishers Weekly*

"Petrie's prose, vivid and almost tactile, is at its loving best in these jazz interludes, writing of a sound 'spontaneous, like water welling up from a spring.' . . . This thriller is all about the thrills, and there are plenty of them." —*Booklist*

PRAISE FOR *THE DRIFTER*

"Lots of characters get compared to my own Jack Reacher, but Petrie's Peter Ash is the real deal."

—Lee Child

"Peter Ash is one of the most complex characters I've come across in a long time. The pace is like a sniper round, extraordinarily fast and precisely calibrated. The prose is fluid, original, and frequently brilliant, the story heart-wrenching and uplifting at the same time. There is grit in this tale that will stay with you. Perhaps forever."

—David Baldacci, *New York Times* bestselling author of *Memory Man*

"[The] lean prose, gritty descriptions, and raw psychological depth give the novel a feel that reminded me of early Dennis Lehane."   —*Milwaukee Journal Sentinel*

"Nicholas Petrie has written just about the perfect thriller. I haven't read such a well-crafted and gripping story in a month of Sundays. If this is Petrie's first novel, watch out for the second one. But why wait? This one's here now, and it's a home run."

—John Lescroart, *New York Times* bestselling author of *The Keeper*

"Captivating . . . [Petrie's] main character has the capacity to become an action hero of the likes of Jack Reacher or Jason Bourne."   —*Lincoln Journal Star*

"A gripping, beautifully written novel."   —*HuffPost*

TITLES BY NICK PETRIE

THE RUNAWAY

NICK PETRIE

G. P. PUTNAM'S SONS
NEW YORK

PUTNAM
— EST. 1838 —

G. P. PUTNAM'S SONS
Publishers Since 1838
An imprint of Penguin Random House LLC
penguinrandomhouse.com

First G. P. Putnam's Sons hardcover edition / January 2022
First G. P. Putnam's Sons premium edition / July 2022
G. P. Putnam's Sons premium edition ISBN: 9780525535522

Printed in the United States of America
1 3 5 7 9 10 8 6 4 2

For my mom, Lucia Petrie, and
my sweetheart, Margret Petrie, and
all mothers who do the best they can
and still feel like it's still never enough

When two tigers fight, one is certain to be maimed, and one to die.

—GICHIN FUNAKOSHI

THE
RUNAWAY

1

HELENE

THEN

Wake up, girl."

Helene startled on the stool and jerked upright, blinking, from the pillow of her folded arms. The magazine under her elbows fell to the floor with a slap.

A man stood on the far side of the register. He wore a faded green John Deere cap over a scraggly blond beard that crept up his cheeks. She'd never heard the bell on the door. Helene was so damn tired she could snore through a tornado. That's what happened when you worked two jobs.

It was four in the morning. She was a few days shy of nineteen.

John Deere lingered a couple of steps back, a six-pack of Coke in one hand and a bag of beer nuts in the other, somehow watching her without staring at her. Not like the other customers, who put their fat bellies right up to the edge of the countertop, trying to get as close to her as they could. Running their eyes all over her like she was theirs for the taking.

"Honey, I could have stole you blind." His face didn't change but she could feel his concern.

"Like I give a crap." She wiped the sleep from her eyes, then waved a hand at the goods on display. "None of this is my shit. Steal what you want. I couldn't care less."

He glanced around like he was halfway considering it. Beer and soda in rattling coolers, bins of half-sprouted potatoes and half-rotted onions, cans of Campbell's soup and Hormel chili with the expiration dates scratched off the labels. Bogaloosa's Gas and Grocery, the crossroads of no place and nowhere.

Finally he stepped up and set his things on the counter, where milky, peeling tape covered the sample lottery tickets. "Well, not today, I reckon. Wouldn't want to get you into trouble." Dirty-blond hair curled out from under the cap, but his eyes were so dark they were almost black. A faded blue farm coat hung unzipped over a plain gray sweatshirt.

"Mister, I got nothing but trouble already," she said. "You can't begin to add to it." Then tried to smile as if it were a joke and looked away. Don't be a complainer, her mom had always said. It scares away the good luck and invites the bad.

She watched him think of how to answer her, then decide not to. She liked him for that. No empty platitudes like the sweaty minister at the food pantry who talked up the rewards of heaven while sneaking peeks down her flannel shirt. She didn't say anything because she needed the mac and cheese. Caught between pride and hunger, she didn't have much choice.

John Deere tipped a thumb toward the door and his coat fell open. She caught a glimpse of a gun on his belt, not unusual in Montana, where half the population carried a pistol and the rest had a rifle in their truck or at home. Somehow she knew he wasn't a lawman. "I need to fuel up, too," he said. "Sign outside says pay in advance?"

Bogaloosa had long ago decided that it was cheaper to be open all night, paying his employees next to nothing, rather than upgrade the ancient pumps to self-serve automatic.

Helene picked up the cheap binoculars chained to the counter and peered out the window into the relentless night. A big four-door pickup was parked on the far side of the pumps, hitched to a long windowless cargo trailer, a newer truck than most driving that lonely road. Judging from the mud splatter and dead bugs, he'd come a long way. She wondered where he'd been and where he was going.

"Gas is free today," she said. "You want cigarettes? A pint of Jim Beam? Video rentals? On the house, I won't say a word."

He took off his hat and used the brim to scratch his head. He had good hair, blond and wavy. Movie star hair, her mom would have called it. He regarded her steadily. "I guess you're some kind of hard case," he said.

"Damn right I am." She stuck her chin out. She had her daddy's gun in her bag. "You want to find out, you just try me."

He smiled then, a bright ray of sun that warmed her in the cold night. "Honey, I wouldn't dream of it."

Most men couldn't stop staring at her tits, full-grown and bothersome in more ways than one, no matter how she tried to hide them under baggy clothes. Back when she'd still gone to school, she watched the way older girls used their bodies, how they arched their backs and twitched their hips to get boys to look at them. By the time Helene turned thirteen, she had the opposite problem. Too many men paying too much attention, thinking they could reach out and touch her anytime they wanted. It only got worse every year. The late-night customers, the food-pantry preacher, the old farts at the library, goddamn Bogaloosa. Especially Bogaloosa.

But this man's eyes hadn't left her face. She wondered how old he was. Under thirty, anyway. She wondered what he looked like underneath that beard. She wondered why she cared, or what difference any of it made.

"My name's not *honey*, or *girl*," she said. "It's Helene. Hella for short." What her mom used to call her.

"Hella," he said. "That certainly suits you." His smile got wider and she found herself basking in its glow. "But I don't guess I'll take your gas for nothing. I wouldn't want the sheriff on my trail." He took his wallet from his hip pocket. "Give me fifty gallons, please."

She raised her eyebrows. "That much?" In this lean and hungry place, most people only bought ten gallons at a time.

"Truck's got dual tanks, sixty-six gallons total," he said. "Gives us a lot of range, even hauling that trailer. We work all over."

She wanted to ask him what kind of work he did, just to keep him talking for a few more minutes. Just to see that smile. But she didn't. He might think he could take something from her, the same thing they all wanted. Better to keep him as he was, a stranger passing through. She could think of him from time to time, that was all. Warm herself with the pretend memory that he wasn't like every other man she'd ever met.

She rang him up and he licked his thumb to slide wrinkled fifties from his billfold. She couldn't help but notice he had a lot more cash in there. After she gave him his change and bagged his groceries, he nodded his thanks and headed out, elbow cocked and coat shucked aside to return his wallet to his pocket, fully exposing the gun in its black leather holster.

Halfway to the door, he paused, his elbow stopped mid-movement. Then he turned around and came back to the counter with the wallet still in his hand.

Helene's heart sank. John Deere was no different

from the rest, thinking she might be for sale like all the other cheap trash in the store, and if they offered enough money she would let them do what they wanted.

He licked his thumb again and slipped a bill partway out, considered it a moment, then added two more. Bent them together lengthwise and laid them gently on the counter. She didn't touch them. They were hundreds, crisp and new. She'd never seen three at once before. When he put his dark eyes on hers, she shivered.

"Maybe this will help with your troubles," he said. He glanced at the door, then back at her, and lowered his voice. "But here's the deal. You don't tell anyone where you got this. You and I never met. I was never here. You got it?"

She nodded, suddenly shy. The shiver took over her whole body. John Deere was definitely not a lawman. The bills lay there on the counter between them. She didn't know what to do. It was a lot of money.

He smiled like he understood everything about her. "I hope you get out of here," he said. "A sharp girl like you deserves better than this."

"I don't need your charity." They were her mom's words and they came out on their own. "I'm just tired, is all. Overdue for a day off."

He tapped the counter with his knuckles like knocking on a door. "It ain't charity, honey. It's a gift, pure and simple. No strings attached. You got something special in you, I can see it. Be a shame to have it go to waste." He gave her one last smile, warm but also somehow sad, then turned to go.

She watched him walk away, broad shoulders in the farm coat, blue jeans that fit his slim hips just right, heels of his cowboy boots on the hard floor like the ticking of a clock.

Just because she didn't want men staring at her tits didn't mean she didn't have some thoughts along those lines herself. She was a grown woman. She'd hooked up with an army-bound farmboy from her school a couple of months ago, after he'd kept showing up all sweet and flirty to keep her company in the middle of the night. She'd grabbed a pack of ancient condoms off the rack and climbed in the back of his car to get her virginity out of the way, see what the fuss was all about. They'd done the deed a few times, but in the end she hadn't been impressed by the experience, or how the boy had thought those few sweaty minutes gave him some kind of claim on her, like she was a prize hog at the county fair.

That wasn't how John Deere had looked at her. When the door closed behind him, the bell on the jamb rang once, a clear, pure chime that hung in the air like the first snowflakes of winter.

Coldwater, Montana, the loneliest place in the world.

2

Maybe it had been more of a town, once upon a time, before Helene was born. Now Coldwater was just a name on a sign at the edge of the plains where two county roads came together, seventy miles from the nearest stoplight. The few surviving buildings leaned into the wind, siding flapping, roof shingles half gone, a little more torn away with every storm. The only remainders were Bogaloosa's Gas and Grocery in the corner of a hayfield and the little tin travel trailer she rented from him that sat up on blocks behind the store. Bogaloosa's half-assed farm was a twenty-minute walk up the tractor path, his swaybacked barn filled with skinny cows she milked at both ends of her twelve-hour shift, seven days a week.

After her mom died, the town population was down to two, just her and goddamn Bogaloosa.

Helene was a month past her eighteenth birthday

and two months into her senior year when her mom fell asleep at the wheel and missed a curve on Highway 2. Deputy Bogaloosa knocked on the trailer door and broke the news, then took her to Glasgow to identify her mom's body.

Driving back, he said he felt real bad about her mom, and that Helene was welcome to keep living in the trailer. He apologized for bringing it up, but said Helene had to consider how she was going to earn a living, now that she was legally an adult. If she wanted, she could just step into the jobs her mom had done. He'd take care of her the way he'd taken care of her mom. As long as she got to work on time, she'd be free to do whatever she wanted. She'd never liked school anyway, right?

Just sitting beside him in the sheriff's pickup that first time, she'd felt acutely uncomfortable. It should have been a warning.

After dropping out of school, it didn't take Helene long to figure out that she wasn't free, not at all. Her mom's accident had totaled the car, and also ruined the phone they had shared. There was no insurance money. Bogaloosa barely paid her for all the work she did. He took the rent out of her check from the Gas and Grocery, gave her a small allowance for food, and held on to the rest of it for safekeeping, he said. For her own good, like a savings account. Besides, what was she going to buy, out there in the middle of nowhere?

When she told him she needed a phone, he just laughed.

She kept track of her hours and knew exactly how much he owed her, to the penny. Not that it made any difference. Every time she asked for more money, he made her tell him why she needed it, what she planned to buy, practically made her beg for her own dollars. He knew what was best for her, he said. She was lucky she had him in her life. He liked to remind her how much she needed him.

She had a driver's license, but no car. It wasn't a problem while her mom was still alive, but Bogaloosa must have said something to somebody, and now people she'd known for years would no longer give her a lift to town. Gas and Grocery regulars all just shook their heads and apologized, knowing Deputy Bogaloosa was petty and vengeful on the best of days.

Which meant she couldn't get to the library or laundromat or drugstore or a real grocery store without sitting beside Bogaloosa in his county pickup, pushing his sweaty hand off her leg every five minutes. "We might as well get along," he'd say with a smile. "Way I see it, we're stuck with each other."

Once she realized how trapped she was, she tried everything she could to get away. She talked to the food-bank preacher, hoping for a cot in the women's shelter, but he'd just said something about how the devil couldn't take your soul unless you invited him in yourself. She'd gone to see the sheriff one day, but he'd just put his long, wrinkled arm around her, knuckles touching the side of her breast, and said that she was welcome to move in with him anytime, he had an excellent wine cellar.

She'd have taken up with that farmboy she'd slept with, but she hadn't heard from him since he left for basic training. Bogaloosa had scared off everyone else.

Last month, in the barn, he finally stopped hinting and came out and said it. Starched brown official shirt tucked into tight jeans, gun on his hip, dip in his lip, he'd backed her up against the stall gate and stared down at her. "I like how you pull them teats, girl. I bet you got real strong hands." His teeth were stained the color of his shirt and she could smell the wintergreen Skoal on his breath.

She tried to ignore him and push past, but he grabbed her upper arm, letting her feel how strong he was. He had a weight bench in the barn so he could pump iron, grunting, while she milked his cows. "You know how much rent I could get for that nice trailer you're living in? How many grown men could use those two jobs I gave you? You gonna have to start showing some appreciation, young lady."

She pulled at her arm, but his fingers just dug in deeper. He gave her the look a cat gives a mouse. "Your birthday's coming up, ain't it? Nineteen's a good age to get married. Why don't we just go ahead and tie the knot? Change your life for the better." She pulled harder and he finally let her go. As she ducked away, he called after her, "What day's your birthday again? Aw, heck, I can just look that up in the department computer."

Her last trip into town, he'd asked her what she wore to bed and told her he'd buy her a nice clean white nightie for her nineteenth birthday. "One more week 'til I give you the best present of your life." He'd waggled his eyebrows at her like it was some kind of game they were playing together.

The worst part was knowing it was coming. She tried to block it out, but her mind wouldn't quit. Every time she closed her eyes, she got flashes of it. Bogaloosa's hands on her naked flesh, the smell of wintergreen dip and fermented armpit, her legs pushed wide and something rough forced inside.

Beneath the fear and sadness and despair was something else, something that burned. She felt it in the tightness of her stomach and the hard pinch between her shoulder blades. Anger at how hard she worked and got nothing back, anger at her mother for dying and leaving her alone and unprotected, anger at Bogaloosa for the way he'd backed her into this corner with no way out.

Above all, anger at herself for putting up with it. As if she had a choice.

She could hear the smile in her mom's voice as she told her it wasn't her fault. *Life hands out a lot of lemons, baby girl. Sometimes all you can do is make some lemonade.*

But it was hard to imagine making lemonade from this.

Sometimes, Helene was sure she'd fight him. Pick up her mom's big cast-iron frying pan and bash in his head. Or take her daddy's old revolver, point it at his face, and pull the trigger until he was a pulpy red mess. Her life was a prison already, what difference did it make if she went to jail?

Other times, she saw herself closing her eyes and giving in. Just this once, she'd tell herself. Then just once more. Then she'd be doing it over and over, for the rest of her life.

The worst was when she saw herself nine months pregnant in that white nightie, now stained and worn, standing at the stove stirring oatmeal while a half-dozen crying Bogaloosa babies clutched her legs like alien parasites.

She turned nineteen in four days.

3

Looking through the glass at the big truck parked outside, Helene watched John Deere open his gas cap and gently fit the pump nozzle into the opening. She grabbed up the cheap binoculars, pulled them to the limit of their chain, and took a closer look. He leaned against the truck while the pump worked, hat tipped back on his head, his face calm and composed.

Double gas tanks, she thought. Sixty-six gallons. How far could he drive on that?

She was suddenly conscious of her heart beating in her throat, her mouth as dry as a July hayfield.

She remembered that hot afternoon when she'd propped open the trailer door, hoping to catch the breeze, and a bird had accidentally flown inside.

She didn't know what kind of bird it was, something small and plain and frantic. It had fluttered around the little one-room trailer, thumping against the window glass again and again as it tried to make its way back out. But it just couldn't find the opening. Finally it launched itself headlong toward the front window as if, with enough speed and power, it could pass through the invisible walls that kept it trapped.

It didn't break through, of course.

It didn't even crack the glass.

It just broke its neck and died.

Outside, John Deere removed the pump nozzle, replaced the gas cap, then began to fill the second tank. Five minutes and he'd be gone.

She felt like that bird, starting that last flight. Headed for something, anything. Do or die.

Before she could talk herself out of it, she popped open the register, scooped up the cash inside, and stuffed it into the pink school backpack that she used to carry all her shit. Bogaloosa had a key to the trailer where she lived, and he used it all the time, so she always carried everything of value with her in that bag.

She added a couple of her favorite magazines, some candy bars, and a handful of those little five-hour energy drinks that gave her a boost when she needed it. Then she zipped up the threadbare fleece-lined sweatshirt that had been her mother's favorite piece of clothing, put her daddy's gun in the pocket, and ran into the late September night.

I don't need a man, she told herself. I just need a ride out of here.

Fortune favors the bold, her mother used to say.

Besides, even if Helene's worst fears came to pass and she ended up dead in a ditch, she was certain that weedy moonlit resting place would be an improvement over what she was leaving behind in Coldwater, Montana.

John Deere must have heard the bell ring when the door closed, because his eyes rose to watch her come. She slowed then, suddenly unsure of herself, not knowing what to say or how to interpret the look on his face, somehow different from the face she'd seen inside just a few moments ago. Now he had a cigarette tucked into the corner of his mouth, the ember flaring bright in the constant wind.

He took the cigarette from his mouth and smiled again and it flooded her with warmth, like stepping in front of the barn heater on the coldest day of the year. "Heck, you caught me," he said. "I know I'm not supposed to smoke at the gas pump."

"You can blow this whole place straight to hell for all I care," she said. "Where are you headed to, anyway?"

He pointed the cigarette in line with the road, west toward the mountains. His coat fell open and again she saw the pistol on his belt. "Thataway," he said. "The land of plenty."

She shivered again. She told herself it was the wind, cutting through her bones.

"Take me with you," she said.

He took a draw off his cigarette and cupped it in his fist. "Where you trying to get to?"

"It don't matter. Anywhere but here."

He turned to look her full in the face, the way she remembered her dad looking at a new colt in the gone-away days. She saw kindness and care and a measure of soft sorrow. "Honey, how old are you?"

She drew herself up, not sticking out her chest, but not slouching to hide it, either. "I'm nineteen," she said. "And my name's Helene, not honey." She took a shaky breath for courage. "Just tell me you're not a serial killer."

A smile teased at the corner of his mouth. "Darlin', I love cereal," he said. "I kill a box of Cap'n Crunch every week. I'm Roy, by the way."

"Roy what?"

"Roy Wiley."

That was a better name than John Deere. The pump clicked off, the tank full. In the newly quiet night, she heard the crunch of boots on gravel and another guy stepped from behind the truck, zipping his fly.

He sighed deeply, as if even the fact of her was a disappointment. "Who's this, now?"

Under the pale sideways glow of the store lights, he was very tall and thin and weirdly shirtless in the cool fall night. His hairless torso reminded her of the drawings in her freshman biology book. She could see every muscle and tendon, as if he'd somehow been run through the wash and his skin had shrunk down a size. His eyes ran across her like the old farmer who ran the mobile slaughterhouse, sizing up Bogaloosa's dairy cows after their milk had gone dry.

That look put a pit in her stomach. She'd felt something good between her and Roy, at least she hoped she had, but another guy changed things. Maybe this shirtless guy especially.

She thought about her mom, working two jobs and falling asleep at her dinner plate, getting thinner every day until she died. Her mom who kept a notebook of scribbled half poems by her bed, who'd left college pregnant at eighteen to marry the man she loved and move to the plains and care for their daughter. Her mom who didn't take crap from any man, woman, or dog, no matter what kind of shit life served up on your plate. She could hear her mom's voice right now. *We can do hard things, baby girl.*

Then she thought of Bogaloosa in the barn, the smell of wintermint Skoal as he pushed her up against the milking stall. She wasn't going to accept that fate. She was going to choose. She would use what she had and make her way out of that place. She had to hope Roy would protect her until she could protect herself.

So she looked the new guy right in the eye like her mom had taught her. "I'm Helene," she said. "I need a lift out of here."

His face was colder than the wind. "This is a bad idea, Roy. We're on a schedule."

Roy just smiled at Helene as if he was interested in what she'd say next. Like this was a test, Helene showing how she could handle herself. And it *was* a test, she knew, because how she responded would set the terms for everything that followed. Now was not the time to show weakness.

"I've got money," she said. "I can pay my way."

"But where do you want to go," the shirtless man said.

"Like I said." She didn't look at Roy. "Anywhere but here."

The shirtless guy blinked his eyes, slow and lazy. "You're telling me you're willing to climb in a truck with two grown men you don't even know?"

She took the old revolver out of her pocket. The walnut grip was cracked, but she knew how to hold it and she knew how to shoot. Her daddy had showed her. "I can take care of myself."

Roy just smiled wider. "Well, I guess I know what you're running from," he said. "Did you kill him?"

"Another few days, I would have."

"Well, you don't need that peashooter with us," Roy said. "I'm not bent that way, and Frank, let's just say you're not his type."

Shirtless Frank just shook his head and pressed his sour lips into a thin line. "You got people going to come after you?"

She raised her chin. "I'm a grown woman, I can do what I want. All I got's a rented trailer and a boss who won't even pay minimum wage." She wasn't going to mention the county badge on Bogaloosa's chest. She was going to leave him choking on her dust.

The shirtless guy sighed as if he already knew how

things would end. "Risk-reward, Roy. I'm telling you, this is a bad idea. We have things to do, remember?"

Roy put the gas nozzle back in the pump. "Relax, Frank. She won't be in the way. I'll put her in a hotel while we work. If things don't work out, we'll drop her at the bus station with money for a ticket, wherever she wants to go. Maybe even a little cash stake to get her started."

Frank yawned, scratched his naked chest, and turned away, his face in shadow. "Whatever. That's on you, not me. I'm going to crawl in the back and get some shut-eye."

Roy opened his door and turned to Helene. "Is that little pink backpack all you've got?"

4

PETER

NOW

The gravel road followed the top of the high, grassy bluff along the river, so Peter Ash saw the car from a long way off in the angled light. It was only the sixth vehicle he'd seen all day.

He didn't mind the lack of company. In fact, solitude was half the point of the trip, getting his old green 1968 Chevy pickup from storage outside Portland, Oregon, and driving it to Milwaukee, which had been home for the last year or so. He had the windows down to feel the cold breeze on his face. The countryside seen through a windshield was, to Peter's mind, one of the finer things in life.

His rule of thumb was to stay off the highway wherever possible. He didn't much like the view of America from the interstate, with its chain restaurants, chain hotels, and chain gas stations with identical corporate snacks, everything the same with only minor variations, coast to coast. He preferred smaller local roads that followed the contours of the land, cracked, lumpy asphalt with no center line and no guardrail between him and the drop-off.

Gravel roads were better yet. There were a lot of them in the great wide open of the western plains. Like this pitted one-lane track, more dirt than stones, which wandered halfway across northern Nebraska before easing down the slope to the wide brown Missouri River. The winter had been hard and the spring came late, so the fields were still sodden with mud. The wind had dried the roads, though, and a plume of dust rose up behind him.

The plain white hatchback sat small and lonely in the vast landscape that carried no other evidence of humanity except for the road itself. Just the rain-swollen river, a few solitary trees climbing the broken bluffs on either side, and the high, pale grasses that still grew in every corner of the plains that hadn't been converted to farmland or pasture, the last hardy remnants of the original ancient prairie.

His first thought was that someone had stopped for a picnic, although the beginning of April didn't exactly offer picnic weather. If it was a fisherman, Peter figured the guy didn't expect to catch anything in the flood. If it turned out to be a couple of teenagers, skipping school in favor of sex education, he hoped they'd ignore him. Peter didn't want to stand in the way of romance.

But he didn't see any picnic blankets by the river. No fishermen or bare-assed lovers, either. No people at all. Just a huge downed cottonwood on the muddy bank, roots exposed and branches worn bare by floodwaters that had torn it up and washed it downstream.

Several years before, swollen by torrential spring rains and rapid snowmelt, pushing a raft of ice like a bulldozer blade, the river had scraped away half the dams and bridges and levees for three hundred miles. The heavy overflow had flooded entire towns, pushed buildings from their foundations, and turned fertile farmland into shallow lakes. The land and its people still bore the scars, from that catastrophe and others more subtle.

Peter took his foot off the gas.

His next assumption was a car problem. Unless his own truck was on fire or he was being chased, Peter made a point to pull over for stranded motorists. He had a truckful of tools and was good with his hands, so he felt he had an obligation, even a duty. Somebody had to help. Why not him?

In the city, that usually meant nothing more complicated than changing a flat or giving someone a lift to the nearest gas station. A half hour out of his life. An opportunity to be useful. With most breakdowns, the other drivers had cell phones and had already called a relative or a tow truck. They would thank him for his kindness, but they didn't need him.

That might not be the case out here, though. Cell

service was spotty in the lowlands along the river. On the winding gravel road, Peter hadn't had a decent signal since yesterday.

The little white car was mostly windows. At fifty yards away, he realized he couldn't see any heads through the glass. If the driver wasn't resting inside, waiting for help, he was probably walking the gravel southeast, the same direction the car was pointed, toward the nearest town. If that was the case, Peter would pick him up on the way, shorten his hike. He scanned the road farther downriver, but saw no figures there, either.

At twenty-five yards, the road curved slightly around a sinkhole, bringing Peter directly behind the vehicle for the first time, and he realized the passenger door was wide open.

Which was strange, he thought. On a cool April evening like this, technically spring but not exactly feeling that way, any sensible person with car trouble would stay in the shelter of the closed car, where the weak sun would greenhouse the interior and block the near-constant wind. When the sun dropped below the horizon, the outside temperature would drop to near freezing, if not below. Winter tended to linger on the northern plains, and this winter had been harder than most.

Peter stopped his truck ten yards back, turned off the engine, and got out. Without the rumble of the big V8, he could hear the wind whispering in the grass, the early blackbirds calling from the reedtops.

The river smelled of wet dirt and melted snow. The clouds were high and thin, the sky the faintest blue, the air so clear he could see into next week.

He was tall and lean, muscle and bone, nothing extra. He wore knee-torn hiking pants and a Milwaukee Tool T-shirt under a blue fleece pullover that June Cassidy had bought him in an attempt to up his clothing game, or at least get him to look less homeless. His hair was dark and shaggy, prematurely silver at the temples, and fell to his collar, covering the slightly pointed tips of his ears. With the bright, thoughtful eyes of a werewolf still recovering from the last full moon, he surveyed the hatchback.

It was newer, small, one of the cheaper imports. The chassis was low and the skinny tires looked fragile on the rough road. A lot could go wrong with a vehicle like that in a place like this. The paint was coated with a layer of road dust.

He stepped forward to get a better look. The car was empty. Nobody reclined in the front or stretched out in the back, earbuds blasting, oblivious to the arrival of Peter's pickup. There was no picnic basket or blanket, no duffel or purse, no food or water, not even an empty soda can or candy wrapper. The keys were in the ignition and the dome light was on. And all the windows were down. Like the outside, the dashboard and carpet and seats were coated with dust, everything except the driver's seat.

Had someone else already come to pick up the driver? That didn't seem likely. Why would you leave your car in the middle of nowhere with the door open, the windows down, and the keys still in it?

Peter turned and took another long slow look around. Not a soul.

Maybe the driver was a kid, gone joyriding and scared of getting caught. Peter was pretty sure joyriding didn't earn you a death sentence in Nebraska, but getting caught in the open without proper gear might just do the job. Peter was already feeling the chill, standing in the wind without a coat.

What if the driver had a medical problem, a heart attack or seizure, and lay crumpled and hurt and possibly unconscious in the grass nearby?

He put his hand on the car's dusty hood. Not warm, but not quite cool, either. The engine had stopped an hour ago, give or take.

"Excuse me."

Startled, Peter spun on his heel and saw a young woman standing on the far side of the cottonwood tree, just past the wide fan of exposed roots. Where the hell had she been?

She was perhaps the most pregnant person Peter had ever seen.

"My car stopped working." She gave him a hesitant smile. "I don't suppose you can give me a ride to town?"

5

She wore a faded print dress that fell below her knees, reminding Peter of a dust bowl photograph from the 1930s. She wasn't full in the face and body in the way of most pregnant women. With those skinny legs below and birdlike collarbones showing above the open neck of the dress, she looked like a teenage girl who had swallowed a beach ball on the way to the junior prom. Either she had the metabolism of a hummingbird or she didn't have enough to eat.

"Uh," Peter said.

She walked toward him around the upturned tree. She wore clunky untied winter boots that looked huge on her feet, but she stepped over the rocks and dirt with a careless, unconscious grace. Over the dress, she wore an off-brand canvas barn coat, faded blue, with the torn cuffs and collar that came from long use. The coat was much too big for her, but she still couldn't close it around her belly.

"I wasn't hiding from you," she said. "I was peeing. When you're pregnant, you pee a lot." Unembarrassed, she gave him a frank, appraising look that seemed strange on her young face.

She wasn't beautiful, not in any conventional way. But even vastly pregnant, with her tangle of straw-colored hair, the pale blush of her skin, the ripe swell of her body, there was something hopelessly, urgently desirable about her. It seeped from her pores and scented the air around her, mixing with and amplifying the rich wet tang of the swollen river and the slick fertile mud of its banks and the heady perfume of the ancient grass. Peter felt stunned at the sight of her, like he'd been kicked by a horse on the first day of spring.

She put her hands in the pockets of the coat and watched his face and waited.

The dress was so tight on her torso that he could see her bellybutton. The swell of her breasts strained the thin fabric, her nipples like gumdrops in the cold. Startled by the hormonal tide that washed over him, Peter made himself look away. He had met many beautiful women in his life, had committed himself to one of them, but he'd never experienced this kind of reaction to a stranger.

Even in that moment, he somehow knew no good would come from this.

But he couldn't just leave her there in the cold.

He closed his eyes and took a deep breath. He brought June Cassidy's face into his mind, the amused intelligence in her eyes, the spray of freckles across her cheeks, that wicked smile. Then he exhaled and the strange desire fell away as if he were an upright ape somehow suddenly granted the power of reason.

"Happy to give you a lift, ma'am." He cleared his throat. "I'm headed your way. Hop in."

Her body shifted slightly, like tension gone out of a spring, and she looked even younger than she had before. "Actually, I need to go west." She angled her head back the way he'd come. "To Lynch, or even Valentine. Is that okay?"

Peter didn't understand. He looked at the little car again. It was pointed southeast, the same as his truck. She'd been heading that direction, hadn't she? Then he saw the pair of handprints on the dusty white hatch.

He glanced down at her front tires. They were turned at an angle, with a small ridge of gravel pushed forward at the leading corners. She'd cranked the wheel before the car had stopped. She'd made a U-turn with the last gasp of the engine.

Or maybe not. He stepped back and peered at the road between the marks of her rear tires. He saw footprints in the dirt, dug in hard.

She hadn't driven the car in a U-turn, she had pushed it.

This skinny young woman, enormously pregnant.

He turned back to her, mouth already shaped to

ask the question, but she was staring away to the southeast, where a plume of dust rose in the distance. Somebody coming.

She shook her head, mouth grim. She gave Peter's 1968 Chevy a critical glance. "How fast can this thing go?"

He smiled. "Fast enough. I've made a few modifications." The dust boiled into the air, garishly lit by the afternoon sun. A mile or two away, he figured. "What are you running from?"

Her face had gone pale. "Trust me, you don't want to find out." She shifted from foot to foot, hands out of her pockets and balled into fists. "Are you taking me or not? Because we need to go right now. Otherwise you best just leave me behind and get yourself out of here."

"I'll take you." As she ran around the front of the truck, Peter climbed behind the wheel and turned the key. The big V8 came to life without complaint or hesitation. He felt its power thrum through the heavy reinforced frame and rise up through the shifter that vibrated under the palm of his right hand.

By then she was in and reaching for her seat belt. He eased out the clutch and made a gentle turn without throwing gravel or raising dust.

"I'm Peter," he said. "What's your name?"

She shook her head and stared out the windshield. "Just drive. Please."

"Yes, ma'am." Peter put the hammer down.

6

The narrow sloping track angled up the bluff, a rough mix of washboard, mud holes, and weed-tufted humps. At thirty miles an hour, Peter palmed the wheel with his left hand as he jockeyed the shifter between second and third, fighting the hill as well as the road. In the mahogany cargo box behind him, tools clattered and banged on their shelves.

Midway up, he shot a quick glance at the girl. She sat easily on the cloth-covered seat, feet spread wide for stability, reminding Peter of a veteran Afghan field commander on his favorite horse. She caught him looking and pointedly reached out the open window to adjust the side mirror so she could see behind them.

Peter didn't need to look in his rearview to know the dust cloud was getting closer.

The road was a little better at the top. When he hit forty, the truck bucked like a rodeo bull and his teeth clacked together hard enough to make him wish for a boxer's mouth guard. The girl had her feet braced against the floor now, one arm cradling her enormous belly and the other hand tight on the oh-shit handle. "This isn't going to do it," she called over the rumble and rattle. "You might as well let me out here."

"I don't want you to go into labor." Peter had combat medical training and too much experience using it, but that didn't include delivering babies, especially not on the bench seat of his pickup in the middle of this ocean of grass.

"Don't you worry about me," she said. "I'm tougher than I look."

Peter was getting that idea. "Is there any kind of clinic in Lynch?"

She bent to look in the mirror again. "We'll never find out at this rate," she said. "Not unless you can drive faster than this."

He put one wheel on the center hump and the other in the grass and pushed the truck harder, hoping to find the sweet spot somewhere in fourth gear.

As a Recon Marine lieutenant, the tip of the spear for eight long years, he found that he was better in a combat zone than he was on leave. His brain had rewired itself so profoundly for the fight that he could never quite turn off the reflex for war.

Knowing he needed to keep himself busy in the short pauses between the long deployments overseas, he'd tracked down the old Chevy in a barn in central California and poured himself into its restoration.

He'd rebuilt the engine from top to bottom, boring out the cylinders for added muscle. He'd replaced the springs and struts and tie rods and anything else that might break under stress. Because he was planning to return home and join his dad and his uncle in the family business, building high-end vacation homes in northern Wisconsin, he'd swapped out the original rusted cargo bed with a custom mahogany box to hold his tools. The focus of physical labor allowed him to step into a kind of temporary peace.

None of that changed the fact that the Chevy was a half century old. It sure as hell wasn't a race car or a dune buggy. It was a four-speed stick-shift work truck, built to carry a load.

The pickup hadn't saved Peter from post-traumatic stress, either. Once he'd mustered out, it rose up in an acute claustrophobia that he called the white static, which kept him from being indoors for more than a few minutes at a time. Unable to function in the civilian world, he'd walked away from everything for more than a year, living out of a backpack above the treeline of various western mountain ranges, sleeping in the open and hoping the purity of the high granite peaks would set him right, take away the static and wire his brain back the way it used to be.

It didn't help.

But meeting June Cassidy did. She'd given him both a reason to change and the kick in the ass he'd needed to put in the effort. He'd also gotten lucky in finding a shrink who was a combat vet himself. Oddly enough, it was a bartender spiking his beer with medical-grade Ecstasy that made the biggest difference. He still felt the static in a closed room, but he was learning to live with it.

Mostly the war lived in him now like a hungry wolf, curled nose to tail as if asleep, waiting always for the chance to spring to its feet.

Like now.

7

At fifty miles an hour, the Chevy felt like an amusement park ride with the safety features removed, bouncing so hard on the ruts that Peter could barely keep his foot on the gas. He had to clamp his mouth shut so he didn't bite off his tongue by accident. Every tool in the cargo box had already fallen from the shelves, but now he heard them rise and fall again with each leap of the truck. Beside him, his passenger held her huge belly tight with both arms, her feet up on the dashboard to lock her into her seat. Her face was flushed pink with excitement, and her tangled hair blew wild in the wind through the open windows.

Peter had allowed himself to hope that whoever was after her would linger by the river to examine the small white car. No such luck. Looking in the side mirror, he saw a dark vehicle crest the rise behind him.

It trailed a boiling brown cloud and grew a little larger in the glass each time he checked. Close enough now that he could tell it was a pickup, a big one, riding high on oversized tires with the heavy line of a roll bar showing above the cab. Better suited to this rough road than Peter's old Chevy.

Not that he was slowing down. In his experience, the deciding factor between success and failure was how badly you wanted it.

He showed his teeth and put his hand on the dashboard. He knew this good Detroit steel. Come on, old girl, he said silently. Let's show 'em what you're made of.

At sixty, somewhere between liftoff and a broken axle, the truck found equilibrium. A kind of levitation over the muddy ruts and weedy humps that made Peter feel like Luke Skywalker in his landspeeder. The grassland flew past in a blur. He checked the mirror and a smile spread across his face. The big black truck was falling behind.

He raised his voice over the wind. "How are you feeling? Okay?"

She nodded. Her arms were supporting her belly, but her eyes were on her fingers, plucking at the hem of her skirt.

He said, "Tell me the best possible way this ends for you."

"Best case?" She leaned to check her own mirror. "He rolls that truck back there, and you get me all the way to Valentine. I catch the first bus to Minnesota."

She took a hand off her belly to rake her hair from her face.

"What's in Minnesota?"

"My aunt. At least, I think she's there."

"Are you going to tell me what you're running from?"

"My husband." She looked away. "Soon to be ex-husband. Turns out he's not a very nice man."

"Why don't we just go to the police?"

She snorted. "They never helped before. Besides, my husband used to *be* the police."

"Then tell me the problem," he said. "Let me help."

She rolled her eyes. "Most of the men I ever met want to fuck me. The rest of them want to fuck me, too, but first they want to feel like they're *saving* me from something. Just like you."

Peter blew out his breath. "Lady, right now I *am* saving you from something. I might do a better job if knew what that something is."

She gave him a look that was older than civilization, probably older than the discovery of fire. A look that every woman knew, that every man hoped to see.

"I'm not wrong about you wanting to fuck me, though. I'll let you, if you get me out of this. I'll even enjoy it."

She closed her eyes lazily, then opened them again, a half-smile on her face, a blush on her cheeks. Nothing more than that, and Peter felt the blood abandon his brain and rush toward his groin.

"Jesus." He turned away and stared out the wind-

shield, more than a little ashamed of his body's automatic response. "What's the matter with you? You're
fifteen years younger than me and seriously pregnant."

The half-smile grew wider. "Never stopped anyone
else," she said. "Might make it sweeter." She angled
her head, suddenly a shy schoolgirl, although he knew
that, too, was a pose. "Why don't *you* drive me to
Minnesota? We could spend a few days at a hotel on
the way."

She was stunning, yes, but it was more than that.
The way she looked right at him, the directness of her
gaze. She was too young for that kind of knowledge.
He wondered at the history that had given it to her.

"No, thanks," he said. "I have someone waiting for
me." And he meant it.

He saw her face change when she realized he was
telling the truth. The sex bomb was gone and she was
just a scared girl, too beautiful for her own good,
pregnant, and desperate enough to drive alone into
the empty plains without food or water or warm
clothes. Now she was stuck in a truck with a stranger,
hoping to get herself free in whatever way she could.

She'd known her husband would come after her.
That's why she'd pushed her car around to face back
the way she'd come. To fool him into thinking she was
just on an afternoon drive, already on her way back
when she'd run out of gas. So if she got caught, she
could deny that she was running.

Peter had known a few cops in his day. They talked
about domestic calls as the worst part of policing.

Loaded with emotion, weighted with a history even the participants didn't fully understand. Violence always simmering right below the surface. The worst of humanity. Conflating love and sex with ownership and domination.

And Peter had stepped right into the middle of it.

June was going to murder him.

Just a nice, slow cross-country drive, he'd told her. Do a little hiking, sleep under the stars. Stay out of trouble, I promise.

He hoped June would understand.

What was he supposed to do, ignore a pregnant girl stuck in the middle of nowhere?

8

The road came to a row of low, grass-covered hills and angled north to run around them. Ahead Peter could see the abrupt horizon of the bluff above the river, where the road turned west into a long narrow cut skirting the edge of the headland.

He remembered this place from earlier in the day. At the end of the cut, the land opened up and the gravel track crossed a two-lane paved county highway. The gravel kept going though hayfields and pastures, but he knew the blacktop would be a straight shot to Lynch, the next big town, where the presence of others might provide some protection. The asphalt would nullify some of the big black truck's off-road advantage, too, and provide no dust trail to follow, either.

He checked his mirror again but couldn't see the other truck. Peter had gained more ground but he didn't doubt their pursuer was still behind him. Even if Peter managed to stay ahead, he couldn't just leave her in town. It was the first place her husband would look.

No, Peter would stay on the highway and keep going. Valentine was only two hours. Or even all the way to Rapid City, someplace distant enough to dilute the search and big enough for a serious hospital. If she didn't go into labor in the next five minutes. If the black truck didn't close the gap.

The road veered around the turn and into the long, narrow passage, curved to follow the arc of the river below. On the left lay a long limestone outcrop like a buttress holding back the hillside. On the right was the eroded bluff edge, thin sandy soil over the same weathered rock, the only reason this skinny strip of land hadn't already fallen into the water a hundred feet down.

The gravel flew beneath their wheels. A half mile, then a mile. The curve made it impossible to see too far forward. Still nothing in the rearview. Maybe another mile to the blacktop.

"Dammit," she said.

Something blocked the road ahead. A big pickup, this one gray with a high cap on the back, parked sideways across the gravel between the wall of stone and the edge of the headland. Two figures stood in the grass. Long guns hung down from their hands.

That was when Peter knew that he hadn't outrun the black truck. He'd been allowed to pull away so that he'd drive into this trap. The husband and his friends had radios or some local cell service that got a signal out here, far from the highway towers.

One of the figures raised his weapon.

"Hang on." Peter hit the clutch and brake and the Chevy slewed to a stop. Their dust cloud caught up and washed over them, pouring through the open windows like dirty river water. Coughing, Peter reversed to the rock outcrop, wheels spinning in the gravel, then cranked the pickup around to head back the way he'd come, hoping the dust might hide them. He needed to get the hell out of this shooting gallery before the black truck blocked the other end. There was more than one way to the blacktop.

"What does your husband want?"

"He wants me." Her fingers worried at the hem of her skirt. The dress was a pale print, but the hem had a faint blue pattern, like embroidery.

"What will he do?"

"Take me back to the home place." Her lips were pressed into a thin line, her shoulders curled forward over her belly like all the air had gone out of her. "He's a bad man. I was leaving him." She didn't look at Peter. "Sorry. You shouldn't have stopped to help."

"Somebody had to," Peter said. "Might as well be me."

As if he had a choice in the matter. He wasn't built to turn away from someone else's trouble. As far as he knew, he'd been that way since he was born. The Corps and the war had only sharpened the edge.

The road curved away from them, the bluff now on his left with the river running fast below. The air was thick with dust. He was in third gear with his foot to the floor and the engine's power rising in his ears. No sign of the black truck. For a moment, he allowed himself to hope.

Then a dark shape materialized out of the haze. The black truck was stopped in its own gathering cloud at a narrow place where the gravel threaded between the sharp-cut bluff and the cracked stone outcrop. Peter hit the brakes again and came to a halt thirty yards from the other vehicle.

Two men slid out of the black truck, driver and passenger. The dust was thick and swirling but Peter could see that they were carrying shotguns. He'd long ago learned to identify that silhouette in all possible conditions. Their big dark bores glared at him like holes in the world itself.

In his rearview, he saw the gray truck come to a stop thirty yards behind him.

He couldn't help but admire the tactics.

They had trapped him at a choke point, the passage too narrow here for him even to turn around. There was no way past either vehicle unless he could physically push one of the larger trucks out of the way.

Reverse would be better, he thought. His back bumper was beefier, and there was no chance that he'd wreck his radiator and render the Chevy undrivable. He didn't even have to move the gray truck very far.

Just get one rear wheel off the bluff and let gravity do the rest. Then find a place to turn around and put the pedal down all the way to the blacktop.

Peter revved the engine and rehearsed the move in his mind. The black truck's passenger swung his weapon up to his shoulder. Peter didn't like how comfortable he looked. The driver patted the air with his open palm, mouth moving as he tried to shout over the Chevy.

"He'll tell you he just wants to talk," the girl said. "Don't believe him."

Peter goosed the gas again. He didn't need to know what the other man was saying, the meaning was clear enough. Turn off the truck and get out. We won't hurt you, we promise. Cross our hearts.

Peter knew his plan was not good.

The instant he put the Chevy into reverse, someone would start shooting.

They might aim for Peter, but shotguns weren't precision weapons. He'd be a moving target, with the girl right beside him.

She was white as a sheet, knees drawn up and pinched fingers still working at the blue-embroidered hem of her skirt. He wanted to tell her to fold herself into the footwell where the engine might provide some protection, but he knew she couldn't fit, not with that big round belly.

He'd be risking her life, and the life of her baby.

She'd said her husband would take her home. Was that better or worse than dying?

Thirty yards ahead, the driver stopped patting the air and raised his weapon. His mouth kept moving, though.

Peter let up on the gas pedal. "Will he shoot?"

"He's already killed two people that I know of. He's cold as ice. And he doesn't know what I might have told you."

The driver of the black truck took one step forward, then another. In Peter's rearview, two men got out of the gray truck with their long guns up. The dust cloud had begun to thin. He had more questions, but not much time. "Where's the home place?"

She didn't answer. She seemed smaller now. As though she were already withdrawing into herself, preparing for whatever came next.

"Hey." He touched her arm. "What's the address? Quickly."

She looked at him, blinking. "I don't know the address. There's no mailbox. It's at the dead end of a dirt road, right on the river. Set deep in the trees. Look for the crosses."

That wasn't much. Peter opened his door and raised his hands through the gap. The driver was still shouting, but Peter ignored him. "What direction and how far?"

"East, maybe twenty miles? Right across the county line."

"Okay." Peter took a deep breath, preparing himself. His mouth tasted of copper. Adrenaline burned in his blood like gasoline. "I'll see you soon."

"Wait." The tendons stood out on the backs of her hands as she ripped the doubled hem from her skirt in a continuous ring. She lifted her feet to free the fabric, wrapped it into a small, tight bundle, and held it out to him. "Take this. For safekeeping."

He had new questions now, but they'd have to wait. The driver stepped closer. Peter was out of time. He took the bundle and thumbed it into his front pocket, then swung his legs out and got his boots planted. He kept his eyes on the driver, but in his peripheral vision, he saw the girl's hands at the neck of her dress, tearing it open.

Then he launched himself out of the truck. Two long fast strides, and he dove headlong off the edge of the bluff.

Chased by the dull booms of shotguns, firing.

9

In the air, Peter's racing mind hoped for three things.

One, that he'd leaped far enough, and the bluff was steep enough, for him to make it all the way to the water.

Two, that the river had risen high enough and carved a channel deep enough to prevent him from breaking his neck on the bottom.

And three, that the road dust had limited the other men's vision as much as his own, or at least enough to keep them from filling him with buckshot while still on the fly. If they were duck hunters, he was fucked.

He'd never jumped from that height before, and had timed his dive badly for the distance. As gravity pulled him down to the churning river, his legs toppled forward, his feet overtaking his head. He heard two more thudding shotgun blasts—*BOOM BOOM*.

Still somehow unpunctured, he had time to close his eyes and take one last breath before he hit.

When the backs of his hands broke the surface, he was already bending himself into a curve, trying to reduce the impact, keep the air in his lungs, and stay as shallow as possible. The water punched him hard on the back, but his breath held and he didn't arrow straight into the bottom. With the taste of wet dirt against his teeth, the arc of his body combined with his momentum tumbled him in a forward roll until his heels slapped something gritty. Then the current took him.

He didn't feel the cold at first, still riding the adrenaline of the jump from the bluff. His heavy boots dragged him down. For the moment, that was a good thing. If he could stay below the surface without getting trapped in the branches of a submerged tree or some other hazard torn loose by the flood, the water would carry him away faster than the gunmen could follow.

It was one thing to see the spring-swollen river from above. It was something else entirely to be submerged in its rough, turbulent power. With his eyes still closed in the churning murk, he couldn't tell up from down. The current pulled at his clothes, rolling him like a drunk on Saturday night. He didn't fight it. He kept his lungs full to stay relatively buoyant and opened his eyes to look for the brightness of daylight, glowing dimly through the silty water. Once he was oriented, he used his arms to get himself faceup, his feet raised and pointed downstream, but he didn't try to swim, not yet.

He wondered how many hours it would be before June began to worry.

Then the cold hit and took his breath away. It was like rolling naked into a snowbank without first cooking in a sauna. His chest seized and he fought for the surface and came up gasping.

POPPOPPOP. POPPOPPOP POPPOPPOP.

The staccato bursts of a semiautomatic rifle. Much better than a shotgun for accuracy over distance and not a welcome development.

He didn't turn to look or try to see where the rounds hit the water. He just sucked in a breath, then swept his arms upward through the flood and pushed himself back down into the muddy flow, hands already aching from the cold, knowing every second was taking him farther away from the shooters. He was just glad they weren't firing in single-shot deliberation. They'd be more accurate that way.

As far underwater as he could manage, he counted to thirty, nice and slow, focusing on the numbers to keep the panic at bay. Rising for air would kill him faster. Now the ache spread to his arms and legs and the back of his skull. Immersion was the quickest way to cool meat. Confusion was the first sign of hypothermia.

Shivering, he counted to thirty once more, as a red rose bloomed behind his eyes and the urge for air became overpowering. He forced himself to come up slow and easy, nose and mouth only, tongue tasting silt as he pulled in one sweet shuddering breath after another.

He turned his head to expose an ear and heard no gunfire. He raised his eyes above the water and blinked away the grit. The bluff appeared in the distance with the blocky shapes of three trucks parked on top. It was hard to tell how far the current had carried him in this wide-open landscape, but he thought he'd gone more than a quarter mile, safely out of effective target range unless the asshole with the semiauto was a better marksman than he'd been a minute ago.

He heard a rush of sound approaching and looked downstream again. White water boiled around a boulder ahead. Before he could navigate away, his feet hit something solid. The current flipped him on his head and into a standing wave that tumbled him like a front-loading wash machine. He swallowed ten gallons of river, then inhaled a lungful of water that burned with cold fire. He somehow resisted the urge to vomit or exhale or clench into a ball. Instead he flexed himself straight and threw his arms outward and, after a vertiginous spin, the wave spit him out.

His face broke the surface. Coughing and disoriented, he felt the seat of his pants grind the gravel bottom. He dug his heels into the sand and the current stood him up and pushed him back. The river only came to his waist. He'd washed out of the main channel. He widened his stance and leaned into the flow and managed to keep his feet.

Half-paddling with hands burning with cold, he struggled toward the far bank, where he fell to his knees shivering in the waist-high reeds and promptly puked up all the water he'd swallowed.

When his stomach was empty, he crouched in the cattails and peered upriver with a sour mouth and shaking limbs. The bluff was farther away now, but still visible in the distance. He could only see two vehicles. With its mahogany cargo box, he'd recognize the distinctive shape of the Chevy anywhere, even in the fading late-afternoon light. Behind it was the gray truck with its high cap on the back.

The black truck was gone.

He assumed the driver was her husband, the ex-cop. Was he also the tactician who'd come up with that choke point trap, back in the cut? Peter had to assume so. Which meant he also had to assume that, if the husband truly wanted Peter dead, he'd be headed downstream, back the way they'd come on that same gravel road. With the best rifle they had and both eyes peeled for a cold, wet man on the opposite bank.

That's what Peter would have done, anyway. He'd done a lot of manhunting, in his years of combat. According to the field manual, that was the job, to locate, close with, and destroy the enemy.

It's what he would do now.

He thought again about how scared she was, how she'd seemed to shrink in size as she curled herself protectively around her pregnant belly.

He didn't even know her name.

10

Roy had said she was safe with him, and Helene wanted to believe it. Anyway, she made herself believe it enough to get into the truck and get the hell out of Coldwater, Montana.

With her experience of men, though, especially Bogaloosa, she figured Roy's hand would be crawling up her thigh before they hit Grass Range. So she kept her daddy's pistol in her right hand, where he'd have to reach all the way across her body to grab it. If he even tried to touch her, she told herself, she'd shoot him. Even if that meant he crashed the truck.

None of that happened. Instead Roy yawned as he pulled his own holstered gun from his belt and tucked it in the door pocket. He glanced into the back seat, where Frank slept in a curl like a snail in its shell, then popped open a Coke for each of them and offered her some beer nuts. "Whyn't you talk to me, honey? We got a lot of miles to cover and I could use some help staying awake."

Settling in, revived by sugar and caffeine, Helene found herself telling Roy about Coldwater and her mom missing the curve above the Milk River. About how she'd gotten stuck working at the Gas and Grocery, about her predatory boss. The big truck was roomy and comfortable and it rolled steadily forward into the night. Roy kept asking questions and never turned the conversation to himself, which, in Helene's experience, was a first. She did learn that he used to be a policeman in Minneapolis, and he told a quick, funny story about searching a guy whose pants fell down, but then he changed the subject back to her.

The night drive reminded her of the year her dad had gone missing in North Dakota. Trying to find him, her mom had hauled Helene across four states in that old car, stopping at every sheriff's office, shale field, and man-camp they came across. Despite the sadness and loss, those long trips had given Helene some of her favorite memories. Her mom always had at least two jobs, sometimes three. We don't sleep, we work, she'd said more times than Helene could count. So Helene had never gotten a lot of time with her. But in those strange, weightless, highway hours between stops, they'd talked the hours away.

That closeness only made Helene feel more lonely later, working nights in the middle of nowhere, with her mom gone and nobody to talk to.

They never did find her dad. Without his paycheck,

their lives got a lot worse. That was how they'd ended up living in that one-room travel trailer behind the Gas and Grocery.

After the Cokes wore off, Roy's yawns got wider and wider until he finally pulled over on a barren roadside and looked in the mirror. "Hey, Frankie, I'm wiped. You okay to drive a little?"

Frank didn't answer, but he got out of the truck, shirtless and barefoot in the cold. The two men stood on the verge to pee, shoulder to shoulder like mismatched brothers, turned away from her in some odd gentlemanly gesture of modesty as the ditch grass blew sideways in the wind.

Roy really was a nice guy, she thought. All that worrying for nothing.

Helene needed to go, too, so she walked behind the trailer, dropped her pants, and squatted, feeling the wind on her backside, making sure not to get any on her shoes. To save money during that long bad year, she and her mom had camped out in parks and fields, often sleeping in the car. Helene had gotten very good at peeing outside. Even now, all alone in the world, she felt like her mom was standing beside her, keeping watch.

When she walked up to her open door, Roy was already sprawled snoring across the rear seats and Frank sat behind the wheel. He gave her a sharp look and suddenly she didn't feel like talking anymore. In the red dashboard glow, his bare chest with its too-tight skin seemed even more like an anatomy drawing. She tilted back the passenger seat and closed her eyes.

When she opened them again, it was broad daylight, Roy was behind the wheel, and they were pulling into the parking lot of a funky old motel. Roy looked different in a way she couldn't quite define but was certain she didn't like. Gone was the handsome, relaxed stranger who had charmed her in the night, replaced with this new man who seemed to look right through her.

Suddenly Helene was afraid again. Before falling asleep, she'd wedged her daddy's pistol under her right thigh, but now it was gone.

At the edge of the asphalt, Roy pulled the big truck and trailer crosswise to the stripes and gave her an empty smile. "Ride's over, honey, we're checking you in." Helene's fear spiked higher. She'd felt safe before but that'd been a lie. She saw herself lying on a bloody bed, naked as a jaybird, her body sliced open wide for the whole world to see.

He hopped out and walked around and opened her door. Her daddy's gun fell out onto the blacktop. Before she could move, Roy scooped it up and tucked it deep into his jacket pocket, then took her pink backpack in one hand and her upper arm in the other, wrapping his strong fingers all the way around her. "Let's go," he said. "You knew this was coming." Even his voice was different, the words coming tight and fast.

She walked beside him into the lobby, already numb. He took her driver's license from her wallet and handed it to the clerk. While the clerk did something on his computer, Helene tried to talk herself into being okay. You can do this, she thought. There's a price for everything. He can't be worse than Bogaloosa. You pay this now and you're free.

Wherever she was, the town looked large enough to have a bus station, right? She knew getting the gun wasn't an option. Absurdly, she thought about her underwear. She'd taken to wearing two pairs at once. It had felt like some kind of protection against Bogaloosa, but now it was the only underwear she had. The Montana farmboy had thought it was fun to tear them off her. She hoped Roy wasn't like that.

"Hey. Hey!" Roy snapped his fingers to bring her back to the present. To her surprise, he held out both room keys and her backpack along with a folded pair of twenties. "Don't forget to lock the security bolt. And get yourself a couple of good meals, I bet you're hungry. There's a few places to eat on the other side of the highway."

She stared at him, not quite understanding what was going on. "Wait," she said.

"Oh, right." He took her daddy's pistol from his jacket and handed it to her, then scribbled something on a scrap of paper. "Here's my number. Frank and I are working tonight. We'll grab a couple hours of shut-eye in the Walmart parking lot. We're heading west again tomorrow, so if you want another ride, set your alarm and be outside by seven. Got it?"

Before she could tell him she didn't have a phone, he was out the door and gone.

11

The room was on the first floor, with a view of the parking lot. As soon as she saw Roy's truck roll out toward the highway, she closed the curtains, stripped off her clothes, turned up the shower, and put herself under the spray.

Helene had never stayed in a hotel before. It was very different from the tiny travel trailer up on blocks behind the Gas and Grocery. The water got so hot that she actually had to turn the temperature down. She soaped and shampooed quickly, like she always did, then leaned against the wall and put her face up to soak in the warmth. She was certain the water would turn cold any moment, but it didn't. Finally she sat on the shower floor and closed her eyes and dozed while the hot water came down like it would never run out.

Wrapped in a giant white soap-smelling towel, she

rinsed her bra and undies in the sink and hung them over a lamp to dry. That part, making do, wasn't so different from home, where it was seventy miles to the laundromat. Then she upended her pink backpack and took stock of what she had.

It wasn't much, considering it was now all she owned. From the smaller pocket, a hairbrush and some scrunchies, her wallet with her driver's license and library card and the few dollars Bogaloosa had given her from her paycheck. The half tube of Bag Balm she'd taken from the cow barn because her hands were always cracked from milking in the cold. A handful of tampons. The candy bars and energy drinks she'd taken from the Gas and Grocery. And her magazines, of course, some new and some dog-eared and creased from reading. Sometimes the only thing that got her through the day was imagining herself in the life shown on those glossy pages.

Most of the stuff in the backpack's larger pocket had been her mom's, carried like talismans against the world. Her mom's favorite mittens and warm thermal top, because Bogaloosa was too cheap to turn the store's heat above sixty. The pair of thick dry socks that her mom had always kept in her own bag, which came in handy more often than you'd expect. But the most important thing was her mom's old notebook with its messy handwritten poems and the many inspirational sayings she was always repeating to Helene. It had a few important phone numbers inside the back cover, and old photos were wedged between the pages, showing Helene and her mom and dad back when she was a little girl and things were still okay.

Scattered across all of it was just over eight hundred dollars in cash, which included the loose wrinkled bills she'd taken from the Gas and Grocery's register and the crisp new hundreds Roy had given her.

She couldn't believe that was less than eight hours ago. It seemed like a lifetime. Maybe it was.

Although she was pretty sure eight hundred dollars wasn't enough to start a new life somewhere else, at least not by herself.

Her mom had basically run away from home at six-teen because her family didn't think women should even have jobs, let alone go to college. Helene had never met them and didn't want to. Her dad's people were all back east somewhere. She had never met them, either, except for her great-aunt Willa, who lived in Minnesota. At least Helene thought she still did. She hadn't seen the woman in years, but she'd always liked her.

Roy had taken her in the opposite direction of Aunt Willa's, but Helene told herself it didn't matter. She was out of Coldwater and away from Bogaloosa, that was the most important thing. As her mom liked to say, You can't control the wind, but you can adjust your sails.

Besides, Roy had promised to buy her a bus ticket. Even if he was lying, or she got scared of him and Freaky Frank and took off on her own, she *definitely* had enough money for a Greyhound to Brandon, Minnesota, even if it was a million miles away. So she wasn't going to worry. She was going to allow herself to hope. The thing with feathers, which was something else her mom used to say.

Aunt Willa could wait a few more days.

Helene's life was changing for the better. She could *feel* it.

She was still afraid, but at least she wasn't alone.

Or she wouldn't be, when Roy came back.

At seven the next morning, when the black truck and trailer pulled into the parking lot, she was dressed and packed and ready to go. Determined to be helpful, she had her pink backpack over one shoulder and three large coffees in cardboard cups from the hotel's complimentary breakfast buffet, carried in a stack. She hadn't gotten the lids on quite right, and hot black splashes spilled onto her hands, but she was used to worse. She never even felt the scald on her skin.

She glanced at the long black trailer. Something in there was humming. Also, the side of the trailer showed a red rectangular sign that she hadn't noticed before. BIG SKY PETROLEUM SERVICES LLC with a phone number below. Now she knew what they did for a living, she thought. Petroleum services, whatever that was. Maybe they had to fix the equipment at night while everyone else slept.

Roy opened the driver's door and got out, wearing

the same clothes and a tired smile. "You brought coffee? Honey, you're a lifesaver." He took two cups and handed one through the door to Frank. "I wasn't sure we'd see you this morning." His voice was an easy drawl, back to the relaxed, charming man she'd met at the Gas and Grocery. Whatever tension had held him the previous afternoon was gone.

She shrugged, playing it casual, and offered up her fistful of cream and sugar packets. "I don't know anybody in Livingston," she said. "Figured I'd stick with you another day."

He looked at her in the worn old sweatshirt. "Honey, you're shivering. Get inside where it's warm. We've got to cover some miles today."

Helene, she wanted to say. My name is Helene. But she didn't. She wanted the ride.

Instead, she walked around to the passenger seat and climbed into the truck. Just like that, they were back on the road. Whitefish, Montana, next stop. He and Frank took turns driving and sleeping in the back. Roy kept asking about her life. Frank never said a word.

The next hotel was different but everything else was the same. By the time they arrived, cold-eyed Roy was back. He handed her license to the clerk and paid for the room with cash peeled from his wallet. He held out the keys and a couple more twenties and told her he'd pick her up at seven. After another long shower, she watched TV in the room until she got bored, then went out and walked around, staring at the huge houses gleaming on the hillsides outside of town. Whitefish was colder than Livingston, though, and even though she walked fast, she never really got warm. The wind blew her hair all over. After finding a sandwich, she went back to the room and lay alone in the dark, thinking.

In the morning, she carried out three more cups of coffee. Warm Roy got out of the truck and gave her a smile with something extra in it. "Hey, I brought you something."

He reached into the cab and pulled out a winter coat. It was emerald green and puffy with down. There was no sales tag, but it looked really expensive. Somehow she knew it wasn't from any store she'd ever been in.

"Roy," she said. "I can't."

"Come on, try it on." He held the parka open for her like she'd only ever seen men do in the movies. "Don't worry, I got it at the Salvation Army yesterday. It was practically free. You wouldn't believe what rich people give away in these fancy towns."

She put the coffee on the roof of the truck, then shed her mom's old sweatshirt and stepped closer to him. She put in one arm, then the other, and before she knew what was happening, he'd spun her around and zipped her into the coat.

It startled her, but as he backed away, she felt the coat embrace her. It was like climbing into a warm bed. No, it was like Aunt Willa's super-soft guest bed with the electric blanket already on.

Her face must have told him something. He laughed. "Guess you like it. Does it fit?"

She nodded, not trusting herself to speak.

He didn't seem to notice. "Well, good. A special girl like you deserves something nice." He tipped his head at the truck. "You coming with us today?"

She nodded again.

He reached for the coffee. "Then get a move on, honey. We gotta be in Sandpoint by three."

When she walked around to the passenger side, she saw that the sign on the side of the trailer was different. It was the same size and shape, but it was white instead of red.

This one read WESTERN RESIDENTIAL SERVICES.

Which was when she realized that every time she asked Roy what he did for a living, he changed the subject.

12

PETER

NOW

Half a mile downstream from the bluff where he'd abandoned the pregnant woman, Peter crouched behind the reeds and scanned the far side of the river for a man with a military-style rifle. He didn't see anybody. But that didn't mean the other man wasn't there.

In fact, Peter felt certain he was, or soon would be.

He had zero basis for this feeling other than his own intuition, but he'd learned to trust his gut and was comfortable with his conclusion. Too much effort had gone into that pursuit. Four men and two trucks. They'd fired at him twice, once while he was jumping off the bluff, and again when he was in the water, coming up for air. He couldn't imagine they'd give up now.

Watching and waiting, he shivered uncontrollably in his wet clothes. The muscles of his stomach twitched as though electrified, trying in vain to warm him. The sun was dropping and the clock was ticking. With the temperature below forty and the wind blowing from the north, he might as well have been standing in a meat locker. He had to get moving soon, before hypothermia set in.

He turned to examine the riverbank behind him, looking for his next place of concealment, then abruptly scrambled behind a low stand of evergreens, where the foliage would break up his silhouette. No rounds flew past. Maybe the man with the rifle wasn't in place yet. Maybe he was waiting for a better shot. Maybe Peter was wrong and he'd gone home.

Untying his boots, Peter found a gap in the branches and peered across the river. The far bank was in shadow. It wasn't yet dark enough to require headlights, but the orange sun was low in the southwest. He didn't see any sign of the dust plume from a fast-moving pickup.

He removed his boots and poured out the water. He stripped off his fleece and T-shirt, then his hiking pants and wool socks and the high-tech long underwear bottoms that had seemed like overkill at noon. He was grateful for them now because, even wet, they would help keep him warm. The temperature would drop below freezing before midnight.

He stood barefoot on a flat rock and wrung the river from his clothes, lean and rough and naked but for the silt on his skin, as if sculpted by some imperfect shaman from no better materials than sacred dirt and snowmelt and mumbled prayers.

As he began to dress again, the fabric still damp and cold, he remembered what the pregnant woman had said about her husband. *He's already killed two people that I know of. He's cold as ice. And he doesn't know what I might have told you.*

Peter thought of the torn piece of fabric she'd given him, the embroidered hem of her skirt. He checked to make sure it was still in his pocket. She'd given it to him for a reason, he supposed, although he had no idea why. Some kind of good-luck charm? He wished he'd had time to ask more questions. It would help to know what he was up against.

A bad man, she'd said.

The fact that the other man had killed people wasn't Peter's main concern. Any idiot with a firearm could take a life. That didn't necessarily make him dangerous. Peter had lived a life of violence himself, in the Marines and afterward, to protect himself and the people he cared for, and sometimes to end a larger threat.

But what was the context for the husband's killings? Outside a bar, in a fit of drunken anger? As part of a greater scheme? He wouldn't be the first ex-cop to turn his skills to some criminal enterprise.

He doesn't know what I might have told you.

Maybe, like a few guys Peter had known in the service, the husband had grown to like the worst parts of the job. Had gotten good at it.

That wasn't the only problem. The way the husband had set the trap in the cut told Peter the other man had excellent local knowledge of the roads and terrain. He also was a decent tactician and had reliable partners with good communications. Between the four of them, now, they had at least three vehicles and two kinds of firearms.

Peter had none of those things. All he had were his wet clothes and the good folding knife he kept clipped inside his pants pocket. But he did have one advantage. He felt fairly certain now that the other man hadn't seen him leave the water. Although a good scope might allow him to see the damp trail Peter had left on the sandy bank, it would dry before long. Peter wondered how far it was to the nearest bridge.

Upstream across the river, the tops of the hills looked different. Softer, as if they'd faded somehow. But downstream, the colors were still bright and sharp. He looked higher, examining the vivid shoals of clouds lowering in the southern sky, and found the faint dusty outline of a gravel plume. The black truck was in motion over there somewhere.

He looked back toward the distant bluff where he'd left his pickup. Because he'd been carried around a curve in the river, he could no longer see the cut where he'd been ambushed. But he could see beyond it, where two sets of headlights appeared, headed downriver. The Chevy's lights were distinctive enough. He'd left his engine running.

Bad enough they'd tried to kill him, now they were taking his pickup.

With his wallet and phone in the glove box.

The shivering in his stomach muscles had spread to his chest and shoulders and back. He was tempted to build a fire, but knew it was a bad idea. Lacking a lighter or flint and steel, it would take time he didn't have, and the flames would be a beacon for the pregnant girl's husband.

Instead, as the dust cloud slowly billowed and his truck's headlights bounced along the bluff top, he leaned against a tree and laced up his boots.

He had twenty miles of open country to cover before daylight.

While four strangers were trying to find him and end his life.

Was it wrong that he might be having a little bit of fun?

13

Peter began to climb the high north bank of the Missouri, which rose in broken hills covered with cedar and pine seedlings, serviceberry thickets, banks of spiky thistles and Queen Anne's lace and a hundred kinds of grass. Taller cedars, along with still-bare oaks and maples, grew in the dense, brushy drainages where water remained in the soil over the long dry season.

Staying in the evergreen cover of the nearest ravine, Peter warmed with the climb. More than half-way up, he came to the ghost of an old road visible only as twin depressions in the soft sandy soil. The tracks rose from a flat spot in the drainage, maybe some long-dead farmer's summer picnic spot, to cross the hill in an upward arc. Following the ghost track was the easiest way to walk out of the river basin to the plains above, but it also would mean leaving the protection of the trees.

He turned and looked across the water. It was relatively narrow here, maybe three hundred yards across the braided channels and grassy sandbars to the top of the far hills. The haze of road dust was already fading. The sun had fallen farther and the slanted, golden light made the vast rolling landscape seem like something from a children's storybook. All that was missing was a princess in a high tower.

He told himself again that the other man did not know where he was. Other than the faint haze before the setting sun, he saw no sign of the black truck. Three hundred yards was a far target for a civilian shooter. Still, Peter felt a faint tickle at the back of his neck as the fine hairs rose in a subconscious warning he'd long ago learned to heed.

He didn't move. Just stood and watched, scanning for anything out of place. As both predator and prey, homo sapiens had evolved to be very good at pattern recognition.

His eye stuck on something dark in the distant dun-colored grass. Before the front of his mind could recognize the shape, his lizard brain told him to step sideways, deeper into the trees.

He saw a small, bright flash and a thin branch snapped by his left ear. Then he heard a faint *crack*, hollowed out by the distance. The shape changed and Peter suddenly saw a man lying prone with his eye to a rifle scope, cycling the bolt to chamber another round.

As Peter dropped to the ground, the dappled light crossed his face and he knew his mistake. He'd counted on the evergreens to block him from view, but the late-afternoon sun shone horizontally through the layered tiers of branches and made his outline clearly visible.

The muzzle flashed again and bark flew off a tree behind him, followed a half-instant later by another hollow *crack*. He rolled down toward the cleft in the hill, chased by two more supersonic rounds, then crashed into thorny brush as the land fell away. He tore himself free and dove into the dense cluster of cedars that lined the ravine's sides, then scuttled up the incline on his belly as more bullets tore through the green branches around him.

Again Peter had misjudged the other man.

The cedars died out below a giant solitary maple, which had killed off the local competition with its thick annual mat of fallen leaves. A lucky shot through the evergreens could still find Peter's vulnerable flesh. The maple trunk, on the other hand, would stop whatever this guy was shooting, unless he had a howitzer in his pocket.

Peter had been counting rounds and the pauses between them. He knew this was a fool's game to attempt with any guarantee of precision, especially while running for his life, but these shots were deliberate, at least a second or two between them, not the rapid semiautomatic fire that had chased him in the river. He'd also seen the other man cycling the bolt, which, along with the weapon's disturbing accuracy at a distance, made the weapon some kind of traditional deer rifle. Even having made this calculation on the fly, Peter was reasonably confident that the weapon had a four-round capacity plus one in the chamber. During reload, even if the other man had multiple magazines, Peter had a short window for movement, maybe four seconds, longer if he was lucky.

At this exact moment, his best guess was a single round left in the chamber. He gathered his feet beneath him, reached far to his left, grabbed a branch of a pliant cedar sapling, and gave it a quick shake. A bullet split the sapling as Peter slipped to the right and scrambled up toward the big maple. One Mississippi. His boots slipped in the slick fallen leaves. He fell to his knees. Two Mississippi. He reached for a raised root and pulled himself forward, legs pumping.

He felt something pluck at his fleece, followed by the hollow *crack* of rifle fire. Then heard the woody smack of another round hitting the edge of the maple's trunk just as he ducked behind it. Splinters bit his skin and fell down the back of his shirt.

He pressed himself against the tree, breathing hard and riding the adrenaline as round after round pounded into the tree. Was he hit? He brushed wood shards from his neck and found only a little blood on his fingertips. He probed his left side where the fleece had twitched and felt nothing wet, no pain. Just a neat pair of holes in the fabric directly below the armpit.

Another inch and he'd be hurting. Two more and he'd be bleeding out.

He'd felt so good about that four-round magazine. It wasn't hard to count to four, especially when you had all your fingers.

Then he had an unpleasant thought. Had the other man timed his shots deliberately in order to fool his target? If so, he'd been very convincing. Peter didn't want to begin to think about facing that kind of tactical planning.

Still, there was no feeling in the world like somebody shooting at you. Not a good feeling, not exactly. But it sure made the world sparkle more brightly while it was happening.

The firing stopped. Peter looked up. A heavy branch was just overhead, protruding opposite the line of fire. He pulled himself onto it, wanting to get a half-decent look at the other man from an unexpected vantage. The maple's trunk was thick enough that he could stay behind it easily. The tree was probably older than the Declaration of Independence. He went up another branch, then another, careful to keep his limbs out of sight.

He was well aware that the other man could be gaming him again, pretending to be out of ammunition. But he wouldn't look for Peter's head twenty feet off the ground, would he? If he did, it would be a very small target. Somehow, Peter wasn't reassured. Still, after a deep breath, he slowly eased one eye past the bark until he could scan the opposite hillside.

At three hundred yards and without optics, he knew

he wouldn't get a look at the other man's face. Whether by accident or by design, the shooter had also positioned himself directly before the setting sun, which shone orange through thin clouds and lit him from behind. So all Peter could see was a dark silhouette standing motionless in the tall grass, right elbow crooked to the side.

Peter had stood that way many times himself, thumb hooked in the strap of a rifle slung over his shoulder, facing downrange toward his quarry, planning how to finish the job.

The wind blew cold from the north. Peter shivered again in his wet clothes. It was a ridiculous thought, but he was sure the other man was staring right at him. And knew that Peter was looking right back.

Finally, the other man turned and strode up the hillside.

This isn't the end of it, Peter thought. Not for him, and not for me.

One way or another, we'll meet again.

It was hard not to take it personally when some asshole tried to shoot your lights out.

Especially when that asshole had come so damn close to succeeding.

Peter waited until a new plume of dust rose above the hills. Ahead of it, the big black truck appeared, flickering across the treeless gaps like a shadow on the plain, headed east.

As he watched, the truck's headlamps came on, along with a set of high bright floodlights that Peter assumed were mounted to the top of the heavy roll bar he had seen earlier. The combination made a distinctive pattern.

Peter jumped to the ground and double-timed up the brushy slope to the faint twin lines of the ghost road, panicked rabbits bounding ahead of him in the grass. He sprinted toward the top of the rise, hoping the high ground would let him track the black truck's path. What he saw confirmed his memory of the map. Perhaps five miles downstream, the distant details clear in the crisp, dry air, a long well-lit bridge rose above the braided river, connecting Nebraska to South Dakota.

The next downstream crossing point was thirty miles east, by Yankton. Upstream, to the west, there was no crossing until the hydro dam at Pickstown, at least forty miles.

The gathering dusk was in his favor. There were few cars visible, but they all had their headlamps on. In Peter's experience, rural drivers tended to be more conscientious about this detail, especially on winding country roads where the center line was more of a suggestion and any added visibility could save your life.

After only a few moments, a fast, dark shape appeared from behind a headland, with two sets of lights in that distinctive high-low pattern. It followed the curve of the highway, then turned onto the bridge.

Peter didn't need to see what happened next. He knew where the other man was going.

He put the river on his right and began to run again. Across the open ground to the east, toward the bridge.

The other two trucks, his own Chevy and the long gray pickup, were gone. The pregnant woman had told Peter that they would take her back to their home base. After that, Peter had to assume that the other men would cross the river and join the hunt.

14

Soon Peter was at the edge of a wide field that seemed to stretch from horizon to horizon. He looked at the setting sun and figured the time around eight o'clock. Other than the river down below and a few distant stands of trees planted by the old-timers to shelter their farmsteads from the summer sun and winter wind, there was nothing but corn stubble as far as he could see. Welcome to South Dakota.

Past the last row of cut stalks, Peter's feet found the smooth ground unbroken by the cultivator's knife. He pushed his pace into an easy, ground-eating lope that he knew he could sustain for several hours without stopping. His legs felt strong and his breath came easily. In his eight years as a Recon Marine, between training and combat, he figured he'd covered at least twenty thousand miles on foot, most of those miles carrying sixty to a hundred pounds of weapons, armor, ammunition, and provisions.

Since those days, still driven by the restless wolf of war that lived inside of him, he'd gone for countless night runs with a sixteen-kilo barbell in his battered old pack. As if, in those dark moments, he still needed the load on his shoulders to keep him grounded instead of careening away into the great midnight empty. Now, carrying nothing but his own emotional baggage, he felt weightless in the falling light, like he could run forever.

He wondered if that exhilaration came because he was moving, inevitably, toward conflict. The thought shamed him, even as it thrilled him. No matter that the conflict had not begun with Peter. Or perhaps it was more thrilling, more acceptable, because this coming violence was not of his own making. He could release the wolf with a clean conscience. As clean as his conscience ever got, anyway, after his war.

The air smelled of damp dirt and dead plants, the true green blush of spring still weeks away. The cropped vegetation crunched under his boots. To the southwest, across the river, a long shoal of clouds glowed deep purple. On the northern horizon, several pairs of fast-moving headlights marked an unseen road far away. None of them had the distinctive profile of the black truck, and none had slowed.

He only needed to run long enough to let his body heat dry his clothes and widen the search area by a few square miles, disrupting the other man's idea of where

Peter might be. A solitary human being, alone in open country, could be very hard to find.

He hoped the pregnant woman didn't disclose that she'd told Peter about the home place. Or that Peter had said he would come for her. If not, her husband would simply think Peter was looking for help, that he'd head toward the nearest house, looking for a phone so he could call the police. What any normal person would do when strangers began shooting at them.

That wasn't Peter's plan.

He wasn't exactly normal.

Although they were correct that he would stop at a farmhouse. He didn't care about a phone, at least not yet. He wanted a decent coat, some food in his stomach, and a long drink of water. A weapon would be nice, too. But what he really needed was transportation. In the last two days of driving, he'd seen exactly zero pedestrians outside the towns. If he crossed that bridge on foot, Peter would stand out like a sore thumb.

Not that he wasn't willing to run twenty miles over the course of five or six hours. But he couldn't exactly eat a giant steak burrito and fall into his rack afterward. He'd still have to recon the home place. Lay up in the fields or trees for hours, maybe days, to find his chance. All while June Cassidy worried and wondered where he'd gone. He was already overdue for a phone call.

A decent vehicle would let him change the whole equation. If he could get past them quickly, and cross back to Nebraska while they were still hunting him in South Dakota, he'd likely have an easier time retrieving his truck and the pregnant woman.

Because he didn't know anything about the others, including what they looked like, he couldn't trust anyone. Maybe there were more than four of them. Maybe some were women. They could have different vehicles he wouldn't recognize. They might even have people in law enforcement. It wouldn't be the first time Peter had run into bad cops. So he would avoid roads and towns, stick to the fields, and try not to get skylighted. At least one of them was very good with a rifle.

Three times, Peter slowed to pick his way through the thin line of trees and scrub that made up the cornfield's eastern boundary, then emerged onto the next stubbled plain and began to run again. In general, these field sections were a mile square, which meant he'd traveled more than two miles from the place where he'd climbed up from the river.

He was fully warm now, and his clothes were beginning to dry, although his heavy leather boots still squelched softly with each step. As the wide purple sky deepened into darkness, he hadn't seen any sign of the black truck. Maybe he'd miscalculated the time it would take to arrive. It wasn't a straight shot from the bridge. Maybe the other man had taken a different route, assuming Peter would head north or west. Peter wasn't counting on it.

He had already passed several isolated stands of the

tall, elegant hardwoods that sheltered farmsteads along the distant road to the north. Soon he spotted another, with a trio of lights shining through the bare branches. He angled across the field to approach from behind. It was a calculated risk, but he figured he'd gone far enough, and didn't see any advantage to waiting.

As he got closer, the steep roof of an old farmhouse materialized out of the gloom, dwarfed by a massive metal barn and a group of fat grain silos clustered along the road. He crept closer still, bent low and careful of the sound of his boots on the stubble, listening for a barking dog or an automobile engine. An owl called above him and the wind whistled through the skeletal trees. He circled toward the front, noting the unmown meadow that had once been a lawn. When he saw the dark, empty holes where the house windows had been, he straightened up and walked in.

Peter had seen his share of these homesteads before, growing up in northern Wisconsin. During one of the many farm crises over the last fifty years, the farmer had likely borrowed more than he could repay. Maybe hail had taken his crop, or drought. The bank didn't care. After foreclosure, some agricultural conglomerate had bought up the acreage and machinery, ignoring the perfectly good century-old house. In the decades since, the weather had rotted out the windows and doors, scoured the clapboard free of all but the most tenacious chips of paint, and reduced the roof to bare boards that did nothing to stop the rain or snow. Only the dry climate, ageless craftsmanship, and inertia kept the house standing.

The new barn, set close to the road, was a different story. It was an ugly sheet metal shed the size of an eight-family apartment building and built as cheaply as possible. Four green John Deere combine harvesters were parked out front, their hunched forms like giant mechanical beetles with wide, toothy corn headers still mounted at their fronts. On the far side of the packed dirt yard, half a dozen thick steel silos squatted close together on round concrete pads, dwarfing Peter with their collective size.

This was no longer a farm, at least not the way Peter thought of a farm. It was an industrial production facility whose output was grain. The owner was a corporation headquartered in a low-tax state, overseeing its operation by satellite and the cameras mounted on the barn gables and light poles. The same thing was happening, or had already happened, across much of the country, multinationals scooping up land anywhere they could create economies of scale. With price supports vanishing and commodity prices dropping, the remaining family farmers could barely break even, let alone turn a profit from year to year. Anyone who worked here would be an hourly employee, subject to firing at the whim of a supervisor. At this time of year especially, awaiting the spring planting, there would be no personal items inside the barn, certainly no food or useful spare clothing.

If Peter wanted supplies, he'd have to keep moving.

Find a functional farm, not just an empty shell, and hope the barn was unlocked. That might be harder than he'd originally thought.

A coyote howled from the direction of the river. Another answered from farther away. He looked at the darkening sky, knowing these were the last few moments before true night. It would be several hours before the moon rose enough to give him any help, and he had a lot to do in that time. Then he heard the soft rush of a big engine in the distance.

He jogged past the far corner of the barn to get a view up the road. To the east, against the pale stripe of gravel, he saw a small dark shape, maybe a half mile away and coming fast. From the high profile, probably a truck. Most of the vehicles Peter had seen in the last few days were trucks of some kind or another.

Whoever it was, they'd forgotten to turn on their headlamps.

The vehicle rolled closer and Peter retreated into the gloom between the huge barn and the combines. He didn't think he would be visible to a passing car, but better to be safe than sorry. Then the brake lights flared and Peter saw a familiar silhouette. A jacked-up pickup with a roll bar mounted above the cab, shedding speed fast.

15

Peter backpedaled down the row of muddy harvesters parked nose-in before the barn, feeling small beside the hulking green beasts.

Before he could get past the final combine and into the cover of the trees, the driver veered into the farmyard, flipped on his headlamps and high bright floods, and began a slow, deliberate turn across the hardpacked dirt.

Peter stepped behind a thick-lugged tire that rose to the top of his head. It was the only available cover, because the big machines stood high enough off the ground that his legs would be visible anywhere else. The fierce illumination crept toward him, blasting each combine in turn and making strange, shifting shadows on the barn. Terrified rabbits zigzagged into the weeds. Peter watched them run and thought of the man with the scoped rifle and considered his options. He liked none of them. He readied himself for a sprint.

But the lights swept across his hiding place without pause. The pickup continued its curve, washing over the stand of maples, the abandoned farmhouse, the shining silos, and the unmown weeds along the road. After the vehicle completed a full loop, it came to a stop in the middle of the yard, facing away from the road and into the trees.

Then a new and more powerful light lanced out, probing the stand of maples and ruined house like an accusing finger. The passenger had a handheld spot, a useful tool for finding escaped livestock and shining deer out of season.

At least Peter knew they hadn't seen him. If they had, they'd have started with the combines.

With the passenger's attention on the trees and house, Peter got a better look at him. Late twenties, angular and pale, sharp features and fair hair brushed straight back from his veined forehead. Despite the cold and his open window, he wore no coat, just a tank top. His arms were thin but hard-looking, like alabaster hammer handles, and he managed the heavy spotlight with ease, playing it across the tree trunks with his left hand across his chest while he dangled a big chrome revolver out the window from his right. From the twist of his lips, he seemed both bored and annoyed, as if balancing someone else's bank account after months of neglect.

Bored was bad. It likely meant this manhunt was a

chore the pale passenger had done before, and with enough repetition to get good at it. Annoyed was especially bad. He was motivated to finish this task so he could move on to something more interesting.

Who the hell were these guys? Peter was acutely aware that he had no weapons other than his pocket-knife. The other men definitely carried plenty of ordnance. In addition to the big chrome revolver, which looked to Peter's educated eye like a .357, one of the most powerful pistols ever made, Peter had already seen shotguns and a very accurate scoped rifle, not to mention the military-style semiauto carbine he'd heard firing at him from the river.

To make things more challenging, the driver had stopped the truck at a point dead center between the edge of the trees, the cluster of silos, and the row of harvesters. Whether that was an intentional tactic or an unconscious one, it had the effect of putting the men at least thirty feet away from any potential threats. That was a long way to run toward a man with a gun.

But if Peter could get his hands on the revolver, the game would change.

The spotlight roved from the trees toward the big new barn, paused on its locked door, then moved on to the row of harvesters, the bright beam poking into the shadows beneath and between them. Peter tucked himself against the hard lugs of the tire and kept himself still. It would be nice to do some damage. If he could come up behind them, he might have a chance.

The spotlight passed him and the truck began to

roll again, now making a slow one-eighty that allowed the passenger to play the spot across the silos, lighting the dark gaps between their shining metal sides. In the relative darkness, Peter crept through the space between the harvesters toward the open yard.

Now the truck was pointed at the road and the driver was in view, but Peter didn't like him any better than the passenger. Also late twenties, his face was focused and intent. His head moved in a smooth swivel, eyes scanning the middle distance with a hard smile playing at the corner of his mouth like there was nothing in the world he'd rather be doing. Tipped up onto a backward ball cap was a night-vision headset. Which explained how he drove in the dark. But the farmyard's pole lights would have flared out the headset, which was why he'd switched his headlamps back on.

At least the driver wore a decent coat. His right hand was on the wheel and his left elbow was bent out the window, a full-sized automatic pistol in his hand.

Peter had wanted the .357, but the driver's gun was just as good. Maybe better, because the automatic's magazine would have more than six rounds. Either way, with a pistol in his hand, Peter would have a shot at the remaining man.

The pregnant woman said her husband had been a cop. Had he also been a soldier? Peter didn't see any obvious signs. None of the usual window stickers, no high-and-tight haircuts or visible military tattoos.

He was certain now that the way they'd handled themselves on the other side of the river, organizing the trap at the narrow place between the hill and the bluff, was not beginner's luck. Nor was the way the sniper had found Peter after he'd climbed out of the water. Someone from the other truck had probably acted as his spotter, using a scope or binoculars to track Peter in the river. And they had used night-vision gear to hide the distinctive pattern of the headlamps, as if they had known Peter would be looking for it. Then the quick turn into this farmyard where they had turned nighttime into day, scouring the shadows with their spotlight.

Each time, Peter had been lucky not to be caught or killed.

Which meant his next step wasn't going to be easy.

But if it worked, he'd have everything he needed. A vehicle, a phone, and, if his aim was good, a warm coat without any holes.

He took a long, slow breath, oxygenating his system as he calculated the distance to the truck. Before they had made the turn, it had been thirty feet. Now it was fifty. Call it sixteen strides at a sprint, with his boots crunching on the dirt with each footfall. Five seconds for the other man to notice. It was a long time.

Another deep breath and the taste of copper in his mouth as he thumbed open his knife and tucked the three-inch blade behind his belt for easy access. The knife was a last resort. He wanted both hands free to control the gun. And he didn't want to get blood on the coat.

He would approach from the driver's blind spot, to the left and slightly behind, trying to stay out of the side mirror and the other man's peripheral vision. But he wouldn't be silent or invisible, and the other man would almost certainly hear Peter coming despite the engine noise, or maybe clock a flicker of motion before he arrived. To bring the pistol to bear on Peter, however, the driver would have to hyperextend his shoulder, reducing his ability to aim. Or he could twist in his seat, but that contortion would also compromise his marksmanship. Worst case, if he noticed Peter early enough, he might open his door and get one foot on the ground. That would give him the best chance to hit a moving target. But if Peter got there first, he could capture the arm and strip the weapon. Then reverse it and pull the trigger.

He'd aim for the legs and then turn to the passenger and do the same. Depending on the length of the struggle, the passenger could have several extra seconds to react, although he would be reluctant to fire, Peter hoped, because the driver would be in the way.

Peter wouldn't kill them unless he had to, at least not both of them. He had questions to ask.

He tried not to think about what might happen if he failed. He certainly wouldn't be able to free the pregnant woman from her husband. June Cassidy would have no idea where Peter had gone or what had happened to him. The other men would want his corpse to disappear, so they'd probably dump it in some untracked creek drainage and let the coyotes pull the meat from his bones. From June's perspective, Peter would simply vanish from the face of the earth.

There was no use dwelling on it. He would simply have to succeed. He took another long breath. The adrenaline filled him up and sharpened his attention into a point. He dug the toes of his boots into the soil for traction. He needed the driver to turn away, just for a moment. Maybe he should find a clod of dirt and throw it.

Then the spotlight went black. The driver took his foot off the brake and the truck began to roll. Peter stepped out from between the two big harvesters, heart pounding hard. He wanted to call out, but he didn't. The truck picked up speed and the driver killed its headlamps and floods. Peter stood in the open, hands flexing at his sides, as the truck turned onto the gravel road and continued west, the engine rising as it carried his attackers into the darkness.

The whole thing had taken two minutes, maybe three.

Kind of a disappointment, really.

Peter thought again about the pregnant woman. Once he kept his promise, once he found his way to her and got her free, he'd have a better idea what this was all about.

When he could no longer hear the truck, he turned east and began running toward the next stand of trees, a mile away.

16

Every day, the routine was the same. In the afternoon, the cold-eyed Roy checked Helene into the hotel, handed her the keys, gave her money for food, then drove off with Frank. Helene took a shower and washed her underwear in the sink, then spent the evening exploring the town, finally warm in her new coat, soaking up everything that wasn't Coldwater, Montana. The next morning, the warm, smiling Roy picked her up in the parking lot. She handed over his coffee and they headed off to the next place.

Each night, a new town. Wednesday in Sandpoint, Idaho. Thursday in Winthrop, Washington. Friday in Leavenworth, Washington. Saturday in Bend, Oregon. Through high mountain passes and dark evergreen forests, fast-running rivers and tilted meadows. All of it so different from where she'd grown up on the Montana plains.

They rarely drove on the interstate. Although the hotels were always clean and comfortable, they were also small and old and somehow faded, like photographs from another time. For lunch, Roy and Frank picked little roadside restaurants, usually taking their meals to go in squeaky Styrofoam containers.

Frank talked to Roy sometimes, but rarely to her. As if Frank was pretending she didn't exist.

Every morning, the trailer had a new sign. SAWTOOTH CONSTRUCTION. WASHINGTON EQUIPMENT REPAIR. NORTHWEST PROPERTY MAINTENANCE. MOUNTAIN RENOVATION. And whatever was inside, it never stopped humming.

She didn't want to ask. She was warm in the green parka. Someone else was paying for her food. She was seeing the world.

Roy gave her other things, too. When he picked her up in Sandpoint, Frank was asleep in the back and a soft leather duffel sat on the passenger seat. Roy said, "I thought you might want something else to carry your things."

Helene picked it up and turned it over in her hands. It wasn't brand-new, she could tell, but she was pretty sure it didn't come from Goodwill, no matter what Roy told her. It was way too nice. Plus, that night, in the bottom of the bag, she found a single men's black dress sock.

Past Spokane, he pulled into the Walmart parking lot on Highway 2. "It finally occurred to me that you'd probably like a change of clothes." He pulled out his wallet and counted out two hundred dollars. She stared at him, speechless. He flashed a tired smile. "Go on, get what you want." He leaned his head back and closed his eyes. "Take your time, have some fun. We're ahead of schedule."

Helene hurried anyway.

In Winthrop the next morning, she found a jet-black sweater neatly folded on her seat, the material like her dad's heavy wool work shirts but softer than anything she'd ever owned. Right there in the cold hotel parking lot, she shed the green coat and her mom's sweatshirt, suddenly very aware of her body in the thin Walmart T-shirt and baggy jeans as she pulled the sweater over her head. All her clothes were over-sized because she hadn't liked the Gas and Grocery customers staring at her, and the black sweater was much more snug in the chest than she was used to.

Still, it fit like it had been made for her, and Roy smiled so warmly that she kept it on. All the way to Leavenworth, she'd kept brushing the soft sleeve across her cheek and glancing at him. Roy kept his eyes on the road.

Day after day, gift after gift, she kept waiting for him to *do* something. To put his hand on her thigh, to kiss her, to walk her to the room and start undressing her, *something*.

Instead, he was the perfect gentleman. He didn't even touch her arm.

She knew he liked women. She could feel him

watching her when she wasn't looking, although she never once caught him at it.

He certainly didn't stare at her the way other men did. Their hungry eyes wandered freely all over her body, feeding greedily as if she was theirs for the taking. As if she couldn't see them doing it, couldn't *feel* it like ants on her skin. As if she wasn't even a damn person, just some dumb object made purely to give them pleasure.

Roy barely looked at her face. When he did, his eyes slipped away immediately, as if on their way somewhere else. Even when he gave her something nice, he only glanced at her for a moment, just long enough to confirm that she liked it.

She began to wonder what was wrong with her. Why hadn't he done something?

He was a lot older than she was, at least seven years.

Did she *want* him to do something?

She didn't know. Maybe.

By the time they were headed south toward Bend, Helene could no longer sit beside Roy without being acutely aware of his presence. She noticed everything about him. The faint smell of sweat when he peeled off his coat as the sun warmed the cab of the pickup. The way he bit the inside of his lip as he peered past her out the side window, maneuvering the truck and trailer into a parking spot. How he ate, even while driving, with a kind of delicacy that she had never seen in a man. He took small bites and didn't lick his fingers. He always used a napkin.

When they walked into the hotel, she was conscious of him at her side, his rough strength and size. When he handed her driver's license to the clerk, she felt the tension humming through him, the change that came every day before he and Frank went off to work. When he walked away from her, out to the parking lot and the waiting truck, she watched the sway of his broad shoulders in the flannel shirt, his narrow hips in the faded jeans.

Then he was gone and she was alone again. Killing time until the next morning when he came to pick her up.

It didn't help that Frank still wouldn't talk to her. When it was his turn to drive, he turned the heater off, then plugged in his phone and played one audiobook after another. Not the kind of mystery stories her mom had gotten from the library, but weird stuff about real criminals and the police who chased them. The latest was a book about someone called the Golden State Killer.

Between Bend and Klamath Falls, she kept sneaking looks at him, still shirtless, his skin pale, not an ounce of fat on his whole body. His irritation at her presence came off him like the stink of spilled diesel, harsh and insistent.

Without the heat, it was cold in the truck. She pulled the green coat over her like a blanket and gathered her courage. Finally, she said, "Frank, why don't you like me?"

"Don't interrupt when I'm listening to a book." He shook his head. "I wish to hell you'd gotten in somebody else's truck."

"I'm sorry." She turned to look out the window. She wasn't going to cry, she just wasn't.

He shifted in his seat. After a moment, he sighed. His finger stabbed at the radio and the truck went silent. "It's not you, all right? The work we do, it's difficult and complicated. Roy never should have offered you a ride. You're in the way." He glanced at her, then away. "Anyone would be in the way."

"Okay." She cleared her throat. "Thank you for saying that." They drove a silent mile. Then she asked, "Frank? What can I do to help?"

He glanced into the back, where Roy was sprawled, snoring, then looked at her and dropped his voice. "The next time he checks you into a hotel? Don't spend the night. Don't meet us in the morning. Just find the bus station and take the first ride out of town."

She lowered her voice to match his. "I don't understand. Is that what Roy wants?"

"No." Frank had that sour look on his face again. "You're not the first girl he's picked up, you know. But he thinks you're different, somehow special. Some kind of good-luck charm."

"Really?" She gave Frank her sunniest smile. "Well, maybe I am."

He shook his head again. "You're not."

She'd gotten Frank talking, so she figured she might as well make the most of it. "What kind of work do you guys do, anyway?"

He flashed her a look. "Dangerous work. Dangerous for all of us. That's why you should get on a damn bus. And that's all I'm going to say about it."

"Can I ask another question? It's personal."

Now he glared. "If I said no, would you shut up?"

"Prob'ly not," she said. "But it passes the time, doesn't it?"

He sighed again. "One last question."

"Roy said he used to be a policeman, in Minneapolis. Is that where you two met?"

Frank nodded. "We were partners."

"So what happened? Why aren't you with the police anymore?"

In the back, Roy smacked his lips in his sleep. Frank glanced over his shoulder. Roy started snoring again. "That's two questions," Frank said.

"Come on, Frank. Please."

He shook his head. "You don't want to know the answer. Trust me on that."

Then he stabbed a finger at the radio and the Golden State Killer came on again.

The rest of the way to Klamath Falls, Helene turned over the conversation in her head. It was nice to know that Frank didn't actually hate her. Had Roy really said she was his good-luck charm?

She hoped it was true. If so, it would be the nicest thing anyone had ever said about her.

God, she couldn't stop thinking about him. He was no farmboy, that was for sure. She wanted his hands on her skin. She wanted his weight on her body. When she closed her eyes, she could almost feel it.

When they arrived at the musty old Klamath Motor Lodge, Roy checked her in, handed her the keys and a pair of twenties, and walked back out to the pickup. She watched from the lobby as he turned the truck and trailer around in the parking lot. Frank held her eyes from the passenger seat, and raised a hand in farewell.

Helene found the room, took a shower, went for a walk, grabbed dinner, and went to bed, thinking of Roy all the while.

The next morning, she met them in the parking lot with three cups of coffee and a smile.

17

After Klamath Falls, they spent a short day driving down into California. The trailer still hummed. The sign on the side read GOLDEN STATE SOLUTIONS.

Before Lake Tahoe, Roy turned off the highway at an open gate with a big red T set in a red metal circle mounted on a pole. After a long, winding drive, they came to a huge timbered lodge set deep in the pines.

It reminded her of the fancy hotel outside of Livingston, where her aunt Willa had taken her after finishing the seventh grade. It was very hot and the pool was the main attraction, but Helene felt awkward in her swimming suit and hadn't wanted to go in the water with boys. She'd thought Aunt Willa would complain, but she had just smiled conspiratorially and taken Helene river rafting and horseback riding instead.

"What is this place?"

"It's a resort." Roy yawned. "They have a heated swimming pool, a spa. Great steaks in the restaurant, too."

Frank got out and stretched. He hadn't spoken to her since their conversation the day before.

She followed them into the lush lobby, eyes wide. This was no funky old motel. A huge chandelier made of elk antlers hung down from the high, peaked ceiling. An enormous stone fireplace dominated the far side of the room, flanked by couches and armchairs made with real leather. On a table in the corner stood a big crystal jar with lemon slices in ice water and three kinds of complimentary wine. The glasses weren't plastic, either.

"May I help you?"

The woman at the reception desk was stunning in a French braid and formfitting blouse. Helene, on the other hand, was on her third day in the Walmart jeans and wrinkled button-down shirt, although she had washed the shirt and her bra in the sink the night before. Even her sneakers came from Walmart. She raked her tangled hair back with her fingers and looked around nervously, feeling completely out of place.

No wonder Roy didn't want her. Even in his beat-up Wranglers and flannel, he walked in like a movie star, like he owned the place. He could have anyone he wanted. The receptionist couldn't stop staring at him.

Roy pulled out his wallet and, for the first time, handed over his own driver's license and a credit card instead of cash. He had reserved three rooms for two nights.

"Wait," Helene said. "You guys are staying, too?"

"We worked hard the last week," Roy said. "I think we've earned a little rest."

Without a word, Frank reached for his key and turned to go. He still hadn't put on a shirt.

Roy put out a hand to stop him. "Why are you so damn grumpy, Frank? We've got a few days off. Live a little."

Frank just made that sour face and walked away, a canvas bag slung over one bare shoulder.

"There is just no pleasing some people." Roy held out a hand, ushering Helene forward. "After you, honey. Our rooms are all right next to each other. I'm going to hand over my dirty laundry, take a long shower, then go for a swim. Maybe get a massage."

Helene didn't know how to ask for what she wanted. They walked down a long hall. Frank was far ahead of them. Roy kept talking. "You can go to the spa, get a mud bath, whatever you like. My treat. Just tell them your room number, it's all paid for." He touched her bare arm with a finger. A shiver passed through her body, but he didn't seem to notice. Had he ever really touched her before?

At the end of the hall, Frank opened his door and stepped inside without looking at them. The door thunked shut. Roy looked at the numbers on the wall, then stopped. "I guess this is me. Which means you're right next door."

He gave her the good smile. Suddenly she was flooded with his warmth, just like the night when she'd first met him at the Gas and Grocery. It was as if he could see deep inside, all her fears and weakness and stupidity, everything she lacked, and he liked her anyway. She hadn't known how much she needed that. How much she needed him.

She knew what her mom would have said. Fortune favors the bold! She cleared her throat. "Um. Roy?"

He had his key card in the lock now. He turned the handle and the door swung open. He looked back at her. "What, honey?"

She didn't care what he and Frank did for work in the middle of the night. She didn't care about the different names on the side of the trailer or the fact that she knew almost nothing about him. She didn't care about anything. She wanted to trust him. Maybe she loved him. She didn't have anyone else. This was it.

Her mouth was dry. "I've been trying to think of a way to thank you for how kind you've been to me."

"Aw, you don't have to thank me," he said. "You needed a hand, that's all. I'm happy to help."

His eyes were bottomless. A faint smile played on his lips. She'd never really noticed his mouth before. She stepped closer to him. "Are you going to make me say it?"

Something changed in his eyes, a flickering shadow rising from the depths. His smile became wide and knowing. "Oh, yeah."

She realized now that he'd been playing with her,

maybe for days. Maybe he wasn't who he seemed. It didn't matter. She put her hand flat on his chest, feeling his heat, then brushed past him into the room. "Well, I'm not going to say anything." She set her things on the bed and did her best to match his smile. She began to unbutton her shirt. "But I'll do absolutely anything."

He walked toward her, the heavy door slamming shut behind him. "Anything?"

Finally, she had his attention. "Everything." She slipped her fingers behind his belt buckle and pulled herself closer.

By the time he was finished, she'd done more things than she'd known were possible.

He was rougher than she liked. Sometimes it hurt.

She didn't mind.

Roy was hers now.

She was safe.

18

PETER

NOW

As Peter worked his way east toward the bridge, wet boots squelching with every step, he saw the spotlight's bright, interrogating finger behind him, again and again. Ahead of him, he saw another.

The lights probed farmyards, investigated the lines of trees and brush between fields, and searched across the stubble. More than once, he had to drop down in the dirt with his head turned away so his face didn't reflect the glare. Waiting while the wind blew through his still-damp clothes and the cold leached up through the soil.

He wasn't worried about the spotlights. Peter was a small figure in a very large landscape. No, his main concern was the night-vision headgear.

Because the other man would understand the size of the landscape, too, and how it might help Peter feel safe in the expanse of night. The other man would use that feeling of safety by sweeping the spotlights across a field, then turning them off to watch and wait in darkness until Peter, believing he was invisible, began to run again. Humans had been hunters since they first came down from the trees, and nothing drew a predator's eye like movement.

Worst case would be if the headgear had a thermal setting. Peter wouldn't need to move at all. After two hours of stop-and-start running on this cold and windy night, his heat signature would be bright as a bonfire.

If he hadn't seen the goggles at that first farmyard, they might have had him already.

If he wasn't careful, they still could.

The itch between his shoulder blades had only gotten stronger. He hadn't forgotten how good the other man had been with that scoped rifle. Or how many times he'd anticipated Peter's tactics and countered them. It was, in fact, a little freaky, as if the guy could somehow read Peter's mind.

But Peter wasn't in a war zone, he was in the upper Midwest. He had no phone to track. The other guy was simply an excellent manhunter who'd gotten a very good read on Peter in a very short period of time. Although Peter had to admit that any dumb-ass who would dive from the seat of his truck, off a high bluff, and into a flooded river was a pretty specific personality type.

The other problem with the spotlights was that,

every time they shone across the windows of an occupied house or trailer, the inhabitants took notice. Lights went on and doors opened and dogs began to bark. Which meant Peter could no longer slip unnoticed into a garage or barn to find an old hunting jacket or a work truck with the keys in it. He didn't want to face down a couple of farm dogs to knock on somebody's door, and he wasn't going to try a home invasion, either. He was willing to bet that every one of these dwellings had at least one firearm, whether for hunting deer or shooting coyotes or simply for sport, and Peter was still unarmed.

Distance remained his best defense, so he fell back from the road but continued east, his legs strong and steady, his clothes getting dry. He'd walk all night if he had to. The exercise would keep him warm, and an opportunity would present itself eventually.

When he came to a small rise and saw a spray of headlamps shining through the next treeline, almost a mile off the road, he smiled and picked up the pace.

Soon he heard the deep diesel roar of heavy equipment. Ten o'clock at night and somebody was still hard at work. By the time he made it to the trees, he could see a yellow Caterpillar track excavator with overhead spots on the cab and lights on the boom and arm. The big Cat's top speed was maybe six miles an hour. Not exactly a getaway car.

But the equipment operator wasn't driving it home, either. He'd have a heavy truck and trailer to transport the beast to the next job and, if Peter was lucky, another vehicle nearby to get him home for the night. The square-mile field sections were subdivided into quarter sections by dirt tractor paths. The operator wasn't going to walk the long cold mile back to the gravel road. His truck wouldn't be far.

Peter slipped into the line of trees, scanning the night for the silhouette of a pickup, but the bright lights on the big machine were messing with his night vision. He could see enough, however, to know that the Cat's operator was an artist, swinging the bucket with the grace and precision of an Olympic figure skater, leaving in his wake a long, straight trench with a clean, flat bottom and crisp sides. Part of some kind of drainage system, Peter assumed, designed to dry a chronically wet field.

He worked his way behind the moving excavator, hopped the trench when the cab was turned away, then jogged toward a blocky silhouette maybe forty yards away. It was a big dump truck parked on the packed dirt access road with a long, low trailer behind it.

There was no other vehicle. But the Cat's operator had done Peter the favor of parking the ten-wheeler facing the road. Peter had never driven a dump truck before. How hard could it be?

He made a wide circle to come up on the far side of the vehicle. He felt pretty good about his chances of finding the keys in the ignition or on the seat. The excavator was facing his direction, so he'd have to move fast once he opened the door and the interior lights came on. Better unhitch the trailer first.

He was curious about the tarp-wrapped rectangle mounted to the tongue, but he didn't have time to investigate. A fuel tank for the excavator, maybe, or some rarely used attachment.

As he wrestled with the trailer's mud-crusted drop-leg jack, he heard the excavator's engine drop down to idle. The work lights, which shifted shadows with every twitch and pivot of the cab, went still. He still couldn't get the damn jack leg free. Looked like he was taking the trailer, too. He abandoned the jack and hustled toward the driver's side.

He had his foot on the step and his fingers on the door handle when something slammed into his lower leg and yanked him away from the truck, the door flying open as he fell.

"Ow, shit." Peter tried to stay upright on one foot while a forty-pound whirlwind growled like a chain saw, adjusted its bite to a firmer grip on his pant leg, and thrashed him like a cheap chew toy with a squeaker inside. "C'mon, really?"

As Peter pogoed across the dirt, trying to figure a way out of this mess that didn't involve putting his butt on the ground and his face within reach of those teeth, he heard the distinct double-click of a round being chambered in an automatic pistol.

"Son, what the *heck* do you think you're doin'?"

19

In the light spilling from the dump truck's open door, the equipment operator's face was a seamed granite boulder over a faded yellow Caterpillar sweatshirt tucked into dirty black Carhartt bibs, topped off by a hot pink trucker's cap with NASTY WOMAN on the front.

She was not smiling. The pistol was steady in a two-handed grip.

"I'm sorry, ma'am." Balanced badly on one leg, Peter tried and failed to rescue his pant leg. "I can explain."

"I've heard that before." Her voice was a rich rasp. The gun was nothing fancy, but her finger was firm on the trigger. "Thieves who get caught always have an explanation."

The dog dug its feet in and pulled. Distracted by the gun, Peter hopped sideways, wondering if he could scoop up the dog and hold it like a shield. He wasn't proud of that idea, nor did he like the thought of putting his hands anywhere near those choppers. Then his boot caught in a rut and he fell sideways and landed awkwardly in the dirt on his hip and elbow.

The dog dropped his pant leg in an instant, fangs flashing white as it jumped for his neck. It got a mouthful of the fleece over his forearm instead, but kept chewing.

"Leave it!" The woman's voice was sharp. "Cupcake! Leave it, girl."

The dog wasn't happy, but she backed off a few steps, legs still bent for a leap, lips peeled back to show a complete set of teeth and mottled pink gums in a full-on display of aggression. Peter had plenty of experience with dogs, but Cupcake was giving off a different vibe, a special kind of angry. His forearm burned where her bite had made it past the thick fabric.

"Thank you, ma'am." Peter stayed down, knowing he'd be less threatening on the ground, although it limited his options for attack. "I'm sorry about this. My name's Peter. What's yours?"

She frowned. "I never did like a smooth talker." She had a good shooter's stance, knees slightly bent, feet firmly planted in the muddy ground. Her right index finger was still on the trigger. "I ought to put a bullet in your head and drop you in that hole. Down so deep you'll never come up."

Peter kept his mouth shut, letting her think. She wouldn't shoot him, would she? Cupcake was still growling, lean and athletic with a tan coat and bushy tail that reminded Peter of a coyote. With all that attitude, the rest of her might as well have been bobcat or wolverine. She wore no collar.

She'd really gone after his arm, too. Peter pulled back his punctured sleeve and exposed the torn, bloody skin where Cupcake had made contact. He'd need better light to see how much damage she'd done.

"That's your own dang fault," the woman pointed out. "Cupcake thinks she owns that old Mack dumper. It sure as heck ain't yours, is it?"

Peter wanted to get up but wasn't going to push his luck. "No, ma'am. My mistake."

"You're dang right it is." She stepped back and glanced around. He could tell she was trying to figure out what to do with him. Any police were almost certainly a long way away. If she let him go, she had no guarantee he wouldn't circle back and answer the dog bite with worse. "Where's your ride?"

"Stolen, ma'am. Along with my wallet and my phone." He figured the short version was best.

"Likely story. Climb to your knees. Slowly. Then lift that shirt and show me your belt and your pockets. And your ankles. One-handed."

Peter got his legs under him, raised his fleece to expose his waistband, then tugged up his pant legs so she could see he wasn't wearing an ankle holster. He pivoted to show her his empty back pockets, then turned out the front ones, and dropped his knife on the ground along with the blue-embroidered hem from the pregnant woman's dress. He still didn't know why she'd given it to him.

"Huh." She looked him up and down. "You're really on foot, way out here? And that's all you've got to wear?"

The wind cut through the fleece, stealing his heat. His clothes were still slightly damp. "Yes, ma'am. It's a long story. I'm sorry to bother you. I've got a long way to go tonight."

"What did you want with my Mack?" The cab light shone on the bulldog hood ornament.

"I was hoping you had a spare jacket in there. Maybe a granola bar or something."

He left out the part where he was planning to borrow her truck. Back in the day, they used to shoot horse thieves in the Dakota territory. From where Peter was standing, on the wrong end of a gun, it didn't seem that long ago.

"If you're hungry, you don't have to steal," she said. "The Methodist church in Springfield serves a good supper every night at six o'clock, no questions asked. Their food bank gives out groceries on Mondays and Thursdays."

"Thank you, ma'am. But that's not my situation. I just want my truck back."

"Well, I guess you've got your troubles. I won't pry." She straightened up and lowered the pistol to her side. "Although if you'd just waved at me and asked for help, you wouldn't have that bloody arm."

"Yes, ma'am. Lesson learned." Slowly, he gathered

his knife and the torn scrap of the pregnant woman's dress and tucked them away. "If you don't mind, ma'am, I'm going to stand up now. I really do need to get moving."

"Where're you headed?"

On his feet, Peter got a better look at her. Somewhere between fifty and sixty, she was one of those women who got more solid with age. "Across the river," he said. "East of the bridge."

She gave him a sideways look. "Is that home?"

"No, ma'am. The men who took my truck live there."

"You know who they are?"

"No, ma'am. I just know where they live, more or less."

"Dangit, I said I wouldn't pry, didn't I?" She took off her NASTY WOMAN hat and slapped it against her leg. Her hair was steel-gray, cut short.

"It's all right," he told her. "I'm going to leave now."

"Hold up." She glanced over her shoulder at the trailer with the tarp-wrapped rectangle strapped to the front. "How far east of the bridge?"

"Maybe fifteen miles? It would help if I could look at a map."

She sighed and stuffed the pistol down into the side pocket of her bibs. "Does that pitiful look on your sorry face work with all the girls?"

He allowed himself a smile. "Just one, ma'am. But she's six hundred miles away."

20

The excavator operator's name was Roberta. "But everyone calls me Bobbie."

Leaving Peter in the open field under the ferocious supervision of Cupcake, Bobbie climbed into the truck's cab and retrieved a blue first-aid kit, a bottle of water, and a creased, coffee-stained Nebraska Gazetteer atlas that showed everything from interstate highways to gravel roads.

She left the door open, put the Gazetteer on the truck's corrugated steel step, parked her backside on it, then opened the first-aid kit in her lap. The dome light shone brightly down. "Let me see your arm."

Peter rolled back the fleece. It wasn't pretty. A half-dozen nice punctures and some torn skin. Bad dog. At least his pants had protected his leg.

While Cupcake watched, growling, her legs still

poised to leap, Bobbie bunched up a large gauze pad and soaked it with water, then wiped the blood away to expose the injury. Then she soaked fresh gauze with mercurochrome and scrubbed the bites vigorously. Peter sucked in his breath at the pain, but resisted the urge to curse. Something told him Bobbie wouldn't like it.

She took a tube of store-brand antibiotic ointment and smeared it generously across new pads and stuck them on his wounds. "Hold these." He did. She opened a roll of gauze and wrapped it around his forearm until it was gone, then ran a few strips of tape to stick it in place. "I'd say I'm sorry, but you know it's your own dang fault for messing with somebody else's things."

"Yes, ma'am." The dog hadn't stopped growling. "But at least Cupcake got to bite somebody."

Bobbie repacked the kit and stuffed the used wrappers in her pockets. "I do believe you made her day." She stood up and handed him the book of maps.

Peter leaned against the dump box and leafed through the Gazetteer's pages. With the pregnant girl's directions in mind, he found a gravel road that looked about right. It dead-ended by the river, just east of the county line. Look for the crosses, she'd said. They weren't on the map.

While he got the details lodged in his head, Bobbie put the first-aid kit back in the dump truck and came out with a brown duck work jacket with a red quilted lining. The right sleeve looked like it had been torn clean off the shoulder, then roughly refastened using copper electrical wire as thread.

She saw Peter looking at it. "My lucky jacket," she said. "Cuff got grabbed by a hay baler. Sleeve tore off and saved my arm."

Peter had heard his share of those stories. Farming could be dangerous work. "Farm strong."

She shook her head. "Farm stupid. Should have turned off the PTO." She tossed him the coat then pointed a stern finger at him. "I want that back."

"Yes, ma'am." He pulled the jacket gingerly over his bandaged forearm. "Where do I find you?"

She gave him an address. "About ten miles west of Springfield just off the Tabor Rec road." She reached for a pencil tucked into her bib pocket. "I better write that down."

Peter didn't want anything with Bobbie's name or address. If he was unsuccessful with the husband and his friends, they might decide to pay her a visit. They seemed like the type.

"No need," he said. "I've got it."

She measured him with a look. "I bet you do," she said. "You figure out where you're going?"

"Yes." He wasn't going to tell her, though. If he ended up leaving a body behind in Nebraska, he didn't want her to connect the dots to the man she met in South Dakota. Although he knew she would anyway. She was plenty smart and he'd already told her too much.

"You were military," she said.

"Yes, ma'am. U.S. Marines. How'd you know?"

"You're not a whiner, for one. A lot of folks go into the service around here. The good ones get something out of it. The bad ones, well. Some of them just get worse."

Peter thought about the pregnant girl's husband. "You got somebody in mind?"

"Not anymore," she said. "What are you going to do about your truck?"

"It's my truck. I'm going to take it back."

And try not to get killed in the process. He didn't see any point telling her about the pregnant girl, either. It would just complicate things.

Bobbie might want to call the police, which was the last thing Peter wanted.

So far this little adventure spanned two states and three counties. If he told the local cops what had actually happened, they would probably bring in the state police, who would need to call their Nebraska counterparts, pull the higher-ups away from their supper tables or barstools, interview Peter eight different times, take eight different sets of notes and maybe videotape everything, then consult with prosecutors and judges about the proper course to take. It would be morning before anything happened, or the day after, while the pregnant girl waited, scared and alone. Or maybe dead.

If the police even believed Peter's story at all.

No, it was easier for Peter just to take care of things himself.

More fun, too. Unless he got killed.

——

Bobbie walked to the long trailer and began to unwrap the tarp from the rectangle on the front. It wasn't a fuel tank for the excavator, it was a hot pink Yamaha 250 strapped into a metal holding frame welded to the tongue.

As he watched, she unstrapped the motorcycle and climbed aboard, then kicked the engine into raucous life and sat staring at him in a blue cloud of exhaust.

"If you want a ride," she said, "you're going to have to tell me where we're going."

With a license plate and headlight, the bike was street legal, but it also had knobby tires and high fenders coated with dried mud. A large wooden box was fastened firmly across the rear half of the two-person seat.

"What's wrong with the dump truck?"

"Too many miles on that old girl already. No reason to add more when I don't have to."

"What about the dog?"

"She usually rides in the crate. I'll have to take that off to make room for you, so I guess she'll sit on your lap."

Cupcake's growl rose above the rattle of the Yamaha, as if she knew exactly what they were discussing. She bared her teeth again, exposing those mottled pink gums and inch-long fangs.

Peter took an involuntary step back and wondered if a dog could be clinically insane. Or develop a taste for human flesh. "I think I'll just walk."

Bobbie gave him a withering look. "Don't be such a scaredy-cat. She's only half coyote."

"What's the other half?"

"Nobody knows, but her momma was the alpha bitch at a junkyard outside of Sioux Falls."

Before he could respond, Bobbie juiced the throttle, popped the front tire in the air, and rode the wheelie down to the dirt.

21

Helene's eyes blinked open as Roy pulled off the road, the truck bouncing on the ruts. "Good, you're awake," he said. "I want to show you something."

Out the window, bare, bony mountains cut the horizon like knife blades. The sun was too bright. She was afraid he wanted to fuck her again.

Their two days at the resort had flown by in a blur. She never made it to the spa. They spent most of that time in bed. She did her best to make Roy happy, even though she was increasingly sticky and sore. At some point, she realized that he was no longer using a condom, but it seemed too late to say anything. After he fed her a few of the pot-laced chocolates in the mini-bar, the hazy glow made it easier.

Every time he led her through the lobby to the restaurant or the pool, she was sure the elegant receptionist knew all the things he had done to her. She would grow to like it, she told herself. Maybe not all of it, but enough. She put her hand on his arm and lengthened her stride to keep up.

The one time she'd seen Frank, he was in a booth in the steak house with two other men, heads bent together in quiet talk. Frank hadn't looked at her, but the other men followed her with their eyes. When she and Roy checked out of the resort, Frank hadn't come with them.

Now Roy turned off the engine and got out of the truck. "Come on, honey."

She'd asked him a half-dozen times to call her *Helene*, not *honey*. Each time, he'd said something like, "Sure thing, honey." It got under her skin like a permanent mosquito bite. As she scooted out after him, she told herself she'd keep working on it. Everyone could change.

The road was gravel. Everything else was brown and dry. She couldn't see the highway or a single living thing except for Roy. The only sound was the humming from the trailer, which seemed much louder than it had in the resort parking lot. The trailer's sign still read GOLDEN STATE SOLUTIONS. "Where are we?"

"Central Nevada. We'll be in Salt Lake in four hours." He took her elbow and guided her toward the back of the trailer. His jacket was off and he still wore the pistol on his hip. His keys jangled as he unfastened two heavy round security padlocks on the rear. The door pulled down to become a ramp. The humming grew louder.

She was expecting tools of some kind, maybe construction supplies. Instead, she saw a packed jumble of goods, everything from old furniture wrapped in quilts to a pair of sleek racing bicycles to narrow wooden packing crates strapped to the sidewall. Behind the clutter, a curvy convertible gleamed in the dark. The humming came from behind the car.

"What's that sound?"

"I'll show you." Roy raised the ramp, then led her around to the driver's side of the trailer and unlocked a door she hadn't noticed before.

She peered inside and saw an enormous white chest freezer, longer than Helene was tall, set against the back wall. It was plugged into a small gas generator that hummed under a square metal duct that sucked the exhaust out through the ceiling. The rest of the space carried floor-to-ceiling plywood shelves filled with U-Haul boxes and plastic storage bins.

"I don't understand," she said. "What is it you guys do for a living?"

She didn't want to know. But she knew anyway. Maybe she'd always known.

"You remember those houses we drove past this morning? Up in the hills looking down on Lake Tahoe?"

She remembered him pointing them out. High in the pines, broad expanses of glass flashed in the sun, making her think of poolside cocktails and magazine models. She'd craned her neck for a better view, wondering at the golden lives of the people who lived there. They were never lonely or scared. They had food in the fridge and more money than they could ever spend.

"They're all owned by wealthy jerks who live somewhere else," Roy said. "They might only visit once or twice a year. But those houses are filled with wonderful things, the kind of things that you and I could work two jobs and save our whole lives and still never be able to afford. Designer watches and fine jewelry. Giant entertainment systems. High-end firearms that have never been cleaned. Power tools that have never been used. Jet Skis and dirt bikes and vintage cars. Just sitting there, all of it. It's a damn shame. It's a crime, really."

He gave her the warm smile that soaked into her bones.

"So Frank and I, along with a couple others, we rob them. Very carefully. We take only the most valuable stuff. We keep the things we like and we sell the rest."

In each town where she'd spent the night on this trip, she'd walked the outskirts looking up at the houses set on the surrounding mountainsides like jewels in the trees. She turned back to Roy.

"That's where my green coat came from," she said. "Not from a resale shop. You stole it."

"Yes." His voice was soft, almost a purr. "But it's a

lot warmer than your old coat, right? Isn't it nice not to be cold? Or hungry? And stay in a nice hotel, with some cash in your pocket?"

She thought about the money Roy had given her, tucked into the bottom of her bag. It made her feel safe, knowing she could take care of herself, at least for a little while. She thought about the money she'd taken from the register at the Gas and Grocery. She'd told herself Bogaloosa owed it to her. And he did, didn't he? He'd held back her paycheck. He owed her that money and more.

She frowned at the long chest freezer. "What's in there?"

"These big houses, sometimes they have a bunch of meat in the freezer, slowly going bad. Really good meat. Elk, venison, grass-fed beef. We take that, too. We can't sell it, but we can grill it ourselves, back home. And we can give it away to people like us, who maybe don't always have enough to eat."

She stepped inside the trailer and tugged on the freezer's lid. It didn't open.

"Sometimes it gets iced shut," he said. "Don't pull too hard, it might not close right. Then all that meat starts to thaw and we have to throw it out."

"What if you get caught?"

"I know how not to get caught," he said. "I was a cop for seven years. Besides, I've saved my share. One more year and I'm done, that's a promise. We can go anywhere we want, do anything we want."

She leaned against the freezer, feeling its subtle vibration in her hips and up her spine. "Roy, why are you telling me this?"

He followed her inside the dark trailer, standing close. She smelled the acrid tang of his sweat, the stale coffee on his breath. "Honey, I don't want us to keep secrets." He put his strong hand on her arm. "If we're going to be together, I want to be able to tell you anything. Total honesty. So here it is."

He looked at the floor, suddenly shy, not the confident Roy she was used to. "I'm no choirboy. I've been with other girls. But you're not like them, honey. You're different." His dark eyes rose to meet hers. "I've known, from the moment we met, that you were special. You might not see it in yourself, but I do. You'll do great things, if you put your mind to it."

She thought he might be joking, but he looked deadly serious. "Roy?"

He held up a hand to stop her. "Honey, you and I are the same. We're not like anyone else." He cleared his throat, eyes brimming. "I've been looking for you my whole life. And now I've finally found you." He dropped to one knee on the trailer floor. He had a blue velvet box in one hand.

"Jesus, Roy. What the hell?"

"Maybe I'm not doing this right," he said. "I know it's probably too soon. But I can't help myself."

He opened the velvet box. Inside was a glittering gold ring with a stone that looked way too big to be a real diamond. She wasn't going to touch it but her hand reached out on its own.

Roy smiled. "Do you like it? The second I saw it, I thought of you. It's worth eighty thousand dollars, at least."

Her eyes popped. "Eighty thousand dollars!"

"Listen, honey, I'm crazy about you and I want to spend my life with you. Elko is less than an hour away. I'm sure we can find a little chapel there. Let's make it official. Will you marry me?"

She made a decision. "On one condition," she said. "I get to come with you the next time you go into one of those big houses."

"Of course!" He beamed. "That's the whole idea. We're partners in everything."

"Then yes, Roy, yes." She stepped into his arms. "Yes, yes, yes."

Then his hands were at her waist, unbuckling her belt and unbuttoning her jeans. "C'mon," he said. "Let's celebrate."

Later, she realized that when he said he wanted total honesty, she should have known he was telling the biggest lie of all.

22

Elko was a spare and dusty town. They were married on a stranger's front porch, a woman with dyed blond hair and a lot of eye makeup who took Roy's money and their signatures and told them she'd file the paperwork with the city on Monday. Helene tried not to wish that her mom could be there, which was impossible, or her aunt Willa, who'd had Helene as a flower girl at her own wedding, years and years ago. The whole thing took less than fifteen minutes, and ended when the woman said, "You may now kiss the bride."

Roy crushed Helene in his arms, his mouth hungry on hers. She had never worn a ring on that finger before, and it felt strangely tight.

After cheeseburgers at a truck stop, Roy pulled behind a line of parked semis, peeled off the magnetic GOLDEN STATE SOLUTIONS sign, stuck it to the trailer's inside wall, and replaced it with PREMIUM PROJECT MANAGEMENT. Then he took a screwdriver and swapped the California plates for a fresh set from Utah. He had a whole box of them. She counted fourteen different states.

Back on the road, he told her they only did a few jobs in each state. "And we never repeat in the same county, or even in adjoining counties. We don't want the locals to get too curious. As long as they think it's a onetime thing, some rich guy's house getting robbed, they don't pay much attention."

"How long have you been at this?"

"Almost four years." He flashed a smile. "If anyone knew how much shit I've done, I'd have an FBI task force on my ass." He laughed and slapped the steering wheel. "But nobody has a clue."

"Really? How can you know that?"

"I was a cop, remember? I still have plenty of connections."

She thought of Bogaloosa, a sheriff's deputy, and all the things he got away with. "What if somebody's at the house?"

"That never happens," he said. "We're very careful."

"Okay, what do you do with all that stuff?"

"Depends," he said. "The tools go to one guy, the guns to a couple others. I know an antiques dealer in Chicago who will take anything I bring him. He even tells me the kind of stuff his clients are looking for. He pays really well, too."

As Roy talked about pioneer-era furniture and

high-end pistols, she realized this was the first time he had really told her anything about his life.

It was midafternoon when they stopped for gas outside of Salt Lake. Roy hung his phone from the heat vent and pulled up a mapping app, then continued east toward Park City. It was a cute little town full of snowboard shops and fancy boutiques and restaurants that she might have seen in one of her magazines. It was the first week of October now, and ski season was still at least a month away. "You really don't want to do this kind of work in the snow," he said. "You leave tire tracks and footprints, which can be used as evidence. And anyone checking on the house will know someone has been there. The longer we can go without the robbery being discovered, the better. Most security companies erase camera footage after a week. Two is even better."

She hadn't even thought about security cameras. "Don't those big fancy houses have alarm systems, too?"

"They do. But I'm smarter than they are."

She still couldn't believe they were actually going to do it, break into a mountain mansion and take rich people's things. It just seemed like talk, a game of make-believe. Even though she had someone else's eighty-thousand-dollar ring on her finger, and someone else's money in her pocket.

Roy stopped talking as they continued through Park City on 189. She watched the muscles flex in his jaw as he bent over the wheel. By the time he turned off the highway at Heber City, he had become the same quiet, cold Roy who had checked her into those motels just a few days before. But it was different now, she thought. She knew what he was preparing himself for.

The road was narrow and followed the slope uphill. A braided river wound beneath them. The mountains were pale green and brushy with trees growing along the creek drainages.

He kept one eye on his phone as they wound farther into the mountains, going more slowly now, window down and heat cranked, peering up driveways and watching his mirrors. Helene hadn't seen another person for the last half hour. The clock said it was just before six.

When they came to a sturdy metal gate between two stone pillars, he slowed to a crawl. She leaned forward to look past him. The driveway was so long she couldn't even see the house. "Is this it?"

He picked up speed and kept going. "Yep," he said. "But we need to check the neighbors first. I'd feel pretty stupid if there were a couple of deputies parked just up the hill."

Five minutes later, the road died at a wide spot with space for a few cars to park and a sign for a hiking trail. Nobody was there. After taking a funny little walkie-talkie out of the center console, Roy jockeyed the truck and trailer around to head back the way they'd come.

At the gate, a big gray pickup sat at the side of the

narrow lane. It had a long boxy trailer, too, just like Roy's. The other driver held up a hand. Roy pulled up beside him, window to window. "All clear behind me," he said. "Anything on your end?"

Frank leaned forward in the gray truck's passenger seat. He'd put on a denim shirt with the sleeves and neck buttoned tight. "Not a soul. Good to go."

Frank's driver was a skinny guy in a camo jacket with long brown hair, bad tattoos crawling up his neck, and a tooth missing at the edge of his smile. His eyes were glued to her tits. "You must be Helene," he said. "I'm Hollywood."

She realized he was one of the men Frank had been sitting with in the resort's steak house the day before. Hollywood had stared at her then, too.

She put one arm across her chest and put the other hand on Roy's leg, wishing she'd worn her old baggy flannel instead of the tight black sweater.

Roy didn't seem to notice any of it. "Pony Boy get off okay?"

"An hour ago," Frank said. "Should be any minute now."

As if on cue, the little walkie-talkie came to life with a crackly voice. "Okay here. Everybody ready?"

Roy checked his watch and raised the radio to his mouth. "We're ready. Pull it." He slipped the radio into his jacket pocket. "Hollywood, you're up."

The skinny guy hopped out of the gray truck with a black toolbag slung over one shoulder. He slipped around the stone pillar and bent down behind the gate, his gloved hands already moving. Frank slid into the now-empty driver's seat.

Roy reached into the center console again, this time for a pair of ski masks and thin blue gloves. He handed her a mask. "Put this on. Make sure you tuck all your hair up inside. You don't want to leave anything behind."

She tied her hair in a knot on the back of her head, then worked the mask down to her neck. It was too big for her and didn't fit right, the fabric covering her nose and most of her mouth so that her breath stayed inside, warm and damp. Roy reached over and tugged at the top and sides, getting the holes lined up with her face. She was having trouble catching her breath. She was about to rob a house. She would be a criminal. She could go to jail.

Somehow, Roy knew what she was thinking. "You sure you're up for this? You can always walk away. Just open your door and go."

She swallowed hard. "No. I'm ready. Besides, we're married now, right?"

"Atta girl." He pulled down his own mask. It had a grinning white skull printed on the front of it. His eyes stared out of the empty sockets.

Behind the stone pillar, Hollywood stood up and pulled the gate out of the way. Roy put the truck into gear and hit the gas. "Put those gloves on. It's time to make some money, honey."

23

The house was a comforting arrangement of sand-colored stone and pale wood under a roof that had the exact same angle as the distant mountains. It was also smaller than Helene had expected, until she realized how much house continued past the crest of the hill to hang out over empty space. As if it didn't have to obey the same laws of gravity as the rest of the world.

A wide-bodied guy in jeans and a black T-shirt stepped out of the bushes at the far edge of the building. He waved them forward, then disappeared around the corner. Hollywood spilled out of the gray truck and followed him at a run. Frank jogged to the front porch and knelt by the door. All three men wore ski masks and gloves.

Helene's stomach fluttered. "Where are they going?"

"That's Pony Boy around the corner. He came up

from below and scouted the house to make sure nobody was here. While we were waiting on the road, he pulled the electrical meter to cut the power and kill the security cameras and sensors. With the power off, we have four minutes until the backup generator kicks in and another two until the cameras come back online. After the generator comes back on, Pony'll let it run for ninety seconds, then kill it before the cameras wake up again. That triggers another reboot. So far the security system's brain, which is still awake, thanks to a little emergency battery inside the panel, thinks this is all completely normal. Power outages happen all the time out here."

"And Frank?"

"He's picking the lock so he can get inside after the generator shuts down. He'll find the security panel and unplug the battery. That puts the system itself to sleep, so it can't call home and tell them the cameras are dead and the power's out. If we left it that way, someone would notice eventually. But on our way out, we just reverse the whole thing. The system wakes back up, the cameras reboot, and nobody knows we were here until weeks later."

She was impressed. "How do you know all this stuff?"

"The house sold a few years ago. The property listing is still up on another company's website, with more than fifty pictures. In one photo, I could see part of the security keypad, so I learned which system they had. There were also pictures of the generator and the climate-controlled wine cellar, so I learned how the power backup works."

She felt like she was missing something. "But you didn't just pick this house at random. So why this house? And why today?"

"Oho," he said with a grin. "I knew you were the right girl. This house is a special order. Sent to me by a man in a position to know certain things. In exchange, he gets part of the take."

Through the open window, she heard an engine cough into life somewhere behind the house. Frank stood up and the radio crackled. "I'm ready." The engine died. Frank opened the door and slipped inside.

She moved to get out of the truck but Roy stopped her with a hand. "Just wait. Two more minutes." His fingers drummed on the steering wheel. "We don't know what the owner might have changed. Maybe he went with a different alarm company. Maybe he added a fat bank of Tesla batteries as a secondary backup to protect his wine in case the generator fails. Either of those might mean the cameras are still live."

"Then what?"

"Pony will cut the ground wires at the meter and short the main feeds inside the socket. That power surge will trip the main breaker, which will give Frank another two minutes, hopefully, to disconnect the alarm system and the backup power. If he's got Tesla batteries, we might take them, too. They're not cheap."

"People do all that just for a few bottles of wine?"

"Honey, nobody builds a climate-controlled cellar

for a few bottles. Last summer I hit a house where Hollywood stole a refrigerator truck just to carry the wine. Four hundred cases. That house was a special order, too. We made three hundred grand on the wine alone. The lawyer in Houston told me it sold for over a million."

She closed her eyes and tried to imagine a million dollars' worth of wine.

The radio crackled again. "We're good."

Roy opened his door and got out of the truck. "Time to go."

They walked inside like they owned the place. Everything was cool creamy white and soothing shades of blue. The carpet was thick and soft underfoot. Her magazines didn't begin to capture this experience.

The back of the house opened up into an enormous room. Floor-to-ceiling windows filled a broad, curved wall. On the other side of the glass was a huge deck and a panoramic view of pale green mountains that seemed close enough to reach out and touch. The distant trees flashed as their leaves turned in the wind, and the grass rippled like the surface of a pond. The effect was mesmerizing.

So this was what money bought, she thought. If it was her house, she'd eat her meals right here. Hell, she'd sleep on this couch, even brush her teeth here. She'd never leave this spot.

After eight years in a sixteen-foot travel trailer that

was an oven in the summer and a freezer in the winter, she couldn't decide if she hated the rich people who owned this beautiful place and didn't even live here, or if she wanted to be rich herself.

Maybe both, she thought. It made her angry and jealous and greedy, all at once.

The radio crackled right behind her. Frank's voice said, "I found the safe room. Lower level. It's major league." She could feel Roy standing at her shoulder.

The radio crackled again as he pressed the talk button. "Hollywood, help Pony carry the tools. I'm on my way." He pressed himself against her and she felt the bulge of his erection. He reached under her sweater and brushed his fingers across her breast, her nipple under his thumb, his voice both soft and rough in her ear. "It's a rush, right?"

She turned into him, eyes closed, suddenly wanting his touch, startled at the hot rush of her desire. Was this how he felt, all the time? Why he couldn't leave her alone? It was as though she'd stepped into his skin, just for a moment. Had she ever been truly awake before right now?

Footsteps ran down the hall. "Roy, stop fucking around." Hollywood was breathing hard. "Work first, then play, remember? Your rules."

Roy's hand slipped away and she stood trembling. He backed toward the stairs. "Go find yourself something nice," he said. "Maybe some fancy underwear."

Even under the skull-faced ski mask, she could tell he was smiling.

And she was smiling back.

Who the hell was she?

Fifteen minutes later, while the screech of a power tool filtered up from the lower level, she stood naked in a closet that was bigger than her whole trailer. She had a lacy white nightgown in both hands, ready to pull it over her head, when she glanced out the window and saw a small blue SUV roll up the driveway and come to a stop behind Hollywood's gray truck.

"Oh, no." She dropped the nightgown and reached for her underwear. "No, no, no."

A woman got out of the car and looked up at the house. She wore black pants and tennis shoes and an open blue windbreaker. She wore something dark on the side of her belt under the jacket.

"Roy." Helene ducked away from the window and fumbled for her jeans. "Roy!" She pulled on her T-shirt, then grabbed her sweater and Walmart sneakers and ran for the stairs. "Roy, where the hell are you?"

24

Helene found the men on the lowest level, inside a large, windowless room with a wrecked metal door. The door and its metal jamb had ragged, burned-looking cuts on the edge.

Frank and Hollywood were transferring guns from a wall full of gleaming glass display cases into plastic storage bins. There were open shelves with boxes of ammunition and canned food and a whole bunch of camping gear. Roy and the wide man in the black T-shirt—Pony Boy, Roy had called him—stood looking at a big metal cabinet with thick lever handles and a keypad. A safe. An orange machine like an oversized chain saw, but with a circular cutting blade, idled at their feet.

"Roy, someone's here." She was still in her socks with her sneakers in one hand and her sweater in the other, breathing hard from the run.

He stepped toward her. "Say again?" The orange machine wasn't quiet. The air smelled of engine exhaust and burned metal.

Helene raised her voice and spoke into the side of his mask. "Someone's here. A woman. In the driveway."

"Crap. Okay. I'll go talk to her. Stay here." He touched Pony Boy on the shoulder. "Get to work on that safe." He turned to Frank. "Keep loading, but don't take anything upstairs 'til I come back."

"Roy," Helene said. But he'd already picked up a toolbag and was out the door.

Hollywood looked at Frank. "What do we do?"

"What Roy told us. You know he'll handle it."

Pony Boy picked up the orange machine and revved the engine. The noise filled the room. He held the blade to the metal cabinet and orange sparks flew.

Helene stepped out into the hall to get away from the sound but there was no escaping it. She went up to the main floor, her socks slippery on the polished wood. The front door was open but she couldn't see Roy or the woman.

She dropped her sweater and shoes and ran up the stairs to the second floor.

She could see the driveway from the closet window.

Roy walked toward the woman, his back to Helene. He'd taken off the skull mask and the blue gloves. He carried the toolbag in one hand, the other raised in greeting. He still wore the gun on the back of his hip.

Helene thought about how charming Roy could be. Not in a slick way, like Bogaloosa when it suited him. More like a good neighbor, someone you'd known a long time. Which was exactly how Roy had charmed her, she thought.

The woman smiled at him. Even from the window, Helene could tell she was pretty. She ran her hand through her hair, then brushed back the windbreaker to reach a hand toward her hip. She had something blocky on her belt. A pistol.

But she wasn't reaching for the gun. She took her wallet from her hip pocket and held it up to show Roy. He set down the toolbag and stepped closer, as if hoping for a better look at the wallet. Then, without any warning, he smashed his fist into her face.

Her head snapped back. She rocked on her heels. The wallet fell to the ground.

Before she could recover, Roy had stepped behind her, snaked the crook of his elbow around her neck, and pulled her head against his chest. He was significantly taller than she was. His face was calm. His lips were moving.

The woman's hands flew down to his arm, pulling. Eyes wide, she fought his grasp. Her nose was streaming blood. A string of pink spittle hung from her mouth. Roy kept talking.

She couldn't move him. She raised her shoe and stomped toward his foot, but he shifted slightly and she missed. Her hand dropped to the gun on her belt, fumbled it from the holster. He twisted it from her fist. He was still talking to her.

He might have been discussing the weather, or the price of soybeans.

Finally the woman released his arm and moved her hands, trembling, out from her sides. She said something that seemed urgent, important. Her teeth were red. Her eyes strained upward, trying to see him.

Roy spoke again. Helene wanted to open the window. She wanted to know what they were saying. What Roy was saying.

Then he smiled to himself. Helene knew that smile. It was the same smile that warmed her from the inside out. The smile that had made her grab her things from the Gas and Grocery and walk out to his truck. A kind smile. It made Helene think that everything would be okay.

Until Roy, in a single quick movement, raised one clamping forearm to the woman's temple and put his other hand on the back of her skull and gave her head a sharp twist, as if pulling a cap from a bottle of beer.

Her arms flailed in the air. Her feet danced on the pavement. A spastic puppet, for just a second or two. Until she stopped.

Roy held her upright, his face beside hers, for a long moment. Finally, he bent his knees and scooped her into his arms like a honeymooning groom. Her head was turned to one side at an impossible angle.

Then he raised his eyes to the house and saw Helene standing at the upstairs closet window, where she had just watched him kill a woman.

From the basement, the sound of the power saw rose into a gasoline scream.

"Helene," he called.

She couldn't hear him, the window was closed, but she could read her name on his lips.

Her legs were wobbly. She stepped back from the window. She began to shiver. She had no idea what to do.

What would her mom possibly have said, at a time like this?

Absurdly, Helene wanted to get her mom's notebook and page through it. To find some useful bit of wisdom to fit this moment.

But the notebook was in Roy's truck. Along with the leather duffel and pink backpack that held her clothes, her money, her daddy's revolver, and everything else she owned in the world. Including the phone number and address for her aunt Willa in Minnesota.

Helene looked down at her feet. She wasn't even wearing shoes. How could she have been so stupid?

She peeked out the window again. The dead woman lay on the grass, her eyes wide open and staring. Roy was nowhere to be seen.

Then she heard a knock behind her. She spun and there he stood, leaning against the doorway.

"I'm sorry you had to see that," he said.

She searched his face, hoping to see some evidence of remorse or distress.

But he didn't seem upset at all.

Instead, his cheeks were flushed, his chest rose and fell. Like he'd just run a race and won.

Helene turned away.

To her back, Roy said, "She was the part-time caretaker for a few houses on the mountain. She said she was going to another place up the hill when she saw the gate partway open. I guess Hollywood didn't close it all the way. Then she heard the power saw."

Roy held out a wallet, folded open to show a bright metal badge. "In her regular job, she was a Wasatch County deputy sheriff."

"You killed her," Helene said. "You didn't have to do that."

"Yes, I did," Roy said. "If she'd pulled her weapon, she could have shot me. Even if she'd just walked away? Well, she'd already seen too much for me to allow that."

Helene knew what Roy was telling her. The dead woman wasn't the only one who couldn't walk away.

Roy kept talking. "It was her or us, honey, and I chose us. Is that so wrong? Do you want to be hunted by the police the rest of your life?"

She didn't have an answer to that.

He stepped closer. He carried her Walmart sneakers hooked on his fingers, the laces hanging down. "Better put these on."

He held them out and she took them. Then, with

infinite slowness, he reached for her face. He put his hands on her cheeks and tipped her head up so that he could look into her eyes. Then he bent down and kissed her. His lips were so soft, his hands so gentle. How could she reconcile that perfect kiss with what she had just seen?

He pulled her close and wrapped his arms around her. He smelled the same as he had just a few minutes before, when he'd put his hand beneath her sweater. He even had the same erection, pressing into her stomach. Just a few minutes before, she'd wanted nothing more than to strip off his clothes and fuck him blind on that soft, beautiful couch in front of that amazing view.

They had been married for six hours.

She didn't want to be married anymore. But she couldn't tell him that, not now.

"We have to get out of here," she said.

"We will, honey. I promise." His voice was soft and kind. "But first, I need you to do something for me."

25

With one arm holding the dog on his lap and the other hand on the grab handle on the back of the bike, it wasn't easy to keep his seat while Bobbie piloted the hot pink Yamaha down the bumpy tractor path toward the road. None of them wore a helmet.

Not only did Peter hear Cupcake's growls over the throaty grumble of the engine, he could feel them vibrating through his chest. Her mouth was open, pink gums and bared fangs just inches from his throat, a long line of drool flapping in the wind.

"Good girl," he said. "Can't we be friends?"

But Cupcake didn't give a shit what Peter wanted. She just showed him more teeth.

The wind blew right through his clothes. He felt the cold spot from the still-damp embroidered hem of the pregnant woman's dress in his front pocket. At speed, Bobbie's beat-up jacket was little help. His head began to ache where someone had hit him with a vodka bottle a few years ago. At some point, Peter thought, he should start making better life choices.

Before they'd left the dump truck, he'd thought about borrowing Bobbie's phone to call June, but decided that was a bad idea. If Bobbie connected the dots between Peter and a body found in some stubbled cornfield, he didn't want to give the authorities any electronic link to June.

But he had memorized Bobbie's number, and borrowed her pencil to write Lewis's burner number on the back of a diesel receipt, telling her, "If you don't hear from me inside of twelve hours, call this number. The man who answers, tell him everything you know."

He didn't ask to borrow Bobbie's gun. He wasn't going to get her in trouble by using her legally registered weapon to shoot a man. He had his own firearm in a hidden compartment under the frame of his Chevy. With any luck, he'd have it in hand soon enough.

When they came to the gravel road, Bobbie twisted the throttle and the bike leaped forward.

The farm roads were a grid marking the one-mile sections. From Peter's memory of the map, it was three miles east to the paved two-lane highway, then two more miles south to the bridge across the Missouri. If the pregnant woman had told her husband that Peter had promised to come for her, the bottleneck at the bridge was the logical place for them to wait for him.

He craned his neck, looking for spotlights in the distance.

One minute the road behind them was empty. The next, a small white car was hard on their rear wheel, its headlamps dark as night. Just like the black truck.

Peter leaned forward and bumped Bobbie's arm. She glanced back, saw the car. Her steel-gray hair held firm in the wind. She cranked the throttle, shifted, and cranked it again. The Yamaha's grumble rose into a howl. It wasn't built for speed, especially not with a passenger. Peter peeked over his shoulder. The white car kept pace easily, ten feet back.

Peter leaned forward again and shouted into her ear. "They're here for me. Get off this road." Peter would dismount and let her get clear. After that, improvise.

But before she could do anything, the car swung out and pulled beside them as if to pass. Bobbie saw it and touched the brake instinctively. The car shot forward. In the glare of the Yamaha's headlamp, Peter saw the pregnant woman's handprints on the dusty rear hatch, clear as day.

The car had seemed fragile and forlorn, by the river, but its rapid acceleration and smooth responsiveness now told him the vehicle was probably a four-wheel drive, tuned for performance.

The driver quickly dropped back to match their reduced speed. Peter saw a small man with long dark hair in the driver's seat, wearing a night-vision headset over the top of his face, the cyclops lens pointed directly at the riders through the open passenger window.

It wasn't a big car, but that didn't matter. All the driver would have to do was pull the wheel hard to the right. Even if Bobbie somehow managed not to dump the bike and grind them into the gravel, they'd be down in the ditch going fifty beside a barbed-wire fence with rocks and stumps and all manner of other shit hiding in the weeds. Either way, they wouldn't last long. A helmet would have been nice.

Bobbie kept her eyes on the road, the highway coming up fast. Ahead of them on the right, a big complex of barns and silos were lit up like Christmas day, brightening the night. Peter pointed. Bobbie nodded and downshifted, shedding speed.

The driver kept pace. Steering with his knees, he pushed his headset up with his left hand and he lifted his right toward Peter, holding a dark rectangle.

A phone. Taking his picture.

Maybe they were going to show it to the pregnant woman. Or compare it to Peter's driver's license, because they also had his wallet from the Chevy's glove box. Just to ensure that he was their target.

The farm complex filled one corner of the intersection. The entrance was wide enough for two tractors. "Hang on," Bobbie shouted. She braked hard and leaned into the turn. Peter tightened his grip on the grab handle and the dog. The white car continued straight for a fraction of a second before it followed suit, sharpening its angle to close the distance.

The Yamaha's rear wheel skated sideways on loose stones and the bike began to tip. Bobbie goosed the throttle and steered into the skid, encouraging the rear wheel's slide as she dropped a leg for support in case the front wheel slipped, too. The dog locked her teeth into Peter's fleece collar and shifted her feet, claws digging into his thighs. Peter's forearm burned where she'd chewed it.

Then the knobby back tire caught on the packed dirt driveway and the bike stood itself up and shot across the rutted farmyard, the white car somehow still right beside them as they ran headlong toward the tight cluster of fat steel silos.

Just when Peter was about to jump, Bobbie braked sharply and tucked them into a narrow gap between the silos and a new metal barn. The white car's wheels locked and it came to a sideways stop, rocking on its springs just outside the gap.

Then Bobbie had the kickstand down and was off the Yamaha, shouting at the slim young driver.

"What the heck kind of game do you think you're playing?" She marched toward the open passenger window, her voice loud and strong, carrying all the authority of her years. The dog flew from Peter's lap, then crouched for a leap beside Bobbie, growling at the car. "Tell me your name, boy. I'm gonna call your momma."

"Bobbie, don't." Peter was off the bike, too, reaching for her shoulder, thinking now they'd also have her picture, a bad development.

The driver looked past Bobbie as if he didn't speak her language, or maybe her voice didn't even register. He stared right at Peter with a shit-eating grin, as if the two of them were having all the fun in the world. A chrome-plated AR-15 clone lay across his lap, barrel pointed toward the passenger door, his right hand on the pistol grip.

His left hand held his phone. An orange two-way radio sat on the dashboard. Bobbie kept hollering at the guy as if the weapon wasn't there. Maybe she hadn't seen it. Her pistol was still tucked deep inside the pocket of her bibs. If the driver raised his rifle, neither Peter nor Bobbie would get to the gun in time. Cupcake growled louder.

The driver's eyes flicked down to the screen. His hand tightened on the pistol grip. He began to lower the phone. Now or never, Peter thought.

Before he could change his mind, he shouldered Bobbie aside, then bent and scooped up the dog. He was afraid Cupcake would take a chunk out of his face, but she was too focused on the driver.

In fact, she jumped from Peter's arms, through the window, and into the driver's lap.

Peter couldn't see what happened next. He'd already leaped onto the smooth roof of the little car and was sliding on his belly toward the other side.

He could hear the action, though. From the sound of things, it wasn't going well for the driver. The rifle was too big to bring to bear inside the vehicle. An angry dog was a much better close-quarters weapon. He hoped Cupcake didn't tear out the guy's voice box, because Peter wanted to talk to him.

Even more, he hoped the guy didn't have a knife somewhere he could reach it.

"Cupcake!" Bobbie shouted, "Cupcake, come!"

The dog wasn't listening.

Peter swung his legs down and dropped to the ground beside the driver's door. The guy was backed up hard against it, night-vision headset somehow still in place. His right hand pushed at Cupcake's neck, trying to hold her at bay while she snapped at him. With his left hand, he was rucking up the side of his high-tech camo jacket. The dog had already torn the jacket's arm into shreds.

Peter popped the door handle and the guy fell backward out of the car. Cupcake gathered herself and leaped for his throat. The guy kicked at her. Peter grabbed a handful of his hair and whacked his skull into the doorjamb. The guy kept kicking, so Peter whacked him into the hard metal again, this time with feeling.

The NV headset fell off and the guy stopped fighting. Peter grabbed the front of his jacket and dragged him clear. Cupcake leaped from the car and went for his crotch.

Peter figured she deserved a treat after being such a good dog, but the femoral artery was in the groin and he didn't want the driver to bleed out, so he blocked her with a knee. She stumbled back, snarling, and went after the man's leg as Bobbie ran around the front bumper. "Leave it, Cupcake. Leave it."

As Bobbie got the dog under control, Peter yanked up the man's jacket and pulled a small automatic pistol from a waistband holster.

The front sight had been filed down flush with the barrel, turning the gun into an ugly little quick-draw weapon, good only for close-quarters killing of people who'd never see it coming.

26

The dead woman had left her keys in the little blue SUV. Helene sat in the driver's seat, the engine running. She could still hear the scream of the power saw. Roy leaned on the open window.

Her pink backpack was on the front seat of his truck. With his fist clamped hard on her elbow, Roy had pushed her past the truck and humming trailer to the blue SUV. Helene tried not to look past him at the woman lying on the grass. She wasn't asleep. Nobody fell asleep with their head at that angle.

"Remember the trailhead?" he asked. "At the end of the road, where we turned around? Leave the car there. Use the tail of your shirt to wipe off the steering wheel and the window button and anything else you touched. Lock the door, throw the keys as far downslope as you can, and find a place nobody can see you."

Helene looked back at the truck. Her entire life was in that backpack, everything she owned in the world. It might as well have been on the moon. "You're not coming with me?"

"I'll be right behind you," he said. "We need to get that safe open."

Her hands were so tight on the wheel, they hurt. "Did you have to kill that woman?"

"I wish I hadn't," he said. She thought of his pink cheeks afterward and wondered if that was true. "Anyway, it's done and I can't undo it. So we might as well get what we came for. With what those guns are worth, that safe's gonna be loaded with cash, probably gold and silver, too." He looked back at the house, distracted.

If she was going to ask, now was the time. "Roy, will you get me my backpack? It's like my purse. I feel naked without it."

His head swiveled toward her. She saw something flash across his face, like irritation but darker. "You need to trust me, honey. You're my wife, remember? Just do what I say and everything will be fine."

She wanted to trust him. She wanted to believe that this was all some horrible mistake. She was only nineteen and she'd roped herself to this man she barely knew, or maybe didn't know at all, with no other means to make her way in the world. She was scared to be with him, and scared to be without him.

He saw her hesitation. "A woman is dead, Helene. Do you want it to be for nothing? We're so close, you and I. Soon we can put this life behind us. Go to

Costa Rica, spend our days surfing and drinking margaritas, just the two of us. How does that sound?"

Helene didn't know how to surf. She barely knew how to swim. She'd never seen the ocean. She wasn't going to tell him any of that. She cleared her throat. "Okay."

"Great." He put his big hand on her shoulder. "One last thing. Don't forget to close the gate on your way out. We're in this together, now. You got my back on this?"

She nodded.

"Good." Roy stood away from the window. "Go on, now. I'll be right behind you."

While he watched, she made a clumsy Y-turn and headed back to the road. At the end of the driveway, she got out of the car and pulled the gate shut. Because she was a criminal now, she used her sleeve to rub the spot she'd touched with her hand. It was getting dark.

At the trailhead, before she left the car, she opened the glove box and found the registration.

The woman's name was Jessica Moore.

Roy was not right behind her. Night had fallen and she was shivering behind a boulder in the scrub below the trailhead, with the keys stupidly thrown away. She was questioning every decision she had ever made when she finally heard the truck's familiar rumble and the quick double-tap of his horn.

By the time she'd scrambled up from her hiding place, he'd already turned the truck around. Before she even closed the passenger door, he took his foot off the brake and let gravity begin to pull them downhill. The truck chimed softly. "Put on your seat belt, honey."

She looked around for her pink backpack, but it was gone. She climbed to her knees and looked into the back, but it wasn't there, either. The black leather duffel was missing, too.

"Where's my stuff, Roy?" Her voice was louder than she'd intended.

"Take it easy. I cleaned up a little. Everything's in the trailer, your stuff and mine, for our own safety." His voice was calm. "If the cops pull us over, they'd need a warrant to get in there. And they won't have cause. Once we put some miles behind us, we'll stop and get whatever you want. Did you wipe down the car and pitch the keys?"

She rubbed her face with her hands. "Yeah. Where's Frank?" The truck chimed louder. She put on her seat belt.

"He's riding with the others. Giving us a little space. This is our honeymoon, remember?"

She looked out the window. "Some honeymoon."

He reached across and patted her leg. "Give it time. It'll be okay."

She pushed his hand away. "Roy, you fucking killed someone. And I watched you do it."

He kept his eyes on the road. "You're upset, I get

it. I already apologized. What else do you want me to do?"

This was all too easy for him. She wanted to ask if he'd killed anyone else, but she was afraid of how he might answer. Instead, she said, "Tell me what you did with her. Where you put her body."

"You don't want to know. Trust me, it won't make you feel better."

"No," she said. "I do want to know. Tell me." Because she didn't *want* to feel better. She wanted it to be real. She wanted it to hurt.

He shook his head like he was reading her mind. "Honey, there's no reason to punish yourself. What's done is done. There's no going back."

"Just tell me, okay?"

Now he looked at her. "It's taken care of."

"What the hell does that mean, Roy? Did you leave her on the grass? Did you throw her off the side of the mountain?"

His look was sharper this time. "I told you, it's taken care of. It's better if you don't know these things."

Her stomach clenched. "Doesn't it affect you? The fact that you killed a woman less than two hours ago?"

"Of course it affects me. It makes me sad, okay?" He sighed. "I didn't want her to die. But she was a cop, she swore the oath, she knew the risks. Also, when she saw the open gate, she could have kept driving, but she didn't. She stuck her nose into something that was none of her business. And in this life, there are consequences."

"Roy."

"No, listen. This is how it is, honey. It was her or me. Actually, the fact that you saw her from that window and ran to get me? That was absolutely the right move. You gave me time to control the situation. Five more minutes and she'd have called for backup. We could all be in jail or dead right now."

He laughed. He actually laughed.

"I really owe you, honey. We all do. I knew you were something special."

Helene felt like she was going to throw up.

He slowed for the curve. "I was a cop, too, remember? I swore the same oath she did. To protect and serve. Well, now I'm a thief, so I have to protect and serve myself." He put his hand on her thigh. "But I'm looking out for you, too. Because we're married, honey. 'Til death do us part, remember?"

Her stomach lurched. Suddenly sweating, she tasted the rush of saliva. Roy must have seen something in her face because he hit the brakes hard. She opened her door and leaned out and vomited a thick, sour stream of sickness, over and over until there was nothing left inside.

"You done?" Roy handed her the bottle of water from the center console. "Feels better, right? I used to puke after every job, but not anymore. Like I said, give it time. You get used to it."

Helene didn't want to get used to it. When she got her hands on her backpack again, she was going to get the hell away from him.

He leaned across her to the glove box and fished around until he found a plastic truck-stop travel kit with a tiny toothpaste and a new toothbrush still in its package. "Here you go."

She was aware again of how big Roy was, how he filled the cab of the truck. The travel kit looked tiny in his hands. The hands that had broken that poor woman's neck.

She realized now that he could do the same to her anytime he wanted.

Like she was nothing at all.

"Oh, Roy." She put her face in her hands. "Thank you. I'm so sorry."

It would help if she could cry, she thought. It didn't take much.

Roy put his strong arm around her shoulder and pulled her close.

"It's okay, honey," he said. "I've got you now."

27

As the Utah night unraveled in the headlights, the tires thrumming on the asphalt, Roy silent beside her, Helene's mind wouldn't leave her alone.

How *stupid* she'd been.

How she'd fled Bogaloosa without thinking, without planning. How she'd gotten into a truck with two strange men. How she'd stayed, drawn to Roy, despite all the warning signs.

Had she thought she would escape without cost, without consequence?

No. She'd known she might pay a price.

She just hadn't thought it would be so damn high.

Well, now she knew.

Yes, Helene had made her mistakes, a whole lot of them. But that didn't matter anymore.

What mattered was how she was going to get her-

self out of this situation, and away from this killer she'd
married.

She turned to Roy. "Tell me about your house," she
said. "*Our* house, I mean."

"The home place? Oh, it's heaven, you're going to
love it. Been in my family forever. Two thousand acres
on the bluff above the Missouri River. Hawks and
coyotes and no neighbors for miles."

She didn't like the sound of the last part. "When
do we get there?"

"Soon." His voice was a warm rumble. "You think
you could drive for a while? I could use some shut-eye.
I know the trailer's big, but as long as you don't try to
back up, it's easy."

"Sure. But I don't know where we're going."

He pointed at his phone mounted on the dash.
"Steamboat Springs, Colorado. Just follow the directions."

"What's there? The home place?"

"One more job," he said.

She worked hard to keep her voice reasonable. "Really? After what happened today? Shouldn't we just
call it quits for a while?"

"It's not that simple," he said. "It's a special order.
We're on a schedule."

Then she imagined walking into a hotel again. She'd
have her purse and her overnight bag, too. Her money,
her daddy's gun, her mom's notebook. She remembered Frank's advice, on the way to Klamath Falls.
Don't spend the night. Don't meet us in the morning.

Just find the bus station and take the first ride out of town.

She shrugged. "Okay." Helene found herself putting a soft hand on Roy's arm and a smile on her face. "I can't wait to have a long hot shower. You know I love hotels."

"Hon, I'm real sorry, but we don't have time for that. Besides, I need you with me."

"Roy, I don't think I'm cut out for your kind of work." He gave her a look. She swallowed and kept going. "I mean, I'm happy to keep you company on the road, I'm happy to drive all night if that's what you need." She dipped her chin and wet her lips and widened her eyes like the popular girls in school used to do. "You know I'll do anything you want, baby. But please don't make me go to work with you again."

He ran his hand up the inside of her thigh. "Really, hon, you're such a big help. The fact that you saw that cop right away? That was huge. You saved us. You're part of the team now. You'll sleep in the truck, with me. Just a few more days."

So much for the hotel.

Roy found a place to pull over and Helene climbed behind the wheel. He sat beside her for a few miles to coach her on driving with the long trailer, then crawled into the back. Soon he was snoring.

Whenever Frank drove, Roy always slept through the gas stops. Well, she could stop for gas, too. Take his keys and open the trailer and find her things and walk away. Find a ride going anywhere. She'd look for a woman or a family, but she wasn't going to be picky. She'd pay whatever price she had to pay. What were the odds that the next guy would be a killer?

Roy's snores got louder. No way someone could fake that noise. When she came to a long, straight section of the road, she turned on the overhead and swung his keyring up into the light. There were fewer than before.

The three trailer keys were gone.

When she reached Colorado, Roy woke and took over the driving again. Low on gas, he stopped at a ratty little place that made the Gas and Grocery seem like a palace. It was after midnight. She asked him for her backpack but he was glued to his phone and shooed her away like a child. She didn't want to make a big deal out of it, thinking she'd have another chance soon enough.

The single bathroom stank of urine, with a beer poster of a half-naked woman on the wall and cases of wiper fluid stacked to the ceiling. She opened the sink cabinet, hoping to find something useful or sharp, and saw only a leaky drain and a wrinkled magazine. The cover showed a woman tied up and blindfolded with a gag in her mouth. Shuddering, Helene closed the cabinet and washed her hands and got out of there.

Before dawn, Roy pulled into the parking lot of an abandoned warehouse and peeled her clothes off in the back seat. She tried to be enthusiastic. Afterward they slept for a few hours. Helene dreamed of the dead woman, her head trapped between Roy's big hands.

They met the rest of the guys outside a hilltop palace of glass and concrete, where Roy and Frank took six paintings off the walls and Hollywood packed them into flat wooden crates from the gray truck's trailer. The paintings were all different sizes and the crates matched. Another special order, Helene thought. For some lawyer in Houston.

She watched the driveway from an upstairs bedroom, trying to slow her pounding heart, praying to God that nobody showed up. Then the house went silent and the men were outside, closing the trailer doors. Frank looked up at the window where she stood alone, then turned away. Roy called from the stairs. "Come on, honey. Time to go home."

On the road again, headed east on a series of two-lanes that wound through the mountains. Roy was different now, less self-contained. His mood was wilder.

It was past dark when they stopped again at a high, snow-dusted crossroads where dirty semis idled in rows outside a long metal building spotted with rust like a stray dog with mange. She wondered about the truck drivers, what kind of men they were. Better than Roy, or worse? A bright sign read CHEAP DIESEL. HOME COOKING. HOT SHOWERS.

"Oh, God," she said. "I could really use a shower."

He reached for her. "You smell just fine to me."

"Roy. Girl stuff? I need my things." When she

opened her door, the cold air pinched at her nose. She wanted to take her coat, but didn't. She'd been fine without it before.

He walked back and unlocked the trailer. "Which bag?"

"Both, Roy. Jeez. I want to change my clothes." The perfect amount of attitude. Actress of the year.

He handed out her pink backpack and the leather duffel. "I'll come with you. I could use a shower, too."

She patted him on the chest. "Yes, you definitely could." She led him toward the building, chattering away. "Boy, I'd love a real meal. How 'bout I meet you in the restaurant? This might take a while."

The shower rooms were small and moldy and you had to put money in the machine to get water to come out. Helene didn't bother. If Roy was going to shower, she had maybe ten minutes to find a ride. She unzipped the overnight bag, looking for her daddy's gun with the cracked walnut grip. It wasn't there. She upended the bag on the plastic chair and went through everything. The gun was gone.

Her heart caught in her throat. She tore open the pink backpack and dug down to the bottom. The roll of bills was still there, now nine hundred dollars, tucked into her spare pair of socks, and her mom's notebook. She found her aunt Willa's address and phone number in Minnesota and read them over and over until she could breathe again.

Moving fast, she stuffed her shit back in the bag and opened the bathroom door.

Roy stood just outside, grinning, as if he'd known exactly what she planned. "That was quick."

She forced a smile onto her face. "Turns out I need change for the shower."

"Thought you might." He held out a roll of quarters. "This'll get you as much hot water as you want."

"Thanks, Roy."

"My pleasure, hon."

When she came back out, scrubbed clean but with a pit in her stomach, he was still waiting. He hadn't showered. He'd been there the whole time.

He reached for her bags. "Here, let me get those for you."

She wrapped her arm around the backpack. "It's okay, I can manage."

"Honey, you're my wife, I should carry your things."

His hands were fast and strong. Before she knew it, he'd stripped the straps from her shoulder and taken the bags.

"Time to go." Smiling, he took her elbow in his fist and moved her toward the door. "If we make good time, we'll be home for breakfast."

She slept fitfully in the back while he drove. She dreamed that the dead woman sat in the passenger seat, dressed in Helene's green coat, her head hanging to the side at an impossible angle.

28

Peter press-checked the hatchback driver's gun and noted the round in the chamber, ready to fire. He tucked the pistol in his back pocket. The driver lay flat on his ass, blinking at bluebirds, his hair thickening with blood where Peter had bashed him. Scalp injuries bled a lot.

Peter peeled off the man's camo jacket without much trouble, then patted him down. He found a wallet, a spare magazine for the pistol, and a pack of nicotine gum. He pitched them into the open car. The man also wore a large fixed-blade knife on his belt. A regular Daniel Boone.

Peter stripped off the belt, tossed the sheathed knife after the other stuff, then rolled the man onto his front and knelt on his bony ass. The man was alert enough to struggle as Peter ran the belt's tongue through the buckle, then captured a wrist in the loop.

The man pulled his free arm under his body and cocked a knee, trying to get loose. He was small and skinny, but strong.

"Hold still, asshole." Peter didn't want to hurt him, he just didn't want to have to chase him halfway to Iowa. The driver began to fight harder, muttering under his breath. Peter shook his head, leaned in, and gave him a short, chopping strike to the kidney.

It was a bad place to take a hard blow. Peter had known big men who had wept from the agony of a good kidney punch. Others wet themselves. The driver gave a guttural grunt, but that was it. Sometimes the skinny little fuckers were the toughest.

While the driver was focused on the pain, Peter captured his other wrist in the loop and tied off the belt. As he ran the remainder through the rear belt loops on the other man's jeans, locking his arms low behind him, he said, "Okay, Bobbie, we gotta go."

Then he looked up and saw her in that textbook shooter's stance again, gun pointed right at him.

The dog was at her side, growling. The fur around her muzzle was tinted red. She'd managed to do some damage of her own. Peter would have to look at the driver's arm.

"You can put the gun down, Bobbie. I've got this now."

Her jaw was set. "I don't think so, sonny boy. You better start talking. And don't give me that bullcrap about somebody stealing your truck."

This was the second time she'd surprised him. Her

tactics were textbook, too, each time standing far enough away so he couldn't rush her. Even if Peter was inclined to try for the pistol in his pocket, she'd have no trouble pulling the trigger before he got his hand on the grip.

On the other hand, Peter could see her more clearly here in the bright farmyard than the last time she had pointed a gun at him, in the darkness by her truck. Her pupils were dilated but her body was still. She didn't look scared or angry enough to overcome decades of social conditioning and put a bullet into a human being. Some people, even after months of military training, still couldn't do it. Peter didn't think Bobbie would, either. This calculation took him less than a second.

"I didn't lie to you, Bobbie. I just didn't tell you everything." He stood and hauled the driver up by the bicep. "Right now we need to move. I'm pretty sure this guy's friends are coming and they're not nice people."

Bobbie didn't relax her stance, but she didn't pull the trigger, either.

The driver said, "Help me, lady. I was just playin'. I wasn't tryna to hurt nobody." The twang in his voice sounded like the dark hungry hollers of West Virginia, where the trees were so thick that the sun never hit the ground. A long way from the empty plains of Nebraska.

Peter towed the guy to the rear of the vehicle. "Clock's ticking, Bobbie. Trust me, you don't want to be here. Get on your bike and go."

He could still see the pregnant girl's handprints on the dusty white paint.

He popped the hatch and it rose like a clamshell, revealing a modest cargo area with a slim hinged cover that would hold a few lightweight items and also conceal what you were carrying beneath. He shoved the guy into a seated position at the edge of the small compartment.

The driver leaned toward Peter, his voice too low for Bobbie to hear. "Dude, you're fucked. We know who you are, who all your people are. You have exactly one chance and it's right now. Let me go and walk away or everybody dies."

Peter thought of the girl's handprints and slammed the hatch down on the guy's head.

"Ow, fuck." The driver bent forward, curled into himself.

"It's always more fun when somebody else gets hurt, isn't it?" Peter scooped up the driver's legs, rolled him inside the cargo compartment, then closed the hatch.

Bobbie watched from five yards away. "This isn't right, none of it." She still had the gun on him, but one-handed. The other hand dipped into her pocket.

"Bobbie, I'm doing my best." Peter hustled up to the driver's-side door, one eye on the roads. How long had it been since the driver had sent Peter's picture to his buddies? They'd be here any moment. Peter grabbed the driver's phone from the dirt where it had fallen.

No texts or calls showed on the phone, but the

orange two-way radio hissed softly on the dashboard. From the speaker, a dark voice. "Three, what's your status?"

Peter removed the phone's battery cover and battery in case they were using location tracking, tossed the pieces into the car, then collected the orange two-way and marched around to the rear of the car again.

When he raised the hatch, the driver stared at him balefully, tied up and hurting in the cargo bay of his own car. Peter showed him the radio. "I need you to tell them something. We're heading north on Highway 37, and you're right behind me."

"Dude, I'm not saying shit. If I lie to him, he'll kill me."

Peter let the werewolf peek out from behind his eyes, just a little. "Imagine what I'll do if you don't."

The driver saw something there and swallowed hard. But his mouth just tightened and he shook his head.

"Okay," Peter said. "I can respect that. But consider this. If they're on our ass and start shooting? You're in the trunk. So you're gonna catch the first bullet." He raised his arm to close the hatch, head on a swivel to scan the roads.

"Wait, wait. How do I know you won't just kill me afterward?"

"Because I'm not like you. Yes or no?"

The driver let out a breath and nodded.

Peter didn't know if this would work, but it was better than nothing. He held the radio to the other man's mouth. "Be good now." Then pressed the talk button.

The driver said, "This is Three. I'm right behind him, headed north on 37."

Peter released the button. A long moment. Then the radio squawked. "This is One. What's your location?"

Peter eyeballed the driver. "At least five miles," he said. The driver nodded. Peter hit talk again.

"Coming up on Springfield."

"Acknowledged. Get it done before Tyndall. On our way."

The driver rolled his eyes up at Peter. They were already purpling from the beating he'd taken.

Peter tucked the two-way into his pocket and closed the hatch. Maybe it would buy them a few minutes. At least until the others realized that Three had stopped answering the radio.

He frowned as he walked around to the driver's side. He'd done snatch-and-grab missions in Iraq and Afghanistan. He hadn't much liked them then, and he didn't like it now. But the alternatives were to kill the skinny little fucker, or to let him go, and Peter didn't want to do either one. Letting him go was putting one more enemy back in the world, and killing a prisoner would make Peter one of the bad guys. Maybe worse.

He collected the night-vision headset and the driver's camo jacket and tossed them onto the passenger seat along with the murderous little pistol. The chrome-plated AR was barrel-down in the footwell. A handheld spotlight was plugged into the power outlet.

The engine purred. As he racked back the driver's seat and climbed behind the wheel, he wondered why the car had died when the pregnant woman was driving it. Had they put gas in it? The tank was half-full. It didn't matter. It was running now.

"Stop." Bobbie had the gun in one hand and her phone cupped in the other. He supposed she could have been recording, but the phone wasn't oriented that way. "We got laws in South Dakota. I can't let you leave with that man in the trunk."

With the door still open, Peter found the window control and lowered the glass. "Then I guess you have a decision to make. Are you going to shoot me?"

Without taking her eyes or the gun off Peter, Bobbie lifted her phone to her ear. "I'm calling the sheriff."

It was the last thing Peter wanted, but he didn't want her to get hurt, either.

"Listen to me," he said. "That guy's friends are almost certainly closer than the nearest police car. When they realize he's lied to them, they'll come here and kill us both. They're after me, so I'm leaving. You should really do the same. Stay off the roads and you'll be okay."

Bobbie stepped away, eyes on the dirt. "Hi, my name is Roberta Davies and I'd like to report a crime in progress at the intersection of Highway 37 and 317th."

Then Peter was out of the car. Before she could

react, he twisted the pistol from her hand. Then he pushed it deep into her bibs' oversized side pocket and shoved her toward the hot pink Yamaha. "Go, Bobbie. You want to wait for the cops, fine, but do it from someplace safe, far away and out of sight." He was shouting now. *"Go!"*

She went. The two-way crackled in his pocket. Peter threw himself into the driver's seat, found first gear, then dropped the hand brake and popped the clutch and felt all four tires bite.

Just past the county line by the river, the pregnant girl had said. Look for the crosses.

As the little VW slewed sideways toward the road, he looked over his shoulder and saw Bobbie climbing on the bike and settling the dog onto her lap.

Peter realized he was still wearing her lucky coat.

29

When Helene woke again in Roy's truck, they were somewhere in Kansas. It was two a.m. She told him she needed to pee and he pulled onto the verge. The narrow road was dead straight and seemed to stretch out forever, both ahead of them and behind. The wind was unrelenting and smelled of manure and smoke. The only other lights were pinpricks at the edge of the horizon.

Because of the truck's huge gas tank, they only had to stop once more to refuel. It was a nameless place with plywood over the broken front window and just one pump working. She went inside to use the bathroom and buy food and coffee, trying to find a back door, but Roy was never more than twenty feet away. It didn't matter, because the only other person there was the clerk, a wheezing old man who never looked away from his tiny television.

The sun came up on their right as they crossed into Nebraska. Her stomach jittered from the coffee and she kept waiting for Roy to ask her to drive. Instead, he shook a few pills from a faded aspirin bottle, washed them down with warm Coke, then drummed his fingers on the wheel and went on and on about what he called the home place, which turned out to be the house he'd grown up in.

"Baby, you're going to love it. I admit, it's a work in progress. But now that I've got you with me, we can really make some changes. A big vegetable garden, and maybe some chickens?"

Helene had stopped talking. She was too exhausted to pretend that everything was fine, but she didn't know what else to do. She sure as hell wasn't going to tell Roy she wanted out. She didn't want to shatter the cheery illusion of their new marriage. She was terrified of what it might turn into.

If Roy noticed her distress, he didn't mention it.

As the sun rose higher, he abandoned the state highway for an unmarked road, then made a series of turns that continued until she had lost all ability to retrace her steps. The farmland gave way to rolling grassland too steep for cultivating crops. Ragged barns and a burned-out single-wide and a faded metal sign that read LEAVING KNOX COUNTY. No cars, no houses.

They came to a slim gravel track that rapidly devolved into rutted dirt. The dried mud formed craters deep enough to drown in. The truck and trailer lurched and bounced and Roy slowed. On the right rose densely wooded hillsides. On the left, an ancient fence whose wire was long rusted or broken, the remaining unrotted posts now serving as crooked supports for a series of homemade crosses.

The first few were straight and tall, made of long, notched timbers that Helene thought had been torn from the bowels of some ancient structure now lost to history. As Roy drove onward, the crosses became smaller, more rickety, until finally they were cobbled together with mere scraps and remnants. At a certain point, the makers switched to tree limbs and branches, bark stripped away to show the undulating, serpentine shapes. Some of these had rough Christ figures hung from them, fashioned crudely from sticks or woven vines and slowly coming apart over the years. Others had been painted with whitewash now faded to pale streaks on the bone-dry wood.

Beyond the crosses, an ancient forest fell away downslope to something she couldn't see. She thought of that old fairy tale, "Hansel and Gretel." Except she didn't even have bread crumbs.

Ahead of her, the road ended.

"Honey, we're hoooome." Roy turned into the trees, piloting the truck down a precipitous dirt driveway with a raised stripe of weeds down the center. At the bottom stood an unmown meadow with a house and a barn and a partial view of the river below.

———

The house was tall and square, made of dark red brick with a wide porch. Its steep black roof reminded Helene of a witch's hat. The barn was red-painted wood and looked like something from a picture book, built into the hillside with a dirt ramp to the upper level. Both buildings looked old but sturdy. Enduring.

The day was warmer than she'd expected, the sun warming her skin. Roy got her bags from the trailer, then led her up the porch and unlocked the front door. "Take a look around," he said. "Get settled. I have a few things to do in the barn."

Inside, the house smelled of dust.

The kitchen was large with a broad porcelain sink, a fridge and stove, shelves for plates and pantry staples, and a big square worktable in the center of the room. All of it had been there a very long time.

She turned the tap and let the water run. After a moment, it warmed.

As if she were considering living here. As if she had any choice.

At least it was nicer than the trailer behind the Gas and Grocery, she thought. Nothing she couldn't improve with a little cleaning.

Then caught herself again. She didn't want to be here. She wasn't planning to stay, either.

She walked into the dining room, then the living room, then mounted the creaking stairs. In the bathroom, she found a clawfoot tub with no overhead shower. The door was new, and only locked from the outside.

She hadn't lived in a real house in a long time, but that didn't seem right.

She checked the bedrooms. Something was off there, too, but she couldn't figure out what. Then she looked at the closet doors. They had the same locks.

She went downstairs with different eyes. The basement door had the same lock as the closets. So did the front and back doors.

If you didn't have a key, someone could lock you in.

And there was no phone.

She scooped up her pink backpack and ran out to the yard, her chest heaving, panic building up inside her like a creek overflowing its banks. She was losing it. She had to get out of there.

Roy had backed the truck and trailer up the dirt ramp and into the barn. He was nowhere in sight.

She ran up the driveway toward the road. She could feel every rock and root through her cheap Walmart sneakers. She'd left her coat in the truck but she didn't care. It was a warm day, she was a country girl, and she had all day to walk. At the top of the drive, she'd get into the woods, where she'd be harder to find. How far could it be to the next safe place?

She slowed to pace herself and heard a *yip*. A dog stood in the trees to her right. No, not a dog. A coyote, tawny and sleek and well fed. Regarding her regally.

She heard another sound behind her and spun on

her heel. A second coyote trotted up the driveway, not ten feet away.

"Hey," Roy shouted. He jogged toward Helene, clapping his hands loudly. "Go on, you. Git. Get out of here."

The coyotes didn't move. They barely looked at him. They were focused on her.

Roy took the pistol from his belt, pointed it at the ground, and pulled the trigger. The sound was loud.

The animals tensed. They didn't leave, but he definitely had their attention. He pulled the trigger twice more. *BANG. BANG.* "Go on, get out of here."

Finally, as if it had thought of something better to do, the coyote on the driveway trotted into the trees to join the other. Although Helene could still see them both, watching from the underbrush.

"Didn't I tell you about them? There's a whole pack. They get kind of bold because I'm gone a lot." Roy flashed his warm smile, put his big hand on her arm, and turned her toward the house. "Better stick close to home."

Up the hill, someone tapped a horn. She looked over her shoulder and saw the gray truck coming down the drive.

30

Hollywood backed the truck and trailer up the dirt ramp and into the barn beside Roy's. Helene stood in the opening and watched while the men reorganized the contents. Roy's trailer took all the antique furniture and crated paintings and guns. The little convertible and expensive bikes and boxes of power tools went in the gray trailer. If there was cash or jewelry or gold, she didn't see it. The chest freezer stayed in Roy's trailer, the generator humming away.

Every few minutes, she felt Frank's eyes on her, his expression unreadable.

There were other things in the barn. A blue Jeep, a small white car, a pair of ATVs, and an old green tractor with a scoop on the front and a bucket on the back. Nothing she could use right now, she thought. But maybe later. If she could find the keys.

Repacking the trailers didn't take long. When they were done, they pulled the trucks into the yard, Pony Boy behind the wheel of one and Frank driving the other. Roy closed the barn door and fastened the pair of fat padlocks on heavy hasps. Then he grabbed her up and gave her a big kiss.

"You're on your own for a little while. A week, ten days. We've got to offload this stuff and get paid."

She stared at him, unable to process this.

"I know, honey, I wish you could come, too. But the people we're going to meet, they don't like new faces." He patted her butt. "Don't worry, I'll tell 'em all about you for next time."

"I need a car, Roy. How do I get groceries?"

"There's plenty of food. You'll be fine." Roy climbed into the passenger seat and gave her a wink. "Best be inside by suppertime. The coyotes get more aggressive after dark."

Frank hit the gas, following Pony Boy up the driveway. And then they were gone.

She walked around the barn. There were two big sliding doors, one at the top of the dirt ramp and another for the lower level. Both were reinforced with new wood and sturdy locks. The lower-level windows were boarded over with planks. She turned to look at the house. The basement windows were covered, too. She wasn't getting inside any of them without keys or some kind of tools.

It wasn't until a cool breeze cut through her T-shirt that she realized her green coat was still in Roy's truck. All she had to wear were the black sweater and her mom's sweatshirt in her backpack. The Walmart sneakers were already falling apart.

She searched the house for something warmer. The bedroom dresser held Roy's T-shirts and jeans, socks and underwear, but nothing else. If he had any other clothing, it had to be in the closets or basement, which were all locked. She checked every drawer for keys, but found none.

Which meant that if Helene was going to get out of this place, she was going to have to do it under her own power. With nothing other than her pink backpack and the clothes on her back.

At least Roy was telling the truth about the food. The fridge held nothing but condiments, beer, and a few Cokes, but the freezer was stocked. Meat wrapped in white paper and labeled with black marker. Loaves of bread, a couple pounds of butter, a half gallon of milk that he'd probably frozen so it wouldn't spoil. The pantry had canned vegetables, instant coffee, and ancient glass jars filled with dried beans, flour, sugar, and other staples.

Helene didn't know how to make anything but microwave burritos, Cup O' Noodles, and mac and cheese from a box. But she wasn't going to be here long, no sirree. She found a cast-iron pan and dropped in a pound of venison sausages directly from the freezer. She ate two of them, half burned and half raw, wrapped in toasted bread with questionable yellow mustard and green beans forked directly from the can. Then made two more sandwiches and wrapped them in waxed paper and set them on the table where she went through the pink backpack to see what she had. The sweatshirt, which she put on over the black sweater. Her money. Her hairbrush. A half-dozen tampons. She added the food, then threw in a couple of Cokes. She had no idea how far she would have to walk.

By the time she'd done all of that and stepped out onto the porch, the weather had turned. In Coldwater, it could happen very quickly, and Nebraska didn't seem to be any different. The sun had vanished behind low, dark clouds and the wind smelled like November.

She didn't care. She was leaving. She'd been cold plenty of times. She stepped to the edge of the woods and found a stout stick to fend off the coyotes. She was *not* going to get eaten.

Thunder sounded before she even got to the road. The clouds flashed bright with lightning. The crosses on the fence line turned dark with rain. She was soon soaked to the skin but didn't stop or turn back. As long as she kept moving, she'd be okay. She'd learned this walking through the snow to Bogaloosa's barn. At least in Coldwater she had a key to her own trailer door, even if Bogaloosa had one, too. Good God, was she feeling nostalgic for the Gas and Grocery? There had to be something better. She walked faster. The ruts were filling with water. Her cheap shoes were coated with mud. She came to the gravel and kept going. Surely if she stayed parallel to the river, she'd find another house.

But she didn't. The landscape hadn't seemed so desolate from the passenger seat of the truck, but now it seemed emptied of all humanity. At least there was no sign of the coyotes. They were smart enough to stay out of this downpour.

How long had she been walking? An hour? With no sign of a single neighbor? This was dumb, to try this in the rain. Roy said he'd be gone a week. The weather would be better tomorrow. Anyway it couldn't be worse. She set the Cokes down at the side of the road to mark how far she'd gone.

Back at the house, she ran a hot bath and hung her wet things by the heater. When she got out of the tub, she had nothing of her own to wear, so she put on one of Roy's T-shirts and wrapped herself in a blanket. She made herself an elkburger and heated a can of baked beans, but couldn't stand to be inside, staring at the locks on the doors. She found a thick quilt from the bedroom and sat on the porch to eat her supper, listening to the rain on the tin roof. It was actually kind of nice, she thought. Then hated herself for it.

She put her dishes in the sink, and found herself washing them out of habit. When she returned to the porch, the rain had stopped and the coyotes prowled at the edge of the trees. She counted five, maybe six. When they began to leap and pounce, making short zigzag sprints through the grass, she thought they were playing. Until she realized they were hunting rabbits. No matter how fast the rabbits ran, how frantically they dodged, the chase always ended in teeth and blood.

She had to get out of this place.

The next morning, it began to rain again.

And every day after that.

Still, she walked.

Her clothes never really got dry. If the rain stopped, even just for a few minutes, she became aware of the coyotes in the woods. Sometimes one or two, sometimes more, they kept pace with her as she hurried along the road. It reminded Helene of the way she herself would stand at the open door of the refrigerator, considering her next meal. She waved her stick and shouted at them and kept moving until the rain came down hard once more.

Most days, even drenched to the bone, she made it a little farther, moving the Coke cans down the road. Despite that, she never came to another house. As if she'd fallen into a hole in the world, a hole without a bottom.

When she became so cold that she could barely control her hands, she went back to the home place, where the panic fluttered in her stomach like a live bird. She tried not to think about Roy walking through the door. She hung up her wet clothes and warmed herself by the heater, then tried to think of new ways to open the locked closets or basement. She had no better tools than a kitchen spatula and a paring knife.

Roy had to have more clothes somewhere. A raincoat would make a big difference. Any kind of coat. And boots, even if they were too big, to replace the Walmart sneakers. She searched the house again and again. Nothing. She paced around the barn, thinking of the vehicles inside, but it was locked up just as tight, the hardware new and strong.

After supper, warm and dry and fed, she sat on the porch while the coyotes howled in the woods. Later she lay in the big bed and listened to the unfamiliar sounds of the house, thinking about tomorrow, praying for sunshine. Wondering when Roy would come home.

One night, she brushed her teeth in the bathroom and wondered what day it was. She'd totally lost track of time. She counted back to her last shift at the Gas and Grocery, then counted forward. It was October now. Roy had been gone nine days.

Then she closed her eyes and counted again, this time trying to picture a calendar.

Oh, this was bad. Her mother would have been *pissed*.

She had no idea how long it had been since her last period.

More than a month. More than two?

The next morning, bright and early, he came home.

31

She had the skillet on the stove, making pancakes from a box, when she heard his truck outside. She took a deep breath and told herself that everything would be fine. She could do this. Time to make some lemonade, baby girl.

From the porch, she saw the first sunshine since the day he'd left, as if he'd known exactly when to come home. She put a smile on her face and waved at him with the spatula, feeling like a picture in one of her mom's magazines. "Just in time for pancakes."

The pickup stood in the yard, the trailer behind it. Roy locked the barn as Frank drove the blue Jeep up the driveway, followed by Hollywood in the little white car. When they were gone, Roy came at her in a rush, stinking and unshaven. His breath was sour and his hands were all over her.

"Hold on, lover boy." She turned her face away and pushed at his chest. "Ugh. You need a bath. And to brush your teeth. After that, I'm all yours."

He squeezed her so hard she could barely breathe. Then he released her. "You're right, honey. I'm sorry. That's no way to romance my wife." He gave her that smile and she felt herself warm despite herself. His charm made it easy to forget she'd watched him kill poor Jessica Moore with his bare hands.

He walked into the kitchen, took a sip of her coffee, then plucked a pancake from the skillet with his fingers and ate it as he walked toward the stairs. "Why're your clothes all hanging up on the chairbacks?"

"I got caught in the rain yesterday," she said. "I get restless all by myself with nothing to do. Give me your keys, I'll bring in your bag."

"Truck's open," he said. "I brought groceries, too." He kicked off his boots and headed up the stairs.

She put on her still-damp sneakers and went out to the truck, heart pounding. She allowed herself to hope his keys might still be in the ignition. She'd hit the gas and go. But no such luck.

Two bags of groceries sat on the floor in the front. His duffel was on the back seat. Her green coat was nowhere to be found.

She left the groceries in the kitchen and carried his duffel up to the bathroom door. "Roy, where's my green coat?"

He grinned at her from the tub. It seemed small with him in it. "Not my day to watch it, hon."

"Seriously? You left before I could get it from the truck. Now it's gone."

He gave her an innocent shrug. "No idea, hon. Sorry."

She dropped the duffel with a thump. "Roy, I have been freezing my ass off for more than a week."

"Honey, will you relax? I just got home."

His dirty clothes lay in a heap on the bathroom floor. She grabbed up his jeans and slapped at the pockets. No heavy rattle of keys. "You leave me all alone, no phone, no car, no coat. No idea when you're coming back. What the hell am I supposed to do? What if the heat went out?"

Then she saw his keyring on the windowsill on the far side of the tub. She'd have to reach across him to grab them. He winked at her, as if he knew exactly what she was thinking.

She balled up his pants and threw them at the pile of dirty clothes. His sweatshirt shifted and his pistol peeked out of the pile, still tucked into its black leather holster.

"Hey." His voice was soft. "Honey. Calm down, okay?"

She didn't look at him. She didn't want to see how strong he was, or think about how fast he could be. Although she was closer to the gun than he was. She'd practiced with her daddy's, but Roy's was different. Not a revolver, and much bigger. Would she even know how to use it? She wouldn't have time to learn.

He'd be out of the tub in an instant. Could she even pull the trigger?

She tried to imagine it. The sound of it in the small room. The red hole in his naked flesh, the blood. There would be a lot of blood.

She closed her eyes and sagged back against the sink. "You live in the middle of fucking *nowhere*, Roy. Your closets are all *locked*. The *barn* is locked, the *basement* is locked. What the fuck is the matter with you?"

"Honey, I'm sorry. I had to go meet a guy, I was in a hurry, and I didn't think. I'm not used to having someone here. And yes, I'm security conscious. It's an occupational hazard. We'll work it out, okay? This is your house, too."

He stood and stepped from the tub, water streaming from his body. He was hairy as an animal. He wrapped himself in a towel. "I want to show you something. It's in the trailer. Let me put some clothes on."

He gathered up his things, walked past her to the bedroom, and took fresh clothes from the dresser. Outside, he took his keys from his pocket and unfastened the padlock on the trailer's side door. "After you." The generator hummed quietly.

Her stomach fluttered as she stepped into the dim space, bounded by plywood shelves, now mostly empty. Behind her, Roy picked up a big cardboard box and set it atop the chest freezer. He unfolded the lid.

It was full of money. Rough bundles bound with

rubber bands, crisp stacks that looked fresh from a bank vault.

"More than two hundred thousand dollars," he said. "Plus another hundred and sixty grand in gold coins. That's our share, you and me, from just one trip. And there's plenty more, hidden away."

He held out a stack of new bills. She took it. It was heavier than she'd thought it would be. There was a printed paper band around the middle labeled *$10,000*. That single packet was more than she'd made in a whole year, working two jobs for Bogaloosa.

"What we do, it's hard work," he said. "And risky. But this is the reward."

He set the box back on the shelf, then flipped through his keys until he found a small one. He reached past her and stuck it into the side of the freezer. She hadn't even realized it had a lock. The first time she'd seen it, he'd told her it was frozen shut.

He took a breath and let it out. "To get the reward, though, sometimes we have to do unpleasant things." He turned the key, tucked the ring back in his pocket, then lifted the lid. "Take a look."

Inside, covered with white frost, surreal in the pale freezer light, lay Jessica Moore, the woman from the blue SUV.

She was on her back with her legs straight and her arms at her side, like a child pretending to sleep. Her eyes were still open, and covered with a thin scrim of ice. The blood on her face looked gray under the veil of frost.

"Roy." Helene clenched her fist around the money. The flutter in her stomach got much worse. She tried to keep her voice steady. She couldn't look away from the dead woman. "Why would you show me this?"

"Well, you're holding the reward in your hand. That cardboard box is full of it. But this here is the cost. And I don't mind paying it. Or I should say, I don't mind other people paying it. Because I want the money. I want what I deserve. And I want you to get what you deserve, too."

Helene frowned. Something in the freezer didn't make sense. What was it?

Roy kept talking. "Don't you want a house on the beach, hon? Someplace warm, with palm trees and fruity drinks? Another year of this and we won't ever have to work again."

Helene looked closer. There were too many feet. She saw an extra hand, too. Then she realized. Underneath the dead woman, there was a second body. The flutter rose in her stomach. Things were so much worse than she'd thought. "Roy?"

"Honey, that night we met, I saw something in you that I've never seen before. It was like looking into a mirror." His voice rose. "You and me, we're the same. We're special. We're not made for normal life, normal rules. We're made for each other. We'll do what we want, we'll take what we want. Sometimes, when we have to, we'll even take a life."

She couldn't take her eyes off the frozen bodies. Her voice was soft. "How many lives?"

"Does it matter?" he asked. "Nobody can stop us." His face was shining. He was a monster.

Helene needed air, she needed to get away from these dead people. Roy stood between her and the door. She put a hand on his chest but he was too big to move.

"Roy, I'm sorry," she said. "I can't do this, I just can't. I'm not like you. I'm sorry."

She looked up at him. His eyes had gone cold, far colder than anything inside that freezer. The air between them crackled.

"Roy, I love you," she said, "I do. But do you remember what you said, that night we met? If things didn't work out between us, you'd just drop me off at the bus station and we'd go our separate ways. Remember?" She swallowed hard. The flutter kept rising. Don't throw up, Helene. "Well, darling, that's what I want you to do. Right now. If you really love me, you'll drive me to the nearest bus station."

He reached out for her, put a hand on her back.

She talked faster. "And you know I won't tell a soul about any of this. Why would I want to? I mean, I was part of it, right? I'm just as guilty. Which means I can't tell anyone, ever. I promise you that. Okay, Roy? Please? Just take me to the bus station. I'll buy my own ticket."

He nodded, almost as if to himself, then leaned in and kissed her gently, his lips soft, his breath sweet. "I'm sorry, honey. This is the bus station. This is your ticket."

And in a single smooth motion, he bent at the

waist and caught up her legs, holding her in his arms like a newlywed, then stepped forward, dropped her in the freezer, and slammed the lid.

"Roy!" She tried to sit up and banged her forehead. It was dark as night. The body beneath her was cold and hard. "Roy!" She was screaming. She put her hands up to the freezer lid and tried to push it open. It didn't move, not even a little. Either he was leaning on it or he'd locked it again.

She couldn't get any air. The freezer was too full, there wasn't room to fight. She was cold and getting colder. The dead woman's frost was seeping into her bones. She pushed again, harder, as hard as she could. Then banged with her fists, bright bursts of pain. "Roy, please! Roy, I love you!"

Through the lid, she heard his voice, thin as a blade. "No, you don't. You want to leave."

She made herself take a long, shuddering breath and hold it a moment as she tried to think of what to say. Of what he might want to hear.

"I'm scared, Roy, I'm just scared. I don't know how to be married. But I don't want to be alone, either. I want to be with you, Roy. Please let me stay. I'll be a good wife, I promise."

No answer. She wondered if he'd left the trailer. If he'd locked the door and gone in the house. If she was going to die in here.

She closed her eyes and felt the frost on her lashes. She was shaking now. The cold had fully penetrated her body. The corpse was like ice beneath her.

"Roy!" she shouted. "I'm pregnant!" Then screamed it as loud as she could. "I'm pregnant, I'm pregnant! With your baby."

After a long moment, the freezer lid opened. She blinked in the sudden light. He looked down at her. "It's my baby?"

"Of course it's your baby, Roy." Her voice shivered. "I've never been with anyone else."

He smiled, then, flooding her with warmth. "Honey, that's wonderful news. I knew we were meant to be together." She didn't dare move. Icy tendrils floated past her into the air. "Hey, let's get you out of there."

He reached down, scooped her into his arms again, and lifted her from the freezer as if she weighed nothing at all. She felt the overwhelming strength and power of him, the hard muscles taut under the thin T-shirt. The power to do anything. The power of life and death.

Shivering uncontrollably, she clung to him with everything she had.

32

The little white car flew across the long bridge at a hundred and ten, a rocket masquerading as a hatchback. Obviously, someone had bought the high-performance package.

Peter hadn't driven a ride like this in years. If he could stay on the blacktop, he'd have no problem keeping ahead of that jacked-up pickup. Too bad he was headed for dirt.

On the Nebraska side, he came to Highway 12 and slowed for the intersection, then headed south. It was almost eleven by the clock on the dash and the roads were empty. The trussed-up guy in the cargo bay was silent, no doubt deep into a truly massive headache. The orange two-way radio squawked in the center console. "Three, we don't see you on 37. What's your location?"

He was up to ninety again on a sweeping curve

when a familiar silhouette materialized on the left. His Chevy, parked on a grassy turnoff above the river. He wanted to stop but knew he couldn't afford the time.

"Three, where the fuck are you?"

The map in his head guided him through the turns, state highway to county pavement to ragged gravel. He had to slow the rocket or risk tearing out the oil pan. The fertile farms had turned to lumpy meadows and slumped hills covered with dense, scrubby trees. The only buildings were dark shapes in the night. By the time he saw the small county marker appear in his headlights, he still hadn't passed a single moving car. He wondered who the hell the sign was for. As far as he'd seen, nobody lived anywhere near here.

He stopped in the middle of the road and grabbed the night-vision gear from the passenger seat. It was a commercial model, not the military-grade stuff he'd used overseas. He found the power button and pulled on the headset. Nothing. He took it off and turned it in his hands, looking for the controls, and saw the cracked plastic. Shit. The skinny redneck had been wearing it when Peter smacked his head against the car.

He killed his headlights anyway, including the dash glow, then dropped all the windows and kept driving by starlight and the low sliver of a moon. He was glad the car's performance-minded owner hadn't chosen the noisy exhaust option. The orange radio had gone silent.

The world was different in the dark, even inside the

car. His other senses expanded. He could smell the river now, and feel the land falling away toward it to the north. He passed a long-deserted farmstead, then another, both overtaken by trees. How long had it been since he'd seen lights from a house or barn? Coyotes called back and forth across the hills. The gravel turned to rutted dirt and he slowed to a crawl, navigating its rough geography. He had to be close. Unless he'd missed it.

Then he saw the crosses, just off the road to his left. He stopped the car and got out.

He wasn't sure what he expected, but it wasn't these rough, leaning forms cobbled together from scraps and sticks. As if representing a flavor of devotion so mean and hungry that it had to cannibalize the world to make itself known, and could survive only in this tangled, empty place.

He walked ahead a hundred yards and found the berm of dirt where the road ended. A long narrow driveway turned between a gap in the crosses, curving downhill into the trees. No lights shone. No sound but the low hum of the little white car. No sign of any kind of life.

He turned the car carefully and returned to the first decent pull-off, a narrow track turned to hip-high weeds that thumped under the chassis. At its end was an ancient cinder-block structure with a swaybacked roof and cracked walls pushed outward at the top like the inverted hull of a ship.

Peter drove to the far side of the building so he'd be

out of sight from the road. At a jumble of wrecked farm machines with full-grown trees rising through their rusted skeletons, he killed the engine so he could hear the sound of the other men's trucks. The orange radio was still silent. That was a bad sign, evidence they thought their comms were compromised. He didn't know if they were still searching across the bridge or if they'd regrouped and were coming home. He'd find out soon enough.

He tucked the lethal little pistol into his back pocket and clipped the orange radio to the neck of his fleece. Then he picked up the driver's big knife and camo jacket, raised the windows, and got out of the car.

When he popped the hatch, the driver looked up at him, hog-tied with his own belt and shoelaces, pitiful as a pup.

Peter wasn't fooled. This was the same man who had threatened to kill Peter and all his people. "Is the pregnant woman at the home place? The house with all the crosses on the road?"

"Roy's place? I don't know, dude. It's not my house and she's not my girl."

Roy must be the husband, Peter thought. "Keep your voice down." Peter showed him the knife. It had a black blade. "I'm in a hurry. Where is she?"

"Dude, I'm tellin' the truth, I don't fuckin' know. When I left, she was in Pony's truck."

"I said keep your damn voice down." Peter pulled

the man's head back by the hair and put the knife to his throat. "Where would he take her?"

"Okay, shit, okay," the driver said in a hoarse whisper. "He'd take her to Roy's place. I don't know anywhere else."

"Would he stay with her? Would anyone else be there?"

"Nobody else lives there, if that's what you mean. Just her and Roy."

"Okay," Peter said. "If she's at the house, and you're off the radio, what's Roy's next move? Will he come for her?"

The driver closed his eyes. "Yeah. He will. He'll know we've had this conversation. Roy's scary like that. And when it comes to that girl, he ain't right in the head."

Peter had already reached that conclusion. "How many in your crew?"

"Me and Roy and Frank and Pony. That's it."

It could be the truth. There were four men at the ambush by the river. Peter had seen the faces of the two men in the black truck, plus now this nasty little asshole. That left the driver of the big gray truck, who could be anywhere.

Peter took the knife and touched the point to the man's cheek, right below his eye. A tiny bead of blood formed. "Next question. Any security measures at the house? Cameras? Booby traps in the woods?"

The driver got very still. "Sweet Jesus, please. I'm

telling you, I don't know. I don't spend time there. Roy's a freaky dude. I got no idea what all he's got."

"Okay." Peter picked up the man's thin camo jacket and balled up one front flap. "Open your mouth."

"Dude, please, I'm tryna help."

Peter smiled. "For your sake, I sincerely hope that's true. Open up."

The driver opened his mouth tentatively. Peter stuffed the wad between his jaws, then wrapped the sleeves around his head and tied them in a tight double knot. "Take a deep breath."

The driver pulled in some air and Peter knew he wasn't going to asphyxiate.

"So here's the deal. I'm going to get that pregnant woman." Peter rolled the man onto his other side, checked the belt around his wrists, then began to strip the laces from his boots. "You are staying in the car. If I die, you're screwed. Nobody will know you're here. Nobody will come looking. Even if you slip that gag, the windows are up, so nobody will hear you screaming."

Peter knotted the laces into one long strand, then tied the man's ankles together and used the extra length to connect to the belt wrapping his wrists. "You'll probably die of thirst, which will take a few days. Not a fun way to go." He rolled the man back to face him. "So. That in mind, do you have anything else to add?"

The man hesitated a moment, then nodded. Peter pulled the gag out.

The driver licked his lips. "Roy Wiley is the smartest man I ever met. He was a Minneapolis cop for years, and he still knows cops in a dozen states. He's mean as a snake, he does not forgive, and he does not forget. I don't know what's the deal with you and that girl, and I don't want to know. I guess I can't blame you, she is one sexy piece. But if I was you, I'd save myself. Walk my ass away right now and get as far from here as I possibly can."

Peter shook his head. "But I'm not like you, remember?" He held up the wet wadded flap of jacket. "Open up."

33

He left the doors unlocked and the keys on the seat, then slung the chrome-plated carbine across his chest and set off for the road at a run, wondering what kind of person put chrome plating on an assault rifle. He'd found a spare magazine for it in the car's center console and tucked it in his off-side jacket pocket beside the extra pistol mag. They swung and bounced with every step.

He was tempted to double-time it all the way to the dead end, then turn down the driveway. It was the fastest way in, but it was also the first place someone would put a camera or lethal self-defense measure. Instead, he slipped past the crosses and into the trees, ears wide open for the sound of a vehicle.

If they're coming, he thought, they'll be here soon. If they aren't here already.

The branches grabbed at his clothes and poked at

his eyes, as if the forest itself was against him. He picked his way deliberately, heel and toe, bent low with the rifle up and ready, silent as the night. Eyes bright for trip wires and motion sensors and cameras. From Peter's limited experience of Roy, the husband, he expected cameras at a minimum. Homemade blackpowder IEDs were a distinct possibility.

Before long, the brush and evergreens thinned and the trees changed to mature hardwoods. Past their thick trunks, he saw the bright rectangles of windows lit from within. The relief streamed through him. At least there's a damn house here, he thought.

He'd covered half the remaining ground when his scanning eye caught on something pale in the growing window light. Several somethings, jutting up from leaf litter. Knobby, irregular, familiar.

Bones.

He looked left and right. They were all around him. Some were scattered and clean as medical specimens spilled from a box. Others were newer, still held together by cartilage and tendon and gobbets of meat. The unmistakable stench of death filled his nose, cloying and sweet.

He stood in a kind of midden. A boneyard large enough to be years in the making and, from the smell of it, still very much in use. The wide, round arcs of a grazer's ribs. The naked hips of a quadruped. The long slender legs of a deer, hooves still attached. Then, a few steps away, something round and white as a softball.

He nudged it with his toe. It rolled to the side.

Not a softball. It had eye sockets.

A human skull.

How many more bodies were here, buried under the leaves?

He peered through the trees and spied a shadowed mass on the ground, backlit by the window light. It was too bulky for bones. Maybe something recent. Something human? He felt the possibility in his stomach. He needed to get a better look. He crept forward.

As he got closer, the shadow shifted. It was not one mass, but several. He saw high triangular ears, long noses. Coyotes, seated around the soft ravaged mound of a carcass as if at the supper table. Which, Peter supposed, they were.

They didn't make a sound. He barely saw them move, floating low like tawny ghosts, although their teeth flashed in the dark. Five of them, maybe more, closing in.

Despite the throb in his arm where Cupcake had chewed him, he didn't want to shoot them. It would be loud, and he was less than fifty yards from the house. But if he wasn't willing to pull the trigger, the rifle wasn't much good to him. Five full-grown coyotes could make a meal of him without much effort.

He didn't have time for this.

But he needed to know what they were feeding on.

So he backed away, reducing the threat without engaging their chase instinct. The coyotes followed at a distance. He kept one eye on the animals and the other on the ground behind him. If he stumbled, bad things could happen.

He made it out of the boneyard and the coyotes faded back. If they hadn't fed recently, they'd be all around him. He supposed he should feel grateful for the carcass. But he couldn't be. Not until he saw it. He needed a good stick, something to fend them off with, just for a moment.

He found himself at the line of crosses. They were wired to old fenceposts. Peter wasn't particularly religious, but he still felt the power of their ancient symbology. He raised his eyes and gave a silent apology to whoever might be looking down at him, then chose one made of crooked branches and gave it a tug. It was sturdier than it looked. He leaned on the crossbar. It was wired in place, too. For the love of God. He moved down the row until he found a cross that had fallen to the ground. He stomped on it. The wood broke with a *crack*. He froze for a long moment, listening. Nothing.

He bent and picked up the branch, three feet long and as thick as his wrist. A nice knot on one end. Solid enough to convince those coyotes that he'd be a painful meal to catch.

He walked downslope again, rifle slung behind him, blood surging in his veins, the club hanging down like an extension of his arm. The coyotes had returned to the carcass. They weren't sure what to make of him now that he wasn't behaving like prey. So they stood and bared their teeth, letting him know they were prepared to defend their food.

One moved to face him, hackles raised, growling. It was almost certainly a male, larger than Cupcake, well fed and wilder in some vast, undefinable way. Peter stepped toward it, club raised, adrenaline battling against fear.

Like many rural Wisconsin kids, he'd been a hunter in his teens, although he gave it up after the war. He wasn't looking to hurt these animals, either, but one dog bite today was plenty. He needed to see what they were feeding on. What happened next was up to the coyotes.

He swung the club, hazing the beast back. A second coyote joined it, then two more. Together, they seemed less concerned about the stick and more pissed off about Peter invading their dining room. They spread out, surrounding him for more vectors of attack. They'd made their living at this for countless millennia. Things were going to get ugly fast. He stepped closer to the ravaged carcass, keeping the club moving, until he got a good look.

Amid the black blood and torn flesh, he saw fur. He saw hooves.

It wasn't her.

He backpedaled away from the dead deer. The coyotes watched for a moment, then went back to their meal.

Despite how ranchers and hunters felt about large predators, Peter knew they rarely killed for pleasure. Most predators were good for the environment, culling the sick and weak, only taking what they needed to survive. They almost never attacked people.

But this boneyard wasn't the result of natural behavior. Coyotes didn't move their kills, they ate them where they fell. They certainly didn't carry them home, not like this.

They weren't responsible for this museum of death.

There was really only one candidate.

Whoever owned the house. Roy, the husband.

Peter moved faster now. He knew there would be no trip wires or IEDs. The coyotes would set them off. More than that, the carcasses were left in the woods to attract them. Because the coyotes themselves were the security system.

Not to keep someone out, but to keep someone in.

34

While Helene was still shivering from the freezer, Roy went for supplies and came home with six bags of groceries, a stack of magazines, and two different pregnancy tests. He sat on the tub while she peed on the sticks and they watched together while the pink lines appeared. Roy crushed her in his arms, tears in his eyes. Helene stared out the bathroom window, thinking furiously.

She'd lied to Roy, earlier. He wasn't the only man she'd slept with. But she was going to keep that fact to herself.

"We need to find a doctor," she said. "Just to make sure everything is okay." She remembered when she'd had her first ob-gyn appointment at fifteen, when the gynecologist asked if she felt safe in her home. A doctor would have to help, wouldn't he?

Roy frowned. "That might be bad luck, don't you think? Let's give it a few months. Just to make sure."

He unlocked the closet in the spare bedroom and brought out armloads of clothes, simple skirts and blouses and old-timey dresses on wooden hangers. Nothing warm, though. Nothing practical. She didn't want to think about why there were at least three different sizes. After she'd made her selections, they sat on the porch holding hands like a normal couple, watching the coyotes stalk rabbits through the tall grass. After one particularly bloody moment, Roy said, "Do you think it's just instinct for them? Or do you think they *like* it?"

Before she could come up with an answer, he scooped her into his arms and carried her up to the bedroom.

As the weeks passed, his appetites were even greater than before. He'd lift her dress at the kitchen table at any time of day. He'd carry her up to the bedroom before lunch and dinner. Sometimes he was rough, other times he was tender. Helene never knew which Roy she was going to get.

The weather only grew colder.

Between cooking and cleaning, she wrapped herself in the quilt and sat on the couch and paged through *Good Housekeeping* or *Pioneer Woman* or *House Beautiful*. Even though the magazines had gone sour for her, they were all she had. The place was old and drafty and she was always freezing. One morning, her mom's sweatshirt had disappeared, along with the black sweater and her jeans. Even her pink backpack was gone, with her money and her mom's notebook. She tried not to panic.

"Roy, I need some warmer things. A real coat, a sweater, some long underwear. It's almost winter."

He was gone an hour and came home with more groceries, a paper sack full of prenatal vitamins, and a skinny little book about pregnancy. No coat, no long underwear, and no more discussion about a doctor. She felt the weather window closing.

October turned to November. She pored over the pregnancy book, but the baby still didn't seem real. Her belly hadn't grown, and she didn't have morning sickness or any of the other early signs. She was terrified the tests had been wrong. She really didn't want to bring a baby into Roy's house, in truth she didn't want this baby at *all*. But right now, she needed it. The baby was the only thing keeping her alive.

Meanwhile, Roy came and went as he pleased. He brought her more magazines, flowers, and chocolate, as if he hadn't nearly killed her weeks before. He spent afternoons in the barn, working on his old tractor. In the spring, he said, after he got it running again, they'd have a big garden, just like his grandparents. They sat together after supper with a seed catalog and a yellow pad, sketching it out. Sweet peas in the spring, watermelons for summer, pumpkins in the fall.

Mornings, he sat alone in the basement, always locking the door behind him. When she wondered aloud what was down there, he told her it was guy stuff, she wouldn't like it. She got a look down the steps before he closed the door and saw an old couch, a table with a laptop computer, and the corner of a workbench with a few tools scattered on top. On an unseasonably warm day, she wandered outside to see if she could peek between the weathered planks over the basement windows, but there were no gaps.

His keys were always in his pocket. He wore the pistol on his belt. At night, he tucked both between the mattress and the box spring. The barn was locked up tight and she couldn't call the police because the house had no phone, she'd never bought a cell, and she hadn't seen Roy's in weeks. He'd thought of everything.

She considered poisoning him, but she had nothing but cleaning supplies and she was pretty sure he'd smell bleach in his coffee. The only other real weapon was the paring knife from the kitchen, and somehow it didn't seem enough to actually harm him. As if he were made of harder metal and his skin would blunt the blade. Even if she tried it, the minute she stepped close enough to use it, she was sure he'd know what she was thinking. There were days when she felt like he could read her mind. And whatever she did, it had to succeed completely. There was no room for *almost*.

The chest freezer was never far from her mind. The two bodies inside and the place she had occupied, third in the stack. At night, she dreamed of it. The cold. The fear. The darkness, closing in.

In the hours he was gone, she searched the house again and again, hoping for something he'd missed. A screwdriver, a claw hammer, a spare set of keys. The only thing she found was a half-completed embroidery hoop on the back of a high shelf in her closet. HOME SWEET HOME in eight colors. It was something to do with her hands while her mind raced. She wondered who had started it. Whether someone else might finish it.

The first week of December, she stood in front of the mirror and realized that she had a small but visible baby bump. She'd practically memorized the pregnancy book, so she knew what that meant. She was too far along for Roy to be the father. The father had to be the Montana farmboy. He was the only other man she'd slept with.

Which was a huge relief, knowing she wasn't carrying a monster's child. But it was also terrifying. Roy could never know.

She had to get away before the truth became inescapable.

That night at dinner, she asked, "How long until we go back to work?" As if she was eager to rob houses again, to put herself in the place where someone else might die. Because if they went to work, Roy would have to get her some real clothes and let her back into the world again. He couldn't watch her every damn minute, could he?

He shook his head. "You're pregnant, honey. I'm not taking that risk with our baby."

Despite the overwhelming urge to brain him with the skillet, she knew she could never overpower him physically. Even if she somehow managed to work up the nerve to stab him with the paring knife, it wouldn't do enough damage to stop him. He'd still snap her neck like a twig. She couldn't find a way. Unless she could get into the barn or the basement.

With each passing day, she could feel herself accommodating herself to him. Adapting. His preferences were clear enough. When she displeased him, he didn't hit her, but he grew cold and rough, especially in bed. She found herself wearing the farmhouse dresses he liked, cooking his favorite foods. She'd tear recipes from her magazines and show them to him. Does this look good? How about this? She'd model the day's outfit for his approval. She learned to make pie.

She was a prisoner pretending to be a housewife. Fucking her jailer with a smile on her face, just to stay alive.

The snow climbed the sides of the house and barn. Her belly grew at an alarming rate, and she was increasingly terrified that Roy would discover her lie. She was always tired and always hungry, no matter how much she ate, burning every calorie just to feed the baby and keep herself warm. She often found herself at the kitchen window, staring out at the yard, mug of tea gone cold in her hand, unsure of how long she'd been standing there. In late January, she watched the coyote pack take down a fully grown deer not fifty yards away, while Roy cheered them on.

Some days, she wondered if she'd ever love this baby that occupied her womb like an uninvited guest, this baby that had saved her life and might get her killed. She was sure there was something wrong with her, that she would be a terrible mother. Other days she was overwhelmed with love. When she felt a twinge in her belly, she became terrified that something was wrong, that the baby would be stillborn or that she would die during the delivery. She worried that she was losing her mind. She asked Roy again and again about seeing a doctor, and he always said he'd find one. But he didn't.

To keep herself sane, she took the embroidery needle and began to work on the hem of her favorite dress. She only did it when Roy was gone. She started with her mother's name. She needed the reminder. To know that, once upon a time, someone had truly cared for her. Later she put in some of the things her mother used to say. Time to make lemonade. Fortune favors the bold. We can do hard things. The only way out is through.

Then found herself adding Jessica Moore, the name of the woman in the blue SUV.

The sun rose earlier and set later. Her belly got bigger and bigger. Her back ached, her feet were sore, she was exhausted all the time. She'd hoped the changes to her body would make Roy leave her alone, but they seemed to have the opposite effect. He put his hands on her whenever he wanted, which was all the time. When she resisted, he got mean, so she didn't resist. Valentine's Day was especially hard.

Every hour, she worried that he would learn the truth about the baby. He was too smart not to figure it out that she was too damn pregnant. If she stayed long enough to give birth, surely he would realize that the child couldn't possibly be his. She told herself that he would let them go, her and the baby, but she knew that was a fairy tale she made up to make herself feel better.

The baby would fit in the freezer, too.

As the months passed, her indifference toward the passenger in her belly faded away. She found herself loving her unborn child with an intensity that often scared her. She stood at the window and cradled the growing belly in her arms as if it were a newborn. She thought about her mom all the time, and the things they had done when Helene was a little girl, making dandelion crowns in the yard and drawing pictures at the kitchen table, long before her dad had disappeared and everything changed. She wondered what kind of mother she would be. She wondered if she would ever get out of there.

Near the end of March, there was a thaw and the snow began to melt in earnest. She could stand on the porch and hear it trickling downhill to the river. She put on her disintegrating sneakers and wrapped herself in the quilt and walked through the wet meadow with frozen feet, just to be outside, realizing for the first time how the cold winter had hardened her.

She found the sagging fence around the old garden, now a riot of wild plants still dormant, waiting for spring. As she high-stepped through a tangle of weeds, her shoe landed on something that rocked underfoot.

Roy was in the basement with the door closed. When he was home, she always knew where he was. She squatted down, not easy with her huge belly and sore back, and worked her hand through the thick mat of vines until she found it. An upturned shovel.

Not a whole one, because the handle was rotted away, but the metal part. The curved blade of the spade and the short tube at the top where the wood handle had been inserted. Rusty, yes, but solid enough.

She left it there, invisible, under the plants.

It was the first thing she knew that Roy didn't.

The first crack in his control.

35

Two weeks later, Roy came home from the grocery store and said, "Frank and the others are coming for dinner tomorrow. Why don't you make something special?"

They all arrived at once. Frank parked his blue Jeep in the barn. Hollywood pulled his white car in beside it. Pony Boy came in the gray truck with the big trailer and left it in the driveway. They came up the porch steps together and walked through the door without knocking.

They threw their coats in the corner and poured themselves drinks and sat around the kitchen table as if they lived there. Frank wouldn't look at her. Hollywood couldn't stop staring at her, as if picturing what she'd done to get herself in that condition. Only Pony Boy, who'd barely said a word to her in the few days she'd known him, asked her when the baby was due.

"I'm not sure. Roy still hasn't taken me to the doctor." But she'd done the math to get the answer that would keep her safe. "Early July?"

He raised his eyebrows. "You are very big for six months."

Her heart pounded so loudly she was afraid all the men could hear it. She'd been afraid this moment would come. She glared daggers at Pony, trying to shut down this conversation. "That's a crappy thing to say to a pregnant woman."

"I meant no offense," he replied, calm as a stone. "My grandmother is a midwife. I have met many pregnant women. Are you certain of the date of conception?"

Roy looked at her. She took his hand in hers. "I'm sure." Then she took a deep breath and played the card she'd been holding for this moment. "Although I've been thinking. Maybe we're having twins? They run in my family."

"Twins?" Roy turned to Pony Boy. "Can that be right?"

Pony only hesitated a fraction of a second. "It could be. I am not the person to ask. You should go visit my grandmother, at Pine Ridge."

"Holy shit." Roy grinned at her, suddenly unguarded. "Twins?"

"I would love to meet your grandmother," Helene said. "There's so much I don't know. I'm starting to get scared about actually giving birth."

"I'm sure she'd be happy to speak with you. Although I already know what she would say about your fears. She would say that women are stronger than men. You have been giving birth for hundreds of thousands of years. Your body is built to do this. Everything will be fine."

She looked at Roy. "Things might get more complicated with twins. We really should talk to her. And probably find a doctor, too."

"Okay," he said. "We'll do that after we get back."

"Wait. Where are we going?"

"Wyoming. There's a job, a special order. We leave in the morning."

She couldn't hide her relief, so she said the first thing that came to mind. "Oh, thank God. I can't wait to see something besides these four walls."

He laughed. "Honey, it's just the guys. You're not coming. You're big as a house."

She stood abruptly, allowing her belly to bump the table, which knocked over Roy's beer. And proved his point, she well knew. "What the hell kind of thing is that to say, Roy? You're the one who did this to me."

"Honey, you know I didn't mean anything by that. Of course I think you're beautiful. We'll only be gone one night. Will you be okay without me?"

She stomped up the stairs, slamming the bedroom door behind her, trying to contain the wild hope that grew within her. He couldn't see that. He would know.

She thought again of her mother. All women are actresses. Roy wanted to be fooled. He wanted to be loved.

Maybe she could do this.

She lay in the dark and listened to the rumble of the men downstairs. She wrapped her arms around her enormous belly and thought about what she hoped to do with twenty-four hours alone.

When Roy came to bed, he was sweet and kind. He wanted to fuck her, of course. As if that were some kind of apology.

She let him have his way, one last time.

The next day, she draped the quilt across her shoulders and waved good-bye from the porch as the two big trucks pulled their trailers up the driveway. When she could no longer hear the sound of their engines, she put on her rotten shoes, walked out to the garden, and scraped through the weeds with her fingers until she found the rusty spade.

If she failed today, she wouldn't be able to hide the evidence of what she'd done. But maybe, with the idea of twins in his mind, Roy would be less likely to put her in the freezer. At least not until after her baby was born, and he learned the truth.

Don't even think about that. You're going to do this. You're going to get out of here.

She'd already considered attacking the basement

door, but it was new and made of metal. She wasn't getting through that with the head of an old shovel.

The basement windows, even planked over, were a different story.

The house was built on a slope. On the uphill side, the windows were tiny. But on the downhill side, one of the windows was much larger. Large enough, Helene hoped, for her and her giant belly.

That window was boarded up like the others, big nails pounded deep. None of the planks were new. They were gray with age and beginning to cup. But the gaps between them were still too narrow for the shovel tip, no matter how hard she pushed.

Her next step was to use the shovel like a hatchet. She hadn't damaged anything yet. She could still turn back. Roy would never know. Was she really going to do this?

On her knees in the cold wet grass with the quilt fallen around her, she raised the shovel in both hands, found the place where the gap between the boards was widest, and began to hack at it with short, chopping blows. It wasn't easy with her pregnant belly pulling her off balance. Her back began to ache almost immediately. But small splinters cracked loose and fell. She was breathing hard. The blade bit deeper. Her arms were strong. She'd carried sacks of feed for Bogaloosa's cattle, cases of canned goods for his store. Little by little, she chipped away at the wood.

Then she could fit the shovel's sharp tip into the

gap between two planks. She still remembered her high school physics class. The curve of the blade was the fulcrum. The metal tube, where the handle had been attached, was the lever.

She put her weight into it. Now the belly was a help. When the big nails finally released with a soft scream, one end of the first plank was free.

After that, the rest of them were easier.

When she climbed over the sill and down into that basement, all she'd wanted was a decent pair of shoes and a coat against the cold. Then she'd stuff her pockets with food and start walking. It wasn't much of a plan. She felt the urgency to flee like a hummingbird in her chest.

She quickly put on an old blue barn coat, even though it didn't close over her belly, and a pair of men's winter boots that fit okay with three pairs of socks. Then she started to think about Roy's money. He'd told her he had a lockbox full of it. A few thousand dollars would make it easier when she finally stopped running.

She gave herself fifteen minutes to search the basement, but there was no cash. She gave herself another fifteen minutes and broke into his old desk, found a metal box in a drawer and cracked that open, too, but the only thing of interest inside was a ring of mixed keys. With another fifteen minutes, she climbed upstairs and unlocked the closets. Still nothing useful.

Not even her old clothes or her old pink backpack, or her mom's old notebook.

It was simply another way that he demonstrated his ownership of her, she realized. He had taken away everything that belonged to her. Nothing remained.

Except for her baby. Who meant more to her than anything else in the world.

She wondered how long Roy had been gone. What if he came back early? What if he caught her? How would he punish her? The fluttery panic grew in her chest. She needed to get moving. On foot, through the woods, in the cold.

For a moment, she fantasized about finding her daddy's gun, with its familiar cracked walnut grip. Then it wouldn't matter when Roy came home. She'd wait in the kitchen. When he walked in the door, she'd point the pistol at his chest.

But somehow she couldn't quite believe that she'd pull the trigger. He would just look at her with those eyes that somehow knew every thought she'd ever had. He'd hold out his hand for the gun, and she'd give it to him.

If that happened, he wouldn't have to trap her at the house. She'd be his prisoner no matter where she went. Because he'd own her mind.

No, she told herself. That wasn't going to happen, none of it.

She looked at the keyring again. She saw car keys. Other, smaller keys.

Maybe she wouldn't have to walk out of here after all.

One of the smaller keys opened the barn's padlock. She rolled back the wide upper door and saw Frank's big blue Jeep alongside Hollywood's little white hatchback. There was a spare Jeep key on Roy's big ring, but Hollywood had left his on the seat. He'd always talked about how fast the car was. That made the decision easy.

The black trailer was already open. The cardboard box of bills was gone, as was the bin of stolen guns. No green coat, no overnight bag, no pink backpack. Just the freezer, humming away like always.

She felt the frost on her skin, just looking at it. She had to get the hell out of there.

She didn't need the money. She still had the ring he'd given her, although she was sure now it wasn't a real diamond. She told herself she'd feel free when she was two states away, but she was lying. She'd still be afraid of him ten years from now, walking through the frozen food section of the grocery store.

She got in the car, started the engine, and drove down the ramp. As she passed the house, she threw the ring of Roy's keys at it, as hard as she could.

36

PETER

NOW

Peter made a quick silent circuit around the hulking barn with its boarded-up windows, reinforced doors, and shiny new locks. Then he circled the house, gauzy curtains over the bright first-floor windows, seeing no shadows or other signs of people. The second floor was dark. The basement windows were planked over like the barn's, except for one, which was covered until recently. The cracked boards lay on the ground beside it, torn away by someone with few skills but a lot of enthusiasm. Or maybe desperation.

The hog-tied hatchback driver had been certain that the pregnant woman was here, and that Roy was coming for her. After seeing the bones in the trees, Peter knew that was right. Roy was tied to this place like an animal to its den. He was dug in. And the clock was ticking.

No vehicles were parked on the driveway or in the yard, but that didn't mean anything. The gray truck could be in the barn, with the man named Pony Boy standing sentry out of sight, and the black truck getting closer by the minute. Or both trucks could have stopped a half mile away, where Peter wouldn't hear them, with the other three men running toward him right now. He was acutely conscious of the night-vision headsets they had worn earlier. He wished he hadn't broken the driver's. It would have been useful.

At the base of the porch, Peter's foot chimed against a big ring of keys. He picked them up and put them in his jacket pocket, then climbed the steps and stood silently beside the kitchen door, the chrome-plated carbine slung against his chest. Peeking through the thin curtains, he saw nobody in the kitchen, nobody visible through the open passage to the dining room. He heard no sound but the wind in the trees.

As his heart thumped in his chest, he tried not to think about Fallujah and Mosul and all the other cruel, dusty places where he'd gone house to house with a three-man fire team at his back. That work had nearly broken him, and here he was, back at it.

No fire team this time. No Lewis, either. None of it mattered. The wolf inside him was wide awake. The static rose, crackling up his brainstem. Hello, old friend. He took a deep breath, oxygenating his blood. Time to go to work.

He put his hand on the doorknob. It turned freely. He applied just enough pressure to part the door from the jamb. The deadbolt wasn't locked, either. He pulled in another breath and felt the adrenaline surge through him. Nobody lives forever.

Then, in a single swift movement, he pushed open the door and slipped inside, rifle up and ready.

Still nobody visible in the antiquated kitchen or the dining room. A deadbolted metal door probably led to the basement. Peter's wallet lay open on the wood table, beside his phone, which stood in a mason jar full of water. So much for calling June. A tactical flashlight was clipped into a wall charger, the same model Peter kept in his truck. He pulled it free, turned it on, held it cupped beneath the rifle's handguard, and kept moving.

Through the dining room into the living room, slow and smooth, heel and toe, quiet as he could. Not a soul. The house was small and cramped with furniture from another age, handmade doilies on the arms of the faded couch and matching chair. The thin curtains worked in his favor now, helping hide him from outside eyes.

He crept up the squeaking stairs into the dark, wishing again for a working night-vision headset. He forced himself to be careful, clearing each room, checking behind the doors and the low, shadowed spaces on the far side of the beds. He only confirmed what the static already knew. The house was empty.

The closets had the same serious deadbolts as the basement. One was locked. He knocked softly and got no answer. The driver was right. Roy was a freaky dude.

Back to the kitchen, he put his phone and wallet in the pockets of Bobbie's jacket along with the big ring of keys, then went to the front door and raised the carbine and slipped outside, alert for any changes.

Kneeling silently beside the ruined basement window, he listened for a long minute. Hearing nothing, he slung the rifle behind him, took out the pistol and aligned the flash along the barrel, then pivoted to point both pistol and light through the opening.

No shots fired. No pregnant woman. He slipped through the opening as gracefully as he could manage. The stairs were right below. His boots crunched on broken glass. He followed the beam of his flashlight around the basement.

He wasn't sure what he'd expected, but it wasn't this cheesy rec room. Except for the fieldstone foundation, it looked like any other improvised working-class suburban man cave, complete with minifridge and sagging couch, a vintage workbench with scattered tools, and an old oak desk.

But whoever had broken the window had done a number here, too. The desk drawers were all open, their locks torn out. Except for a few loose pens and a half bottle of high-priced Japanese Scotch, they were empty. A hammer and prybar lay on the rug beside a metal strongbox, its lid standing open. Inside were folders with bank statements, the deed to a house, and an empty manila envelope labeled SPARE KEYS. He took the ring from his pocket, recognizing matches for padlocks, residential locks, and several different vehicles.

He worked his way through the boiler room, then the laundry, then a storage area full of hunting and fishing equipment, but no guns. And no pregnant woman.

Maybe he was wrong about her being here. Maybe she was dead in some drainage gully, or facedown in the river. Hell, maybe she was riding around with her husband, laughing about the whole thing.

Any of those possibilities would explain why she wasn't here, and why nobody else was, either.

But that wasn't a useful assumption.

Because if Peter was wrong, he was dead. And maybe she was, too.

He turned off the flashlight, then returned to the basement window and listened.

Still no sound of trucks. Which meant the other men, if they were coming, were almost certainly coming through the woods. This was the worst-case scenario, because there would be no engine noise to announce their arrival. They would just be there, in the trees, watching through their night-vision headsets. The sniper from the river, who Peter was almost certain was Roy, probably had a night scope, too.

He could almost feel the itch between his shoulder blades. He wouldn't even hear the bullet. He might not even feel it, not if it was a head shot. He would just die.

He hoped they had the same NV gear as the driver, because it was cheap stuff. Poor resolution, and no thermal setting that he had seen, either.

Then it occurred to him that, if they thought Peter had the car, they might think he had a headset, too. They wouldn't know he'd broken it. They'd also figure he had the driver's chrome-plated carbine, which was a decent weapon, even if it was ridiculous. They might wonder if he'd set up somewhere, waiting to ambush them. They'd be taking their time. So maybe he wasn't completely screwed.

He quickly went back to the desk, picked up the hammer and prybar, and climbed out into the night.

He had one more place to look. But he'd better hurry.

The barn was built into the slope of the land in the old style. On the broad uphill side, facing the road, it had a wide dirt ramp to a vehicle door on the upper floor. On the side facing the house, the land was partially cut away for a second vehicle door to the fieldstone lower floor. Both were exposed to the open meadow. Bobbie's coat, pale from years of washing, would be a light spot against the wood and stone and clearly visible to the naked eye. Not to mention the shiny-ass chrome-plated carbine.

On the downhill side, however, nestled under a stone-pillared overhang, facing the tangled woods and the drop to the river, was a third door, sized for people. Reinforced wood like the others, with a heavy-duty hasp and a round, thick-bodied padlock, the hardened-steel shackle impervious to normal bolt cutters. Roy took his security seriously.

Peter fished out the fat ring of keys. The hammer and prybar were his backup plan. They could get him inside, but would take time and make noise that Peter could not afford.

The trees were close overhead here, and the sliver of moon didn't penetrate. He couldn't see a damn thing. But he wasn't about to turn on the flashlight. Not if Roy and his crew were out there somewhere. On a dark night like this, the glow would shine in their headsets like a movie marquee.

He began to flip through the ring, checking keys, mostly by feel. His dad and uncle were custom builders, with similar padlocks on their tool trailer, so he knew the key he needed would be shorter than a house key. One of Peter's jobs as a teenager was installing every lockset in a new home, and he could tell a Schlage from a Kwikset in the dark. The long, double-sided keys would be for vehicles.

He found a small key that fit the lock. It went in, but didn't turn. He jiggled it, thinking the lock might just be stiff from lack of use. No good. He was grateful for the sound of the wind in the trees.

"Roy, is that you?" The pregnant woman, calling from somewhere inside. He'd found her.

"Shhh." Peter's fingers flipped frantically through the rattling ring, still searching.

Either she didn't hear him or didn't care. "Goddammit, Roy, I am so *pissed* at you right now. Is this any way to treat the mother of your twins?"

"Shut up," he hissed. "It's Peter, from the river. I'm here to get you out."

Blessed silence from the barn.

The keys clinked. He tried another. No luck. This was going to take forever. Maybe he should use the flashlight.

Then the wind died. As the silence descended, Peter closed his eyes and listened. The night magnified all sound. Trees creaked as they settled into the stillness. It was still too early for spring peepers. An owl called, looking for a friend. Fifty yards downslope, the river rushed faintly against its banks. Then came the faint prolonged scrape of a branch.

Peter knew that sound.

He had made it himself, with the sleeve of Bobbie's coat as he pushed through the tangled brush.

He slipped sideways behind the stone pillar of the overhang.

Then all hell broke loose.

BOOM BOOM! A shotgun shouted, partnered with the tight *POPPOPPOP* of a semiautomatic rifle, something similar to the one Peter carried slung at his back. Stones cracked and splinters flew from the reinforced door. He didn't have long. One of them would circle left or right until they'd flanked him. Then the pillar would no longer provide shelter.

He stuck the tactical light around the corner and hit the switch twice for strobe mode. The rapid flashing would make their NV gear flare and buy him a few precious seconds. As their guns went silent, he swung the carbine around and fired a few volleys into the trees, just to remind them he had teeth of his own. Then he flicked the rifle to single-shot, jammed its muzzle against the padlock's shackle, turned his face away, and pulled the trigger.

The hardened steel was no match for a high-velocity round. The shackle cracked and he peeled the lock away, firing into the trees again as he hauled the door open, waiting for the shot to pierce his flesh and end his life.

Then he was inside the darkened barn, the white static flaring as he clicked the light to red to make himself less visible, then cast about for some way to brace the door shut. "Stay down," he shouted. "Where are you?"

37

In the barn, Helene heard gunfire. Then a man called out to her. He didn't sound like Roy or Frank or the others. "Back here," she shouted, hoping he could follow her voice.

Locked in a stall like livestock, like a damn brood cow. Maybe that's what she really was to Roy. The door had another one of those round padlocks on it, as if keeping her here was a possibility he'd considered from the beginning. Ever since he'd learned she was pregnant, or before.

Maybe there were worse things than the freezer.

It was only a few hours ago, when the driver of the old green pickup leaped off the bluff and into the river. She'd already been tearing open the neck of her dress, her mind in overdrive.

She heard the *BOOM BOOM* of Pony and Frank firing their shotguns at him. She watched Hollywood run to the bluff's edge with a shiny rifle, sighting down into the water below. Then Roy opened her door, grabbed her arm, and pulled her out.

"Thank God you're here," she said. She didn't need to pretend to be scared.

He dragged her toward Pony's truck, his face cold. Even if she wanted to resist, she couldn't. He was too strong. Instead she made herself walk faster than him, as if it were her idea, holding the ruined front of her dress together with her free hand.

She felt bad about the guy who'd jumped into the river, but there was no way he was coming back for her, no matter what he said. She had to save herself. She had her story ready.

She was afraid she'd overdone it with the ripped dress, but Roy didn't even look at her. Maybe he hadn't even noticed. He reeled her back in with a yank on her arm, then gave her a sharp slap across the face.

"You broke into my barn and stole a car? What else did you take?"

Her cheek burned like fire, and her eyes watered. Showing fear wouldn't help her now. She reminded herself that she'd been kicked by cows a dozen times and it hurt worse than this. Then let herself convert the pain into anger and attitude. "I took this warm coat and these boots, because it's *cold* out and I've been freezing my *ass* off *all winter*. And by the way, Roy, you steal for a damn *living*. So don't you dare lecture me."

His mouth was tight as a fist. She knew he could do more than slap her. Much more.

He pushed her up against the gray truck. She let herself rebound against the door as if he'd shoved her harder than he really had. Her grip on the dress relaxed. She felt the fabric part as her giant pregnant boobs spilled out of the torn top. She didn't have Roy's muscle, but she had these tits. Roy really liked them, especially the pregnant version.

Hollywood's mouth fell open at the sight. Pony Boy turned and walked away. Frank stared at the distant clouds as if praying for rain.

"Dammit," she said, and pretended to try to pack herself back into the dress that her belly and breasts had outgrown two months ago. She hadn't fit into her bra for longer than that. The dress had torn more than she'd planned. She hoped it would be worth it.

Roy stepped between her and Hollywood, shielding her with his body. "Helene, what the hell happened?"

"I just wanted to get out of the house." She glared at him, trying to channel crazy pregnant lady, rather than a woman terrified that her husband would kill her. "You never take me anywhere. After these damn twins get born, I'll never get to go anywhere again."

"Never mind that," he said. "Why were you in that guy's truck?"

"I went for a ride. I was headed home when the car died." She looked over Roy's shoulder and turned the glare on Hollywood. "Your car sucks, asshole."

Roy grabbed her chin and turned her head. "What happened?"

His fingers dug into her jaw. She used the pain and fear, let it show now in an Oscar-worthy moment.

"He offered me a ride. He, ah . . ." She cleared her throat and looked away. "He wanted more than that. He tore my dress. I saw the dust cloud and told him my husband was coming to pick me up. He threw me into his truck and took off." She leaned into Roy, trying to find the tears she needed. "I was really scared, Roy."

"If the tracker on Hollywood's car hadn't pinged him, that guy would have you halfway to Colorado by now."

"The tracker?" She didn't understand.

"Dude, my car didn't die." Hollywood leaned in, eyes flicking down at her chest. "I put a GPS locator on it, and a kill switch on the ignition, all controlled by my phone. That's why we came home."

"Wait. Hollywood, this is your damn fault?"

"No," Roy said. "It's your fault. If you'd stayed home like you were supposed to, none of this would have happened. What if he'd hurt the twins?"

Now she let herself get mad. That was much easier than tears. She pushed him away. "What about me, Roy? What if he'd hurt me?"

"Did you tell him anything about what I do for a living?" he demanded. "About that woman in Utah?"

"No, Roy, never," she lied. "You're my husband."

For the first time, his eyes softened. He believed

her. He didn't think she was trying to run. She was going to live.

"Okay, honey. I'll take care of that guy. He won't ever hurt anyone again. But right now, you need to go home."

He opened Pony's truck door for her. She climbed inside. He closed the door, then motioned Pony Boy and Hollywood closer for a quick conversation.

They dropped Hollywood at his car, which started right up. He smirked at her from the open window. Then Pony Boy drove her back to the home place without saying a single word. He'd waited at the bottom of the stairs while she changed her dress, then walked her outside and locked her in this damn cow stall.

She was afraid Roy hadn't believed her story after all.

"I'm back here," she called again, and rattled the heavy door. "Get me the hell out of here."

38

She heard a thump and a crash, then a faint red light appeared and grew brighter as it bobbed toward her.

"There you are." It was the guy from the river, with some kind of fancy flashlight. He wore a brown coat she hadn't seen before. His voice was quiet but it carried in the dark of the barn.

"I put some junk in front of that door. We'll hear them if they try to break through." He turned the beam on the stall's padlock. His face glowed from below as if lit by burning coals. "Let's get you out of there."

"What about the big doors?"

"I can't do anything about those. I'm just glad they stopped shooting."

Peter, she remembered, his name was Peter. She heard a dull clinking sound and realized he was flipping through the ring of keys she'd left behind. Now she felt bad that she'd set Roy on him.

"You really came for me."

"Told you I would." He was focused on the lock.

She cleared her throat. "Why?"

"Well, your husband jacked my truck and tried to kill me." His tone was perfectly reasonable, as if that kind of thing happened every day.

"But why come for *me*?"

His teeth flashed bright in a crimson smile. "Seems like you should get to decide for yourself whether you want to stay married. Besides, I don't like bullies."

She heard a hard click and the stall door creaked open.

He was big and rough-looking, like the solitary tree in the meadow across from the Gas and Grocery, grown tall and wild in the prairie wind. He had a shiny rifle slung over his shoulder. She felt vulnerable and exposed. She was worried about her baby. But she wasn't going to show him she was scared. If only she had some pants instead of this dress.

But he wasn't even looking at her. Instead he stared down the center aisle toward the doors, then up toward the ceiling. "They'll be coming, soon as they get themselves organized."

"Why'd they stop shooting?"

"They don't know where I am," he said. "But if they have to guess, they'll figure I'm with you. And they probably won't want to hurt you or the baby. So as long as we stick together and I've still got ammunition, we're both okay." He flashed the smile again. "Unless they get close enough to put a bullet in my head. Then it's over."

She didn't know anything about this Peter guy. If she left with him and Roy caught her again, it would be very bad. Worse than if she stayed now.

"What if I don't want to go?"

He looked at her now. "Your call," he said. "I can't make it for you. But I'm getting out of here."

"How are you going to do that?"

The smile grew wider still. As if he were actually enjoying himself. "Good question. You got any thoughts on that?"

She made a decision. "The big doors are locked from the outside. But there's a Jeep on the next level. And I think you probably have a key."

"Well, hell. That sounds remarkably like a plan. How do we get up there?"

She pointed. "The ladder's right around the corner."

He backed up to give her room to leave. "Ladies first."

She shook her head. "You first. I'm wearing a dress."

"Oh, sure," he said. "But stay close and keep moving. Those assholes won't wait forever."

The ladder was just a series of narrow wooden crossboards nailed between two posts, much like the one in Bogaloosa's barn that she'd climbed many times, to fetch hay bales for his cows. Peter vanished up the rungs and left her alone in the dark. Then the red glow shone down, lighting up the way. It was a harder climb than it used to be. She was climbing for two, after all.

She followed Peter to the Jeep. He opened the door and flipped through the keyring in the dome light. Then stopped, slid one into the ignition, and turned it far enough to get the dash lights on. He put down the windows. "We're in business. Better buckle up."

She hustled to the passenger side, but he'd left the Jeep. He'd gone to the pair of four-wheelers and bent over the first machine.

"What are you doing?" she hissed.

"Making it harder for them to follow us." He took something from his jacket pocket, jammed it into the four-wheeler's engine, and pulled hard. Then went to the second machine and repeated the gesture. She smelled gas.

He set a prybar on the dashboard. "Those won't run long with broken fuel lines." He unslung the rifle and slid into the driver's seat with the barrel pointed out his window.

She was breathing hard. Her heart was pounding so loud she could practically hear it. She didn't know how he could be so calm.

He closed the door softly and put on his seat belt. "When I start the engine, things will happen very fast." He reached his hand toward her. There was something in it. A pistol, extended butt-first. "You know how to use this?"

She took the gun. "I'll figure it out." She turned it in the dashboard light.

"The safety is off. There's a round in the chamber. All you have to do is pull the trigger. When we get through that door, they'll start shooting. I want you to shoot back."

She stared at him, eyes wide.

"You don't have to hit anyone," he said. "In fact, you shouldn't. We just want to keep their heads down and make it harder for them to aim at us."

She blinked. "Okay. I can do that."

"Good. You ready?"

She nodded.

"Okay. Here we go." He turned the key.

39

The Jeep's engine roared to life and he threw it into gear. But instead of stomping on the accelerator, he just goosed it a little and let the Jeep jump forward until the bumper came into contact with the door. Then he goosed it again.

In the ambient glow of the dashboard lights, she watched the wide wooden door flex. The left side bent, bowed, and finally buckled as the padlock and hasp tore loose. The whole thing took only a few seconds. Then he hit the gas and she felt the back of her skull smack against the headrest as the Jeep surged ahead. The front bumper pushed the whole bottom of the door outward while the heavy-duty rollers at the top, mounted atop the iron track bolted to the barn, acted like a hinge.

They shot forward. The bottom of the door scraped up the hood of the car, then the windshield, leaving long vertical scratches as it rose to the roof. The Jeep rocked with its weight. Then the rollers let go and the car sank on its springs as the full weight of the wood came down on top of them with a long splintering crash. But they were moving fast down the dirt ramp and the door flew away behind them.

Then she heard other sounds, the hard rattle of gunfire and a thump like a hammer on metal. Glass shattered behind her. "Shoot," he shouted. "Fire out the window."

She pointed the pistol at the house and pulled the trigger, not knowing if she hit anything and not caring, just loving the leap of the gun in her hand and the noise it made loud in her ears, as if her anger had turned into something real and powerful and dangerous. Then the house was out of sight and the Jeep flew up the driveway and the gun stopped firing because she was out of bullets, which only made her more angry.

He turned fast onto the dirt road with the headlights still off. The crosses flew past on her right. The engine started making a weird clattering noise. "C'mon, girl, you can do it." It took her a moment to realize he was talking to the Jeep.

The dirt changed to gravel and he turned on the running lights. Soon she saw the back of a pickup tucked into the trees ahead on the left. "Shit," he said. He looked in the rearview, then at her. "Are you okay? You're not hit?"

"I'm good," she said. And she was. Maybe better than she'd ever been.

Peter grinned at her and she knew he was feeling it, too. He'd stopped in the center of the road, behind the pickup. She realized it was Roy's black truck, with bushes rising up on each side.

He glanced at the rearview. "This engine's not right," he said. "I don't know how long it will last. I've got a car hidden up that old driveway, but the truck is blocking it. I'm going to see if I can use the Jeep to clear a path through the brush. You okay with that?"

She looked over her shoulder at the blackness behind them. "Yeah, sure, just go." The euphoria was fading, replaced by creeping panic.

"Okay." He turned the Jeep and rolled up beside Roy's truck, the fat tires crushing the brush. When it got thick, he popped the gas and the lugged rubber spun, grinding up the vegetation and pulling them forward. Past the truck, he reversed quickly to flatten the stubborn remaining bushes, then pulled ahead again until she saw an old cinder-block building with the roof coming down. He dropped the keys in his coat pocket and leaped into the night, calling low over his shoulder, "Time to go. Bring the gun."

Hollywood's car was parked in the weeds out of sight from the road.

"No, wait," she said, but he'd already slipped inside the little hatchback with the rifle on his lap. The engine started with a low growl. She opened the passenger door as he bent to shove her seat back. "This is a bad idea," she said. "I found out Hollywood can turn the car off from his phone."

"That's his name, Hollywood?" Peter gave her that grin again. "He's tied up in the back, so he's not doing shit right now. Come on, get in."

"Really?" She heard a muffled complaint from the cargo area as she wedged herself into the seat. She tried to feel bad for Hollywood but couldn't. Peter was in reverse and rolling before she had her door closed.

The car dinged at them. "Seat belt." He turned the car around, then revved the engine up high and hit the smashed bushes in second gear, their speed carrying them across the high spots with a squeal of branches.

He stopped on the gravel and got out. The headlights were still off.

"What are you doing?" she hissed.

He bent to Roy's truck with the rifle. She heard two loud pops and the truck settled on flat tires. Then he was back in the car and accelerating hard, eyes on the rearview, saying, "Get down, get down."

She tried to hunch over but there was only so far she could go with her huge belly. Even the dashboard lights were dark as they rocketed forward into the endless night. Then, just for a moment, everything seemed to glow. "That damn spotlight," he said.

She heard a cracking sound. Suddenly the windshield had a jagged hole and the wind whistled strangely through it. "Whoops," he said, and shifted into a higher gear.

The acceleration pushed her back into her seat. The car lurched and leaped on the rough gravel. She pressed both hands against the dash to stabilize herself, then felt something in her hair and raised a hand to touch sharp splinters of glass. She turned in her seat to peer out the back window but it, too, had a hole. Past the spiderweb, she saw the bright white circle of a powerful light.

"Down!" Peter pushed her head toward her knees as the window cracked again and glass flew everywhere. She peeked forward, saw the pale incline ahead, and knew where she was. In all her walks, she'd seen this hill from a distance, but never made it this far. As they crested the rise, she felt a kind of weightlessness, unburdened by her belly and everything else she carried, as they became briefly airborne, held aloft in the brightness of the light.

Then the car dropped, bottomed out on the gravel, and she was pregnant again. She straightened up and craned around to look out the back. The white circle was gone behind the hill.

With a final bump, the road changed to pavement. Peter turned the car's headlamps on. Suddenly the pale world flew toward them at terrifying speed. He bent over the wheel, head turning left and right, eyes methodically searching the landscape ahead. "Where's the other truck? The gray one?"

"What do you mean?"

"Your husband is a planner. A tactician. I only heard two guns, back at the barn. So probably only two men. The third man, the driver of this car, is tied up in the back. But I haven't seen the gray truck. So where is it? Where's the fourth man?"

Her whole body felt tight. She wrapped her arms around her belly and shivered in the cold that whistled past the punctured glass. "I don't know. Roy's never let me leave the property. I've never been anywhere else."

Peter must have heard something in her voice. Without looking, he reached over and patted her hand, then turned up the heat all the way. "We can handle this. I have an idea. Who drives the gray truck? Can you describe him?"

"They call him Pony Boy. He's not as tall as you, but he's thick and strong, with long black hair. He wears a black coat, hip length. I think he's an Indian."

Peter slowed as the road turned left, then picked up speed again, head still swiveling back and forth. "What's he like? Smart?"

"I don't know. Maybe. He's quiet."

"Is he a killer, like Roy? Maybe not as bad? Or worse?"

She frowned. "He did what Roy told him to do. He's the one who locked me into that stall like a damn milk cow." She looked away. "He also offered to take me to see his grandmother, who's a midwife in Pine Ridge. But Roy wouldn't let him."

Peter nodded, as if that detail meant something. "Okay."

He turned right and the asphalt got better. Then he turned again and they were on a smooth two-lane that carved long arcs between the hills. He had the hatchback up to ninety. There were no other cars. She glanced at the clock on the dash. It was almost midnight.

"When I was coming in," he said, "right after I crossed the river, I saw my truck pulled off the highway. If Pony Boy is waiting somewhere, I think that's where he'll be. I think Roy put him there as a backup. I'm going to stop. I can let you out here if you want."

"No, please." She didn't want to be pregnant and alone in the bottomless Nebraska night.

"All right. I'm just going to drive right up to it. Keep your head down. I want him to think there's only one person in the car."

"What are you going to do?"

Peter gave her a wolfish smile. "That depends on him."

They descended toward the river. He dropped the windows and opened the sunroof and the cold air rushed in. Ahead on the right, in the middle of a sweeping curve, she saw an old work truck parked well off the road at the edge of a shaggy meadow that looked like it hadn't been mown or grazed in a long time. Just past the truck was a thick stand of evergreens, maybe where a house or barn had been long ago. She didn't see Pony Boy or his pickup.

"Okay," he said. "This is it."

She put her head down as he braked and left the road a few lengths ahead of the old truck with the wood cargo box. As he pulled into the meadow so that the truck stood between him and the highway, she turned her head and saw him slouched down in the seat, maybe to seem smaller, more like Hollywood. Then he showed his teeth. "There you are, you sonofabitch."

He picked up a little orange walkie-talkie and spoke into it. "That you, Pony? Dude, it's me." He'd made his voice higher and put a little twang into it. Then he stuck his right hand out the sunroof in a wave as he flashed his brights with his left. She wanted to look but she didn't. He slowed more. She heard a voice. Then he hit the gas and turned the wheel. The engine rose up loud and she felt a thump from the front.

She raised her head and watched Peter leap from his seat with the rifle. He stood over Pony Boy, who lay in a crumpled heap with his hair in his eyes. Pony raised a palm and tried to sit up but couldn't. He tried to keep the pain from his face, but failed. Something was wrong with his leg.

The gray truck was parked well behind the stand of evergreens, hidden from the road.

40

Helene watched as Peter took a few steps and kicked something away into the grass. He slung the rifle behind his back and returned to Pony Boy and began to pat his clothes.

She was already out of the car when Pony grabbed at Peter's arm, trying to pull him off balance. Peter leaned in close, hands moving too fast for her to follow, and the other man fell away into the grass. Then Peter snatched up Pony's wrist and bent it backward, forcing him to roll onto his chest with a hard grunt. "Okay, damn," Pony said, his face sideways in the grass. "Enough."

Peter didn't let go. "Take off your belt. Slowly."

Pony Boy just stared up at him with one eye.

Peter bent the wrist farther. "I can break something else, or I can tie you up and leave you for the cops. Your choice."

Pony flexed his jaw. Then he reached for his belt buckle.

Peter tied Pony's wrists behind his back and quickly went through Pony's pockets, taking a wallet, keys, and a knife from his pants and a phone from the coat. He popped the battery from the phone, then walked a few steps into the meadow to collect a black revolver. It was like her daddy's gun, but bigger.

He opened the cylinder, checking to see if it was loaded, then snapped it closed and handed it to her. "I'm going to move the car out of sight. If he moves, shoot him. If Roy comes, shoot them both."

She nodded and raised the revolver in both hands, remembering how it had felt to fire the other gun at Roy's house, over and over. The beautiful red bloom of anger, finally released. She heard her mother's voice in her head. *The only way out is through.*

As Peter drove the hatchback behind the trees, Pony Boy cocked his good leg beneath him and struggled onto his side. "I never wanted anything bad to happen to you, Helene."

"But you didn't actually do anything about it, did you?"

"Frank said he warned you, but you didn't listen."

"Frank didn't tell me what would happen if I stayed."

Pony Boy looked away. "Roy is stronger than all of us put together. He knows where my family lives. Hollywood's, too."

"What about Frank?"

"Roy's all the family Frank has."

"That is fucked up," she said. "You're all fucked up."

Peter returned on the run through the knee-high grass and put his hand under Pony's armpit. "On your feet. Ready?"

Pony needed help to hop across the meadow to the old pickup, where Peter propped him one-legged against the door, mostly out of view from the highway.

"Keep the pistol on him, but don't get too close," he told Helene. "This'll just take a minute." Then he dropped to the dew-damp grass and scooted under his truck.

Pony Boy stared across the meadow to the bluff rising on the far side of the river. "You could just let me go," he said softly, as if speaking to the night. "I can't hurt you, not all broken up like this. I can't even walk."

Peter's voice came out of the darkness. "Stop talking, Pony Boy."

The air was still and cold. Helene was shivering again. The gun was heavy. She lowered it a little.

Pony leaned toward her, his voice low. His long black hair fell forward, framing his face. "Right now, the cops don't know anything. We're all clean."

"Shut up."

"You were there, remember? Part of the crew. You got rid of her car. That makes you guilty."

"Shut up, Pony." She raised the gun again.

"And if you talk, you'll go to jail, too. You'll give

birth in prison. They'll give your babies away. If you're really having twins, that is."

She jammed the pistol into the hollow of his cheek. His eyes were bloodshot and his breath was sour. "Shut the fuck up."

Pony held himself firm against the barrel of the gun. His voice was a rasp. "Unless Roy kills us first. He knows a lot of cops. Once we're in the computer, he's got us. Let me call my sister. She'll pick me up, hide me on the rez. You drive far and fast and hope he never finds you and your baby."

Her finger was tight on the trigger. She was ready to do it. Her mouth was dry as dust and her whole body trembled. Then Peter was beside her, with his big hand wrapped gently around the revolver.

"Please," he said. "Don't." He smelled like spring grass. "You'll see it every time you close your eyes. Believe me, he's not worth the hurt."

She didn't move. She was breathing like she'd just run ten miles. All she had to do was squeeze. She wanted it so much. As if killing Pony would end her fear and pain and keep her baby safe. But he wasn't the source of it, not really.

Finally she stepped back, pulling the gun free of Peter's grip. Pony had a red welt on his cheek. His eyes were hooded and dark.

Had she ever been this gloriously angry? It felt so good, so freeing. She raised the gun to smash Pony in the face, but Peter caught her elbow and turned her away. "Don't give in to it. You don't want to be like them."

She shook herself free and glared at him. His face showed specks of grit and he carried a dirty plastic bag in one hand. Without another word, he got Pony to his feet and hopping one-legged to the rear of the truck. He fished a set of keys from the bag, unlocked the cargo box, and swung the door open. Inside, the floor was filled with a mess of tools and toolboxes spilled from the shelves built into the sides. "Up you go."

Pony shook his head, his face impassive. "No."

"I said I'd leave you for the cops. I didn't say I'd leave you here."

"I'm not getting in there."

"Not a discussion. We're in a hurry." Peter put two fingers against Pony's shoulder and pushed.

He toppled sideways toward the truck, twisting as he fell to avoid falling on his bad leg. He landed with his butt above the bumper and his back on the bed of the box. Before he could react, Peter put an arm under his good knee, then lifted and shoved at the same time. The big man slid forward on the varnished wood floor, ramming the fallen tools aside with the top of his head.

Peter grabbed a zippered pouch from the clutter and removed a handful of long plastic zip-ties. He zipped Pony's ankles together with one, then tucked the rest in his pocket and closed the door.

"I've got to grab one last thing from the hatchback," he told her. "Then we need to talk."

—————

He drove the pickup across the ragged meadow and parked next to Hollywood's car. They weren't entirely out of sight from the road, but it wasn't unusual to see a truck parked in a field in farm country. In the dark, she thought, the only person who would take notice was Roy.

When Peter popped the car's rear hatch, Helene barely recognized the man inside. His hands were strapped behind his back and his ankles were tied to his wrists so that he was bent backward like a bow. He was rocking in place and trying to talk but his jacket was knotted around his mouth, so all she heard was an angry mumble.

Peter took a knife from his front pocket and thumbed open the blade. When he cut the string between Hollywood's ankles and wrists, the smaller man groaned and curled himself forward into a ball.

Peter pulled Hollywood into a sitting position, then bent and hoisted him over one shoulder like he weighed nothing at all. He carried him the half-dozen steps to the rear of the old pickup, where he opened the doors and laid Hollywood down next to Pony, back-to-back. "Everybody comfy?" He checked the belts around their wrists, then connected them with a zip-tie, locking the two men together.

"Where are you taking us?" Pony asked.

Peter just shut the door and locked it, then turned

to Helene. She still held Pony's pistol, heavy in her hand.

Peter held out a set of keys. "The gray truck is yours if you want it. The hatchback, too, but I'm sure the troopers are already looking for it. Even if you make it to another state, every cop you see will pull you over because of the damage to the windshield."

She liked the hatchback. Faster on the highway, and better gas mileage. "Can't I get the glass replaced?"

"Sure, but it won't be cheap, and Roy must know he hit us. He'll start calling body shops first thing in the morning. Plus maybe he's got access to the remote tech on Hollywood's car. Maybe all their vehicles have it, including the gray truck. And after I hand Pony Boy over to the cops, they'll be looking for it, too."

The wind sighed in the trees. She closed her eyes.

"The alternative," Peter said, "is to ride with me and find the cops. They're not all great, but most of them really want to help. They'll also connect you to a social worker, who can get you medical and financial assistance. You can have your baby in a safe place. It's up to you, but you should decide now. We need to go. If Roy has a vehicle we don't know about, he could be here any minute."

Helene frowned. She didn't like her choices. Roy was worse than Bogaloosa. She didn't know Peter at all. What if he was worse than both of them? And right now, she had zero faith in the police.

But Peter was right about the car and the truck,

and also about leaving. She could feel the urgency like spiders in her veins.

She raised Pony's pistol and pointed it at Peter. "Okay. Let's go. You're driving. But I'm in charge. And no cops."

He shook his head, a wry smile forming. "Lady, you are something else."

"Helene," she said. "My damn name is Helene."

41

Peter turned the truck around and headed toward the road. "Where are we going?"

He'd already wiped down the hatchback when he drove it into the evergreens. It wouldn't help with the DNA traces they'd left behind, but Bobbie's 911 call and an empty car, even one full of bullet holes, were probably not enough to generate a full investigation. Plus they'd have to find it first.

As they came to the highway, Helene licked her lips and looked right, then left, then right again, worry etched on her face. He reminded himself how young she was, and how desperately alone. She clearly had no plan. Nor maybe even a way to devise one.

They had to keep moving. He let out the clutch and turned right.

"Stop," she said. She was half-turned against her door with the black revolver held tight in both hands, braced against her pregnant belly. "You do what I say."

"Absolutely," he said. "But the direction doesn't matter right now. We just need to get out of here before Roy shows up." He shifted to second and let the engine wind up.

By the time he hit fourth gear, they came to saw a sign for the bridge. He pointed. "That'll take us to South Dakota. We'd hit I-90 in an hour, give or take, the fastest route east or west. Straight ahead is three hundred and fifty miles of Nebraska. Which way?"

She opened her mouth, then closed it. Then said, "The freeway."

He downshifted for the turn, then headed toward the long concrete span, his third time crossing that day. On the far side, the two-lane bent toward true north and he saw lights ahead, flashing red and blue. He glanced at the cheap little clock stuck to the dash. He'd commandeered the hatchback at the farmyard barely an hour before. It seemed like much longer. He shouldn't have gone this way. There was another bridge forty miles upriver. But it was too late now. If the police saw his headlights make a U-turn, they'd come after him.

"What the hell." Helene was wide-eyed beside him. "Why are you slowing down?"

"Because that's what a normal person would do. Slow down and get a good look."

A full-sized police SUV was parked across the highway just past the farmyard entry, not completely blocking the road but still claiming the territory, the way cops tended to do. A uniformed woman stood beside it, hips wide with her duty belt, eyes on the approaching vehicle. One hand went to the radio mike on her shoulder, her head turned and lips moving, and she held the other hand out, palm forward, for them to stop. From the flat-brimmed hat, Peter took her for a state trooper.

Helene was hunched over, shrinking into herself. "Dammit, dammit."

"It's okay," Peter said. "Put the gun out of sight. Try to relax."

Helene moved the revolver down behind her leg where the trooper wouldn't see it. Peter really didn't want to stop, either. The cops wouldn't know to look for the vintage Chevy, but Bobbie would have given the police his name. She'd have told how he'd locked Hollywood in the trunk of his car, then stolen the car. If Pony Boy started shouting in the back, Peter would be in serious trouble.

As they came to the farmyard, he saw three SUVs with three different jurisdictional markings standing haphazardly on the dirt, engines running, doors open. Three men stood in a loose group, talking. The state trooper probably got stuck on road duty because she was a woman. Or maybe she preferred that to dealing with the men.

There was no sign of Bobbie or her motorbike. He hoped she'd gotten out of sight, that Roy and his guys hadn't found her. Peter still wore her coat. He told himself she was on the far side of the group or getting warm in a patrol car. If they asked her to take a look at his face, they were done for sure.

Approaching the trooper, he pulled in a deep breath to calm himself, then downshifted again to slow the truck to a crawl. The trooper stared right at them, her face stern and serious under the wide brim of her hat. She was at least ten years older than Peter and thick in the body the way cops got when they spent a lot of time in the car. Again she tipped her head toward the mike on her shoulder, this time listening. Helene shifted on the seat and let the coat open, showing her huge pregnant belly.

The trooper saw her through the windshield, noted her condition, then swung her arm in a circle, gesturing for them to keep moving. Peter gave a nod as they passed, and the trooper nodded back. She'd remember Peter's truck and the woman in the passenger seat, but there was nothing to be done about that. If things went the way Peter wanted, it wouldn't matter anyway.

He brought the Chevy back up to speed and the police lights disappeared into the rearview.

She said, "What are you going to do with Hollywood and Pony Boy?"

Peter scratched his stubble. "My plan was to find a cop I could trust and hand them over. It's still our best bet for taking Roy off the board. I saw a human skull in Roy's woods. That will get their attention for sure."

"No police." She brought the pistol up and pointed it at him again. "Definitely not."

He wanted to look at her face but kept his eyes on the road. "I heard what Pony Boy said about Roy knowing a lot of cops. Also about you being part of his crew, being guilty. I don't know what you did, and right now, honestly, I don't care. But maybe if you told me about it, I could help you figure out what to do."

"No," she said. "Just keep driving. Head to the freeway."

"Okay," he said. "But I need to make a quick stop along the way. I borrowed this jacket from someone. I have to return it."

"No," she said again. "Do it later."

"Helene, I made a promise. It's a little out of our way, but that's probably a good thing, avoiding a direct run to the freeway." Bobbie had done him a favor and he'd repaid her with trouble. He wasn't going to steal her lucky coat, too. "After that, we'll take a few minutes and find you some warmer clothes in the back. Get something to eat, too, and coffee. We're going to need it."

Helene stared at him a moment, then finally nodded. But she remained wedged against her door with the black pistol pointed at him, her fingers white on the grip, muscles clenched tight in her jaw.

Fear and anger were chewing her up, Peter knew. It was a powerful and volatile combination. He wondered again what had happened to her. What she'd had to do.

He understood that she didn't trust him. She didn't know him. Maybe he shouldn't have given her the revolver, but it helped her feel more in control. When he'd checked the gun earlier, he'd seen that there was no round under the hammer, which might buy him a second or two. He could still take it from her, but he wasn't fooling himself. He'd have to be very fast. She was pulled tight as a bowstring and ready to break.

At least the hard run from Roy didn't seem to have done the old Chevy any harm. As it rumbled along and ate up the flat prairie miles, he dug into the big Ziploc that he'd taken from the hidden compartment and pulled out a cheap backup phone. He plugged the charger into the cigarette lighter, waited for the screen to come to life, then pulled up the mapping app to find Bobbie's place. The road was arrow-straight and the Chevy's alignment still near-perfect, so it was easy enough to work the phone and stay in the right-hand lane with just the occasional touch of his knee. He could have taken a nap and not touched the wheel until North Dakota.

When he'd gotten the directions in his head, he sent June a quick text. "Are you awake?"

June, who was never far from her phone, replied immediately. "Just leaving for the flamenco contest with my lover, Raoul."

Which meant she was in bed, probably still working. But willing to talk.

He looked at Helene. "I need to call my friend."

Helene tightened her grip on the pistol. "Not the police."

"No. A friend. You'll like her."

He touched in the number and put the phone to his ear. "Hey, sweet lips."

"Your damn phone went dark four hours ago. Tell me you're not in trouble."

He smiled at the sound of her voice. "Who, me?"

He didn't need to see June's face to know she was giving him an epic eye roll. He could sure picture her, though, slouched down in bed, the deep green eyes, the spray of freckles across her cheeks, the wide mouth always ready to flash that wicked grin.

At the moment, however, she was pissed. "Where the fuck are you, Marine? What happened to your phone?" June had spent five years as a crime reporter in Chicago and had learned to curse from the best.

"South Dakota. My phone got wet." He glanced at Helene. "I picked up a hitchhiker. She's young, pregnant, and on the run from her husband. I don't know the whole story, but I met the husband. Not a nice man."

She sighed. "Let me guess. He tried to kill you?"

"Only a little. But he's got friends."

June was well aware of Peter's tendency to step into other people's problems. She knew it was one of the things that kept his post-traumatic static from raging out of control. It provided the periodic doses of atonement he needed to keep washing himself clean of that war. Plus his inner Marine liked the adrenaline.

June understood the impulse. She was an investigative journalist for Public Investigations, an online nonprofit. She'd put herself in harm's way chasing a big story the previous fall, and only Peter's actions had kept her alive while she dug into the truth. It wasn't the first time. June was a bit of an adrenaline junkie herself.

After that, they'd come to an agreement. Peter would do what he needed to do, but he would tell June the truth about it, always. And he would let her help. She'd saved his life several times, too. He was well aware that June was smarter than he was about many things, and in her own way, probably tougher.

He heard the weird digital silence on the line as she made the emotional adjustment.

"Okay, Marine. I'm in. What do you need?"

He felt his chest expand again, just knowing they were good. He didn't like it when she was mad at him. "Juniper, you're the best. Can you reach out to Lewis and see if he's up for a road trip?"

"I was hoping you'd say that," she said. "Gimme a sec, I'll text him."

"If so, just tell him to get on I-90 and head west. Once he's rolling, he can find me at this number."

"Wait." Helene raised the gun again. "Who's Lewis?"

Peter kept his voice calm. "Another friend. He's good at this kind of thing."

"He's not the police?"

"Oh, no." Peter smiled. "Lewis is most definitely not the police."

On the phone, June was silent for a moment, either

still typing or waiting for a response, then laughed. "I just got a text from Dinah. She says, 'Please take that man off my hands for at least a week. He's driving me crazy.' I guess that's a yes." June paused to type again. "Okay, what else?"

"See what you can dig up about a guy named Roy Wiley. He's a former Minneapolis police officer, maybe late twenties? He owns a property in Nebraska, I don't have the address but I can send you the location when we stop, along with a couple other names."

"Got it. Anything else?"

"Yes." Peter glanced at the young woman in the passenger seat. "Can I ask you to talk to Helene? She doesn't exactly trust me. Having met her husband, I can't say I blame her."

"My pleasure. Give her the phone and don't eavesdrop."

Peter did what he was told.

When it came to June Cassidy, he'd found that was usually the best course of action.

42

June was good with people. It didn't take long before the words were pouring out of Helene. Peter wasn't going to drive with his fingers in his ears, so he couldn't help but listen. It wasn't hard to get the picture.

A young woman tried to get herself free of a predatory boss and took a chance on the wrong person. A worse predator. The fact that she'd joined Roy in robbing houses was on her, for sure. Legally, the murder was, too. Peter understood why the law was written that way, but he wasn't going to dwell on it. Not when Roy was still out there, looking for Helene. And Peter, too.

They talked for less than ten minutes. Peter didn't know what June had said, but whatever it was, it seemed to have helped. Helene still kept hold of the black revolver, but she wasn't pointing it at Peter anymore. At least not directly.

After that, they drove in silence.

Bobbie had told Peter that she lived south of Highway 52, off the Tabor Rec road. He didn't have to look long to find her mailbox and the modest hand-carved sign for DIRT WORKS EXCAVATION AND DRAINAGE.

Flanked by broad, muddy fields, the long driveway led past a modest brick ranch-style house to an enormous metal barn, painted hot pink and lit up like daytime by a half-dozen bright sodium lights. The buildings were tucked into a notch in the trees, so you couldn't see the road, and behind them the land fell away in wrinkled folds toward Lewis and Clark Lake, formed at a wide spot in the Missouri River when the Corps of Engineers dammed the river at Gavins Point.

He nosed the truck into the trees beside the barn, then turned off the engine and pocketed the keys. Whatever else Helene might be, she was also clearly some kind of outlaw, and Peter didn't want his truck stolen twice in one day. He got out and pulled a fleece-lined blanket from behind the seat, and handed it to her. "Would you mind staying put? I'll just be a minute."

He didn't see Bobbie's Yamaha anywhere. He walked to the back door and knocked. No answer.

They were thirty miles from the bridge. The night was quiet. The temptation to stay a few minutes was strong. He still hadn't eaten since lunch, and he was willing to bet Helene was hungry, too. If he pulled the bad guys out of the back, he could get to his cooler and cookbox, make sandwiches and coffee, find Helene some warmer clothes from his duffel.

Instead, he sat on the porch step and emptied Bobbie's coat of the things he'd accumulated since he'd borrowed it. The orange radio, the nasty little quick-draw automatic and spare magazine, plus the spare mag for the world's ugliest chrome-plated AR-15, along with Hollywood and Pony Boy's wallets and disassembled cell phones and keys. He was lucky the coat had a lot of pockets.

He hung it on the doorknob, reloaded the pistol, then put all the other crap into the Ziploc bag from under his truck. When they found a good place to pull off the road and regroup, he'd text June photos of the contents of the wallets, so she could start getting a better read on these guys. When Lewis showed up tomorrow, they'd figure out what to do next.

Then he heard the blast of a dirt bike's exhaust carrying on the cool night air.

He tucked the pistol into the back of his pants, then walked to the Chevy. He dropped the plastic bag behind the seat and shoved the rifle after it. Helene raised the revolver. "What's the matter?"

"Someone's coming," he said. "A friend, I hope, but keep out of sight until I come get you." If she stayed in the truck, the trees would mostly hide her from view.

He closed the door, then turned and watched Bobbie roll up the long driveway with Cupcake riding in her lap, the dog's forefeet braced on the instrument cluster and her tongue hanging out happily.

Bobbie slowed the bike when she saw the unfamiliar pickup, and came to a stop thirty feet away. Cupcake jumped down and showed Peter her teeth. Bobbie stayed on the bike, engine running, her face pink from the wind and cold.

"What the heck are you doing here?"

"I was just leaving." Peter pointed to her coat. "I told you I'd return that." He had to raise his voice over the sound of the Yamaha. "Actually, I'm glad you came home so I could say thank you in person, and to apologize for pulling you into this thing. Did anyone show up at that farmyard?"

She nodded. "Two big pickups, just a few minutes after you left. Three guys with those same goggles pushed up on their heads, guns hanging out the windows." She frowned at the memory. "They didn't see me. I got behind the grain bins, like you suggested. I'm grateful for that. They looked around for a minute, then took off to the north." Hollywood's lie about chasing Peter had worked.

Cupcake stopped growling and sniffed toward the Chevy, stiff-legged and wary.

Peter said, "How long until the first police arrived?"

"Twenty minutes or so. It's a big county. Right before they showed up, those pickups rolled through again, headed south toward the bridge."

Bobbie looked past Peter at the dark horizon while the Yamaha rumbled and popped.

"Used to be the main problem was the weather, ruining your crop. Can't do anything about that, right? Then it was the banks and people losing their farms, people going hungry. Then came meth. Oxy. Heroin. On top of all the original problems we still got, too much rain, or not enough. Wind and hail and rivers flooding. The wrath of God."

She shook her head. "You show up for your neighbors, you volunteer at your church. You try to help people. You hope you're making a difference. Used to be, we all pitched in together. But this? Marauders on the road with automatic rifles and night-vision goggles?" She sighed. "This country. It's not the one I grew up in. Your dang car breaks down and nobody stops anymore."

"You do your best," Peter said. "That's all you can do."

"Well, I gave *you* a ride," she said. "I ain't even sure *that* was the right thing to do. Whatever the heck you're involved in."

"I'm a good guy." He tried a reassuring smile. "I promise you that."

She glanced behind her at the house, then turned back to Peter. "What about that guy you tied up and stuffed in the back of his car? What'd you do with him?"

"Better you don't know," Peter said. "He's no worse off than he was an hour ago, if that's what you're asking."

Thankfully, Helene was staying out of sight. Better that Bobbie didn't know about her, either. Cupcake had sniffed a circle around the Chevy and begun to growl at the cargo box doors.

Bobbie glanced at the house again. No, she was looking up the driveway, toward the road. Shit.

Peter followed her gaze. He couldn't hear anything over the sound of the Yamaha. "Bobbie, who's coming?"

But he was too late. A big SUV with a lightbar and the heavy push bumper of the highway patrol turned onto the long gravel drive, then accelerated as it drove toward them.

"Bobbie, what's going on?" He was very aware of Helene, pregnant and vulnerable. Not to mention the two captives in the back of the truck. No matter his motives, it wouldn't look good. He felt the weight of the little automatic in the small of his back.

Bobbie licked her windburned lips and turned off the bike. "Please be cool," she said. "I didn't plan this. I didn't know you'd be here."

The big SUV came to a stop behind Bobbie, and a state trooper got out, bareheaded.

She was the same trooper he'd seen partially blocking the highway. The Mountie hat was designed to be intimidating, and without it, despite the brown uniform coat and radio and duty belt loaded with gear, she looked more like a person. Sun lines bracketed her eyes and mouth, and her thick chestnut hair, streaked with gray, had begun to fly free from the ponytail that hung down her back.

When she walked to Bobbie and put a hand on her shoulder, Peter understood why the trooper had come. She wasn't here for Peter. She was here for Bobbie.

But she stared at the Chevy, and then at him. "Didn't I see you a few minutes ago, coming across the bridge from Nebraska? With a pregnant woman?"

They weren't really questions. She already knew the answers. Cops were trained to look for coincidences, and doubt them.

Peter nodded and kept it simple. "That's us," he said. "I'm Peter. Helene's napping in the truck. We're on our way home from Denver. We like the back roads."

The trooper smiled politely. Her name tag said FALK. "And how do you know Bobbie?"

Peter silently cursed the lie detector in her eyes. You didn't make it as a female state trooper without being very good at your job. "My dad's a home builder in Wisconsin. He's friends with Bobbie on some online group. We were hoping to camp on her land tonight. But it's late and probably too cold for Helene. We were just headed out to find a hotel."

Trooper Falk glanced at Bobbie, whose face had gone sweaty and pale, as if she had a bad case of food poisoning. No lie detector necessary. The trooper's right hand drifted toward her service weapon as she shot a quick glance at the house.

When she saw Bobbie's faded coat hanging from the doorknob, she knew exactly who Peter was, and what he had done.

She was fast, but she also had to unsnap her holster.

Peter had plenty of time to pull the ugly little automatic from his waistband.

43

"Hands up," Peter said. "You, too, Bobbie, please. Let's keep this nice and easy."

He couldn't afford to let Helene go to jail right now, not even an overnight holding cell, not with Roy still out there. Peter wasn't crazy about the idea for himself, either. The last time he'd been in handcuffs, the white static had gotten out of control. The werewolf had taken over. People had gotten hurt. Peter didn't want that to happen again.

The wind whistled across the naked branches. Bobbie was frozen on the bike. Falk's hands were steady, held out from her sides while the muscles flexed in her jaw. She was living every trooper's nightmare. "What about the guy you beat down and threw in the trunk of his own car? Was that nice and easy, too?"

"He ran us off the road," Peter said. "He had night-vision goggles. He was hunting us. He was raising a military-style rifle. I was unarmed, so I did what I had to do to protect myself and Bobbie. When I hauled him out of the driver's seat, he was trying to draw this pistol. It's got the front sight filed off."

Falk looked at Bobbie, who nodded.

Peter knew Bobbie would have told the cops at the farmyard about the other three men with guns and night-vision headsets. That fact would help validate Peter's story. Plus any trooper worth a damn would want to take those guys off the road on general principle. Although Peter was pretty sure he'd blown all available goodwill by pointing a gun at her.

"Let me ask something else," he said. "Do either of you know someone named Roy Wiley? Lives on the other side of the river?" He watched Falk's face. She was the one with the badge. Bobbie would follow her lead.

Falk shook her head. "I'm stationed here, but I'm not from here. I grew up in Leola, four hours north." Her emotions were locked down tight, because she was a law enforcement officer and Peter held a gun on her, but he saw a flicker of something cross her face. Not recognition, he thought. He hoped it was curiosity.

"Bobbie?" he asked. "How about you?"

"No. We both work a lot. Our free time, we mostly keep to ourselves." Bobbie's face was tense, but she wasn't lying.

Falk hadn't relaxed, but he could tell she was thinking hard. Unlike big-city cops, who usually had fellow officers nearby, state troopers often worked alone, in the middle of nowhere, with little or no available backup. As a result, they had a lot of autonomy in decision-making, and were taught to rely on their own judgment.

Peter was hoping Falk would use some of that judgment now.

He had to trust someone. These two seemed like a good place to start.

Also, he was running out of room in the back of the truck.

"I apologize." He rotated the pistol in his palm and offered Falk the butt. "Ma'am, I need your help."

Before he'd finished the move, Falk had her weapon free and aimed at his chest. "Drop the gun and turn around. Hands on the truck."

He'd known that would happen, and was okay with it. She'd feel safer in control, and he needed her to feel safe. At least her finger wasn't on the trigger. She had a radio on her lapel, but she didn't use it. Maybe Peter had some goodwill after all.

He laid the pistol down. She kicked it skittering away across the dirt. He turned and leaned against the truck, waiting for her to grab his wrist and pull it back for the cuffs, but she didn't. A good sign. Instead she patted his clothes, dropped his phone and folding knife into her pocket, then opened his wallet. She missed the embroidered hem of Helene's dress. Anyone could have.

"Peter Ash, huh? Your license is expired. By a couple years."

"I keep meaning to renew it."

She snorted. "Bobbie said you were a real humdinger. Okay, turn around. Let's hear your side of things."

Peter told her how he'd picked up a young woman, stranded and pregnant, on the Nebraska side of the river. The way two trucks had boxed him in on the bluff, four men with long guns, Helene saying they'd kill him. How they'd fired on him as he'd jumped, then again when he was in the water, and once more on the far riverbank. Then he described the two men in the pickup with a spotlight searching the South Dakota side, and almost everything that happened after that. He left out the part about the two men tied up in the back of his truck. She'd ask about Hollywood soon enough.

As he spoke, the wind turned to the north, carrying the smell of snow. Falk slowly lowered her pistol to her side. "Who is this Roy Wiley?"

"Helene's husband," Peter said. "She was trying to leave him. She told me he'd already killed two people. He runs a crew that cleans out luxury houses all across the west."

"Maybe I should hear this from her." Falk made a small gesture with her pistol. "Why don't you ask her to get out of the truck." It wasn't a suggestion.

"I'm right here." Helene stepped out of the trees, led by her belly. Clutching the blanket around her shoulders with one small fist, holding Pony Boy's heavy revolver with the other. The barrel wandered in the air, not exactly pointed at Falk, but not pointed away, either. "I had to pee," she explained.

Face calm and still, Falk stepped toward her. She kept her weapon down and slightly behind her. "Ma'am, please put down the gun."

"No!" The barrel stopped wandering. Helene looked far more ferocious than any young woman should ever have to, and far more scared.

"Helene, it's okay," Peter said. "Put the gun down. We can trust them. We have to."

"I said no. I'm not giving it up." Helene made a face. "I'll put it in my pocket, okay?" She tucked it under the blanket.

Falk let out a breath and backed off, throwing all recognizable procedure out the window. Peter liked her very much right then.

She asked, "Helene, did you hear what we were talking about? Did your husband really kill two people?"

The younger woman nodded. "It's true," she said. "I saw him do it, one of them, anyway. She was a deputy in Utah. He broke her neck."

"What about the other one?"

"I don't know who it was, I just saw the body." She looked away. "He kept them in a big freezer, one on top of the other."

"Dear Lord," Bobbie murmured.

"He took away my money, all my warm clothes. I was stuck in that house." The blanket didn't cover her pregnant belly. Tears fell down her cheek. She was shaking. "I thought he was a good guy."

She turned to Peter. "I lied to Roy," she said. "I told him you made me get in your truck. I tore the neck of my dress so he'd think you tried to, you know. Force me. I'm sorry. This is all my fault."

Falk glanced at Bobbie, then back to Helene. A vein pulsed in her temple.

"It's not your fault," Peter said. "They'd tried to kill me at least once before you had time to tell them anything."

"Wait." Falk raised a palm to Peter. "I want to hear her say it." Her voice softened. "Helene, why did you lie to Roy? Why did you tell him Peter tried to, ah, force you?"

"I was afraid he'd kill me if he knew I was leaving." She looked at the ground. "He almost did, the last time."

The trooper nodded sympathetically. "Now tell me about the robberies."

"Falk, look at her," Peter said. "She's practically turning blue. Can we do this later? Let her go inside with Bobbie to get warm."

"I'll put her in the cruiser," Falk said. "It's warm in there."

"No." Helene's voice was high and sharp. "I'm not getting in that car, I'm not going anywhere with the police." She was tough, but she was also nineteen, pregnant, and scared to death.

"Helene." Peter held out the keys to the Chevy. "Why don't you get back in the truck and crank the heat. You'll be warm in no time. I'll be with you soon."

As Helene climbed into the pickup, Falk's eyes were hard. "This Roy Wiley," she said. "Why'd you ask if I knew him?"

Peter was glad Falk was smart. It saved time. "Helene said he used to be a cop in Minneapolis, that he talks about having law enforcement connections in a dozen states. Can you get your unit commander here?"

If Roy had his hooks into anyone, it would be one or more of the small departments near his base of operations. Peter figured he was less likely to own a state police captain.

"Commander's in Sioux Falls," Falk said. "That's ninety minutes away. If he'll even get in his car this time of night, which he probably won't. He'll just tell me to take everyone to the sheriff's office in Tyndall, put you in the greybar hotel, and sort it out in the morning. And he'd be right."

"That's a problem," Peter said. "The sheriff will take names and run backgrounds and write reports. With Roy's contacts in law enforcement, if we're in the system, he'll be able to find us. Helene won't be safe."

"I don't believe that," Falk said. "The system isn't perfect, but it works well enough."

"What about the sheriff? Do you trust him?"

"Sheriff Johns? I'm stationed in his county, we talk most days. He's okay."

"Just okay?"

Falk raised a shoulder. "He's young and he's trying. It's just him and two deputies to cover almost six hundred square miles. I'll say this for him, he'd get his butt in the car if I called. He only lives ten miles from here."

Peter looked at Bobbie. "Do you know the sheriff?"

"He invited us to his house for dinner with his family," she said. "Twice in the last year. He knows Lisa and I are together and it doesn't seem to matter. And he's got three girls. So yeah, I agree with Lisa, he's trying."

Falk gestured with her service weapon again. "I can't just let you get in the truck and drive away," she said. "You oughta be in cuffs right now. You understand that, right?"

Peter nodded. "Call the sheriff. Get him out here."

44

Sheriff Johns climbed out of a department SUV that had seen better days. He had the narrow hips and heavy shoulders of a man who came of age throwing hay bales, and wore his official coat open over a plain white T-shirt and jeans, with a gun and cuffs on his belt. If he felt the cold wind raising dust off the driveway, he didn't show it.

Bobbie had taken Cupcake to the house. Johns and Falk stood under the bright sodium lights while Peter told the story again, including what Helene had told him about the robberies, but without identifying Helene's husband by name or mentioning his possible connections to law enforcement. Johns watched Peter's face the whole time, fingers idly rattling the cuffs in their leather pouch. Falk listened without adding anything.

When Peter was finished, Sheriff Johns said, "Why aren't you giving me his name?" He was younger than

Peter, but the bags under his eyes were big enough for a round-the-world trip. Like he hadn't slept since puberty.

"Let me ask you a question," Peter said. "What would you do if somebody you knew had committed a crime?"

The sheriff glanced at Falk, eyebrows raised, then turned back to Peter. "I'm gonna pretend you didn't just accuse me of being a crooked lawman, in front of a state trooper, no less, and say this. I was born and raised in this county. We've got a population of seven thousand people, and I know most of them, especially after running for sheriff. But if anybody does wrong, I arrest and prosecute them all the same. I won't get elected again if I don't, and for some damn reason, I kinda like this job. So who all are we talking about?"

Peter took a breath and let it out. "Roy Wiley. That's the husband, an ex-cop. One of his guys told me he's still got law enforcement connections."

The sheriff ran his tongue across his teeth. "Actually, I do know Roy. Used to be Minneapolis PD, a few years back. First I heard he was married, though. He gave a thousand dollars toward my campaign. He also donated the meat for our law enforcement barbecue."

Peter didn't like that answer at all. "He ever ask you to solve a legal problem?"

"Not yet," Johns said. "But he doesn't live in my county. I can't speak for my counterpart across the river. I know for a fact that Roy gave money to his campaign, too."

"What if I told you I saw a human skull in the woods outside his house?"

The sheriff's face went still. "I'd say that was a very serious accusation."

"Not hard to verify, though."

"No," Johns said. "It isn't."

"Another of his guys said Wiley could get to anybody. I'm worried about Helene. I want to keep her off the computer and out of the system. Can you do that?"

He glanced at Falk. "For the moment, yes. And let's keep Roy Wiley between us, too. We don't know who all he might be connected to, and there's no need to let the man know we're coming." He turned back to Peter. "Now, what else aren't you telling me? Who are these guys you've been talking to?"

Peter took a breath and let it out. "Part of his crew. Maybe I should show you. I'll just grab my keys."

Peter shut off his truck. Helene climbed out frowning and stood kicking at the dirt while Peter opened the door of the mahogany cargo box. When the light hit the two men in the back, Hollywood made muffled noises around the sleeve of his jacket and wriggled like a caught fish. Pony Boy just closed his eyes in resignation.

The sheriff took in the scene. "You know South Dakota is no longer a frontier territory, right? We got all kinds of laws against this."

"I know," Peter said. "I'm sorry. I just did what I thought was right at the time."

"Heck, you're not sorry," the sheriff said. "If you're

actually telling the truth about all this, I ain't sure I'm sorry, either."

Behind them, another county SUV rolled up the drive. "Who's this?" Peter asked.

Johns sighed. "My deputy. Late as usual."

"Do you trust him?"

"Well, he's not the sharpest tool in the shed, but he's honest. And he usually doesn't start drinking until the end of his shift."

The deputy got out of his rig and stood two steps behind Peter staring at the two captives with his palm on the butt of his gun. It had mother-of-pearl grips. He was middle-aged with his shirt half untucked and the smell of hot dogs on his breath. "What in the heck is this, Sheriff?"

The sheriff frowned. "Glad you could make it, Doug." He took a radio from his pocket. "Dispatch, this is the sheriff. Call Officer Glenn in Springfield, tell him I'm sorry but he's deputized again, then get him to my location ASAP."

He turned to his deputy and pointed to the two men tied in the back of Peter's truck. "We'll need to keep these two separated while we get their initial statements. When Glenn gets here, get them untied, make sure they're not bleeding to death or anything, then back in cuffs and over to Sacred Heart to get them checked over."

"Not the ambulance?" asked Deputy Doug.

Sheriff Johns shook his head. "It'll take twice as

long, even if they're not on another call. Just make sure the big guy is comfortable. That leg's gotta hurt."

Falk said, "I'll take Helene's statement. She can ride with me."

"Oh, no," Helene said. "I'm not going anywhere with you."

"I stay with her," Peter said.

"It's not up to either one of you." The sheriff's voice was firm. "The lady's pregnant and apparently she's never seen a doctor. We have a responsibility to protect, and that extends to her baby." He turned to Helene. "Ma'am, you are not under arrest. My three girls were born at Sacred Heart, so I know you'll be in good hands. Don't you want to make sure your child is okay?"

Helene's face softened. Falk looked at Peter. "I'll be with her the whole time. I'm good at my job. You have my word."

"Then I'm coming, too."

"No," Johns said. "You're coming with me."

"Dammit, Sheriff—"

Johns cut him off. "Right now, Mr. Ash, we're being real nice and neighborly. But you and I both know that's just pretend, right? Because I'm the law and you're just some cheesehead who crossed state lines with two people trussed up like chickens in the back of his funky old pickup. Regardless of your story or your good intentions. Which, for the moment, I believe to be genuine. So here's how it is. You can get in my cruiser on your own, as a cooperating witness, or

I can put you there in handcuffs and under arrest. What's it gonna be?"

Peter looked at Johns and felt his pulse rise.

They both knew it was an open question whether the sheriff could carry out his threat by force. Peter had assaulted armed police before and been very successful. He'd been on the FBI's Wanted list because of it. He hadn't enjoyed either experience, and he didn't want a repeat. Nor did he want June to have to live through it again.

Plus Deputy Doug, for all his untucked shirt and pearl-handled pistol, had positioned himself at Peter's back, where he could step in quickly. So it wouldn't be easy. Not to mention Falk, who stood twenty feet away. Somehow Peter knew she was an excellent shot. And Helene would have to watch the whole thing.

Even if Peter did succeed in staying free, they already knew his name and plates. If he took Helene with him, he'd make her an accessory. If he left her behind, she'd be on her own. With Roy out there somewhere, looking for her.

Johns gave Peter a polite smile, having read Peter like a book. He'd already run all the scenarios and knew exactly how it would play out.

Peter closed his eyes. He was out of options. He was going to spend the rest of the night at the sheriff's office. Even now, he could feel the static crackle and spark at the thought. "Sure," he said. "Let's go."

Falk put Peter's things in a plastic evidence bag and passed them to the sheriff.

45

P eter waited in the back of the sheriff's cruiser while Johns and Deputy Doug and Officer Glenn, the Springfield cop, got Hollywood and Pony Boy untied and organized. Helene sat inside Trooper Falk's car, where it was warm, talking with Falk. This was how the police worked, Peter knew, separating people to take their statements where they couldn't hear or influence each other.

He remembered the hem of Helene's skirt that was still in his pocket. He'd meant to ask her why she'd given it to him, but had forgotten. He pulled it out now to look at it. The blue embroidery wasn't just pretty stitching, he realized. She'd written two women's names, along with a few inspirational phrases that Peter quite liked. "Fortune favors the bold" and "We can do hard things" were much better than his drill instructor's version of inspiration, which was more like, "Suck it up, you worthless maggots!"

It was well after one before they headed out, a convoy of four big law enforcement SUVs rolling up Bobbie's long driveway toward the road. Deputy Doug had the lead with Pony Boy cuffed in the rear, followed by Glenn hauling Hollywood. Trooper Falk and Helene had third position, with Sheriff Johns taking up the rear with Peter in the back seat. Johns was on the phone, telling his dispatcher to reach out to the South Dakota Department of Criminal Investigation.

Peter wasn't happy about any of it, but in truth this was a best-case scenario. Four cops from three different jurisdictions, with two bad guys in custody, all headed for a regional medical facility to get Helene checked out and meet with state-level investigators. Peter wasn't looking forward to the long hours of questions and waiting and more questions, but he was happy that there were now too many people involved for Roy to make this go away.

At the end of the driveway, they turned right, one by one, headed for Highway 52. The road was gravel but smooth from recent grading. There were no other headlights, few lights at all that Peter could see, although the quarter-moon was up and the sky was clear, so the bare, empty fields were lit with a spectral glow. He felt the relief that came from knowing Helene was in somebody else's hands now. Johns turned up the heat in the cruiser, and Peter still hadn't had anything to eat since lunch. The day was catching up to him, the hunger and adrenaline aftermath making him sleepy. He leaned his head against the door and let himself drift.

The sheriff's voice cut through the fog. "What are you doing, Glenn?"

Peter opened his eyes. They were on the crest of a slight rise, so he could look through the windshield and see the other three vehicles lined out ahead of them, spaced a half-dozen car lengths apart. The first vehicle was veering to the left. Johns shook his head. "Kid's always on his phone. He's got a girlfriend in Mitchell, they're getting married in May."

Johns picked up the radio, but before he could speak, the second vehicle's brake lights flickered, then went out. Glenn's left tires were in the ditch. Then Falk's brakes flared bright as her voice came over the air. "We are under fire, I repeat we are under fire. Glenn's been hit and so has Doug." She cranked the wheel to put the big SUV into a U-turn. She didn't get far before Peter heard a loud thump and the cruiser lurched to a halt. Another thump and a plume of smoke rose under the hood.

It could only be Roy. Somehow he'd found them and had come for Helene.

"Sniper at your twelve o'clock," Peter said. "Step on it, Johns, we have to help them."

Johns was already pushing his own cruiser forward, angled to come up on the protected side of Falk's vehicle. Peter couldn't see Helene, although Falk's uniformed bulk filled the front seat as she struggled to cross the center console to get away from the gunfire. Falk was good at this, Peter told himself. She would protect Helene while Peter and Johns went on the attack.

He looked ahead, searching for a muzzle flash to get a position for the sniper. The rifle would have to be suppressed or they'd have heard it already, but Peter was directly in the line of fire, so he should see something. There, he saw it, closer than expected, just as the windshield splintered and shards of glass flew inward directly in front of the sheriff.

The bullet went right through his head. A chunk of bone and brain matter splattered wetly through the security grate along with a broad wet crimson spray. The smell of iron was strong in the enclosed space. The sheriff was long past steering and the SUV continued forward and crashed into the rear corner of Falk's vehicle, knocking it sideways and rocking it onto two wheels.

The impact threw Peter forward. He caught himself against the seatback, but not before his head crunched into the steel security grate. The world flickered and he slumped into the footwell. For a moment, he couldn't get his arms or legs to work. He tasted blood in his mouth, and wondered idly whether it was his own or the sheriff's. Then his brain reengaged and he pulled himself onto the seat, clawing at the door handle until he remembered it would only open from the outside.

Johns was gone. This was up to him and Falk. He

hooked his fingers through the grate and pulled as hard as he could, but the metal wasn't moving. It was designed to cage a man indefinitely. "Falk," he shouted. "Get me out of here. Falk!"

Through the cracked windshield, he saw her front passenger-side door open. Falk got a leg out with her pistol in her hand and turned to say something to Helene. Then a dark form appeared at the crushed rear corner of her cruiser, arm extended, slipping forward over Johns's front bumper like a shadow.

Something flashed twice with the cough of a suppressed handgun and Falk slumped slowly to the ground. Then the shadowed form turned to look at Peter.

He saw a white skull with fangs for teeth and black holes where the eyes should be. A face mask. With Helene's asshole husband hidden beneath.

Roy plucked up Falk's pistol and took aim.

Peter dropped to the floor and made himself as small as possible, knowing it was useless.

46

BANGBANGBANG! The gunshots were so loud they blocked out all thought.

BANGBANG! Glass shards flew like shrapnel. *BANGBANGBANG!* Peter flinched on the floor, shaking, out of his mind, waiting for the pain. *BANGBANGBANGBANG!* He knew what pistol rounds would do at close range. *BANGBANGBANG!*

Then the firing stopped. His heart hammered and his ears rang. He opened his eyes, hoping he hadn't pissed himself. The shooter was at the side window now. He'd taken off his mask, revealing tousled blond hair, a rough blond beard, and ice-cold eyes that examined Peter's reaction without expression.

The engine block hadn't protected Peter. Roy had just been fucking with him, while also destroying the dashboard and interior cameras, which were now useless plastic shards.

He lingered a moment longer. A cold smile appeared abruptly, flicking on and off like a switch. Then he pulled the mask down again and walked away.

Peter scrambled up to the seat, breathing like he'd lost a footrace, trying to push down the panic. Roy was headed toward the first two cruisers. Peter looked for Helene. Through the wrecked windshield, he saw her stuck in the back of Falk's SUV. Frozen in place, eyes wide, surely terrified, and trapped just like he was. But he couldn't help her until he got free of this fucking car.

He was hyperventilating. His vision began to narrow as the static rose up inside him, crackling like a thunderstorm. He couldn't catch his breath. It would be so easy to give in, to let go. But he couldn't afford to lose it, not now. Hang on to your shit, Marine. This is no time for the werewolf.

He forced himself to take one long, slow, controlled breath. In for a count of four, hold for a count of four, then out for a count of four. Then he did it again. And again. And felt the panic turn to focus, his brain back in gear. Okay. Find a way out.

Gunfire had gone through the windshield and out the rear window. Both were fragile enough now to kick his way through, but he couldn't get to either one because of the pair of security grates enclosing the back seat. Their metal mesh was torn by Roy's rounds in a half-dozen places, but nowhere structural, not where the grates attached to the side pillars.

Maybe one of them was weak enough to bend. Peter hooked his fingers through the front mesh, ignoring the blood and brains that dripped behind the sheriff's ruined skull. He braced his feet, took a deep breath, and pulled as hard as he could. His hands screamed and his back howled and black spots swam through his vision. The metal flexed slightly but stayed firmly bolted in place.

He tried the same with the grate blocking the cargo area. Also nothing. Then he heard the cough of the suppressed handgun. He looked for Roy and saw him at the forward cars, leaning inside and shooting out their cameras.

Now Peter turned his attention to the side windows, which were closed and untouched by gunfire. Their controls were on the driver's door, but none of the holes were big enough for him to get a hand through. He lay on his back and kicked at the passenger side, hoping his heavy bootheels were hard enough to start a crack. The side windows were actually stronger than the bigger panes, because they were smaller and would flex less. What he needed was something hard, like rock or metal. The floor was clean and his lightweight hiker's belt only had a soft plastic buckle. The stainless handle of his pocketknife would do nicely, but it was in the evidence bag on the front seat, out of reach. Along with everything else.

His legs ached with the blows, but he made no discernible progress with the glass. Maybe the other window would have a flaw.

As he turned to attack the driver's side, he saw an older truck parked just past the police cruisers, a backup vehicle Roy must have kept hidden somewhere on his property. The front license plate was missing, no doubt because of the dashboard cameras. Peter was certain it would be registered in a different name. Roy was definitely a planner.

The fourth man, who had to be Frank, was helping Pony Boy out of the lead cruiser. Hollywood was already free and rubbing his wrists where the handcuffs had chafed, apparently forgiven for helping Peter escape. Roy gave him instructions with short, chopping hand gestures.

Hollywood nodded with a fierce grin, then opened the nearest SUV and began to rummage for equipment, laying out the Springfield cop's duty bag and shotgun and medical kit on the road, then reaching in for the man's notepad, phone, and badge. Pony Boy just leaned against a fender and closed his eyes. Roy spoke with Frank and pointed up the road, toward Bobbie's house.

Oh, God, Peter thought, as Frank set off at a jog, the chrome .357 in his hand.

Peter began to kick harder.

Then Roy walked around the back of Falk's cruiser. This time, he opened Helene's door, smiled warmly, and extended a hand. "Come on, honey. You don't belong in there."

The ringing in Peter's ears had mostly subsided. He could hear clearly through the shattered windshield.

Roy took her hand and helped her from the car as

if she were a starlet arriving at the red carpet. "What did you tell the police, honey?"

"Nothing, Roy. I didn't say anything." She stared at Falk's crumpled body.

Roy shook his head sadly. "Look at this mess." Helene tried to turn away, but he grabbed her upper arm and held her there. "No, honey, take a good look. This state trooper, shot in the head? That's your fault. The cop over there?" He pointed through the windshield at Sheriff Johns. "You did that."

Her voice broke. "I didn't make you kill anyone."

"Oh, honey, of course you did." He put a hand on her belly. "You walked away with our twins. What on earth did you think would happen?"

She shook her head. "I told you, I just wanted to get out of the house for a few hours. I was on my way home when that car died."

"What about him?" Roy tipped his chin at Peter.

"He said you tried to kill him. He took me to get back at you. I didn't want to go, but I couldn't stop him."

Her eyes darted away from Peter as she spoke. She would say whatever she needed to survive, and Peter didn't blame her one bit.

Roy gave Peter a glittering smile. "Well, he'll be as dead as those cops in a couple more minutes. But if you'd just stayed home and done what you were told, they'd all still be alive."

Tears streamed down her cheeks. Roy put an arm around her broad waist and drew her to him. "I'll tell you a secret, honey. Those people don't matter. Nobody matters but you. Because you're special."

"Roy, please." She put her hand on his arm and tried to dislodge him.

He just held her tighter. "Do you know what makes you special, honey? It's your pain. It burns inside you, like a furnace. I saw it the moment I laid eyes on you."

She turned away from him to slip his grasp, but he caught her slender wrist in his hard grip. She said, "Roy, you're hurting me."

He stepped in close behind her and wrapped his arm around her neck, tightening the choke as he ground his pelvis against her backside. "Oh, honey, we're just getting started." His voice came through the ruined windshield. "To be truly special, you need more pain, not less."

Helene's eyes got wide and Peter realized she couldn't breathe. She tore at his arm but it made no difference. Her helpless mouth gasped like a fish on a dock, her body held rigid in his overwhelming power. Roy's smile fell away and he stared at Peter, his eyes filled with darkness, a shadow aroused and exultant, for what seemed like forever.

Finally Roy released Helene and spun her around with his arm across her shoulders like a lover. As she gulped air, he walked her past the dead bodies and away.

Locked in the cruiser's cage, Peter began to kick at the window again, as hard as he possibly could.

It made absolutely no fucking difference.

47

By the time the driver's door opened and the overhead light came on, Peter had taken off his belt and wrapped it around his heel, trying unsuccessfully to use the plastic buckle to create a weakness in the window.

Hollywood peered into the prisoner compartment with a grin. "That ain't gonna work, dude. Shoe's on the other foot now, ain't it?"

He reached past Sheriff Johns's body, put the transmission into park, and turned off the engine, which had been purring along despite everything. The heavy push bumper had protected it in the crash. "Roy's got plans for you. It ain't gonna be pretty."

"Why don't you open this door and get your own damn revenge?" Peter growled. He wasn't worried about Hollywood. He just needed to get out of the car. To get to Helene.

"Oh, no. Roy's pretty clear on that." Hollywood got a grip on the sheriff's shirt and pulled sideways. The corpse didn't move. The sheriff still wore his seat belt. "This is fucking gross," Hollywood said under his breath. He leaned gingerly across the body and fumbled for the release, then grabbed the sheriff's arm and pulled him out of the car. "Dude, you are heavy."

Peter went back to kicking at the side window.

Hollywood returned with a roll of paper towels and began to wipe up the blood, muttering, "I sure as hell hope Roy appreciates this."

When the seat was clean, he slid behind the wheel. The police radio squawked and Hollywood turned down the volume. "I don't need to listen because Roy's got a killer scanner," he told Peter. "That's how he found you. These rural counties don't have the budgets for encrypted radios, and Roy knows the frequencies for every department. He's way smarter than the cops."

Which meant that someone had screwed up and given Bobbie's address over the air. In retrospect, with three different jurisdictions' dispatchers operating on incomplete information, it was almost inevitable. Peter wrapped the belt a little differently around his boot and began to kick again.

Hollywood started the engine again, shifted the transmission into two-wheel drive, then backed the cruiser around to face the way it had come. "Always wanted to drive a cop car." He took care with the placement on the road, getting out to check, then climbing back in to make an adjustment. "This is a neat trick, what I'm setting up," he said. "Too bad you won't be around to appreciate it."

"Your mother must be very proud." Peter was breathing hard from the exertion.

"Dude, it's part of the job." Hollywood frowned. "Roy's real big on payback. He calls it punishment." He stared through the shattered windshield. "I mean, sometimes it gets out of hand. Roy ain't like the rest of us. But he's the one knows where the money is, so I just let Roy do Roy. We all do."

Peter tuned him out and kicked harder. Did it sound different, now? Maybe he'd gotten the buckle in the right place this time.

"Listen, what I said earlier, about going after your people? I was just talking. I wouldn't actually do that. I mean, they didn't do nothing to me, right? But Roy, he's different. He gets biblical, dude. Like real Old Testament stuff. Anyway, that ain't me. I just wanted you to know."

"But here you are, rigging the car, taking Roy's orders," Peter said.

Hollywood opened his mouth, as if he might say something more, but he didn't. Instead, he just got out of the car, then walked around to the cargo hatch, pulled it open, and began to rummage through the gear. Peter changed position and went back to work on the window.

It definitely sounded different. A thump, but also a faint *tik*.

Behind the car, he heard the tinny clank of metal on gravel, then a thump against the rear bumper. He didn't know what the smaller man was doing until he heard the rachet of the jack handle. After a moment, the back of the car began to rise.

Frank appeared in the road beside the cruiser, back from Bobbie's place. He must have run the whole way. Shirtless, painfully thin, muscles standing out on pale skin like carved marble. Frowning, he stood watching Peter work on the window.

To Hollywood, he said, "You better hustle up, he's waiting on you."

"I know it. Two minutes."

Roy's voice came through the open driver's door, getting louder as he closed in. "You find anything, Frank?"

"The house was open, but I didn't see anyone. State trooper uniforms in the closet, though." He tipped his chin at Falk's body, crumpled beside her open cruiser a dozen yards away. "I think it was her place."

At least Bobbie was safe, Peter thought. She must have heard the gunfire. He hadn't stopped kicking. He wondered if his foot would break before the glass. Thump, *tik*. Thump, *tik*. Thump, *tik*.

Roy appeared in the window, watching Peter as one might watch a bug trapped under a drinking glass. Hollywood ran around to the driver's door with a long adjustable snow scraper and a heavy-duty rubber bungee. "Almost there, Roy."

Roy gave Peter a cold smile. "I heard drowning is the worst way to die."

Peter's foot ached from the blows, but he didn't ease off. "Fuck you, Roy. Let me out and kill me yourself, the old-fashioned way. Or maybe you're afraid of me. Maybe you can only hurt women."

Something flashed across Roy's face, that dark, triumphant shadow again. "Oh, no. I want you to think about the girl while the water floods into the car. About what I'm doing to her, what I'm making her into. She's already just like me, she just doesn't know it yet."

"Not gonna happen," Peter said grimly. "I'm gonna put a stake through your heart and leave your bones for the crows."

Frank stood a few steps behind Roy, watching and listening.

Hollywood had already rolled down the driver's window and closed the door. Now he leaned into the car and did something with the bungee. Tying the steering wheel to the door's grab handle, locking the car on course.

Peter was starting to get an idea of what that trajectory might be. He didn't like it at all.

Hollywood looked at Roy. "Ready, boss?"

Roy's cold smile grew wider. "Absolutely." He never took his eyes off Peter.

Hollywood shifted the cruiser into drive, then pressed the blade of the snow scraper against the accelerator. The jacked-up rear wheels spun freely in the air.

As the big motor wound up, he extended the scraper's handle and wedged the brush end into the seam between the seatback and the headrest.

The engine grew louder as it cycled up through the gears. The heavy cruiser rocked slightly, front to back.

Peter kicked frantically. A faint crack appeared in the glass.

Hollywood extracted himself and got some distance from the car.

Frank took another step away and closed his eyes.

Roy walked around to the rear of the cruiser. The engine roared, nearing redline. The accelerator would be pressed to the floor.

Roy didn't say another word. He just set both hands against the back of the SUV and gave a push.

The jack tipped forward and the rear wheels dropped.

The tires spun on the gravel, then grabbed.

The cruiser took off like a shot, with Peter locked in the back and nobody at the controls.

The road ahead was perfectly straight for almost a mile.

Directly after Bobbie's driveway, it ended.

48

The cruiser sped up and the world slowed to a crawl.

Peter had driven that road. He knew what would happen.

After the driveway, there was no dirt berm, no fence or guardrail.

Just a short stretch of grass and the long, steep, broken hillside falling down to the river.

The speedometer was already at forty.

The world grew slower still.

With infinite adrenaline clarity, he knew a terrible truth.

He had failed Helene.

He had also failed the two people in Roy's freezer. He had failed the person whose bones lay in those tangled Nebraska woods. He had failed the four dead officers on the road by Bobbie's house, along with everyone Roy would go on to harm tomorrow, or the next day, or the day after that. There would be more deaths, Peter was certain.

But mostly, he'd failed Helene. Who had given him her trust. Her faith.

He had condemned her to a bottomless pit of pain, hell on earth.

The speedometer needle hit fifty.

He thought about his last conversation with June, her voice over the phone, the way he could picture her face as if she were right there beside him. Her green eyes, the freckles spread like a galaxy across her face. The strength of her arms. How often, when he had stumbled, she had carried his weight so he did not fall.

He thought about Lewis, well on his way to South Dakota now, who would probably have to identify Peter's body, mangled though it might be. Lewis was so very different from Peter, except for all the ways that mattered. How many times had Lewis saved Peter's life?

In his mind, Peter shouted at his friend. Turn around, Lewis. Go back home. Hug your wife and children. But Lewis couldn't hear him. Even if he could, he wouldn't listen. Just like Peter wouldn't turn away from Lewis or June or Lewis's family, Lewis wouldn't turn away from Peter.

Even if Peter was dead or damaged beyond repair. Perhaps especially.

Lewis would want to avenge Peter. He would need to.

With June, Lewis would hunt Roy to the ends of the earth. Nothing Peter could say or do would change that.

Maybe they would succeed.

Or maybe Roy would kill them, too.

He thought then of what Hollywood had said, just a few minutes before.

Roy gets biblical, real Old Testament stuff.

Peter had seen the shadow in Roy's eyes. He knew what Roy was.

Roy had seen Peter's driver's license. He's been a cop. He could find out where Peter lived.

Staying home would not keep June safe, or Lewis.

The needle hit sixty.

Even as the cruiser accelerated and these thoughts rocketed through Peter's mind, he lay on his back and kicked at the window.

The crack grew. He kicked again and the crack turned into a spiderweb.

He had to make a choice.

Air rushed through the wrecked windshield. Gravel pinged off the underside and rattled in the wheel wells. The cruiser was heavy. Even with the pedal to the floor, it needed time to pick up velocity. But the same principle applied in reverse. At speed, it would be like a missile in flight, impossible to stop.

So Peter's choice was complicated.

Break out the glass and try to jump?

Or stay inside and ride it out?

If he tried to jump, but didn't have time to fully launch before the cruiser hit, he would get crushed or cut in half on impact.

Even if he did launch, he could bash his head on a rock or wrap his spine around a tree. Or simply get beat to death by meeting the earth at highway speed.

If he stayed inside, the car could protect him from those things.

But what would protect him from the car?

The cruiser would roll, or tumble end over end. Probably both. For a long time.

It might hit a tree or fly off the bluff. He might survive the crash to drown in the Missouri.

The engine roared louder.

The needle hit seventy.

His boot went through the window.

He pulled it back and kicked again, widening the opening.

With the glass gone, the sound of the rushing air changed from a sibilant whistle into a kind of howl, a companion to the rising engine noise. The two together were so loud it was impossible to think.

Peter climbed to his knees and looked through the jagged hole.

The night was a blur.

The needle reached eighty.

He felt a thump as the road ended.

The meadow was lumpy. The cruiser bounced wildly, lurching on its springs. The engine rose and fell as the wheels spun and caught, spun and caught.

Peter put an arm through the broken window and yanked the outside door handle. The door opened. The car bucked and roared beneath him. He pulled himself into the juddering gap, hands grasping, feet slipping. The door pounded his shoulder with every jolt of the car.

He looked forward and saw the dark pointed tops of evergreens.

Time to choose, Marine. Stay inside or take the leap?

Below his feet, the grass fell away.

The cruiser was airborne.

His stomach felt the lift of freefall.

49

HELENE

Locked in the back of the second police car, with the suffocating smell of blood from the dead officer in the driver's seat, Helene watched through the rear window as the red taillights grew smaller and smaller.

A moment later, they vanished over the edge of the hill, as if they'd never been.

Roy raised both arms in the air as if his team had just scored a touchdown.

Peter was gone. She was on her own.

She'd always been on her own, she knew that now. Even her mother hadn't been able to help, not really. She was no match for the ruthless, murderous world.

Helene's neck ached from Roy's fingers on her throat, and it hurt to swallow. Her wrist throbbed where he had grabbed her. She was beaten and broken. She'd run out of tears.

Roy was too strong for her. It would be so easy to give up. To give in.

Then she thought about what her mother might say. What Helene had embroidered on the hem of that dress, so she'd be sure to remember. *We can do hard things.* She wrapped her arms around the baby in her belly.

Maybe she couldn't fight Roy, not now. But she would bide her time. She didn't have long before Roy learned the truth of her pregnancy, but she would watch and wait. She would keep herself ready.

When the time came, he wouldn't catch her again.

One way or another.

Roy led Frank and Hollywood toward her, talking to the other men over his shoulder. She could hear them clearly because Hollywood had left the front doors open after searching the car. She remembered how he'd stuck the officer's pistol in his waistband after taking the cash from his wallet.

"We've bought ourselves a few hours," Roy said. "We better make good use of them. First thing, we'll get across the bridge and drop Hollywood and Pony at Pony's truck."

In front of her, Pony Boy leaned against the side of the first police car, eyes up to the night sky. Beyond him, an older truck stood silent. She'd never seen the truck before.

Roy reached the cruiser, opened the door to her cage, and held out his hand. She didn't take it.

"Be nice, honey. I know I was harsh before, but it's

for your own good. You needed to learn how things were. Now, do you want to ride inside the truck? Or I can wrap you in a tarp and throw you in the bed. It's up to you."

She took his hand. Gently, he helped her from the cruiser. Frank walked ahead, averting his eyes. Hollywood passed them, headed for the older truck. The pistol was in front, with his shirttail raised up and tucked inside the grip.

"Frank, would you help Pony? He can sit with Helene up front, where it's comfortable." Roy gave her a wink and took his hand from hers. Then his elbow bent and he reached for his holstered gun. Without a word, he raised it and shot Hollywood in the back of the head.

Hollywood's legs collapsed and he fell forward onto his face. It was strange. She'd never seen someone fall without trying to catch themselves.

Frank had turned and raised his big chrome revolver so quickly that it seemed instantaneous. But he didn't seem to know where to point the gun.

"Relax, Frank." Roy lowered his gun, took her hand again, and led her past Hollywood, who lay splayed and twitching on the gravel.

Pony Boy still hadn't moved from where he leaned against the lead police car. His pants were bloody along one leg. Beneath the wet cloth, the limb was crooked and wrong. He regarded Hollywood, now still. "You didn't need to do that, Roy."

"Of course I did. He screwed up. You did, too. That's why you're all messed up."

Pony pushed himself off the side of the car and straightened up as much as he could. He looked Roy full in the face. "My money's all spent," he said. "Gone for food and rent for uncles and aunts on the rez. You got no reason to bother them."

Roy raised the gun again. "I don't need a reason. I do what I want."

He shot Pony twice in the chest.

Pony slumped back against the cruiser, eyes wide open, good leg still locked and holding him up. Then he began to tip to one side, at first slowly and then faster, like a toppling tree. When he hit the dirt, he didn't move again.

Frank stood with his head bowed, the big revolver hanging at his side. He pinched his fingers at the bridge of his nose. "They deserved more than that, Roy. Both of them."

Roy's voice was cold. "You know better than me now, Frank?"

"That's not what I'm saying. It's just—we went through a lot together, the four of us. We made a lot of money."

"Are you getting soft?" Roy asked. "They knew too much. We never needed them anyway. It's you and me, Frankie."

"What about her?"

"She's special, I told you that. She comes with us."

Helene turned from Pony Boy to Hollywood, then back. She couldn't stop staring at them. She'd shared food with them, had cooked for them. Now they were dead on cold, hard ground. But she felt nothing.

No, that was wrong. She did feel something. The faintest of tugs, deep inside her. Like when a loose baby tooth, hanging by a thread, finally falls free. The sweet taste of your own blood in your mouth, the soft, tender socket that you probe with your tongue. Where something important had once been. Her soul, maybe.

"Honey," Roy said. "What do you think? Was I right to kill them?"

She looked him in the eye and showed him her teeth. "Yes."

Roy elbowed Frank. "See?"

From the warmth of his smile, she knew it was the right answer. And she meant it.

She wondered what else she would have to say or do to protect herself and her baby.

Roy helped her into the truck. Frank palmed the wheel in a U-turn and left the carnage behind them. "Galveston's a thousand miles," he said. "If we push it, we can be there by suppertime."

Helene sat in the middle. Roy had his hand on her thigh, sliding under her skirt. "We're not going to Galveston," he said. "Not yet."

Frank said, "Roy, it's over. We don't know how much the police have, but they know who we are, or they will. We left four dead cops back there. We can't wait, we have to stick with the plan. Swing by that other place and pick up what you need. Then drive south and get a boat like we talked about. Make our way to South America. Swim in the ocean every day, let it wash everything away. Wash us clean, Roy. That's what you always said."

"You're right, Frankie, I did." Roy gave him the warm smile. "And we'll get there, I promise. I just have a few things to do first."

Roy turned the smile on Helene. "A little family visit. After all, we're married. What's yours is mine, right?"

They came to a crossroads. "Head east," Roy said.

Toward Minnesota.

That's when she knew Roy wasn't done punishing her yet.

50

June Cassidy had her phone in her hand, looking from the map to the road and back. Beside her, Lewis kept his foot down and the rented Explorer leaped forward.

It was almost four a.m. They'd flown into Sioux Falls ninety minutes ago. Lewis knew a guy with a plane. Lewis always knew a guy.

June had tried to nap in the little single-engine turboprop, but she was too worried about why Peter hadn't responded to her follow-up texts or voicemails. He had plenty of shortcomings as a boyfriend, but communication wasn't one of them, at least not anymore. She'd distracted herself with research online, looking for Roy.

Her screen showed a blue location marker for Peter's phone. Either the GPS was acting up or the tower coverage was wonky, because the dot was in the middle of the Missouri River. She'd started tracking his phone the year before, when he and Lewis had hitched a ride on the roof of a semi and needed her to pick them up. She'd kept their phones linked since then because Peter was a magnet for other people's troubles and he liked it that way.

Despite the worry it caused, June had to admit Peter's need to be useful was one of the things she loved about him. They'd met when Peter had stepped into June's own problems a few years back. Since then, they'd saved each other in more ways than one.

June wasn't about to lose him now.

So when Lewis turned onto the gravel road and she saw a cluster of red and blue flashers two miles ahead, she felt a pit open in her stomach.

Lewis just drove faster.

Sunrise was still a long way off.

June counted nine police vehicles and two unmarked white vans.

Someone saw them coming and sent a state trooper on foot to stop them. Lewis looked at her and took her pale hand in his dark one, then dropped his window and came to a respectful stop.

The trooper's face was white and drawn under his flat-brimmed hat. His palm hovered above his pistol grip. "Road's closed, folks. You'll have to turn around."

June squeezed Lewis's hand and leaned toward the trooper. They both knew that a white woman would be more effective talking to a white South Dakota cop than the large Black man at her side.

Like Peter, Lewis wore his capacity for violence like an invisible tattoo that only others like him, including most police, could see. Also like Peter, Lewis now used that capacity to find a kind of redemption for the life he had lived before. The two men came from very different backgrounds, but that part of them was very much the same. It was a bond every bit as powerful as the one she shared with Peter, maybe more so. Unlike a tattoo, it went all the way down to the bone.

June gave the trooper a tight smile. "What's happened here?"

He shook his head. He looked very young. His eyes were bloodshot. He cleared his throat. "I'm sorry, ma'am, this is a crime scene. You'll have to turn around."

The vehicles were in several groups. The white vans were outermost, followed by a half-dozen SUVs in a protective half circle on the road and in the fields. Their lightbars were still going. Past them stood three more SUVs, two in the ditch and pointed her direction, another sideways beyond them. Their lights were off.

She let go of Lewis's hand and raised the small binoculars he'd brought. A sturdy-looking woman in black overalls stood by a cruiser talking to a man in a windbreaker. The two cars in the ditch had holes in the windshields, the rear glass was smeared with something dark.

The young trooper didn't like the binoculars. His

voice got sharper. "Ma'am, please put those down. What's your business here?"

Lewis looked at her again. She nodded.

He put the Explorer in park and laid his hands on top of the steering wheel, where the trooper could see them. "Sir, I have ID in my jacket pocket. May I reach for it?"

June opened her door and got out.

"Ma'am. Get back in your vehicle. Ma'am."

She ran toward the flashing lights.

Behind her, the trooper got on his radio. His voice cracked as he called for help. Whatever had happened, it would be very bad. She wished Lewis could be with her now. But if he got out of the car, that freaked-out trooper might just shoot him.

She made it past the vans before an older man with a long, creased face intercepted her. He wore a string tie and a blue western-style suit and a badge on his belt. "Ma'am, this is a restricted area." Then he caught her upper arm. "Ma'am."

She didn't let him swing her around. She was breathing hard. She saw boot soles, toes pointed up. Four pairs, which meant four bodies. Two more heads showing in the driver's seats of the two far cruisers in the ditch. "Who's dead?"

"I can't tell you that. This is an ongoing investigation. Please—"

"Who's fucking dead?" Her voice was louder than she intended.

She heard a noise at her back and turned to see

Lewis arriving beside her and the young trooper climbing up from the ground by their rental. The older cop reached under his suit jacket. "What did you do to that trooper?"

"He tripped," Lewis said. "We're looking for a man named Peter Ash. White, mid-thirties, six-two, black hair, lean build. He might not have ID."

The older man relaxed, the creases softening on his face. June didn't know what that meant. Maybe she didn't want to know. She let him turn her away from the bodies.

The trooper hustled over with his hat off and his mouth set. The older cop put up a hand. "Ease up, Trooper." He looked at Lewis, then June. "Who is this Ash to you?"

June couldn't quite speak. Lewis put his hand on her arm. "A friend who's gone missing," he said. "Is he here?"

"Listen, I can't—"

Lewis stared at the older man. "Is Peter Ash here?" His voice, usually low and liquid, was sharp enough to cut.

The older cop blinked and took a step back, probably unconsciously. Lewis had that effect on people. "No," he said. "Nobody by that name or description."

June let out the breath she hadn't known she was holding. "Okay," she said. "Okay." She looked at Lewis. "Then where the fuck is he?"

When the older cop frowned, the creases turned into canyons. "Who the hell are you people? I've got four sworn officers dead plus two civilians, shot execution-style. Is your guy responsible?"

Lewis shook his head. "Not my man's style," he said. "How about a young woman, pregnant?"

The older cop shook his head. "No."

Lewis looked at June. "Maybe they're still together."

June still had her phone in her hand. The blue dot was still in the river. She pointed past the bodies. "We need to go that way."

"There's a cruiser in the water," the older man said. "It's upside down. I wouldn't hold out hope. We're waiting on the dive team."

June closed her eyes. The fear and sorrow would only get in the way. She pushed them down. Lewis touched her shoulder. "Come on," he said. "We'll go around."

The Explorer crunched across the corn stubble until they were past the last car, then lurched back onto the gravel. At the end of the road, the headlights showed a trail of torn grass and broken bushes as clear as day.

Lewis dug into his luggage and handed her a flashlight.

They continued on foot.

51

The slope was gentle at first, although the surface was rough and uneven. The flashlights were very bright. June could see places where the tires had slipped or dug in as the cruiser had bounced forward.

The hill steepened and the trail grew more spotty. June moved faster, her hiking shoes sliding on the crushed grass and flattened bushes. Lewis stayed by her side, keeping pace. Below them, the slope flattened out again, then rose in a modest hump. Past it, the land fell away abruptly.

The trail ended there.

She shone her light downhill. Sixty feet away, she saw a great dark slash of wet earth where something large had hit hard, torn away the vegetation, then taken flight again. Beyond it, another black wound in the grass, and another. After that, the slope crested and she could see no more land. Just midnight water far below.

Four tires, just barely visible in the murk, marked the rectangular underside of a submerged vehicle. "No," she said. "Please."

Lewis played his light across the grass at their feet. "June, look."

To the left of the cruiser's path, something glittered amid the stalks. She walked over and picked up a few shards of glass. They were small squares.

"That's auto glass." Lewis played his flash back and forth across the hillside to the left, working his way down.

"Wait." June spotted a single bush nearly torn from the ground. She ran to it, struggling to keep her feet on the worsening grade. The roots were exposed and the soil was still damp.

Lewis was beside her, shining his light ahead. "There."

The grade was too steep to run. June picked her way through the thickening scrub, keeping her eye on the spot Lewis had picked out. The bushes were bent, as through a deer had slept there, but something long hung across the leafless branches. It was a belt. She recognized the fabric. It was the backpacker's belt she had given to Peter. The plastic buckle was cracked and marked with tiny glass splinters.

"Lewis," she called.

"Coming." He shifted his light and slipped through the brush.

She turned her bright beam down the steepening decline, searching for another sign. "There." A long divot in the low evergreen shrubs, twenty yards ahead. "You see it?"

"Got it." Lewis picked up speed and passed her effortlessly.

She crashed in his wake. The scrub was thick now. Bushes tangled her feet. Blackberry canes snatched at her clothes and scraped her skin. Then she was beside him in the spiky junipers, looking at a swath of cracked branches. She leaned in, found a dark spot on a hard stem, and touched it. Her finger came away red.

As she turned her light toward the lake, Lewis put his arm out across her shoulders, stopping her.

They were at the edge of a high drop.

Below them was nothing but water.

She swept her beam across the surface. "Peter," she called. "Peter!"

Because the surface was forgiving, the water was in some ways the best possible landing place. But it was also the worst, because if he was unconscious when he hit, he could have drowned. If he was lucky, the shock of the cold water might have woken him. It depended on how hard he'd banged his head, and whether his body was still intact enough to swim.

Lewis tugged at her arm. "We need to get down there. This way." Farther to the right, the slope eased toward a tree-lined drainage. They followed it down to the lake.

They found Peter on the muddy bank, his boots

still in the lapping shallows, his cheek planted in the dirt.

"Hey, Marine." She knelt beside him in the mud. His cheek was cold. "Marine! Wake up!"

No response. Lewis was beside her. "Been here a couple of hours. Wet clothes, probably hypothermic. Help me roll him."

They got Peter on his back and laid him flat, then Lewis put a finger to Peter's neck. "Got a pulse." He put his hand flat on Peter's chest, feeling for rise and fall. "Shallow, but he's breathing." He ran his hands gently around Peter's skull and neck, then down his limbs and torso, including the armpits and groin, periodically checking his fingers for blood. "No major head trauma, no sign of massive bleeding, no compound fractures."

June bent over him. "Should we move him?"

"I ain't waiting on the locals." Lewis stripped off his jacket, a matte-black high-tech raincoat. "Let's get this on him. It'll help keep his heat until we get to the car."

When they sat him up, he mumbled something. She grabbed his face in both hands. "I'm here, Peter. Lewis is here."

Peter's eyelids were at half-mast. His voice was thin, and he sounded a little drunk. "Helene," he said. "Find Helene. He took her."

"First things first." June picked up Peter's arm and tried to fish it through a coat sleeve.

"Sleep," he mumbled, and pushed June's hand away.

"Oh, no, you don't." She grabbed his nose and twisted.

His eyes popped open. "Ow."

"Put on the damn coat, Marine. Make yourself useful." She got his arms in the sleeves, zipped him up, then pulled the hood over his head and cinched the strings.

She and Lewis each got a shoulder under an armpit and a hand on his belt, and raised him to his feet. June's knees shook. He was heavy, almost deadweight. "He can't stand on his own," she said.

"I got him." Lewis pivoted swiftly to face Peter, dropped his head under Peter's left armpit and wrapped his arm around Peter's left knee. Then he straightened with Peter slung across his shoulders in a fireman's carry.

Peter let out a long groan.

"Imagine how I feel, Jarhead." Lewis's voice was strained. "You one heavy motherfucker."

Then he turned and began to climb the ravine, one step at a time, with June right behind them.

At the top of the hill, they loaded Peter in the back of the rented Ford and June climbed in beside him, using her body heat to raise his temperature, or at least not let it drop any further. She couldn't tell if his skin was getting cooler, but she didn't like that he'd stopped talking.

Lewis cranked the heat up high and hauled ass

toward the cluster of cars gathered around the dead. By the time Lewis diverted into the corn stubble to avoid driving through the crime scene, June was already on her phone, trying to find the nearest medical facility that would be open in the small, cruel hours of the night. There wasn't anything nearby.

As they bounced across the ditch and back to the road, the pasty-faced young trooper stepped in front of the car, waving for them to stop.

Lewis dropped the window. "We found our guy. He was thrown from the car. He's hypothermic and banged up and needs medical attention."

The trooper peered into the back. "You better take him yourself. I can't get you an ambulance for forty minutes or longer."

"Hey, Trooper." The sturdy woman in overalls stood up and pointed across the field. "My house is right there. I got a bathtub and big water heater and a good first-aid kit."

Lewis looked at June, who nodded.

"Thanks, we'll take you up on that," Lewis said.

The woman had already pushed the young trooper aside and opened the passenger door. "I'm Bobbie." She climbed inside. "What are you waiting for? Step on it already."

"Stay at the house," the young trooper called. "The investigator will need to talk with you both."

Lewis hit the gas as Bobbie peered over the seat-back, first at Peter, then at June. "I met this guy earlier," she said. "He's tough, he'll be all right."

"Thank you." June reached out a hand and Bobbie took it. "He means the world to me."

"I know how that is." Bobbie's voice was rough. She looked back at the wrecked police cruisers for a moment, then turned to look forward through the windshield again, her back straight and strong, one hand still holding on to June, her other hand tight on the grab handle as if holding on for dear life.

They laid him in the big tub and ran the water warm. Lewis peeled off the coat, fleece, and T-shirt while June untied his boots and stripped away his pants and underclothes. One knee was swollen and spongy. His shoulders and arms were already turning black and blue and dotted with a dozen small puncture wounds. His back was worse.

There was a knock at the door. "Ma'am?" It was the trooper.

"Would you deal with them?" June asked Lewis. "I'm staying here."

He nodded and stood. "I'll be right down the hall."

June closed the door behind him, then turned out the overhead light. She stripped down to her underwear, then stepped into the tub and wrapped herself around him.

He needed all the warmth she could give him.

52

PETER

Peter sat on Bobbie's couch, June at his side, drinking coffee and watching through the picture window as the sun peeked over the horizon. The static whispered low in the back of his head. He wore dry clothes that Lewis had taken from the back of the Chevy, and was wrapped in a thick down blanket from Bobbie's spare room. He was still very cold, and very tired.

Across from them, on hard chairs taken from the dining nook, sat two South Dakota Department of Criminal Investigation agents, asking questions. Lewis leaned lightly against the wall, perfectly balanced, ready for anything, missing nothing. Two state troopers lurked on the back porch to make sure nobody made a break for it.

When Peter had leaped from the sheriff's cruiser, he'd curled into a ball with his arms wrapped around his head. Like a stone rolling downhill, he'd bounced hard a half-dozen times as he picked up speed. Then he was flying, and then underwater, too disoriented to know up from down. Because it was night, he didn't have daylight to guide him. Lewis and Clark Lake was a lot deeper than the river. Somehow he managed to keep his head enough to follow the bubbles to the surface. By the time he made it to shore, he was already shivering uncontrollably.

After he was warm enough to get out of the tub, June had soaked his minor puncture wounds with mercurochrome, then dressed them with gauze and tape from Bobbie's first-aid kit. He was pretty sure he'd broken a bone in his right forearm, and his left knee felt like someone had bashed it with a baseball bat, but none of that bothered him much at the moment. He knew it could have been far worse.

What bothered him was Bobbie. After he got dressed, he'd found her at the kitchen table, staring into her mug, with Cupcake's head on her lap. He sat beside her and told her how sorry he was about Falk. That it was his fault, all of it. Bobbie just shook her head and turned away. A moment later, she stood up and left the house, taking the dog with her. Framed photos of her and Falk, smiling and happy, hung on every wall. He had asked for Bobbie's help just a few hours ago, and her generosity had taken the heart out of her life.

Worse still was thinking about Helene. She appeared in flashes as if he were still trapped in the back of the sheriff's cruiser, watching through that shattered windshield as Roy assaulted her. The pain on her face, and the hopelessness that filled her eyes as she realized that nobody would come to save her. Difficult as that was to witness, Peter knew it was nothing compared to Helene's experience, living through it. Peter had failed her twice, and he had no way to find her again.

"I'm sorry, son, could be I'm dim or something, but why didn't you just call the law when this whole thing started?"

This was Campbell, the older of the two DCI investigators. With his long, seamed face, his blue suit with contrasting stitching, and a folksy way of talking, he reminded Peter of a singing cowboy from a black-and-white movie, except he never sang a note. Instead, he was polite and patient and doodled in a large black book as he asked question after question in no particular order, looping endlessly forward and back, waiting for the misplaced or altered detail that would tell him Peter was lying.

Peter wasn't lying. Four sworn officers were dead, and Helene had disappeared. He'd told them everything he knew, including what he'd learned from Helene, and the fact that Roy was obviously the leader of the group, with Frank his second in command. He'd identified the men he'd known as Hollywood and Pony Boy from pictures on Campbell's phone. Their real names, or at least the names in their wallets, were Bradford Pitts and Arthur White Horse.

Peter looked at Campbell. "Because Helene said Roy was connected to a bunch of cops. Hollywood and Pony Boy each said the same thing. Sheriff Johns said Roy gave money to his campaign, and was a guest at his annual county law enforcement picnic. I've told you all of this at least four times. Maybe now you can let me know what you're doing to find Helene."

"Mr. Ash, that's not your concern." Buckley, the younger DCI investigator, didn't talk much. He was dressed in designer jeans, running shoes, and a silvery tracksuit jacket. He had a digital recorder going on the coffee table, and he sat watching Peter with one ankle propped on the opposite knee, his foot twitching like the tail of a cat. Unlike Campbell, Buckley didn't even try to conceal his hostility.

"Not my concern?" Peter's voice was loud in the small room. June put her hand on his thigh but Peter kept talking. "Roy Wiley killed four police and almost strangled a pregnant woman right in front of me. And obviously you don't have shit. Was he even on your radar before this happened?"

Buckley gave Peter the hard eye, radiating anger. "We're asking the questions, Mr. Ash." But his foot began to twitch faster.

Peter's eye flagged the movement. He leaned forward. "Wait. You knew about him?"

Now Buckley's foot flapped like a bird's wing. Campbell looked at him, then at Peter. He stood up and tucked his black book under his arm. "Folks, give us a minute. Buck?"

Buckley followed the senior investigator into the kitchen.

Peter heard a low murmur, then Campbell's voice cut through the partition. "When in the hell were you planning on telling me this?"

Two minutes later, Buckley left the kitchen, opened the back door, and walked out of the house without a word. Peter heard a car start. Taillights disappeared down the driveway.

When Campbell returned to the living room, the old-fashioned country cop was gone. "Agent Buckley joined the DCI ten months ago. Before that he was a Sioux Falls police investigator, and part of a monthly poker game, along with local cops and state troopers and even a few DCI guys." He gave Peter a bitter smile. "Roy Wiley was a regular player. Buckley said he was well liked, even admired. Folks would do little things for him, like run license plates or find somebody's address. And he always asked what cases people were working. Because he missed being on the job."

June squeezed Peter's hand, telling him to restrain himself. Lewis just looked at the ceiling.

Campbell picked up the chairs and carried them back to the dining nook. He switched off the digital recorder and tucked it into his pocket.

"You were right to say we don't have anything, but we've only had his name for a couple of hours. Half my office is already working this case. By noon we'll know everything there is to know about Roy Wiley. I can tell you already that he has no criminal record. So no, Wiley was not on our radar or anyone else's. But we will find him, I promise you."

"Unless someone in your office lets him know where you're looking," Peter said.

Campbell's jaw worked. "You can bet I'll be talking with my people about that, too."

"One last thing," Peter said. "Tell the media that a seventh man died in that car in the river. Just don't release my name. I don't want my folks to freak out."

Campbell gave Peter a steady look. "Now why on earth would you want me to do a thing like that?"

Peter angled his head at June. "I don't want Roy coming back to finish what he started."

"No harm in that," Campbell said. "For a day or two, anyway."

He went to the door, put his hand on the knob, then turned back to Peter. "You didn't call the sheriff when this first began. Instead you took things into your own hands. I understand your thinking and your motivation, and given the last five minutes, I can't say I blame you. But as of this moment, you are done with Roy Wiley. He is my business now. If you get in my way, I will charge you with obstruction and whatever else I can think of, and put you in a cell until we find him. Do you understand me?"

"Loud and clear," Peter said.

"Good." Campbell's face softened. "Please tell Bobbie again that I'm sorry for her loss." Then he walked out and got in his car and drove away, with the troopers' cruisers behind him.

Peter watched them go. He knew Campbell and the rest of the DCI were highly motivated, because this happened to their people in their backyard. But Roy and his crew had been active in at least eight or nine states. He could be headed anywhere now. And the people who would be chasing down Campbell's leads in rural Oregon or Montana wouldn't have the same level of motivation. They already had their own cases to work and not enough time to do it.

When the sound of their engines died away, June put her hand on Peter's forehead, checking his temperature. "You're not quitting," she said.

Peter looked at her helplessly. "I can't."

"I know." She reached for her bag. "I have a couple hours' lead on Campbell and his people. Let me tell you what I found."

Lewis rubbed his hands together, then went into the kitchen to make another pot of coffee.

53

"First things first," June said. "I ran Roy Wiley through my subscription databases and found almost nothing. Two bank accounts with less than a thousand dollars combined. A loan on a four-year-old pickup that'll be paid off in August. He owns that Nebraska property outright, and credit reports show he's never had a mortgage. Like Campbell said, no criminal record."

They'd moved to the kitchen table. "That's it?" Peter was at the stove, grilling turkey and Swiss sandwiches. He was going to have to buy Bobbie some groceries. She was still outside somewhere, working through her grief as best she could.

June looked from her laptop to her notepad. "He owns a business called Midwest Services, probably to help launder his cash, but I can't find any account in that name. Helene said he showed her a box filled with money, and that he claimed to have a couple of million put away, but if it's overseas, in the Caymans or someplace, it could take years to find. The only phone I've got is a landline at that same property, but it's no longer in service. If he had an electronic account with the auto loan or bank or phone company, he'd have to provide an email, but he must have kept it all on paper, because I've got nothing. And no social media, either, not even tagged on someone else's."

"Never?" Lewis sat balanced on a high wooden stool. He'd stripped off his starched blue button-down, exposing a white silk undershirt. The articulated muscles in his arms and shoulders bunched and moved under the thin fabric like pinions of a dark machine, restless for work.

June tapped her pen on the pad. "Not fucking ever."

"Is that a surprise?" Peter flipped the sandwiches. The cheese bubbled on the hot pan.

"Jarhead, you got to work hard to stay low profile," Lewis said. "How many people you know got absolutely zero electronic footprint? Even an internet primitive like you leaves a trail. These web scrapers know every physical and electronic address you've ever been associated with, every phone number you've ever had, going all the way back to when you were just a smile on your daddy's face. June, are you saying there's absolutely nothing?"

"I do have some education and employment history," June said, "although it's not recent. When Wiley was a teenager, he worked at a slaughterhouse in

Madison, Nebraska, for eighteen months. During the same span, he got an associate's degree in Criminal Justice from Northeast Community College in Norfolk. His next job was at the Minneapolis Police Department. He was there for seven years. After that, nothing."

Lewis chewed his lip. "I'm guessing you can't get personnel records from the cops."

June shook her head. "They're not public. Like most departments, the MPD works pretty hard to protect their rank and file, including the problem cops. The MPD's contract with the police union's a big part of that. I know a few journalists who'd crowd-sourced the names of officers with complaints against them, then filed a bunch of Freedom of Information lawsuits with the department, trying to get access to the department's disciplinary records. I reached out to them, hoping to get some dirt on Wiley, but he wasn't even on their complaint list."

"'Course not," Lewis said. "Roy's too slick for that. You get a former phone or address in Minneapolis?"

June shook her head. "Like he lived in a cave," she said. "Or under a bridge."

"Probably an informal sublet," Lewis said. "Nothing in his name that way. For seven years?"

June nodded. "Means he's smart. And he thinks ahead."

Lewis frowned. "Like he been working toward this since he was a kid."

Peter didn't like the sound of that.

Almost every murder, he knew, was an impulse or accident, often committed under the influence of alcohol or drugs, in a haze of anger or pain, then regretted for a lifetime. Even soldiers sanctioned and trained for combat by their government had trouble getting out from under their war, as Peter knew too well. True premeditated murder was rare. But premeditation for a decade?

Then another thought occurred to Peter.

"What if he wasn't working toward it? What if he's been killing this whole time?"

June stared at Peter, green eyes bright. "That's my assumption, actually. He took out three cops long distance, and one more with a gun to the head, not to mention his own guys. Helene said he broke a woman's neck with his bare hands. He's way too good at this to be a beginner."

A charcoal smell reminded Peter to take the sandwiches off the skillet. He cut them in half and set them on plates, then refilled the coffee cups and sat.

"Okay," he said. "Knowing all that, are you still okay with me going after him?"

"Not *you*, Marine. *Us.*" June thumped him on the sternum with her forefinger. She put some force behind it. "*We* are going after him."

He caught her hand and held it. "Maybe you should sit this one out. This guy's really scary."

She pulled her hand away, freckles flaring as her face flushed. "I don't need your *permission*, Peter. Helene needs a woman on her side. And I can take care of myself."

After someone had tried to kill June several times in Milwaukee, she had doubled her time at a mixed martial arts gym and at the gun range Lewis had built in the basement of an old industrial building he owned. She'd even spent a couple of weeks at a private military training facility in Tennessee, practicing tactics in the field. But it didn't change how Peter felt.

"June, please. I can't take on Roy and worry about you, too."

Lewis gave Peter a tilted smile. "Jarhead, she already a better pistol shot than you. Hand to hand, she as good as half the instructors at that gym. Plus she an actual investigator, unlike you and me. Short answer, she a dangerous woman, and we need her."

June beamed at him. "That might be the nicest thing anyone's ever said about me."

Lewis gave her a fist bump. "It ain't a compliment if it's the truth."

Peter just shook his head and bit into his sandwich.

54

Chewing, Peter said, "So if we don't know anything about Roy, how do we find him?"

June drank some coffee. "If he were a normal person, I'd say look at family and friends. The only relative I found was his grandfather, who was the last owner of that property on the river, and he's dead. If Wiley has parents or siblings, I can't find them. We don't have a last name for Frank. Hollywood and Pony Boy are dead. And you won't find his friends by mining his socials, because he doesn't have any socials."

"I don't think he's got any actual friends," Lewis said. "Everyone he knows, he's using for something. Like his poker buddies, milking them for information. He sure ain't telling them anything real."

"I agree," Peter said. "Campbell and the DCI will be all over those guys. But if we're right about Roy, why is he so attached to Helene? He killed four officers just to take her back."

"I've been wondering the same thing," Lewis said. "Why didn't he kill her, too?"

Peter thought about what he'd heard Helene tell June. "He almost did, once. He put her in the freezer with two other bodies. But he let her out when she told him she was pregnant."

"You think this asshole wants to have a kid?" Lewis asked. "I don't buy that."

"Don't underestimate the desire for family," June said. "Even for assholes. But I don't think that's it, or not all of it. This kind of abuse isn't about sex or love. It's about power. Imagine the control he would have over a pregnant woman. She'd be afraid not just that he would hurt her, but that he'd hurt the baby, too. It would be that much harder for her to escape. Once the baby was born, he'd have even more power. She would do anything to protect her child."

"So he didn't kill her today because he still likes that power," Peter said. "Or needs it."

June nodded. "That's my guess."

Peter rubbed his eyes. His forearm ached. His swollen knee itched and throbbed. He wanted to break something.

Lewis got up and began to clear the table. "Maybe we going about this the wrong way," he said. "Wiley could have walked away. He'd have a couple bodies on him, and that's not nothin'. But he made things a lot worse when he killed those cops to take Helene back. This ain't local heat anymore, it's national. And it's all for Helene. So what do we know about her?"

"A lot less than we know about Roy, actually." June picked up her notepad and flipped through the pages. "She told me her last name was Wiley, and using that for my search, I got nothing. She's only been married a few months. I can't believe it didn't occur to me to ask her maiden name, but I didn't. And I'm not going to learn anything without it."

"I never got that, either," Peter said. "Falk would have asked, and written it down, but I saw Hollywood search the bodies and take their phones and notepads. On Roy's orders, I'm sure, trying to control the flow of information."

"How about a marriage certificate," Lewis said. "That would require her maiden name. It's a legal document."

June shook her head. "Helene told me they were married in Elko, Nevada, but their records aren't online. I can request a certificate from the county recorder with a phone call, but without the date and her name, they might not give it to me. I'll try them in a few hours, after they open. Worst case, I go there in person."

Peter scratched his chin. "How about the town she was from, Coldwater, Montana? The county would have birth records, right? Or we could look up death records, find her mom that way. We know she died a year or so ago."

June looked at him. "Peter, I can't find any Montana town by that name."

"Did she make it up?" Lewis asked.

"I don't think she was lying," June said. "More likely Coldwater used to be a town, probably unincorporated. Sometimes if those communities lose enough population, they kind of fall off the map."

Just like Helene, Peter thought. "What about a missing persons search?"

"Tried that, too. There are a lot of missing women online, some on social media, some even with their own websites made by their families or friends who're still looking for them. There are a few named Helene, but none of them line up with what we know about her. Plus she's over eighteen, so legally, she's not even missing. She's just gone. Like she fell through a crack in the world."

"Damn." Lewis put his hands on his hips. "You sayin' we got nothing? Not even a scrap to follow?"

"Hey." Peter stood up abruptly. "Where are my pants? The ones I was wearing earlier?"

June gave him a look. "I threw them out. They were shredded, even by your minimal standards."

"Where'd you put them?"

"The trash can in the garage."

Feeling every ache, Peter limped barefoot through the breezeway and turned on the light. The waste bin stood directly inside the garage door. He opened the lid. His pants were right on top, still damp.

In the left front pocket, he found a slender ring of torn fabric, embroidered with bright blue thread.

55

They kept to the back roads, driving slow, headlights showing narrow pavement. With Helene sitting between them, Roy and Frank didn't talk. Her throat ached from when he had choked her, and it hurt to swallow. She was exhausted from the horrors of the day, but she didn't want to sleep. Each time her eyes closed, she watched Trooper Falk—Lisa, she'd told Helene to call her Lisa—slide across to the passenger seat, saying, "I'm getting you out of here. Are you ready?"

Helene had seen the shadow coming from the other direction. She knew who it was. She knew what he'd do. She opened her mouth to speak but no words came.

Lisa pushed open the door, but the shadow was right there, lit from behind by the other police car's headlamps. Helene heard two popping sounds and Lisa fell. Helene knew she was dead. The shadow turned its head and Roy's skull mask looked at her through the window. He rolled the mask up to his nose and smiled at her. Not the warm smile or the cold one, but something different. Something new.

It was that smile that jerked her back to wakefulness, over and over.

Now he said, "Pull over, Frankie." He patted her knee. "Let's get you more comfortable, honey."

Frank stopped and Roy helped her out, then opened the truck's little back door. The rear bench seat was barely wide enough for a grown person to sit with their knees raised high, certainly not wide enough for a pregnant woman's belly. But she could fit laying down, so she crawled inside, cradled her baby in her arms, and slept.

When she woke again, they were parked in a barren field, with Roy and Frank asleep sitting up in the front. It was still dark but the horizon had begun to turn crimson. The land was flat and she could see no sign of life. She got out and walked a few steps, then raised her skirt to pee. She put her hand to her chest, just to feel herself breathing. She supposed she was lucky to be alive, but she sure didn't feel that way.

By the time she straightened up, Roy was awake again, staring at her from the passenger seat. She couldn't read his expression. It made her nervous.

She climbed back in, hungry and shivering. "Is there anything to eat?"

Roy shook his head. "Sorry, honey. We'll get some food soon." Frank started the engine and put the truck in gear. Roy turned in his seat to look at her. "Hey, those are my old boots you're wearing, right? Let me see them."

As the truck picked up speed, she lifted her legs. Roy unlaced the boots and pulled them off, one by one. "Those are my socks, too." He peeled away the heavy wool socks and took her bare feet in his big, rough hands, rubbing the soreness away with his strong fingers.

It actually felt good. She closed her eyes, thinking that this was just like him, to perform a small kindness after doing something horrible. He rubbed up her calves for a moment, and she was afraid of what he might do next. Her whole body tensed.

Then his hands went away and she heard the window hum down. Freezing air poured into the cab. She opened her eyes. Roy held the warm boots and socks in his lap, watching her.

"You don't need these anymore," he said.

"Roy, wait."

But she was too late.

One by one, he threw the boots and socks out the window into the new day.

Frank never said a word.

"**W**ake up, sleepyhead."

It was light and Roy was behind the wheel, turning onto a tree-lined residential street. When she saw the small blue house, she realized where she was. A pit opened in her stomach. She didn't want to ask, but she did anyway.

"Roy, what are we doing here?"

"A family visit." He held up her mother's notebook, which she hadn't seen in months. The Parkview Avenue address was in the back. "I've never had an aunt before."

He opened his door and got out. "Come on, honey. Maybe she'll make us some breakfast."

Frank, in the passenger seat, didn't move. She touched him on the shoulder. Softly, she said, "My aunt doesn't have anything you need. Will you please talk to Roy?"

Frank shook his head. He wouldn't look at her. "There's no talking to him, not anymore."

Roy leaned into the truck. "You can stay here, Frank. Get some sleep. But keep your phone on."

"Please, Roy." She put her arm around her belly. "Let's leave. I'll do anything else you want, if we can just keep driving. How about we go someplace warm for a change?"

"And not see family?" He gave her the new smile, then reached out and cupped her breast. She flinched at his touch, and he saw it. He caught her nipple between his thumb and forefinger and squeezed. She tried to pull away, but he just squeezed tighter. His fingers were strong. "Family is the most important thing."

The pain was electric. Her eyes watered, but she clenched her jaw and pushed down the tears. She could endure this. She would endure everything.

Roy peered into her face, watching. "See how strong you are? You can do this, honey. It's just a friendly visit." Then he released her, opened the truck's narrow back door, and pulled her out.

The pavement was cold under her bare feet and the wind blew right through the thin dress. She wondered what her hair looked like, then hated herself for it. Roy pulled her arm through his and marched her up the steps to the little front porch, where he rang the bell. Frank watched from the truck.

Please, Aunt Willa, Helene thought, don't be home.

The door opened. A woman stood behind the screen. "Yes?"

Roy elbowed Helene. She looked down at her feet.

"Can I help you?" Aunt Willa's voice was sharp as she peered through the mesh, first at Roy, then at Helene, her forehead wrinkled in suspicion.

She was shorter than Helene remembered, maybe because Helene hadn't seen her since middle school. She would be in her early sixties now, Helene thought. But Aunt Willa had the same square, stern face, maybe a little more severe with the added years. She wore a black suit jacket over a white dress blouse, and Helene realized it must be a workday. Her aunt worked at a bank, or at least she used to.

"Helene? Is that you?" Aunt Willa unlatched the screen door and pushed it open. She was staring at Helene. "It *is* you." A broad smile transformed her completely. She stepped out and pulled Helene into her arms for a hug. "Oh, my dear girl."

The other woman's body was warm and welcoming. The strong arms held her tight. Despite herself, Helene began to cry.

Aunt Willa held her tighter. "It's all right, Helene. Everything's all right." After a long moment, she relaxed the hug but kept an arm around Helene, looking at Roy. "Is there some kind of problem, Officer?"

Helene realized that Roy had pulled his coat back and put his hands on his hips, exposing a badge on his belt. He must have taken it from one of the bodies back in South Dakota.

Roy chuckled. "Not at all. I'm her husband, Roy."

Aunt Willa looked back at Helene. "Your husband." Her face was carefully neutral, but her eyes were the same piercing blue.

I should have brushed my hair, Helene thought. Maybe she wouldn't have looked so closely at the dress and the bare feet. She wondered if her neck was bruised.

"Show her the ring, honey."

Helene raised her right hand. Aunt Willa took it in hers. "Oh, my. That's quite a ring. I suppose congratulations are in order." She held the door open wide. "Why don't you come inside and I'll put on some coffee."

Helene looked at Roy. Please, she said silently, moving her lips.

Roy ignored her and turned up the warmth on Aunt Willa. "That's so kind of you, ma'am." He took the door and gestured to the opening. "Ladies first."

56

She could feel Roy behind her as she followed her aunt through the small, neat house. Pastel-colored walls and delicate furniture and fresh flowers on the small round table in the kitchen, just like in *Martha Stewart* or *Real Simple*, Helene thought. Outside the big glass doors, brown garden beds filled the backyard, the dormant plants just waiting for the warmth of real spring. A blue Volvo wagon sat inside the open garage.

After turning down the volume on a little counter-top TV, her aunt filled the coffeemaker with brisk, efficient movements, although her eyes kept returning to Helene and Roy, as if trying to make sense of them. Roy eight or nine years older, the stone in the ring too large to be real. The men had changed into clean jeans and shirts somewhere along the way, but Helene still wore the faded print dress, tight as a drum across her enormous belly.

"Helene, you look radiant. How far along are you?"

Her aunt was too polite to say it, and had too much self-control to show it on her face, but the unasked question was obvious. *What on earth are you doing pregnant at nineteen, after everything your mother taught you? And by this man?*

Roy heard it, too. He gave Helene a warning glance and put his arm around her. She managed not to flinch. She wanted, more than anything, to fool her aunt into thinking everything was okay. She knew what Roy was capable of.

So she forced herself to smile, and tried again to believe the lie that had saved her life so far. "About six months," she said. "And with twins. It was an accident, but a happy one. We were already married."

The TV muttered softly on the countertop. The coffeemaker burbled and hissed. Aunt Willa took mugs from a cabinet. "And how did you two meet?"

Helene opened her mouth, unsure what to say. Roy filled the silence. "I came into the store where she worked. I guess you could say it was love at first sight. We got married a week later."

"I see." Roy's warm smile didn't seem to work on Aunt Willa. "And what brings you to Brandon?"

"Well, Helene hasn't stopped talking about her aunt Willa since the day we met. We just had to come visit."

"Really?" She fixed her eyes on Helene. "I've been worried about you. I spent months trying to find you after your mom's accident."

Helene didn't understand. "You tried to find me?"

"Ever since your dad disappeared, I did my best to convince your mom to leave Coldwater and move here with me. You know your mom, she was too proud to accept help. But I'd finally convinced her, and she was just about to quit her job, but then she had her accident. I only found out because her phone kept sending me to voicemail, and she didn't return my calls. I got worried and called the sheriff's office, and a deputy told me what had happened.

"So I asked the deputy to put me in touch with you. He called me back later that day, saying he'd spoken with you and given you my phone number. He said you were legally an adult, so that was all he could do. But you never called."

Helene stared at her. "Nobody talked to me. Nobody ever gave me your number."

"Well, the deputy also gave me the address where you were living, so after a week I got in the car and drove to Montana to find you. The man at that address said you'd gone to Missoula to stay with a family friend. He didn't have their information, but he said you'd be home soon. I left him a letter for you. I invited you to move here to Brandon, to come live with me."

Helene felt her heart breaking. "You did?"

If she'd gotten that letter, everything might have been different.

"I wrote a half-dozen more after that," Aunt Willa said, "but I never heard from you. I was afraid you were lost."

"I never went to Missoula," Helene said. "I never got any letters." She didn't need to ask, but she did anyway. "Do you remember the deputy's name?"

"I do, because I wrote it down," Aunt Willa said. "Bogaloosa. Deputy Bogaloosa."

Roy laughed, a strange, guttural sound. "Wow."

"How is that funny?" Aunt Willa asked. She turned her piercing blue eyes on him. "Roy, what's your last name?"

He laughed again. "You think I'm Deputy Bogaloosa?" He patted the badge on his belt. "No, I'm a South Dakota state trooper. The name's Wiley."

"Wiley," her aunt said. "South Dakota?"

The little TV was still on. Aunt Willa's eyes flicked to it, just for a moment. Then she cleared her throat and glanced at her watch. "Actually, I do have some appointments this morning." She reached into her jacket pocket for her phone. "Why don't you two have a seat in the living room while the coffee brews, and I'll call my assistant and see what she can reschedule. I can scramble some eggs if you're hungry."

But Roy wasn't fooled.

With a sweep of his left hand, he knocked the phone from her grasp, then raised his right and punched her hard in the face.

She grunted and reeled backward against the counter, scattering the mugs with her splayed arm. But she didn't waste time on the pain or the blood that began to flow from her nose and lip. Instead she turned and reached into the sink, then spun to face Roy again with a kitchen knife held tight in her fist, a plump sixty-year-old woman in a tailored pantsuit.

Roy smiled that new smile, as if something had gotten loose inside of him and was trying to get out. "Aunt Willa! You're really something." He moved back and bent to pick up her phone. "You got 911. But you forgot to hit send."

"Roy, stop," Helene said. "You've done enough."

Turning the smile on her, he said, "Oh, honey. You have no idea."

He slipped the phone into his pocket, then took a step toward Aunt Willa again. "Do you know how to use that knife?" he asked her. "Where to stick me for the most damage? Because I'll tell you right now, you'd better kill me quick."

Helene's aunt didn't say a word, and she didn't take her eyes off him. She just stood in a slight crouch with the cabinets at her back and the blade forward in her hand and blood dripping from her chin.

Roy took a step, then another. Then the older woman leaped forward and Roy moved faster than Helene could follow. The knife flew away and Aunt Willa was spun around with Roy behind her, his arm wrapped tight around her neck. Her teeth were bared and her face was red. She clawed at his sleeve and her feet kicked wildly in the air.

Slowly, deliberately, Roy put his free hand on the

opposite side of her head and raised his other forearm so that his palm was on her temple. Helene realized that she'd seen him do this before, in the driveway in Utah.

She'd seen his lips move, too, but now she heard the words. "It's okay, little rabbit," he murmured softly. "I've got you now."

"Roy, stop," she said, stepping forward. "Roy!"

With a startling abruptness, he twisted Aunt Willa's head sideways, much farther than it was meant to go.

Helene heard a wet snap, like a green branch broken from a tree.

Her aunt's eyes rolled back in her head and she trembled all over.

It seemed to last forever.

Roy held her like that, pressed against him, with his eyes closed. Helene thought he might be smelling her hair. Finally, he bent to lay Aunt Willa gently down on the kitchen floor.

When he straightened up, he looked at the ceiling and shook himself like a dog. Helene saw the bulge in his pants and realized he had a huge erection.

Then she knew. This was the moment he'd been planning all along.

Aunt Willa dead and Helene even more alone in the world.

It was no accident that he'd told her aunt his real name. He'd wanted her to know. He'd wanted a reason to kill her.

The knife lay under the little round table, just a few

feet away. It hadn't done her aunt any good, not with Roy at the height of his powers. Even if she managed to get her hand on it, Helene would fare no better.

But the coffeepot was right there, filled to the brim with scalding liquid. That would slow him down. Then she would get the knife. She grabbed the handle and pulled it from the burner.

"What are you doing with that, Helene?" Roy's eyes were locked on hers, bottomless and black. She couldn't turn away. She was frozen. She was powerless.

Still holding her gaze, he scooped a coffee mug unerringly from the counter and held it out.

"Why don't you pour me a cup, honey?"

And, God help her, she did.

57

After Roy sat Helene in the chair behind the little round table, he put the knife back in the sink and called Frank, who was still in the truck. "Bring in the bags. We're in the kitchen. This is a good place to rest up for a while."

Helene felt strange, as if she were looking down a long tunnel. Aunt Willa was at the other end, and Helene couldn't stop staring. She wanted to kneel beside her and smooth her clothes and hair and wash the blood from her face. But the tunnel was too long and her aunt was too far away.

Frank came down the hall with a frown on his face. Aunt Willa's death did not seem to be a surprise. "Really, Roy? Was this a good idea?"

Roy leaned against the counter with his mug of coffee. His coat hung on the back of a chair and his gun was on his belt. He'd had it the whole time. "My face was on the news, Frank. She was about to call the law. What was I supposed to do?"

"Go to Galveston," Frank growled. "Like we planned."

"This is better," Roy said. "We take a few days, let things cool off."

Frank sighed. "With four dead cops in South Dakota, we're gonna need a lot more than a few days."

"Quit complaining, Frankie. Have I ever steered us wrong? Or are you losing the stomach for this work?"

"I do what needs to be done," Frank said. "But this isn't work. Whatever it is, it stopped being work the minute you decided to kill four cops, plus the rest of our crew."

"You're just tired, Frankie. Have some coffee. Make some breakfast."

"I'm serious, Roy. When does it stop? What's the endgame here?"

"You know me, Frank. There's always a plan."

There was a pause. "Is she okay?" Frank appeared at the end of the tunnel. "Helene, are you okay?" He touched her face with the back of his hand. "She's freezing."

"She's just tired. I'll feed her some scrambled eggs and put her to bed."

"Roy, she's in shock. Did she just watch you kill her aunt?"

"Her great-aunt. And Helene's tougher than you think. She's just saving her strength."

"I don't get this, Roy. You've picked up girls before. You take the truck, and the next day, or the day after that, you drop them at some remote bus station and we meet at the next job. But this thing with Helene, how do you think it's going to turn out? A house in the suburbs with a white picket fence?"

Helene was having trouble staying upright. Maybe she'd put her head down on the table. But her belly got in the way. She closed her eyes and felt herself tilt.

"Hang on, honey, let's get you up."

Then the table was gone and Roy was there. "I've got you."

He picked her up in his arms as if she were a child, as if she weighed nothing at all, and carried her away.

She lay on her side, curled around her belly. Forgetting the lie of twins for a moment, she wondered whether she was having a boy or a girl. Would living with Roy turn her baby into a monster? If she and her baby even lived, after Roy discovered the truth.

"Frank, would you look in the fridge, maybe scramble a couple eggs?" Something soft fell over her, wonderfully smooth against her bare skin. The back of his big hand pressed against her forehead, the knuckles rough and hard. "Is she sick?"

"You should have taken her to the doctor months ago. Pony's grandmother, at least."

"That's real helpful, Frank. Thanks a lot."

"Don't blame me, she's your wife. You need to take care of her."

Helene pulled the blanket closer, beginning to warm. The bed was so comfortable, even better than at the resort in California. What would it have been like, to live in this house with her aunt? She would have finished high school. She would have gone to college. She would have been loved.

Frank's voice was low. "How do you know she's not going to run again?"

"She won't run. She just needs a little time to get used to things. Once the twins come, she'll be fine. Besides, where's she got left to go?"

"All she has to do is find one person with a phone, Roy. The cops will be all over us. I hate to say this, but we should go. Leave her here and get back on the road. It's not like she'll tell them anything they don't already know."

The curtains sighed on their rods and the room dimmed. "I'm not leaving her, Frank. I'm telling you, she's special. She'll come around."

Frank sighed. "Who exactly did she think she was marrying?"

"A high-end thief. I didn't tell her that meant sometimes we had to kill someone."

"Well, she knows now. You doubled your body count in the last twelve hours."

"You understand how it is, Frank. The first one's hard. After that, it gets easier."

"Maybe for you."

The light went out. She heard the click of the latch as the door softly closed. She lay in the dark and realized that Frank didn't understand. He hadn't seen Roy kill Aunt Willa, or Jessica Moore in Utah. He didn't know how much Roy liked it. How Roy felt when he did it, what he really was.

Or maybe Frank didn't want to know. Because he needed Roy, or thought he did.

She examined this new fact in her mind, just as she'd examined that rusted shovel head she'd found under the weeds.

Helene was smaller than Roy, and she didn't have his muscle.

But that didn't mean she was powerless.

58

She must have been out for at least four hours, because when she opened her eyes, it was noon. She still hurt, but less so. A plate with a turkey sandwich sat beside the bed. She picked up the sandwich and started to chew.

Something had changed while she slept. She wasn't sure what, exactly, but she could feel it. Like she'd gone to sleep one person and woken up another. A kind of revelation.

Maybe it was watching her aunt with the knife, ready to fight for her life. Maybe it was watching her aunt die, and realizing that she was truly alone. Maybe it was watching Roy as he killed her, and seeing what that did to him, or for him. Maybe it was understanding that Frank didn't know about it.

Maybe it was all of those things. Whatever it was,

it was clear that she had to step up. Step into this next version of herself. She had nothing left to lose.

She knew what her mother would have said. Fortune favors the bold.

She found Roy sitting in the kitchen, staring out the window. There was a foul smell. Aunt Willa lay where Roy had left her. Helene let her indignation rise.

"Really, Roy? You just leave her there?"

He startled at the sound of her voice. "Well, she's dead, honey. She doesn't care."

"I do, Roy. She's still my aunt. Go put her somewhere. On the bed, and be nice about it." Maybe a body on the bed would keep Roy from trying to fuck her. Although maybe not. She suppressed a shudder.

"I guess you're feeling better," Roy said.

"No thanks to you." He'd always liked it when she was spunky. She was something else now. She tapped her bare foot on the floor beside her aunt. "Are you going to move her, or make me do it?"

He raised his eyebrows at her. "I've got it, honey." He pushed his chair back, bent to pick up the older woman in his arms, then carried her out.

The knife was still in the sink. She left it there and opened the fridge. She didn't want another sandwich. She found a container of leftover spaghetti and put it in the microwave, then opened a window and rummaged through the cabinets looking for cleaning supplies.

The noise brought Roy back in a hurry. He found

her spraying Lysol on the floor where her aunt had been. The fresh air and chemicals helped counteract the smell of death. She took a wad of paper towels and used her foot to wipe up the Lysol because she was too pregnant to bend over.

"You're like an animal, Roy. You need to learn some human skills. We can't live like this when the twins are born."

The microwave beeped. She threw away the paper towels, washed her hands, then opened a drawer and found a fork. She'd been worried about what the red sauce might look like warmed up, but it had no effect on her. In fact, it was delicious, with big meaty chunks. She shoved in bite after bite, barely chewing, not caring if she got sauce on her chin.

Roy looked at her like he wasn't sure what to think. "I guess you're still hungry."

She pointed the fork at him. "This is what happens when you don't feed a pregnant woman, Roy. I'm eating for three, remember?"

He held up his hands in surrender. "Lesson learned, honey. I'm glad you're on the mend."

She polished off the last of the noodles then opened the fridge again. "Where's Frank?"

"Asleep on the couch. Honey, are you sure you're all right? You seem a little worked up."

She liked him on the defensive. "A little worked up?" She took out a plastic half gallon of milk and set it on the counter with a thump. She tuned her voice low, because she didn't want Frank to come in, not for this. "Of course I'm *worked up*, Roy. The police were going to take my babies and put me in jail. And it's your fault. You dragged me into this mess. I didn't kill anybody. That was you."

She sighed, put a little extra drama into it. "But now I'm not going to jail. So am I sorry those cops are dead? Not really. Like with that woman in Utah. I'm not happy about it, but I'm learning to live with it."

She took the cap off the milk and drank right from the jug. "Now, Hollywood, he was a liability," she said. "He never shut up. It was only a matter of time before he talked about your business to the wrong person. And he always looked at me like he was picturing me naked. So I'm not mourning him. And Pony Boy, well, he wasn't loyal to you, Roy. He was loyal to his own people. He just used you to make money to give to them."

She dropped the carton back on the counter and put her hands on her hips. "No, what I'm *really* pissed about, Roy, is how you treat me. Like I told you yesterday by the river, the only reason I took Hollywood's car was to get out of the house. I was heading home when the stupid car died. You wouldn't even let me have a winter coat or a decent pair of boots because you were afraid I'd leave. What kind of man does that, Roy? What the fuck is the matter with you?"

He looked startled, as if she were speaking a foreign language. That was good. She kept talking.

"I'm having your *babies*, Roy. And this is how you treat me? You practically break my wrist, and then you almost choke me to death? How do you think that makes me feel?"

He came forward, reaching for her. "Listen, honey—"

"Oh, no." She let her voice rise. "You do *not* get to touch me right now. In fact, if I see your dick in the next week, I'm going to tear it right off, you hear me?" She glared at him. "When you killed all those poor cops, you just made things worse for all of us. And I am *not* going to jail. So I am going to be involved in the decisions going forward. Is that clear?"

She looked at Roy and had no idea what he was thinking. Had she gone too far? Then she heard a snort and turned to see Frank in the kitchen door.

"I guess you were right, Roy. She's tougher than you think." He held up his phone. "Have you seen the news? They've got my name and picture, now. And it's gone national. Seven dead in South Dakota."

"Seven, now?" Roy smiled. "Good. Anything else?"

Frank shook his head. "If they know about Helene, they're not saying. They're still not releasing the names of the dead."

"Might be a good time to split up, Frankie."

She saw the hurt cross Frank's face.

Before he could respond, the doorbell rang.

Then she heard the sound of a key in the lock.

59

JUNE

It was the hem of her dress," Peter said. "She tore it off and gave it to me when she knew her husband had caught her. When she knew I was going to make a run for it."

Outside the front window of Bobbie's house, the clouds in the east were crimson, bright from the rising sun.

June sat on the couch, with Peter on one side and Lewis on the other. She ran the slender strip through her fingers. It was still damp. The fabric was yellow with age, and thin from many washings. But the fine blue embroidery thread was bright and new.

Lewis picked up one end. "Look at the level of detail. This took her a long time."

"She probably made it for herself," June said. "When she was feeling hopeless. I mean, these sayings are reminders of her own strength and determination, right? *We can do hard things. Fortune favors the bold.* And these two names, whoever they are, they mean something, too."

"Then why on earth would she give it to me?" Peter asked.

"Maybe it's like a message in a bottle," June said. "When you're stuck on a desert island, you're lost and alone. You don't know if you'll ever make it home. But when you put that note in that bottle and send it out to sea, you hope maybe someone, somewhere, will know you're alive. Or at least that you once lived."

They were all silent for a moment. Thinking of Helene, June figured, and what that poor young woman had been through. Then remembering their own desert island times.

They'd each had them, she knew. Peter, right after he mustered out of the Marines, when he was living in a tent in the mountains because his claustrophobia was so bad he couldn't be indoors for more than a few minutes at a time. Lewis, when he was running and gunning, before he met Peter, before he reconnected with his childhood sweetheart and adopted her boys as his own. June, when she was a teenager, stuck living with her mentally ill father after her mother fled, unable to take June with her.

But those days were gone, for all of them. They had each other now, and much more.

June reached out and put her arms around them, these two dangerous men, and pulled them close. She didn't have to try very hard, because they leaned into her. She felt the weight and force of them beside her. Not holding her down, she thought. Lifting her up. Keeping her safe.

Then she let them go and picked up the strip of fabric again. A few expressions of hope and two women's names. She could work with that.

"Okay, here's the plan," she said. "Peter, you and I are going to the nearest major hospital to get you checked out. I can do some digging into these names while they run you through the MRI. Lewis, maybe you'd stay here and watch out for Bobbie? I doubt Roy will come back here, but you never know."

Lewis nodded. "I'm surprised they didn't leave a trooper standing watch."

Bobbie's voice surprised them. "I told Campbell I didn't want any protection."

They looked up to see her filling the kitchen doorway. None of them had heard her come in. She held a double-barreled shotgun in one hand and the other was clenched in a fist. Her eyes were red.

"If that jackwagon comes back," she said, "I don't want anyone standing between him and me. I want him for myself."

Lewis eyed the weapon appreciatively. His voice was gentle. "Okay with you if I stick around, Bobbie? An extra pair of eyes might help."

She nodded. "You got something to shoot with?"

"Just a pistol." Lewis tipped his chin at the shotgun. "I was hoping you had another one of those."

"I'll find you something," Bobbie said.

June rubbed her face with her palms. Her eyeballs felt like they'd been dipped in sand. She hadn't slept in twenty-four hours and neither had Peter. He was starting to sink into the couch. Lewis, on the other hand, had napped on the plane and still looked fresh as a daisy in his creased black jeans and white silk T-shirt.

Lewis caught her looking. "Hospital's a good idea, but maybe you two should get a little rest first."

"Oh, twist my arm," she said. "Come on, Marine."

But Peter had already fallen asleep sitting up.

Three hours later, feeling more rested, they were on their way to Sioux Falls, a hundred miles away. They took the rented Explorer because Roy wouldn't recognize it, and also because it was an automatic, so Peter could drive with his good leg while June ran searches on her laptop. Along with a big Stanley thermos full of coffee, Peter had a loaner pistol from Bobbie, along with the high-end tactical vest that lived in the back of his truck. June didn't know if Peter's taking the vest made her feel better or worse.

June had the Glock 19 that she practiced with at the range and always kept in her bag. Some days, she had trouble believing that she once hadn't liked guns. All you had to do was fire one to fall in love with it. The feeling of power, like lightning bolts from your fingertips. The more practice and training she had, the stronger the feeling. She was still afraid, sometimes, when the memory of her attacker flashed into her mind. But less so, as the months passed.

The two names embroidered on the dress were Jessica Moore and Celeste Johansen. It took June thirty seconds to find Jessica Moore. After four online news articles, she made three phone calls to reach the investigator and learn the rest.

"Jessica Moore was a deputy sheriff in Wasatch County, Utah. That's near Park City." June's laptop had an image of a competent-looking woman in a neat uniform. "She went missing in October. They found her car in the parking lot at a trailhead, but they haven't found her body."

"Because she's in Roy's freezer," Peter said. "She's the woman Helene saw murdered, right?"

"Has to be," June said. "The sheriff's office thinks she got lost on a day hike. They pinged her phone, but couldn't find it with GPS. There was no activity on her credit cards after she got groceries that morning. So no evidence of foul play. They wouldn't tell me anything about any burglaries in that time frame. But how else would Helene even know her name?"

Peter nodded. "Why embroider her name on a dress?"

"I think she's keeping track," June said. "It's a kind of memorial."

"Unless Roy made her include the name. As a kind of trophy or souvenir. Or a reminder of what could happen to her."

June felt a shiver pass through her. "Oh, yuck. I mean, yuck, Peter."

He shrugged. "Well, we already know the guy's a freak. The question is, how big of a freak is he?"

"With just the evidence we already have? I'd say world-class. Now I'm going to start looking for Celeste Johansen."

She found multiple women with that name online. She worked her way through unpromising results until she came to a mention in the *Glasgow Courier*, a small newspaper based in Valley County, Montana. "Celeste Johansen was killed in a car wreck eighteen months ago. She went off the road and into the Milk River and either died on impact or was drowned."

"Sounds familiar," Peter said.

"Well, according to this article, the Valley County sheriff thinks she fell asleep at the wheel and missed a curve along the Milk River. Nineteen people have died on that same curve over the last twenty-five years. The reporter writes about ongoing efforts to get the county to put in a guardrail, even though there's no budget for it."

There was a grainy photo of the dead woman. June usually felt pretty good about her own looks, but the image of Celeste Johansen made her feel like the ugly stepsister. "Wow, she was gorgeous."

Peter leaned over to get a look at the screen. "She looks just like Helene. Same eyes, same cheekbones, same wild tangle of hair."

June scrolled down and kept reading. "Celeste Johansen is survived by an aunt, Willa Sundstrom, in Brandon, Minnesota. And also a daughter, Helene Johansen, who had just turned eighteen."

"Aha!" Peter said. "You're a genius."

She gave him a look. "It's the internet, you idiot."

"But you did the typing part," he said. "And spelled their names correctly."

She poked a finger into his ribs.

"Ow, ow, don't do that." He bent himself away from her.

June put her hand on his. "Crap, I'm sorry. I forgot."

Usually Peter seemed invulnerable. He hadn't given any sign of the pain since she'd gotten him dressed. It was easy to forget he'd come close to dying just twelve hours before.

60

They zigzagged over to the small town of Beresford, where they hopped on I-29. Twenty-five miles to the north was Sioux Falls, the largest city in South Dakota with over a quarter million people in the metro area.

June stared out at the flat brown landscape. The clouds hung low and threatened rain. "I'm glad to know Helene's full name," she said. "It gives her a real identity, you know? Separate from that asshole Roy, I mean."

"I agree," Peter said. "But how does it help us?"

"No idea," June said. "But Campbell has the manpower to look into everyone Roy and Frank have ever known. Also the DCI will have access to their MPD personnel files, which we'll never get. But Roy will have planned for all of that."

"Yes," Peter said. "So if he's looking for a place to hide out, you think he might use Helene's contacts."

"He's already using her for everything else," June said.

There were a few Helene Johansens in the world, but other than that mention in the *Glasgow Courier*, June could find no more information about Helene Johansen, age nineteen, from Valley County, Montana. No social media, and not tagged on anyone else's, either. What kind of teenage girl wasn't on social media? Someone without any friends, June thought, or who can't afford a phone. Or both.

Even June's subscription databases yielded no results. No past or current phone number, no past or current address. No bank account, no job history. She turned to Peter. "Didn't Helene tell you she had a job?"

Peter nodded. "She was scared of her boss. He kept grabbing her, threatening her. She thought it would get worse. That's why she left."

Great, June thought, another asshole. "What's the name of the place where she worked?"

"She called it the gas and grocery. I don't know if that's the name or just the type of business."

She searched for "gas and grocery" and "Montana" and found five names. None of them were anywhere near Valley County or even on that side of the state. One of them was on a state website, showing the business had been shuttered almost two decades ago. Of course, there could be others, maybe informally named, but she wasn't going to find them on the internet.

What the hell was she looking for? She didn't know.

Sometimes you just had to poke around and see what showed up.

With that in mind, she called the Valley County Sheriff's Office, hoping for a little local knowledge. The clerk had a slow, midwestern drawl with a smoker's rasp. "The sheriff's in court on and off all day," he told her. "What's this regarding?"

"I'm a reporter with Public Investigations," June said. "I just have a few questions about a missing young woman." She gave her name and number, and thanked the clerk, who promised the sheriff would return her call.

Her phone chimed with a news alert. "Campbell's people have identified Frank," she said. "Last name Seavers, Roy's former partner at the Minneapolis PD." His face was pale and sharp-featured, with intense eyes and hair combed straight back from a high, veined forehead.

She scrolled down to take another look at Roy Wiley, still at large and considered extremely dangerous. In the photo from his police file, he was blond, clean-shaven, and handsome, with a hint of a smile on his lips, a young Robert Redford playing hero cop.

He looked like a good guy, she thought.

Helene had probably thought so, too.

Unlike Helene, her great-aunt, Willa Sundstrom, was easy to find. Her LinkedIn page listed her as a senior VP at a big regional bank, a Fortune 500 company headquartered in Sioux Falls, South Dakota. The article in the *Glasgow Courier* had said the aunt lived in Brandon, Minnesota, which was slightly confusing until June ran a map search and learned that Brandon was a small satellite community just across the state line.

"The aunt is local," she told Peter. "We should visit after the hospital. Maybe she can give us some more names."

They were approaching the southwest side of town. They'd turn onto the 229 bypass and take the Western Avenue exit. Sanford Medical Center was a few miles north toward downtown.

A quick run through her databases provided a current address and phone number. She called the number. No answer. It was probably the woman's landline or personal cell. Today was a workday, after all. She found the bank's website and worked her way through the phone tree until she got Sundstrom's office.

The phone rang a long time before someone picked up. June had the phone on speaker so Peter could hear.

A young woman answered. "Hello, ah, this is Ms. Sundstrom's office. Can I help you?" She seemed a little flustered.

"Hi," June said. "I'm trying to reach Willa. I'm a friend of her niece."

"Actually, she, ah, she didn't come in this morning. Would you like to leave your name?"

June looked at Peter, who raised his eyebrows.

"That's funny," June said, "Willa asked me to call her today. Was she expected in the office?"

"Actually, she *was*." The young woman lowered her voice, as if telling a secret. "She had a big meeting. But she never called in sick. And she's not answering her phone. I guess that's not like her? Anyway, her assistant Beth has a key, so she drove over before noon to make sure she's okay. I'm just filling in until Beth gets back."

Peter shook his head. June didn't like it, either. "How long has Beth been gone?"

"About an hour. Actually, closer to two. Which is a little odd, I guess? Because it's only ten miles."

"You should call her," June said. "I'll stay on the line."

After a minute, the young woman said, "Okay, that's weird. I got sent to voicemail. Beth is like, *glued* to her phone. Should I go over there?"

"I'm sure she's just taking a long lunch," June said. "I'll swing by and check on them."

She ended the call. They were on the I-229 bypass now, looping east around the low-slung city. Peter had already glanced at the rental company's map and found the town of Brandon. Now he blew past the hospital exit and was steadily increasing his speed. "We're fifteen minutes out, maybe less."

"Marine, you can barely walk. I'm calling Campbell."

"Please don't," Peter said. "Campbell doesn't have his own door-kickers, not enough for something like this. So he'll call the city or the county or both, and they'll send their tactical squad, just itching to use all their toys and training. Protecting Helene won't be their first priority." He glanced over his shoulder and changed lanes, sliding effortlessly through the gaps in traffic. "And if Roy sees them coming? What do you think he'll do to Helene? She's the only witness against him."

"I don't care about Helene," June said. "Not as much as I care about you, anyway. If we've actually found Roy, let the police deal with him."

Peter didn't answer. She closed her eyes. She could feel the car rocketing forward, faster than it was meant to go. The tires thrummed on the sun-faded asphalt. More than anything, she wanted Peter to be wrong. But he wasn't.

She opened her eyes and looked at the tall, raw-boned man beside her, intent on the road and the traffic and the car he was pushing hard. She knew that hungry look.

"That's not all of it." She raised her voice over the engine noise. "It's also about you and Roy. He tried to kill you."

"True," Peter admitted. "But it's more than that. You know what he's done, but you haven't met him. I don't know how to explain it. You know I'm not big on organized religion. But meeting Roy in person kinda made me believe that evil actually exists."

She had no idea how to answer that. But she knew who Peter was the day they met. Right now, she didn't like it. But this was the bargain they had made with each other. This was the life he needed, to put himself at risk to help people who couldn't help themselves, to stop bad things from getting worse. It was part of what had put him back together, after his war. It kept him whole, now.

The worst thing was that she wanted to go with him. She'd killed a man once, to protect herself. She still dreamed about it. They weren't good dreams. But she would do it again in a heartbeat if she had to. To protect Peter. To bring him home in one piece.

So she reached into her bag and pulled out her pistol. Peter took her hand and together they flew toward the merge onto I-90, maybe ten minutes out with the speedometer past a hundred and ten.

61

PETER

By the time they got to Brandon, the adrenaline was burning in Peter's veins like gasoline. It lubricated his muscles and damped down the pain from the beating he'd taken leaping from the car, although the bone-deep ache was still there, beneath the urgency.

He forced himself to keep his speed down on the exit ramp and rolled through the inevitable commercial strip. He took the second right and coasted past low-slung warehouses on a busy two-lane, where he promptly got stuck behind a slow-moving semi.

He unlatched his seat belt to pull on the Kevlar and ceramic vest June had bought him before his trip to Memphis a few years back. June strapped on a similar vest he had given her after that weird thing in Milwaukee.

It had felt like a romantic gesture at the time. Now

it just seemed like a bad idea. He wanted her to stay in the car. He knew she wouldn't.

He followed the curve to the left and the neighborhood turned residential, tract houses with vinyl siding and attached garages facing the street. Two more quick turns and he was on Parkview Boulevard. The aunt lived four blocks down on the right side of the street. Peter knew from the map that her backyard ended at a large state recreation area. He didn't mind that. Fewer neighbors to get hurt if things went wrong.

If the county tactical team was running this, they'd take an hour to assemble, get briefed, and check weapons and gear in a parking lot nearby. They'd block off the roads and have plainclothes officers knock on doors for a stealth evac of any neighbors' homes in the middle of a workday. They'd send a few people down the side yards to cover all the exits, with a drone in the air and a second team in the rec area behind the property in case the bad guys somehow managed to slip the noose. Then they'd throw flashbangs through the windows and go in shooting.

Roy had killed four of their own. No matter that the dead had worn different uniforms. It was how these things were done, part of the mentality. An eye for an eye. Not to mention that anyone who would deliberately target law enforcement was by definition the most dangerous kind of criminal.

It was hard to argue with any of that, in theory.

In practice, however, Peter wasn't willing to sacrifice Helene, who was there through no fault of her own.

Coming up on the aunt's place, he saw that it was older and smaller than the rest, a simple one-story bungalow that sat comfortably behind a trio of mature maple trees, still leafless from winter. The garage was in the back, down a long and empty driveway.

Peter drove past without slowing or turning his head. Peripheral vision was surprisingly good at collecting details, if you paid attention. The curtains were drawn over the windows. The garage door was up and no vehicles were inside. The only car visible for several blocks was a tiny yellow subcompact parked directly in front of the place.

Then he realized what he was seeing. The werewolf growled its disappointment. "They're gone."

"What?" June craned her head to look behind her. "How do you know?"

"The little yellow hatchback? It's the only vehicle. That's not Roy's getaway car." Peter used the next intersection to make a U-turn. "He'd want something big, fast, and powerful."

"Well, it's not the aunt's car," June said. "A VP at a big bank drives something nicer than that."

"So it's probably the assistant's car." Peter pulled the rental to the curb a few houses shy of the aunt's place. "Maybe you should stay here."

"You think they're dead," June said.

"The only person Roy hasn't killed so far is Helene and his old patrol partner, Frank. Why would he stop now?" He put his hand on hers. It was smaller, but strong. "What I'm saying is, you don't need to see this."

She gave him a look. "I know you're trying to be kind, but you're really just being patronizing."

He held up his hands. "I'm trying to spare you the nightmares."

"Too late for that, Marine. And it's not your fault. I chose this life, remember?" She racked the slide on her Glock to chamber a round, then opened her door and stepped out. "You coming or not?"

Peter shook his head. Another reminder of how hard Juniper Cassidy could be. Anyone who called women the weaker sex had never really known one.

Still, there was no point taking unnecessary risks. With vests hidden under baggy shirts, they went up the neighbor's walk as if they belonged there, then slipped along the front of the house toward the aunt's. Peter's knee hurting but mostly functional. Weapons in their hands but held down along their legs and out of sight.

Up on the porch, the white static crackled as he eased the screen door from the frame. June stood behind him with her hand on his shoulder. A gentle twist of the knob told him that the entry was unlocked. He turned his head to catch June's eye. *Go,* she mouthed.

His right forearm throbbed, but its only job was to steady the gun. The static turned to sparks, sharpening his focus. He pushed the door open with his elbow and slipped inside with the pistol up and ready.

Heel and toe, quiet as a mouse, with June two steps behind him. They moved through the rooms like ghosts.

The house was empty.

No Roy or Frank or Helene. No sign of Willa or Beth. No chest freezer in the basement, either. Peter checked.

"What the fuck?" June called from the rear bedroom. "We weren't wrong, were we?"

"No." Peter looked around the kitchen. The dishwasher was running. "Roy's just hiding his tracks. A missing person doesn't generate the same police interest as a murder victim."

June sniffed the air. "What's that smell?"

"Cleaning products?"

But June always had a better nose than he did. "Not there. In here."

Peter followed her voice. When he got to the bed, he recognized the odor, faint, but distinct. He'd smelled it before, too many times. Voided bowels, but with something else beneath it.

June pointed to a long depression in the comforter. "There was a body here."

Peter nodded. He stepped into the bathroom. Water droplets dappled the tub and sink. The ceramic was still warm to the touch.

"We didn't miss them by long," Peter said. "What kind of sick fuck kills two women, then hangs around to take a shower?"

June stepped past him and looked into the tub. She

pointed at several long, pale strands of hair near the drain. "Both Roy and Frank have short hair, right? The aunt does, too, according to pictures in this house. Beth doesn't seem a likely candidate for a shower. So who does that leave?"

Peter didn't like that at all.

Helene, what are you becoming?

62

HELENE

The poor woman didn't have to die, Helene had thought. But she had a key to the house. Once she let herself in, it was all over.

"Hello, Ms. Sundstrom? It's Beth. Are you home?"

Helene had followed Roy into the front hall, with Frank at her heels. Beth's widening eyes told Helene that she knew something was very wrong.

Before the plump young woman could react further, Roy stepped past her and locked the door. Then he'd looked at Helene. As if asking her permission. As if it made any difference.

She'd said, "Go back to the kitchen, Frank." She heard his footsteps recede. She wanted to go with him, but she made herself stay and watch.

She didn't allow herself to show anger, fear, or disgust. She didn't let herself react at all. Because she needed to be stronger, and she needed to understand.

He did it the same way with each woman, she realized. Jessica Moore in Utah, then Aunt Willa, and now poor Beth. The quick hard blow to the face, the controlling arm around the neck that lifted her off her feet. Then the murmured words, *It's okay, little rabbit*, followed by the twist of the head that broke her neck.

Again, even after the woman died, Roy held her close. On his face, a strange, flickering emotion. And when he laid her down, Helene saw again the erection straining his jeans. This time she saw a damp circle in the denim.

She wanted to throw up. She wanted to scream. She wanted to run.

But she knew Roy would just catch her up again. *I've got you now, little rabbit.*

So she pushed all that down deep where it couldn't touch her. She made her eyes linger on his, noting the flush on his cheeks. She dropped her gaze down to the damp bulge in his pants, then back to his face. She curled a corner of her mouth in the slightest of smiles, and let Roy see it.

He looked away, almost shyly.

In that moment, Helene saw a way forward. If she could somehow bring herself to walk down that path.

She heard her mother's voice as if she were standing right beside her.

We can do hard things.

She turned toward the kitchen and raised her voice. "Frank? We need to get moving. Looks like this isn't such a good place to lay low after all."

———

She told them what to do next. Frank stared at her but didn't move.

Roy gave Helene the warm smile. "What are you waiting for, Frank? I told you, she's a natural."

"Take blankets from the hall closet," she said. "Start with poor Beth here. I'm going to grab a quick shower and find some clothes that fit. When you're done, pack up some food, then get rid of any evidence that we were ever here. We need to be gone in fifteen minutes."

She walked into the bedroom where Aunt Willa lay stretched out on the comforter. She thought about what her aunt had tried to do, after her mother died. The letters she'd written, the trip to Montana, all to bring her here to Brandon. To save her.

She took the woman's hand. It was cool to the touch. "I'm sorry," Helene whispered. "This is all my fault."

There was nothing more to say after that.

She went through the dresser and removed underwear and socks and a half-dozen T-shirts. Not the kind of clothes she saw in the magazines, but they would do. In the closet, she found a small suitcase, along with a cardigan, a warm fleece jacket, and sturdy hiking boots. The jeans would never fit, but the oversized sweatpants could accommodate the belly just fine. No more old-time farm dresses, that's for sure. Those days were over.

She heard Roy and Frank talking as they carried

Beth down the hall. In the bathroom, she ran the shower hot, leaving the door cracked six inches. She took her time removing the dress. She was naked by the time the men came back inside and Roy stopped outside the bathroom, watching her silently through the gap.

She didn't look at him. She didn't say anything. She just reached out a hand and pushed the door shut. Telling Roy that he didn't own her.

When she was clean and dressed, she put the extra clothes in the suitcase, added a framed photo of her aunt with her mother from the bedroom wall, and walked out to the garage.

The Volvo wagon was quite roomy. The two blanket-wrapped bundles fit in the back with plenty of room to spare.

Roy made a last trip to the house for the black duffel that he called his go-bag. Frank looked at her and said, "I hope you know what you're doing."

"Well, you sure as hell don't seem to." She put her hand on his arm. "I'm sorry," she said. "I don't see any way out of this mess. I'm just trying to help. You know my husband can be his own worst enemy sometimes."

Roy pulled the door closed with his shirttail. "Frankie, why don't you follow us in the truck?"

He kept looking at her, but he didn't say anything until they were on the freeway.

"You've changed," he said. "What happened?"

She snorted. "You happened, Roy." She made herself soften. "You changed the way I saw the world. The way I saw myself, I guess. I realized there was no reason not to have everything I desire."

His go-bag lay on the floor at her feet. She pulled it onto her knees and opened the flap. She saw a change of clothes, a revolver with a cracked walnut grip that she knew was her daddy's, and two cell phones and chargers in plastic bags. Another bag held banded stacks of used bills, fifties and hundreds. Before he grabbed her arm, she counted eighty thousand dollars.

"Hey." His voice was sharp and his grip was tight. "Close that up and put it in the back seat."

She glared at him and pulled her arm away. Then she held out her right hand, brandishing her wedding ring. "Didn't you put this diamond on my finger? You're my husband and I'm your wife, Roy. That means we share everything. Unless you're just going to kill me, too."

"Of course not." He turned back to the road. "You're the mother of my children."

"You bet your ass I am." She returned the bag to the floor at her feet.

She let a mile pass before she said, "I heard Frank say something about the other girls you picked up on the road. How many were there? Or have you lost count?"

He opened his mouth, then closed it. He shook his head. His cheek was turning pink under the beard.

She knew she was right and gave him a toothy grin. "Are you blushing, Roy?"

"I don't want to talk about it," he said. "That was before I met you."

"I'm not sure that's true," she said. "What about that girl Beth?"

He didn't answer.

"I watched your face, afterward. Frank doesn't see it, but I do. It turns you on, doesn't it?"

He kept his eyes on the road. "I had to kill her. We would have gotten caught."

She laughed. "Roy, you could have locked her in the closet. My aunt, too." She let the silence thicken, then softly said, "You wanted to kill her. That's how it is with you, isn't it? That's what you like best."

He looked at her then, his face suddenly naked as a newborn's. She knew she had seen something inside him, something deeply private, that he'd never allowed anyone else to see. There was power in that intimacy, she thought.

She put her hand on his upper thigh, ran her fingernails lightly across his groin. The damp spot had not yet dried. "I'm not offended, Roy. It's not like you're cheating on me. You're my husband. If that's what you like best, well, maybe I can help."

She was still a prisoner, she thought. But she wasn't going to run. She was going to thrive.

After all, she'd told Roy the truth about at least one thing.

She'd had a revelation.

There really was no reason why she shouldn't have everything she desired.

It was up to her. It had always only ever been up to her.

63

Peter and June went through the house, wiping fingerprints from the few things they had touched, then left by the back door and walked up the driveway toward the car.

Peter's knee ached badly. He tried not to limp, but June knew him too well. "The hospital is our next stop," she said.

"No problem. You can lie to Campbell on the way."

"You think he'd really arrest you for obstruction of justice?"

"Let's not make it too easy," Peter said. "I want to make him work for it."

He got behind the wheel and June put her phone on speaker. "Agent Campbell," she said. "June Cassidy. Any progress?"

"We're putting their lives under a microscope, but we're not finding much. Roy Wiley and Frank Seavers appear to be very smart and very careful. I'm hoping we get some help from the public."

"That's why I'm calling," June said. "I got a last name for Helene. It's Johansen, and she's from Valley County, Montana. I'll send you an email with the details."

"Thank you," Campbell said. "Do I want to know how you figured that out?"

"I'm good at my job," June said. "There's more. Helene's great-aunt lives in Brandon, Minnesota, east of Sioux Falls. She didn't show up at work today and she's not answering her phone. Her assistant, Beth, went looking for her a couple of hours ago. Now the assistant's not answering her phone, either."

"I guess you are good at your job," Campbell said. "I'm grateful. I know the Brandon chief of police. I'll get him to send a few units."

They hung up and June made another call, also on speaker.

"Valley County Sheriff's Office."

June introduced herself and waited on hold for Sheriff Janacek as she flipped her interview pad to a fresh page. "Sheriff, thanks so much for your time today."

"Always happy to talk to my friends at the press. This is an election year, you know." Janacek had a rich, deep baritone, like an old-time radio announcer. "So, you're looking for a woman, right? Did Sheriff Day suggest you call me? She bent my ear about her task force a few weeks ago."

"Yes, the task force." June made a note, her voice casual. "What's your take on that?"

"Oh, Sheriff Day's got this idea about missing young women, thirty-some girls across eight or nine states. I'm sure she means well, but between you and me, I don't know if that's worth a task force. These girls are almost all adults. Grown folks leave town every day in this country, get tired of the life they're living and make themselves a new one somewhere else. We're Americans, that's part of who we are. Just because you don't tell people you're leaving, it doesn't mean you're dead."

"Well," June said, "the woman I'm looking for is Helene Johansen."

"Oh, Helene. Heck, she's not missing, either. She stole a few hundred dollars from her job and took off, probably with some no-account man."

"Do you have any idea where she might go? Friends or neighbors she might stay with?"

"Mm, I doubt it. I'm told she wasn't the friendly type. I can't imagine we'll ever see her anywhere near these parts again. All her people are dead."

"Yes, I read in the *Courier* that she lost her mom, Celeste. A few years ago, right?"

"There's a sad story for you," Janacek said. "She went off the road and drowned in the Milk River. That curve is notorious in this county, and I'm sorry to say it's taken far too many lives. My investigator was convinced it was a simple accident, like the rest of them."

He stopped talking, but June didn't fill the silence. He wasn't done yet. Sheriff Janacek liked to tell stories.

He cleared his throat. "I guess it won't hurt anything to tell you, the state forensics people didn't agree at first. Something about the skid marks being too long and in the wrong place. They thought she might have been bumped by another vehicle. But there was no wrong-colored paint on her car, or what was left of it. We called every repair shop in five counties, but didn't find any damaged front bumpers we couldn't account for by other means. I don't mind saying, it took a lot of man-hours. But it all came to nothing. I guess my investigator was right after all. And he knew Celeste, so he was motivated to figure out what really happened."

"He knew her?" June's pen flew across the paper. "What was their relationship?"

"Celeste worked at a country store he owns, and lived in a trailer on his property. He was kind enough to give Helene a job and let her keep living there after her mom passed. Although it's just a travel trailer, a tiny little thing. It was his money Helene stole." He gave a whiskey chuckle. "I must confess, I don't wonder why she hightailed it out of there. Once you get outside town, Montana can be mighty lonely."

Peter wanted to ask a question, but June did it for him. "Your investigator, what's his name?"

"Anthony Bogaloosa. He's also my chief deputy. A good man, a hard worker."

"I'd love to talk to him," June said. "Maybe he can shed some light on where Helene might be. Do you have his number handy?"

"Oh, I can't give that out," the sheriff said. "I'm happy to pass on your information and suggest he call you. He's got the store to run, plus a barn full of milk cows, so it might be a few days. Not like it's an active case, am I right?" Then he paused. "Funny thing. I had a similar conversation just this morning."

"Really," June said. "With who?"

"An insurance adjuster from Minneapolis. Real nice fella. Said he was cleaning up his files."

"Did you get a name for this guy?"

"Sure, I wrote it down. Peter Ash."

June looked at Peter. Wide-eyed, he shook his head.

Apparently Sheriff Janacek listened to silences, too. "Lady, is there something else I should know about this case?"

"If I figure it out," June said, "I'll let you know."

64

HELENE

Helene pointed up the road at the ruined farmstead backed by a broad swath of evergreens. There were no other houses in sight. "That looks like a good place."

Roy touched the brake and the Volvo began to slow. "It's perfect, honey. Nice call."

As they approached the overgrown driveway, she glanced behind them. "Frank's still following."

"Did you have any doubt?" Roy sighed. "Frank's a born follower."

"He's devoted to you," she said. "Like a puppy. It's kind of sweet."

Roy shook his head. "Frank's useful, but he's weak inside. Not like you."

She gave Roy a look, hair blowing wild from the window she had dropped to vent the smell of the bodies in the back. "Is that what you told the other girls, Roy?"

"No." His voice was soft. "It wasn't like that. None of them saw what you saw in me."

"Because you never let them." She took his hand and put a sunny smile on her face. "I guess we're just lucky we found each other."

Roy turned onto the long, rutted track with Frank right behind them. The weight of the dead made the station wagon bounce on its springs. Behind the splayed gray wreck of a barn, they were invisible from the road. The old farmyard had long ago reverted to weedy meadow, and all around them grew dark pines and tall cedars full of birdsong. The wind blew cold, but Helene was warm in her aunt's sweatpants and jacket. With Roy and Frank at her back, she opened the Volvo's hatch and reached for the duct-taped end of a blanket.

With the size of her belly, she could barely bend over far enough to get a grip. "You're not going to make the pregnant lady do this all by herself, are you?"

Roy still wore the dead trooper's badge on his belt. "Let's just leave them in the car and get on our way."

"Roy, she was my aunt. Have some respect."

He sighed, then smiled indulgently. "Whatever you say, honey. Come on, Frank. Be gentle, now."

Roy took the head and Frank took the feet and they placed her dead aunt in the matted grass. It was pale and dry, still dormant from the harsh winter, but with a little sunshine and a little rain, Helene knew it would soon be green and lush.

Beth, the larger bundle, was next. After a moment, the two oblong shapes lay side by side. Helene was at once glad that she couldn't see their faces, and sorry. At least the blankets were white, she thought.

"We can't bury them," Roy said. "No shovels."

"This is good enough," Helene said. "They're past caring anyway."

She wondered if she'd feel something later, or if she was past caring, too. She hoped so. She couldn't afford to be sentimental.

Frank stepped back. "Roy, we need to make some decisions."

He'd taken off his shirt on the drive, and the muscles and veins stood out under his pale, too-tight skin. His pistol nestled in a holster on his right hip. Helene remembered how fast he had drawn it, after Roy shot Hollywood on the road by Bobbie's house.

"You're right, we do," Roy said. "Tell me how you see it."

"Well, I was thinking. Our faces are all over the news. What about your other house? I'm sure you've got some food stored. Even if we only stay a week, it'll be less dangerous to travel."

Helene had heard Frank mention another place, but she'd forgotten. She wanted to ask, but now wasn't the time.

Roy didn't even glance at her. "Not an option. Too close to the home place."

"I get that," Frank said. "So we head south, like we talked about. Galveston, then South America. But it'll be rough for a while, getting there. Don't you think it would be best for Helene and the twins if we set her up in an apartment for a while, someplace with a good hospital? Omaha, maybe, or Kansas City."

It was tempting, Helene thought, but it wasn't enough. She put her hands on her hips. "Omaha? You think I want to live in Omaha? When you guys are going to live on some beach in South America?"

"Hey, Omaha's nice," Frank said. "I live in Omaha."

"Hell, no," Helene said. "You're not getting rid of me that easily. I'm sure they have doctors down there. Besides, Roy and I are married. We should be together."

"Be smart," Frank said. "We'll leave you plenty of money. The police don't even know you exist. Which means you'll be safer alone than with us. When things ease up, we'll come back. Six months at the most."

She shook her head. "You need me, Frank. You can't show your faces, remember? So who's going to pump the gas on your way to Galveston? Who's going to get you food?"

"It's not up to you, Helene." Frank turned to Roy for support. "It's up to me and Roy. It's not a great solution, but we'll make it work. We know what we're doing."

"Oh, I can see that." She spread her hands to encompass the bodies on the ground, the old pickup, their entire situation. "It's all going so well for you guys."

Frank wouldn't look at her. His face was twisted up. "Come on, Roy. Don't be reckless. We were doing fine before you picked her up. She's the one who got us into this mess. Don't let her get us caught now."

"Hang on," Helene said. "Now that I think about it, you're right. We do need to split up. But not the way you're thinking. You two in a truck, you're real easy to identify as the cop killers on the news. But Roy and I together?" She beamed at her husband. "We're just a handsome couple."

Roy gave her the warm smile. "She's got a point, Frankie."

Frank shook his head. "Don't do this, Roy. It was always you and me. All the other girls, you just left them at the bus station. It's better when it's just the two of us."

Helene smiled at Roy. "Frank doesn't get it, does he?"

"Not now, Helene." Roy's voice was sharp.

She laughed. "He really thinks you put those girls on a Greyhound? He doesn't know you at all."

"Of course I know him," Frank said. "He's my oldest friend. I know everything about him."

Frank didn't want to know, she thought. He needed Roy too much. It would wreck his world. But she could see the doubt festering in his eyes. She said, "He killed them, Frank. And he liked it. And you helped him do it."

"That's a lie. Roy, tell me that's a lie." But some

part of Frank knew it wasn't. She watched the unwanted knowledge settle on his face and turn sour.

Then Roy had his pistol out, held low but aimed at Frank's chest.

Frank, normally fast as a whip, didn't even reach for his own gun. Pain washed across his pale face and he sighed like all the air had gone out of him. "Roy? Say something."

Roy's face was cold. "We were never friends, Frank."

When he pulled the trigger, birds clamored up from the trees.

Frank collapsed with a red puckered hole in his chest and tears in his eyes. His voice was a croak. "You deserve each other."

Roy pulled the trigger again. Frank's head jerked back onto the grass in a splash of red.

Helene stared down at him, her heart pounding. "Oh, Frank."

Roy stood with the pistol hanging down while the wind blew cold and the dark birds whirled above. "You didn't have to do that, you know."

She didn't allow herself to look at the gun. "Do what?"

"Tell Frank our secret, to get me to kill him." He holstered the pistol and took her hand. "All you had to do was ask."

"I wasn't sure," she said. "You and Frank were together a long time."

He shook his head. "You were right about him. Frank never really knew me. Not like you do."

Then she understood. Just like with her aunt, Roy had seen this coming. In fact, he had set the stage for it, for her to do what was necessary to get him to kill Frank. All part of Roy's plan.

She should have felt horrible, she thought. Racked by guilt and shame. But she didn't. Instead she felt giddy and wild. Almost free.

The birds circled back to their branches and started calling again. The trill of red-winged blackbirds, singing for a mate. They liked water. There would be a swamp somewhere back in the trees.

Roy said, "Did you want to pull the trigger yourself?"

"No," she said. "Frank never did anything to me. But he wanted to split us up. I couldn't let that happen."

Roy stared at her with those midnight eyes. "Do you ever wonder what it might be like?"

"Well, I wanted to kill you a few times," she said with a laugh. "When I was really angry."

"Should I be worried?" A smile played on his lips.

She patted him on the chest. "You better be good to your wife, buddy. That's all I'm going to say." Then she stood on her tiptoes, gave him a peck on the lips, and headed for the truck, leaving Frank and her aunt and the other woman behind.

At the passenger door, she turned. "What about Frank's share of the money? I mean, he won't be needing it now, right?"

Roy bent and took Frank's pistol from its holster. "Honey, you are really something else."

"You should know, Roy. You made me."

"I'm just helping you become who you already are." He stalked toward her through the grass. "We should get back on the road. I have a surprise for you. I think you're gonna like it."

65

Peter and June were back on I-90, westbound toward Sioux Falls. Ahead was a sign for the bypass exit, which was the shortest way to Sanford Medical. The adrenaline had drained away and Peter hurt all over. His knee wasn't getting any better, either.

"It's got to be Roy who called the Montana sheriff," he said. "Pretending to be the insurance adjuster. Who else would use my name?"

"Of course. He thinks you're dead, right? It's just his way of saying fuck you, one last time." June tapped her pen on her notepad. "The real question is, why would he care about Helene's mom?"

"I don't think it's about Helene's mom. We know Roy's a planner, right? He finds Helene at that place in Montana. She's all alone, and scared of her boss. Somehow, Roy gets her to trust him enough to climb into a stranger's truck."

June nodded. "He gives her money and gifts and helps her feel safe—he basically grooms her, like a pedophile with his victim—until she becomes his sexual partner. Apparently sociopaths can be very charming."

"He didn't seem so charming to me," Peter said. "Anyway, he gets her to marry him and join his crew, robbing high-end houses for some lawyer in Houston. Maybe the pregnancy was an accident. Maybe he didn't intend to keep her around that long. But it helps him control her, keep her under his power."

"He isolates her at the farmhouse. He doesn't even let her see a doctor." June pointed her pen at Peter. "I think he went to her aunt's for the same reason. To take away her only remaining family. Now she's truly alone, except for Roy. But that doesn't explain the call to Sheriff Janacek." She frowned. "Unless it's about Deputy Bogaloosa."

"That's my guess," Peter said. "He killed the aunt. Now he's going after Bogaloosa. Maybe trying to show Helene that he's on her side. While at the same time, making it so she can never go back to the place she used to live."

"So why did he call the sheriff? Roy already knows where the store is."

"I don't know," Peter admitted. "I haven't worked that one out yet." The exit ramp came up on the right, but he ignored it and continued west.

June didn't seem to notice. She turned in the seat so she was facing Peter. "He's already had every chance to kill her. He took a huge risk to take her back from the police and keep her in his life. Do you think he actually has feelings for her? Twisted as they might be? Do sociopaths fall in love?"

"You're asking the wrong guy," Peter said. "I keep thinking about what Roy said to me the other night. That he was making Helene into something. That she was more like him than she knew."

He remembered the strands of her hair in the still-wet bathtub. He wondered if Roy was right.

"What if Roy's lonely?" June asked. "We're pretty sure he's been killing for a long time. What if there's more to it than Roy trying not to get caught? Maybe he gets off on it. Maybe he wants someone to share the experience with."

"I can see that," Peter said. "He wants Helene to be his partner. That's what he's making her into. A killer. For a freak like Roy, though, it wouldn't taste as sweet if he had to force her into it. She'd have to make the choice of her own free will. That way, Roy gets to both destroy her and remake her in his own image at the same time."

"So how does he do that? How does he get Helene to want to kill someone?"

Then Peter knew. "Offer her a person she already fears and hates. The person she ran away from originally. Her old boss, Anthony Bogaloosa."

June was silent for a minute. "Do you think Helene is capable of that?"

Peter kept his eyes on the road. "Under the right circumstances, anybody is capable of anything." He wasn't going to mention the man June had killed the year before.

He didn't need to. "Killing to protect yourself and the people you care about, that's one thing," she said. "Killing proactively, for revenge? Or pleasure? That's something else."

"Speaking of that," Peter said, "I know Sheriff Janacek didn't buy into that whole task force thing, but it sounded like a pretty good idea to me. Thirty missing women and no bodies?"

She looked at him. "You think that's Roy."

"The guy who likes to stack his victims in the freezer? And leave them in the woods for the coyotes? Don't tell me it didn't occur to you."

"Of course it did," June said. "I think you're right about Roy and Bogaloosa, too. That's why you missed our exit. We're headed to Montana."

"Unless you got any better ideas?"

"I think you better step on it, Marine. They're only an hour ahead of us."

Peter put the pedal down. "We need to get the cops involved. Janacek won't take us seriously. But he might listen to Campbell."

June made the call. Campbell had clearly put her number into his contact list. "Ms. Cassidy," he said. "What else have you got for me?"

June described her conversation with Janacek.

Campbell was unimpressed. "You just told me Wiley was at the aunt's house in Minnesota. I got a tactical team on their way. Now you're saying he's headed to Montana? Because an insurance guy with your boy-friend's name called a county sheriff?"

Peter spoke up. "Campbell, it doesn't cost you any-thing to get on the phone. Valley County is where Helene used to live. That alone is reason enough to take a look. If we're right, Roy's got a ten-hour drive, maybe more depending on his route. That gives the locals plenty of time to get ready for him."

"Oh, I'll make the call. But these rural sheriffs are stubborn. They don't even like their *own* state investi-gators bigfooting on their turf. A DCI guy from a neighboring state isn't going to get much traction."

"What about the FBI?" Peter asked.

"So far, the feds are staying out of it. Waiting for us to screw up, no doubt. How much help would they be, a couple of suits from the Omaha office? They don't know the lay of the land out here, anyway." Ru-ral sheriffs weren't the only ones who didn't want to share their turf.

June rolled her eyes at Peter. "Listen to me, Camp-bell. Roy's killed eight people that we know of, at least four of them law enforcement. The feds have agents with decades of homicide experience. Now is the time to suck it up and pull in all available resources."

"You're not wrong," Campbell said. "But this comes from the governor. We hang on to it until they take it away from us."

June ended the call. "Fucking bureaucrats and pol-iticians." She sighed. "I'm pretty sure we're on our own."

Peter felt the werewolf begin to stir again. "Not entirely." He picked up her phone. The number was on speed-dial. "It's me. Pack your shit, we're going hunting."

Lewis gave a low chuckle, slippery and dark. "All *right*. Where we headed, brother?"

Peter told him the county. "We'll make a plan when we have an address. Did Bobbie have a spare shotgun?"

"Motherfucker, Bobbie got everything up to surface-to-air missiles. She says cleaning guns calms her nerves. Did you know Lisa was state target champion five years in a row?"

66

Roy stayed off the interstates, avoiding the most likely areas for police roadblocks. They made decent time west despite that, pushing the truck fast on the long, straight roads.

He was quiet, gone someplace inside himself where Helene didn't want to follow. She was still tired, and nervous about what was coming, and didn't trust herself enough to make conversation. Her back hurt and her feet were sore. Before long, she climbed awkwardly into the back to get some sleep. She knew she'd need to take over the driving eventually.

She had a hard time getting comfortable, though. The baby had a mind of its own, swimming around inside her belly like a hungry fish grown too big for its tank. Closing her eyes didn't help. First she saw Trooper Falk slumped on the gravel with the side of her head blown off. Then she saw her aunt Willa held in Roy's hard embrace. Then she saw Frank with the puckered red hole in his chest. You deserve each other, he'd said.

He was right about that, she thought.

Finally she dug into the cooler of food from her aunt's house and found the rest of the sliced turkey and a tub of potato salad. The men hadn't packed any silverware or napkins, so she ate with her fingers, then licked them clean. That seemed to settle the dead, and calmed the baby enough for her to sleep.

When she woke, it was dusk. She sat up and peered through the bug-speckled windshield at the deep blue of the western horizon. Behind her, to the east, the stars would already be out. "Have you been driving this whole time?"

"I figured you needed the sleep," he said.

Music played softly on the radio. She was reminded again of the long trips through the shale country with her mom, when they went looking for her dad. The coziness inside the car, just the two of them, a tiny island of light in a vast ocean of darkness.

Then she remembered who she was with, what he had done. What he meant for her to become. What she planned to do.

She wondered if she would have the courage to act, when the time came. Or if courage was even what she lacked. It seemed to her now that she lacked something else, something harder to name but somehow more essential. She wondered when she'd lost it. Or whether she'd simply given it away.

It would be so easy to surrender to Roy's desires.

She could feel herself slipping toward him, even now, like a needle toward a magnet. It wouldn't be surrender, would it? It would be more like acceptance, like shedding her original skin and allowing herself to inhabit the new one that had been growing beneath. It suited her, that new skin. Far more than she cared to admit.

She had to resist. It was up to her now. It had always only ever been up to her.

She wished she'd kept the embroidered hem of that dress. She used to run it through her fingers, as if she could read the words through the faint pressure of her skin. *We can do hard things. Fortune favors the bold. The only way out is through.*

Then Roy slept and Helene drove, her belly touching the steering wheel as she followed the directions on his phone. When she stopped for gas and coffee in Mobridge and Williston, the baby kicked like a mule until she got the truck back up to speed. Roy only woke to tell her to check the oil and pull his green John Deere hat farther down over his eyes. She could have walked away twice, but she didn't.

She paid the clerk with bills from Roy's wallet in the center console. His go-bag was in the wheel well at his feet. Frank's was in the back. Even if she managed to get the money from both bags, it still wasn't enough for her to run. Roy was too smart to get caught. He would never stop chasing her.

She might have been able to shoot him as he slept, but even if she succeeded, and that was a big if, it wouldn't solve her bigger problem, which was what the law would want to do with her. No, her other choices were gone. She would stick to her plan.

She crossed the Montana line long after midnight. She began to recognize towns, the names of rivers, the numbered county highways. When they crossed into Valley County, she woke him.

His coffee had gone cold. He drained the cup in one go anyway, then smacked his lips like she'd made his favorite meal. "This is great, isn't it? I feel like we could drive forever, just the two of us. Go anywhere we want."

"If we can go anywhere, what are we doing back in Coldwater?"

"You have unfinished business here. Something you need to do before we ride off into the sunset together."

She knew, of course. "Bogaloosa. Because of what my aunt said."

Because of the letters her aunt had sent that Helene had never received. Because he had lied to her aunt when she had come in person to take Helene home to Minnesota. Because Helene's whole life would have turned out differently, if not for that goddamned Bogaloosa.

"That's right," he said. "This is your moment, honey."

She was terrified of it. She was also counting on it.

She drove to the crossroads. Before she got to the Gas and Grocery, she saw a darkened sheriff's pickup parked behind it. "That's never been there before." She didn't like this development.

"Keep driving." He craned his head for a better look as they passed. "No engine exhaust. Looks empty." He gave her that new wild smile. "Looks like they figured out who you are. How do you suppose that happened?"

The smile scared her. It told her that she and her baby still weren't safe, that maybe they never would be. She was out of choices. She was committed.

She gave him the truth. "I don't know. Does it matter? Let's just go, it's too risky."

"No, it's too important," he said. "Whatever comes, we'll handle it together, I promise."

She turned out the lights and pulled over. "No more cop-killing, Roy. It only makes things worse for us."

He leaned toward her, seeming to grow in size until he filled the cab of the truck. "This one's different. This one's for you, honey." The smile spread across his face. "Come on, it'll be fun."

She felt the pull of him. She didn't want him to be right. But her own smile grew anyway. "Okay."

He hopped out of the truck to fuss with something in the cargo bed, and returned with a weird-looking rifle with a huge scope. He climbed back into his seat with the long barrel out the window. "Keep the lights off, and drive by his place."

The moon was a bright sliver and the roads were empty. After the turn at the Gas and Grocery, the farmhouse was only a mile ahead. Roy had the rifle up with his eye to the scope. "What do you see?" she asked.

"Another sheriff's pickup by the house, probably your deputy's." She passed the farm and the field beside it. After the windbreak, he said, "A police cruiser tucked into that line of trees. Again, no exhaust, so in this cold, it's probably empty."

She went two more miles but he saw nothing else. She turned around and headed back.

"Either they're trying to scare us away or they're not taking us very seriously," he said. "Are you scared?"

Her baby stirred in her belly. She knew what her answer should be. "Yes. And angry." She flashed her teeth. "But I'm excited, too. When are you going to give me a gun?"

"When the time comes."

67

The cluster of farm buildings was set off the road in the corner of a hayfield. When she had walked from the store to milk Bogaloosa's cows, she had taken the tractor path along the far edge of that field. It seemed like a lifetime ago. It had only been seven months.

She saw a flat spot in the ditch and pulled the truck over without asking. The barn blocked the view from the house, and the ditch put the truck slightly lower than the tops of the winter grasses. Roy looked around approvingly. "You really are a natural, honey."

He walked up from the ditch and stepped through the waist-high line of bushy weeds along the barbed-wire fence. "You coming?" His voice quiet in the empty night.

"Give me a minute," she said. "I have to pee."

"Just remember not to slam your door." He slung

his long legs over the fence and stepped into the grass to give her some privacy.

She dropped to her knees as if squatting, and reached across the driver's seat to pull the plastic bag of money from Roy's go-bag. Her hand groped through the clothes and phones and ammunition, feeling for the revolver, but didn't find it.

"Honey?"

"Hold your horses, mister." She stood and pretended to adjust the sweatpants, then closed the truck door carefully and tucked the plastic bag under the armpit of her jacket. At the fence, she put one foot on the wire while Roy watched from twenty feet away.

"You want a hand?"

"I can do it." She turned sideways so he wouldn't see the money fall under a particularly broad bush, then kicked it farther in as she grabbed the fencepost and hoisted herself over the wire with a grunt. "Everything was a lot easier before you knocked me up."

They set off together across the meadow. The belly slowed her pace across the uneven ground, but he didn't pull ahead or try to rush her. The night air was crisp but the wind smelled of wet dirt and the coming of spring.

Roy carried the rifle across his chest. His pistol was holstered on his belt, and his coat pocket swung with the weight of what she assumed was her daddy's revolver. Helene's hands were empty, but they wouldn't be for long, not if this went the way she hoped it would.

Despite the lack of sleep and the long drive and the general exhaustion of her pregnancy, she felt more awake now than she had in a long time. Maybe ever.

She smelled manure and heard the complaints of the cows through the walls of the old barn. Roy put his finger to his lips and led her quietly around the side. A man in a winter parka and wool cap sat leaning against the weathered planks with his hands in his pockets. He was asleep.

Roy raised the rifle, but he looked at her. "That's not Bogaloosa," she whispered as softly as she could. "Don't kill him."

The man stirred. He looked up, saw them, then fumbled under his coat.

Roy took a single step forward and fired at a downward angle. The gun coughed quietly and the man's head exploded.

It was easier not to flinch this time. *We can do hard things.* She put her hands on her hips. "Roy," she said softly.

He sighed. "What exactly did you think was going to happen?"

"I'm not here for them," she said. "They never did anything to me. I'm here for him."

"They're part of the package," he said. "Trust me, you'll get used to it."

She realized she'd lost count of the number of the dead.

The only way out is through.

The farmyard was dark, but the house was lit from

inside. They walked up to a window and looked into the kitchen from a few paces away. It was empty. She pointed to the left and they moved to the next window, a much larger one. In the living room, an older man pulled himself to a sitting position on the couch, reaching for his phone, fully dressed except for his cowboy boots. A police utility belt hung from a chairback. She remembered him putting his wrinkly arm around her, his knuckles pressing into the side of her breast.

She put her lips to Roy's ear. "That's Sheriff Janacek. Bogaloosa sleeps at the end of the hall."

Roy raised the rifle, aimed through the glass, and shot Janacek twice.

The gun was quiet, but glass fell clattering to the floor and the unmown grass outside. Roy poked the barrel through the hole and raked the remaining jagged shards from the frame, making even more noise, then ducked down out of sight next to the house, motioning for Helene to do the same. It wasn't so easy with the belly.

After a moment, a shadow appeared as someone came to the window. She could hear his breathing. Roy stood up and grabbed the man's belt and pulled him, toppling forward, through the opening.

He twisted in midair, maybe trying to control his fall, but landed hard on his shoulder with a sharp grunt as the air got knocked out of him. He managed not to drop his pistol, but Roy stepped in and kicked it out of his hand, then kicked him in the crotch for good measure.

Even curled around his balls, she knew it was Bogaloosa by the glossy black mustache and the smell of wintergreen Skoal that seeped from his pores. He wore ratty jeans and a white undershirt that showed the soft mound of his gut. His feet were bare.

He'd had no idea what was coming for him, she thought. None of them had.

Roy rolled him over and cuffed his hands behind his back. "On your feet, Deputy. You owe the lady an explanation."

Bogaloosa's eyes were stuck on Roy. Helene stepped in and kicked him in the ribs with her aunt's hiking boot. "Don't be scared of him, you fucker. Be scared of me."

68

PETER

Keeping his speed down, Peter approached the small square building. It had a distinct backward lean and a pair of antique gas pumps in front. According to the state of Montana, it was called Bogaloosa's Crossroads, but the faded sign along the road said Bogaloosa's Gas and Grocery in uneven hand-painted letters. June had found both the store and his farm by searching her databases using his name.

Behind the building, poorly hidden, was a four-door pickup with a push bumper, a lightbar, and a sheriff's logo on the door. Through the window, Peter caught a glimpse of a young woman with long black hair behind the counter. Helene's successor, he thought. Flee while you can.

They had met Lewis and Bobbie in a dirt lot behind the fairgrounds outside of Circle, Montana. The four of them stood around the Chevy's square hood drinking cold coffee as June pulled up a satellite image on her laptop.

"Two ways to drive in." Peter pointed at the screen. "From the driveway on this road to the north, and along this tractor path from the east, by the store. On the other two sides, it's all hills with no vehicle access for miles. Helene is too pregnant for a hard hike, so they won't like that route."

"But you could walk across those fields," Bobbie said. "They're wide open."

"And that's what we'll do," Peter said. "Move in slow and careful and see what we can see. We get close, June will call the sheriff and let him know where we are."

"Are the locals taking this seriously?" Lewis asked.

"Hard to tell," June said. "Campbell talked to Janacek about eight hours ago. He told Campbell he'd put two people at the house overnight, with a pair of state troopers coming in to spell them in the morning. I guess it's a long drive from pretty much anyplace."

"They found Frank," Peter said. "Dead. Couple of kids went to play in the woods and found him with two dead women. Initial ID is the aunt and her assistant. So we're down to Roy and Helene, as far as we know."

"Did you ask Campbell about the task force?" Bobbie asked. "The missing women?"

June nodded. "He had to dig for the email, but the victim profile seems about right. Women, late teens to late twenties. Rural counties across nine states. They worked evenings or nights at gas stations and restaurants and bars. No evidence of violence. In some cases, evidence they may have gone willingly. They're all still missing. All thirty-three of them."

After that, there wasn't much else to say except good-bye and good luck. They got back in their vehicles and drove the last sixty miles to Coldwater.

Peter didn't think it had ever been a real town. It was barely a wide spot where two roads came together, with buildings scattered at the four corners. The only structure still habitable was the Gas and Grocery.

He pulled the rented Ford into the tall grass behind a long shed. Its roof was partially collapsed and whole sections of siding had come loose and rattled in the wind. Lewis and Bobbie had taken the turn and continued on toward the farm to recon the northern perimeter.

He followed June across the blacktop and slipped behind the store. His banged-up knee had gotten worse on the long drive. His forearm was still swelling nicely.

A beaten dirt path led past the dumpster to an old travel trailer, its metal shell peeling at the corners, the small tires long ago eaten away by rot. Aside from the Gas and Grocery and Bogaloosa's farmhouse a mile away, there were no lights in sight. Peter wasn't sure he'd ever seen a lonelier place.

The tractor path was two hard-packed ruts with a

tuft of weeds grown up beneath. The quarter-moon gave enough light to see. Rounded hills on the left and a meadow on the right, both behind raggedy wire fences. They walked each to one side, keeping close to the fence lines where the waist-high scrub and weeds might provide some concealment.

June seemed fine, Peter thought. He wasn't worried about her physically, she was fit and strong. He was worried about what she'd have to do if they ran into Roy. He reminded himself that June had put on her vest again, and had her Glock in a holster and Bobbie's scoped Ruger .22 rifle over one shoulder. It didn't have to be a big round if you could put it where you wanted it, and June was very good at a hundred yards. But a paper target wasn't the real thing. Paper didn't shoot back.

Along with his pistol, Peter had a Benelli shotgun with five rounds of double-ought in the tube and another in the chamber. He hoped he didn't have to use it. It was not a precision weapon. On the other hand, if he did pull the trigger, anything downrange was unlikely to remain a threat.

He swept his eyes across the darkened landscape, his lizard brain scanning for patterns of danger. The weeds thwacked against his pantlegs as he walked. The exercise wasn't improving his knee. More like the opposite. Peter was not exactly a precision weapon himself at the moment. The ibuprofen was keeping him mostly functional. His only concern was that he might fail June and Lewis and the others. He put it out of his mind. He'd make it to the doctor tomorrow, or else he'd be dead. Either way, why worry?

The house was closer now. Halfway there, he figured. Lewis and Bobbie would be finishing their recon, then find a place to drop the Chevy. On foot, they would move a lot faster than Peter.

His phone buzzed, a cheap burner he'd bought at a Flying J outside Bismarck. Voice low, Lewis said, "I got a pickup in the ditch with Nebraska plates."

Peter closed his eyes. "They're here. Watch your ass."

"Roger that. You, too, brother. We're going in."

"Hold up." He kept Lewis on the line and slipped across the tractor path to June's side. "Lewis saw a truck. Nebraska plates. Better call the sheriff."

They kept walking as she put her phone to her ear. After a few moments, she shook her head. Peter told Lewis, "No answer. See you there."

Then they heard, a half mile distant but carried clearly on the cool night breeze, the high pealing sound of breaking glass.

"Go," Peter said. And began to run, bad knee and all.

69

HELENE

Roy shouldered open the front door and hauled Bogaloosa into the living room. The sheriff lay dead on the crimson couch. Kicking away the coffee table, Roy dropped Bogaloosa in a torn leather recliner, hands cuffed behind his back.

How small and soft he looked beside Roy, Helene thought. The baby swirled in her belly.

Eyes wide, Bogaloosa stared at the sheriff. Helene said, "Look at me, fucker." He turned his head, fear all over his face. She liked it. "Do you know who I am?"

He nodded. "Helene." He cleared his throat. "Johansen. What are you doing here?"

At least he recognized her. After all he'd put her through, if he hadn't even recognized her face? She might have killed him just for that.

"You were going to rape me," she said. "On my

birthday. Like it was a gift you were giving me. Do you remember that?"

His eyes flicked to Roy, then back to her. "It was just a joke," he said. "I'm sorry. I would never have done that."

She remembered how he'd pushed her up against the milking stall in the barn, his fist clamped around her arm. All the times he'd brushed up against her, fingertips touching her breasts and butt. She leaned closer to him now, smelling fear in the stink from his armpits.

"Then why didn't you give me the letters from my aunt? When she came looking for me, why did you tell her I'd gone away and you had no way to reach me?" Her voice was loud and getting louder. "I spoke to her yesterday. She was going to take me back to Minnesota. I was going to have a normal life. Instead you trapped me here. With you."

He squirmed in the chair, sweating freely now. "I couldn't help myself, Helene. You were so beautiful. I was in love with you. I wanted to get married, remember?"

It struck her, again, that Bogaloosa had the same urges as Roy. Maybe all men did.

She drove a fist into his balls. He cried out. She smiled. She could get used to this.

"That's your fucking reason? You were in love with me?"

He nodded desperately. He was weak. She couldn't believe how scared he'd made her feel. But she had been scared. Because he hadn't been joking. No matter what he said now, she knew the truth. He would have taken whatever he could. And gotten away with it, because he was the law.

"Honey, there's more." Roy stood watching, calm and still. "Do you remember what your aunt said? That your mom had agreed to move to Minnesota with you. And right after, she ended up in the river."

"Yes," Helene said. "It was an accident."

Roy tipped his head at the body on the couch. "I talked to the sheriff after you fell asleep yesterday morning. He said the state forensics people didn't think it was an accident. The skid marks were all wrong. They were convinced that your mom's car was pushed into the river."

She blinked at him. "Pushed?"

"Deputy Bogaloosa ran the investigation. He couldn't find another car with the right kind of bumper damage. So after a few weeks, he declared it an accident. Blamed it on the curve in the road."

"I didn't know any of this." Helene's heart was racing.

Roy was calm and still. "But you know what kind of vehicle can push a car off the road without damage? Using a front bumper specially designed to do exactly that? A police cruiser. Like the one parked right outside. And nobody would ever know."

"No," she said. "Wait." She turned to Bogaloosa. The look on his face was enough.

She was trembling, furious. Incandescent.

"You killed her," Helene said. "So you could take me."

It was all Helene's fault. Her own fault that her mother had died.

Her body clenched like a fist. The voice in her head rose into a shriek. No, she screamed to herself. It's *not* your fault. All she had done was exist. Goddamned Bogaloosa had done the rest.

With that scream came a kind of clarity. When her aunt had told her about the deputy's lies, she'd seen Roy's reaction. She'd known he would turn that information against her somehow. She had thought she could withstand it. But not now. Not this.

She didn't know which was worse. Knowing Bogaloosa had killed her mother, or knowing that Roy was using that glorious, shining rage against her. To get her to kill Bogaloosa.

And truthfully, it didn't matter. Her plan would still work. She would just add another step.

She would do what Roy wanted her to do. And more. *We can do hard things.*

She was no longer the girl she had been. That girl was long gone. Shed like a skin that no longer fit.

In her towering fury, Helene was bright and shiny and new.

She turned back to Roy. It was as if he had read her mind, had seen the evolution of her thoughts from then to now. That new wild, gleeful smile had spread across his face.

She matched it, tooth for tooth.

"Give me the gun, Roy."

He took his big automatic from his holster and held it out.

"Not yours," she said. "The revolver."

"I thought you might want that one." He fished it from his pocket.

She took it in her hand, felt the cracked walnut grip against her palm. "This was my daddy's gun."

"I saved it for you," he said. "For this exact perfect moment."

She remembered the times she had stood with her daddy behind their old house and he had taught her to shoot tin cans at twenty paces. The gun felt good, heavy, familiar. She checked the cylinder as she'd been taught. "Only two bullets?"

"One to start and one to finish." Roy stood easily with his automatic hanging down at the end of his arm. "Whenever you're ready."

She snapped the cylinder shut, then thumbed back the hammer and pointed the pistol at Bogaloosa. One-handed, with her elbow bent, not the way her daddy had taught her. "Like this?"

"You're six feet away," Roy said. "You can't miss."

She no longer doubted that she could do it. Whatever she had to do.

70

PETER

Peter's knee was on fire, but he covered the distance as fast as he could. June could have gone ahead, but she kept pace beside him, and Peter was glad. He would have happily given his life to end Roy's, but he wouldn't sacrifice June. Never June.

He slowed as they came to the farm. The yard lights were dark, but the lights from the house cast a dim glow across the area. Another four-door sheriff's pickup was parked in the open. He spotted a forlorn shape on the ground by the barn door. Even at thirty yards, Peter knew a dead body when he saw one.

He scanned for Lewis and Bobbie, but didn't find them. It would be smart to wait. June's hand on his arm told him the same thing.

He heard voices from the house. The windows were bright, one of them brighter where the dirty glass had been broken out. He put his lips to June's ear and patted the rifle in her hand. "Stay here. Look through the scope. If you see Roy and have a shot, take it."

Without waiting for an answer, he ran again, limping but grateful for the unmown grass to quiet the scuff of his boots. Roy's eyes would be adjusted to the interior light. Peter hoped the yard was dim enough to hide his own movements. Nearing the house, he wondered how many strides he had left before the knee gave out completely.

Then he was crouched against the waist-high foundation, listening. Helene, angry. Then Roy's smooth voice, explaining something.

Peter didn't hear everything, but he heard enough. His suspicion from June's conversation with the sheriff was confirmed. Helene's mother's death was no accident.

June bent behind the hood of the sheriff's pickup, the Ruger's barrel braced on the hood. He looked again for the others and this time saw a midnight phantom glide from behind the barn. Lewis was the only man Peter had ever seen move like that. On the far side of the driveway, Bobbie's bulk materialized out of the darkened meadow. Peter held up a fist, then patted his palm toward the ground, telling them to hold. The more of them who came to the house, the greater the risk of Roy noticing.

Or Helene, Peter thought. He still had no idea how compromised she was. Whether Roy's violence had made her his creature entirely, or whether some other, more innocent person remained, Peter had no idea. Either way, he wanted to avoid a brute-force assault on the house. The risk to Helene and her baby was too great.

On his screaming knee, Peter scrambled sideways until he was directly below the big broken window. He could feel the shards of glass through the thick fabric of his pants. If he stood, the sill would be at the level of his chest. Helene was talking again, her voice gone quiet. She sounded almost happy. Peter leaned the shotgun against the house where he could snatch it up if necessary. With his pistol in his hand and his knee twanging like a broken banjo, he slowly raised himself up.

Through the frame, he had a clear view of the room and the people inside, arrayed as if in a tragic play. At the center against the far wall was a blood-soaked couch with a crumpled body on it. To the right of the couch, a fat man with a mustache cowered in an easy chair, his arms apparently restrained behind him. Peter only had a partial view of Roy in the near left corner with a big automatic held down along his right thigh. Whether by instinct or design, Roy's sheltered position both gave him a clear line of fire on the rest of the room and took away any decent firing angle from someone standing outside.

In the middle of the human triangle, by the left side of the couch, Helene stood with a black revolver in one hand, aimed awkwardly at the fat man.

Peter's heart sank.

"Like this?" she asked, and made a half pivot toward Roy. The gun was still pointed toward the fat man. She wore a madwoman's smile.

Don't do it, Peter wanted to say. Wanted to shout. But that wouldn't help her.

He could fire through the wall and have a decent chance of hitting Roy, even though the bullet would be slowed by the building. But Helene was directly opposite. He couldn't guarantee he wouldn't harm her or the child in her belly.

Instead he crept backward into the unmown grass. All he needed was a running start. He would launch himself over the windowsill and into the room, where he could empty his pistol into Roy. And hope that Helene wouldn't empty hers into him.

He stood and set his feet and began to sprint. Immediately he knew that his left knee was very bad. Three steps to go, then two. The knee gave way. He caught himself with the right leg and pushed off hard.

He didn't make it as far as he'd planned. The sill caught him at the tops of his thighs. The remaining glass in the frame bit through his pants into his skin. He curled himself forward and fell into the room, scrambling to his side to bring his gun to bear.

But he knew he was too late.

71

Already half turned toward Roy, Helene completed the pivot, no longer awkward as she straightened her arm to find her new target and brought her other hand to the butt of the revolver as if she'd done it a thousand times. With her smile turned electric, she pulled the trigger and shot Roy high in the left breast and again just below the sternum.

Roy's eyes widened and he began to raise his pistol.

Laying on his side on the floor, Peter got his finger inside the trigger guard and began to take up the slack, but Helene ran to Roy and collided with him.

Peter had no shot, Helene was too close. Roy bounced away and stumbled out of his corner, but the gun kept rising, and Helene kept after him. Peter still had no shot.

With a scream of animal rage and pain, she grabbed

Roy's arm with both hands. Even with two bullets in him, he was still too strong for her to really control him. All she could do was pull herself close, her pregnant belly hard against him as she trapped his wrist and gun hand at her side, under her armpit.

He tried to pull away, but she didn't let him, only held him tighter. They staggered in a circle, Roy backward, Helene forward, as if in a reversal of some ancient dance. Helene's scream rose higher as Roy pulled the trigger, again and again.

As they turned, bullets flew outward, uncontrolled, like droplets of water from a slow-motion sprinkler.

Peter flattened himself to the floor. Round after wild round sprayed across the room. Plaster cracked from the walls, feathers flew from couch cushions, the television screen shattered, it went on and on and on. Until, finally, the gun was silent.

Peter looked and saw Helene holding Roy upright. It seemed impossible, because he was so much larger than her and his knees had begun to buckle. But she held him on his feet anyway, perhaps by force of will alone. Roy's eyes sagged and his head dipped and he spoke into her ear. Just a few words, his fading voice too soft for Peter to hear.

Then she let him go, or maybe she pushed him, because he fell backward from his heels like a poorly planted tombstone. Dead, he hit the floor hard enough to rattle the dishes in the china cabinet.

The chest and shoulders of Helene's zip sweatshirt were smeared with his blood. On the round dome of her belly was a bright red handprint. She was breathing hard, as if at the end of a long, hard, race. Then she began to cry.

In the leather chair, the fat man with the dark mustache stared at her, but he didn't share his thoughts with the room.

He was too busy bleeding out from the bullet holes in his neck and stomach.

72

Waiting for the Montana state troopers, Bobbie and June clustered with Helene in the kitchen, out of sight of the dead. Peter and Lewis, temporarily unwelcome because of their gender, sat on the porch drinking Bogaloosa's instant coffee and watching the light gather in the east.

After photographs and initial statements, with reassurance from Agent Campbell's Montana counterparts, the troopers had escorted Peter and Helene to the hospital in Glasgow, where Peter got a cast on his forearm for his broken ulna and a referral to a knee specialist in Rochester, Minnesota.

He had no desire to hang around the waiting room, so he and Lewis and June sat on the picnic table outside the emergency room entrance. Helene was still inside the hospital with Bobbie, who had appointed herself Helene's protector and advocate, getting a comprehensive ob-gyn workup.

Peter drank some bad vending machine coffee. "How much trouble is she in, do you think?"

"Hard to say." June was typing up her notes on her laptop. "Legally, Helene's an accessory to murder, but she's not without leverage. This is already national news. If we're right about Roy and all those missing women, the story will only get bigger. I'm hoping she'll let me help tell her side."

Lewis chuckled. "Once people read about the coyotes in the woods and the bodies in the freezer, won't no prosecutor indict her for anything. 'Cause she slayed the monster and no jury will vote to convict."

Peter looked at his friend. "When are you headed home?"

"Depends," he said. "You need me to drive that antique pickup? Hard to use the clutch with that knee."

"I knew the Chevy was growing on you."

"Jarhead, it don't even have a radio," Lewis said. "Or cruise control. It's like you're some kinda monk."

Still typing, June said, "I need to stay with Helene. Can you get him to Rochester, Lewis? It's the only way I know he'll keep the appointment."

"Sure," Lewis said. "I'll try to keep him from jumping outta the car along the way."

June snorted. Peter looked at his knee, which had swollen up like a softball. "I'm pretty sure I learned my lesson."

Lewis twitched his lips in a tilted smile. "No, you didn't."

Peter sighed and swirled the dregs of his coffee. "After all that, did we actually make anything better? Couldn't I have found a way to get Helene free without getting all these other people killed?"

"Jarhead, you didn't get nobody killed. Roy pulled the trigger. That's on him, not you. Now the dude's dead and Helene got to be the one to turn out his lights. How is that a bad outcome?"

Peter shook his head. "I'm just worried about her. How much damage did he do to her?"

Lewis put a big hand on Peter's shoulder. "Brother, you and I both know the damage don't matter. We all got damage. What matters is what you do with it. Helene's a strong person, right? Got to be, to get free of Roy. He tried to break her, but she wouldn't be broken."

"You didn't see her, at the end," Peter said. "Right before she shot him, she smiled like she was having the time of her life." He looked into his cup as if trying to read something in the grounds. "What if Roy was right? What if Helene is just like him? And now she knows it?"

June stopped typing and looked up. "Peter, there's a world of difference between Roy and Helene. He killed cops and innocents. She killed a murderer. Trust me, that woman's a survivor."

73

HELENE

'm worried about you," Bobbie said. "I really don't think it's a good idea for you to live here."

They stood in the kitchen of the home place, cleaning up after the potluck supper. The last of the church's weekend volunteers had left, and the house smelled of the fresh paint they had rolled over the cracked plaster walls. They'd also brought second-hand furniture to replace Roy's things, which they set alight in a pyre in the yard, adding the planks removed from the windows and downed deadfall from the woods until the fire blazed hot enough to burn even the stained old mattress down to a fine gray ash.

Like an exorcism, Bobbie had said. To get rid of the memories.

After staying in Bobbie's guest room for six months, Helene knew those memories would be with her until the day she died, if not beyond. No matter where she lived.

"I'm fine," she told Bobbie now, as the smoke swirled outside. "Really."

And most days, she was, especially with her daughter to care for.

She'd named the baby Celeste, after her mother. Any concerns about how much she might love the little girl evaporated once she held her daughter in her arms. It overwhelmed her, that love, despite how Celeste stole her sleep and sometimes gnawed on her nipples while breastfeeding. She would do anything to protect her daughter from the pain of the world. As it turned out, Helene was more capable than she'd ever imagined.

She had already driven Lisa's pickup back to Bogaloosa's farm, where she'd retrieved the plastic bag of cash that she'd kicked under a bush along the fence line. It held a hundred and eight thousand dollars, which went a long way when you didn't have to pay rent or taxes.

Her lawyer, a firecracker from Denver, had forged agreements with prosecutors in eleven states. In exchange for Helene's full cooperation with investigators, she would not be charged with any crimes. The authorities had confiscated Roy's truck and trailer and anything else that might be connected to the murders or the burglaries. They had even taken Helene's diamond ring, which turned out to be quite real and valued at almost a quarter million dollars.

But despite their best efforts, the ring was all they could find of Roy's share of the proceeds. A few detectives directed their frustrations at Helene, who got a lot of practice reminding them, with a soft, vulnerable smile and a baby on her lap, that she had been Roy's victim, not his partner. How could she possibly know where Roy had put the money?

The home place and the surrounding acreage had been in Roy's family since long before he was born, so the authorities had no real grounds for confiscation. As for who owned it after Roy's death, the law was clear. The marriage in Elko had been real. Helene was Roy's wife. She inherited everything.

Except for what lay under the soil. After the county had trapped and killed all but one of the coyotes, who was too smart to get caught, a group of forensic archeologists from the University in Lincoln had used ground-penetrating radar to locate multiple informal gravesites on the property. So far, they had dug up what they believed to be thirty-seven distinct sets of human remains, with many more to come. Most of the remains were recent, but at least three sites appeared to go back for generations.

But now the weather had turned too cold for digging, so the archeologists had packed up their tents and trowels until the spring. Even though the lone coyote, a female, still sometimes prowled through the trees, Helene didn't mind the solitude. It was better to be alone for what came next.

She still remembered that scrap of conversation before Frank died, probably because she'd turned it over in her mind every day. Frank had mentioned that Roy had a second house. Roy had said it was too close to home to make a good hiding place.

She'd already gone to the county registrar and figured out the rough borders of the family property. She'd walked the acreage many times now, with Celeste slung across her front and a daypack on her back, and was certain the police had already searched the many derelict buildings it contained.

So the second house was not on the property, but it was nearby. In Helene's mind, it had to be accessible on foot, or there was no upside to having it close. And you had to be able to get there through the woods, because Roy would want to be able to stay off the roads. So she made a guess about how far Roy could travel cross-country in a couple of hours, then looked online for satellite images of the area. With twenty-three candidates, she strapped Celeste into the Baby-Björn and began walking.

In her warm clothes and good boots, with a new phone in case she got truly lost, it was entirely different from that first week at the home place, coatless and freezing in the cold rain, desperate to escape. Little Celeste loved being outside, staring transfixed at the trees rising overhead.

The first six places were either in ruins or obviously occupied, with barking dogs or laundry on the line. The seventh house, set back off the road, featured heavy security screens over the windows and doors and a dirt driveway that was starting to sprout saplings. She knew right away, this was the one.

She was certain that Roy had hidden a set of keys somewhere close, but she didn't bother to look. After copying everything on Roy's big keyring, the police had given her back the originals, which she carried in her backpack with diapers and wipes, her mother's old notebook, and the new revolver Bobbie had given her. She unlocked the back door with no trouble at all.

Stepping inside was another matter. She was deeply afraid of what Roy might have left behind. A bank of humming freezers, stacked with more bodies of women he had killed. Or a box of trophies he had kept, pieces of jewelry or scraps of clothing. The worst, she thought, would be photographs of their faces. She imagined them blown up larger than life and hung on the walls as souvenirs.

But she found none of that. The kitchen cabinets were stocked with jugs of distilled water and packets of freeze-dried food, and the mudroom shelves were loaded with guns and boxes of ammunition, but otherwise, the house was empty, echoing, soulless. She walked from room to room, the floors creaking underfoot, dust rising as she passed. She wondered if this vacant shell was all that remained of him. Except for the memories she carried like tumors inside her.

But it turned out that Roy did leave something behind. Inside the smallest closet of the smallest bedroom, she opened the door to discover a black fire safe the size of a file cabinet.

Celeste was snoring softly against her chest. Helene carefully removed the BabyBjörn and laid it gently down on the floor with the little girl still sleeping inside. Then she shucked off the backpack and knelt beside the black box and sorted through the ring of keys until she found the right one.

The door swung open silently.

The bottom shelf held roll after roll of gold and silver coins. On the middle shelf, she saw dozens of rubber-banded bundles of cash, hundreds and fifties, enough to last her a long time. The narrow top shelf carried only two slim manila envelopes, one with a deed to the empty house in a name she'd never seen before, the other with a handwritten list of logins and passwords for numbered accounts in six different banks in countries she'd never heard of.

Helene sat back on her heels, closed her eyes, and went back to those moments in Coldwater, Montana. Sometimes the memory returned on its own, usually when she least expected it. More often, like now, she called the memory back deliberately.

She felt the pleasing weight of her daddy's revolver, leaping in her hand like a living thing when she pulled the trigger. The blast of fear as Roy did not fall, but instead raised his own pistol toward her. She ran to him without thinking, grabbed his gun arm with both hands and pulled him close, as if slow-dancing in the high school gym.

Even as he fired his pistol, over and over, she knew he was dying. She kept him on his feet beside her because she wanted to feel the life leaking out of him, wanted to know for sure when the fucker was really dead. But that wasn't all of it.

While she held him tight with every ounce of her strength, she also knew where his pistol was pointed, and where Bogaloosa sat in his chair. She made sure Roy's last bullets found Bogaloosa's soft, worthless body.

Of course, Roy had known, too.

When his pistol was finally empty, he had stopped fighting and leaned into her embrace. He had put his bloody hand on her pregnant belly and she had felt that wild, gleeful smile against her cheek. Then he spoke into her ear.

His voice was reduced to a rattle, but his words were clear enough.

I've got you now, little rabbit.

The asshole couldn't even use her name at the very end.

"Fuck you, Roy," she said now, louder than she intended. "My name is Helene."

Celeste startled awake and began to cry. Helene sat on the floor of that empty house, took her daughter in her arms, opened her shirt, and offered her a breast.

Outside, the last coyote paced restlessly through the trees, waiting for the sun to set so it could howl into the darkness, hoping for another predator to howl in reply.

ACKNOWLEDGMENTS

I'll start with a big thanks to Margret, who spent a long pandemic trapped inside with her annoying husband. I blame COVID-19, but to be honest, I was pretty annoying before the pandemic and no doubt that will continue into the foreseeable future.

Next, thanks are due to my mom, who was a philosophy major at Michigan, for the many inspiring quotes over the years. When I was a kid, she used to wake me up by throwing back the curtains and saying, "It's time to rise and experience the day!" (I quickly learned that if I didn't get out of bed ASAP, the covers were next.)

Thanks to the rest of my family and friends for their help and support despite having to listen to hours of whining on my part.

Thanks also to the many talented crime writers I am privileged to know, for their boundless generosity and kindness. If you've never met a crime writer, you're missing out.

Thanks to writer/memoirist Glennon Doyle for the phrase *We can do hard things*. Margret is a big Glennon Doyle fan, and that phrase has found its way into our family lexicon. I find it especially useful when finishing a book seems more impossible than usual.

Thanks to my cousin Dr. Arion Lochner for taking time from his actual medical career to help me detail Peter's injuries after leaping from a speeding car. Due to plot changes in the book, I ended up ignoring his advice and winging it. I imagine he's used to that in his work in the ER. All medical errors in the book are mine, obviously.

Valley County, Montana, is a real place, as is Bon Homme County, South Dakota, but my fictional versions of both are not intended to be true depictions of those places. The law enforcement officials depicted in this novel are, as always, entirely fictitious products of the author's imagination.

For those of you who are concerned about strict geographical accuracy, I have taken some elements of the Niobrara River and others from the Missouri River for this book. The river itself and the landforms around it is the Missouri as I have seen it. The roads and fields, especially at the beginning of the book, are more true of the Niobrara.

My apologies to the citizens of Brandon, South Dakota. I moved your community a few miles east into Minnesota only because it made Aunt Willa's house seem farther away from Coldwater. No hard feelings, I hope.

Thanks to Sheriff Mark Maggs of the real Bon Homme County, for a conversation on policing with a small force in a rural area. He has a ridiculously hard job.

Thanks also to Peg Maciejewski and Detective Chris Erickson of the Princeton, Illinois, Police Department, for the same conversation from an entirely different perspective.

Thanks to Sergeant Adam Plantinga for his own take on policing. Read his great book, *400 Things Cops Know*, for a humorous and insightful look at the life of a street cop.

Many thanks to the talented burrito makers of Jacky's Burrito Express in Sioux Falls. Your fine work kept me going on a long, hot day.

In the infrastructure department, thanks to Barbara Poelle of IGLA for her big brain and sharp teeth.

Thanks are definitely due to the fine folks at Putnam. My first editor, Sara Minnich, has stepped away from publishing, and she will be missed by me and many other writers. My new editor, Danielle Dieterich, stepped into the void with verve and panache. Thanks to Claire Sullivan, Scott Bryan Wilson, Nancy Resnick, and Steven Meditz for making this book both gorgeous and readable. And thanks to the rest of the world-class crew, including Katie Grinch, Emily

Mlynek, Alexis Welby, Ashley McClay, Christine Ball, Sally Kim, Benjamin Lee, Ivan Held, and the superb PRH sales team for getting my books into the world.

Extended and enthusiastic thanks to the many wonderful independent booksellers for putting my books into readers' hands, including (but by no means limited to) Barbara Peters of The Poisoned Pen in Scottsdale and Daniel Goldin of Boswell Books in Milwaukee. Indie stores are the lifeblood of the book world, and the recommendations of these dedicated booksellers are what help bring new writers into the mainstream. As a bonus, indie stores keep your book-buying dollars—and jobs—in your community.

My deepest and most profound thanks are due, as always, to the many veterans who have spoken with me about their experiences both during and after their wars. These conversations were and are still instrumental in forming Peter's character and attitudes—these books would not exist without you. If there's some part of the veteran's experience that you think I have misunderstood or not included in these books—or if you just want to tell me your story—please don't hesitate to message me on social media. I'd love to hear from you.

I've also talked with far too many vets who are suffering from PTSD. Your suffering is real, and you are not alone! If you are a vet having trouble, please consider the Veterans Crisis Hotline at (800) 273-8255. Special thanks to reader Tim Morgan for reaching out with this suggestion, and please accept my sincere apologies for not thinking of this six books ago.

Last but not least, thanks to you, dear reader. Without you, I'd be just another whacko spinning stories in his head.

NICK PETRIE

"Lots of characters get compared to my own Jack Reacher, but [Petrie's] Peter Ash is the real deal."
—Lee Child

For a complete list of titles and to sign up for our newsletter, please visit prh.com/NickPetrie